To Camille Cotton
For your love, your friendship, and your inspiration

ALTERED

THE MADE ONES SAGA BOOK ONE

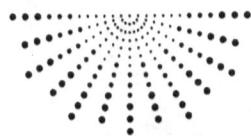

VICKI STIEFEL

"I have dreamed in my life, dreams that have stayed with me ever after, and changed my ideas; they have gone through and through me, like wine through water, and altered the color of my mind."
—Emily Bronte

PRAISE FOR VICKI STIEFEL

"The story is fast-paced, with non-stop action. The plot is complex and intriguing with unpredictable twists." —Sujitha Alexander

"*Chest of Bone* was full of action, magic, suspense and deception. The magic was mysterious and intriguing, and the way it was described was beautiful... I highly recommend this book if you're a lover of the fantastical with loads of mystery and lots of explosive kisses!" —Tiffany Roberts, author of *Dustwalker* and The Kraken Series

"*Chest of Bone's* writing style is innovative, the world is very interesting and provocative. It's a great story! I's a bunch of crazy, but it's GOOD crazy, with some super vivid scenes and fascinating characters." —Nocturnal Book Reviews

The Tally Whyte series
"This is an amazing thriller with action on almost every page. The heroine is strong, independent and sees things nobody else does... Vicki Stiefel writes a brilliant psychological thriller." —Book Review.com

"Tally is a compelling protagonist—edgy, compassionate and vulnerable—with a clipped narrating style that keeps the tricky plot in focus. She can hold her own against genre heavyweights like John Sanford and Patricia Cornwell." —Publishers Weekly

"Compelling, touching, and a pleasure to read." —Robert Parker

"Three words describe the Tally Whyte series: Intense. Addictive. Chilling. Tally's personality will draw you in as surely as the mystery does in this series." —Fresh Fiction

"An interesting read that concludes in an unexpected, dramatic fashion." —RT Book Reviews

A WOMAN ALTERED

A dying world
A woman altered
A warrior's vow

The Eleutians are dying out, one female at a time. To save their species, the powerful Alchemic Clan conscripts women from parallel worlds, altering them into the perfect breeding stock.

Kitlyn, a retired circus equestrian broken in both body and spirit, awakens on a strange world in her own much-younger body. She has been transformed into a Made One, but the gift of youth and the promise of a new life come at a terrible price.

Rafe, the Wolf Clan's warrior champion, vows to find the cause of the species' decline. He's certain the Alchemics' bid to save the Eleutians is but a thin veneer masking a dark purpose.

That vow becomes hard to keep with the threat of an

inter-clan conflict and the arrival of the proud Made One named Kitlyn.

To save herself and those like her, Kit must carve a dangerous path in this new reality and make a choice that may cost her her freedom, her life, and the life of the Eleutian warrior she's come to love.

PROLOGUE

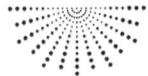

That sunny July day in Maine, the serrated blade of death inched ever closer. Kit knew that only too well as she and her sisters, Sybi and Bree, struggled to hike the Flying Mountain Trail to the top of Acadia's St. Sauveur Mountain. Yet the forest of tall pines, the blaze of summer sun, the twitter of birds made the day a glorious one.

Her accident, her illness—two thieves who'd robbed her of choices. But she could still do this, still could *choose* to walk Acadia's trails, paths she'd trod hundreds of times that never grew old. Her chest expanded, inhaling the scents of pine and sea.

As they ascended, the air grew thicker, closer, muffling bird song and the skitter of small forest animals, an oddity. The towering pines prohibited all but a thin strip of blue above their heads, but the life-affirming sun remained. She savored the forest's embrace. Startled by a seagull's caw, she leaned on her staff and paused, recalling how Elphaba, the wicked Appaloosa she'd loved so dearly, had insisted on chasing seagulls trolling for crumbs. So long ago. She smiled, and the tug on her scars ached in response.

Her hand instinctively rose to her face to touch the ugly map of her accident. Some parts were shiny and hard, others ridges her fingers climbed with seasoned knowledge. She dropped her hand. How foolish to revisit those planes and angles, yet their familiarity soothed her, proclaiming her Kit, and no other, her life's joys and sorrows embedded in her flesh.

A mosquito bit her thigh and she slapped it away. "Damn you! And damn me for wearing shorts."

As the trio climbed, Kit's breath came harder, sweat beading her brow.

"You guys okay?" she called back without looking.

"Doing fine," her sisters chorused.

No, they would not die today, though she cursed the aberrant gene that had stolen their tomorrows—Huntington's took no prisoners.

A friend once asked if she'd considered suicide. Suicide? They wanted to *live*. They might be in their 50s, but there was still so much to explore, to feel, to taste.

Kit paused to catch her breath. Sybi and Bree's heads were bowed as they scrambled up the mountain after her. "Hurry up, lazybones! I'm the gimpy one here. We might be dying, but we're not dead yet!"

Bree and Sybi laughed. She joined them, drinking in their joy like a fine cabernet. Their happiness made her feel free, and she released the clip binding her silver-streaked auburn hair, letting the breeze play with her curls.

Her nose wrinkled at the scent of ozone, her ears catching murmurs whispered through the trees. Stepping forward, an odd pressure rippled through her. *What the hell?* She turned, and her ankle gave, the pain searing. Kit clutched her staff, stopping her fall. If she didn't pay attention, she'd land on her ass and with her luck, break her other leg. That damned weak leg had been acting up again, curbing her martial arts practice, one of the few things stitching her sanity together.

Kit marched up a rise, around a bend, and froze. *Impossible.* Before her yawned a jagged crevasse where far below a river raged.

Sybi and Bree stepped beside her.

"Holy shit!" Bree said. "Where'd that come from?"

Sybi crossed her arms. "This can't be real."

"No?" Kit scooped up a stone and dropped it down the fissure, watching it disappear into the abyss.

Which was when the granite bank they stood upon vanished.

Kit clamped her jaw, refusing to scream as she tumbled toward the raging river hundreds of feet below.

CHAPTER ONE

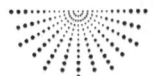

Enveloped by calm waters, Kit sputtered to consciousness, kicked, and broke the surface with a gasp. She tread water in a lukewarm pool surrounded by boulders and towering rock walls the color of burnt sand. She scrubbed her face. Dizzy, she swam, hindered by the strange flowing tunic that covered her neck to ankle, shoulder to wrist.

But… She'd been wearing shorts and a tank top when she'd fallen.

How am I even alive?

She scanned the pool.

My sisters!

"Sybi!" she screamed. "Bree!"

Panic choked her. They'd fallen, too. She saw neither of them, though her eyes scanned the bank. She plunged beneath the surface, the water clear as she searched for Sybi and Bree. Her body shivered, her eyes combing the empty depths. No fish, no plantlife, no sisters.

Hands and feet growing numb, Kit scissor-kicked to the surface where snowflakes drifted down from a gunmetal sky. Her sisters weren't there.

Where were they? Dead? Alive? What if they were hurt?

Snow continued to fall. If she didn't get out of the water, she'd die.

Using the protruding rocks as handholds, Kit tugged her way to the bank and paused. Gathering her strength, she crawled out of the pool, her efforts earning her bloody knees, and she rolled into a sitting position. Walking along the bank would be useless. She saw no exit, no path or steps.

Half frozen, she trembled as the snow continued to fall from a leaden sky. With dread, she peered up the cliff face. Could she climb it? Would she make it? Did she have a choice?

Hand over hand she scaled the rock face, made awkward by the drag of the strange tunic. Given the weather, she would be a fool to remove it. Adrenaline gave her the juice to put one hand above the other, one foot after another pushing her upward, finding hand- and foot-holds, scraping shins and breaking nails.

Clawing her way onto the summit, she collapsed, panting with relief, the icy ground cold against her cheek. How she'd climbed with her crippled side, she didn't know, didn't care. Once she caught her breath, she lay prone as she scoured the terrain for shelter. All she saw were jumbles of rocks and a dead leafless tree, a skeleton reaching toward the snow-burdened sky.

Not that it mattered. She was done, so exhausted she couldn't even pull herself beneath the dead tree's limbs.

No. I will try.

She stretched out an arm and curled her toes, attempting to push and pull at the same time. An inch. Then two.

Her shivering worsened, and yet something within her was growing warm, comfortable even.

Kit wished she'd seen her sisters one last time. Her horses and pups and the Maine Coon cat who woke her each morning with his ridiculous tapping. Or perhaps…

Radulfr was royally pissed. First off, he wished he'd ridden Nightfall for the retrieval. The mistral would have served him better than driving the hovercraft into the Pellopine mountains' unforgiving wilderness. The choice of transport was on him. But the second was on his father, who'd pulled his Alpha card and ordered Rafe to do cleanup for the Alchemic Clan's mess.

The Alchemics had brought over another Made One, much to his dismay, and sent her to the wrong convergence point. Or perhaps the Anti-Made Ones' faction had interfered. Either way, even using the coordinates the Alchemics had given him, he'd been scouring the mountains for hours.

Where the fark was she?

Rafe was tired. He'd fought too many battles of late. Hard to miss the irony of him fetching a Made One.

Should he fail to find her before sunset, she'd die, a priceless treasure taken by the wild country. Teams should have been out searching. Legions. But the *shoting* Alchemics insisted on him—only him—all to keep the Alchemics' mistake under the radar.

Even as Wolf Clan's best tracker, he couldn't perform miracles. He'd prayed to the Fates to guide him. So far, they hadn't listened to his plea.

Far up the mountain, an incongruous light snagged Rafe's attention, the glint coming from a shelf near the mountain's peak. His keen eyes took in the long, shiny tube high above. It didn't belong.

He slipped his binocs from the hover and raised them to his eyes. A frozen object lay within a giant cocoon of ice. Unnatural and strange.

His blood fired.

Rafe retied the strip binding his braid, then hauled the coiled rope from his hovercraft and slung it over his shoulder. He locked crampons onto his boots, then strapped claws onto his palms. Even now, the goddarts could be watching. The semi-sentient simian predators were the bane of the Pellopines. Which was why at the last minute he shoved his laseblaster into his shoulder holster.

His phone chimed. "Hush!" he said, silencing the annoyance. He peered up the rock face, memorizing the best foot- and toe-holds, then began to ascend. Inching up the frigid mountain he tried to imagine the Made One.

What would she look like? Would her voice be low or high? Her hair blond or blue? Her smile warm or chill?

His imagination failed, so he climbed faster.

Rafe stared down at the six-foot length of ice melting beneath the sun's warmth. Not fast enough. Dropping to one knee he examined the thing again. Encased in the ice lay a woman, clothed head to toe in golden-yellow, lying on her belly, one arm outstretched. Dead.

His heart thundered. A tragedy of epic magnitude.

Even so, he would never leave a Made One in her icy prison.

The laseblaster would release her in seconds, but it would damage her flesh, and that he wouldn't do. The task called for delicacy.

Rafe's strapped-on claws ripped apart the icy upper layers, then he slowed, taking care not to hurt her flesh. Gradually, the woman emerged as auburn-haired and lovely, her face heart-shaped, with high cheekbones and plush lips, and he somehow knew she smiled often. *Had* smiled often.

He worked with even greater care, unwilling to injure her, though she was long gone. Intolerable. He paused, panting, vapored puffs bursting from his lips. He wanted to touch her. Badly. But if he did so, her iced flesh would confirm the truth, no matter how much his heart wished otherwise.

Clouds darkened the sun, and it began to snow again. *Fark.* He'd better move it. Once she was fully revealed, her thin gown clinging to her lush curves, he shucked off his coat and wrapped it around her.

An inhuman cry sliced through the keening wind, maybe fifty yards to the east. He settled her over his shoulder and began his descent.

At the very least, she deserved a pyre to guide her way to the Other land.

Three-quarters of the way down the cliff, an arrow zinged by his cheek. *Shote*. Those farking goddarts. He returned fire, clamped the woman tight to his chest, then plunged the remaining distance.

Fark!

A jutting rock sliced his arm, making him tumble out of control, trees, mountains a blur. One, two, *now*—he flipped, landing with a thud, knees bent, and dashed behind the hovercraft, narrowly avoiding the goddarts' lethal "stings."

A long, calming breath later, he slid inside the hover, placing the Made One onto the passenger seat with care. Once settled in the driver's seat, he wrapped a kerchief around his bloody bicep.

Thunk. Thunk. Pause. *Thunk.*

Fark those creatures and their poisonous arrows. Even if they never left the mountains, they caused destruction wherever they went. *Fark them. Fark them all.*

The adrenaline receded, and his shaking hands fisted. This wasn't the goddarts' fault. They hadn't killed her. Those *shoting* Alchemics, screwing up the coordinates, had done so.

The snowstorm's intensity increased, his climbing rope flapping in the wind. No way to retrieve it now, so he punched the start button, his craft rose, and he turned up the heat. Though chilled, he was unwilling to remove his coat from the Made One. He punched the nav's Home button and sighed.

His lids grew heavy, and he leaned back in the seat and stretched out his legs. But like a fished reeled in by an angler, the Made One drew him. One more look.

She was lovely, and so easy to picture alive. He'd bet she'd been determined, with that strong chin and bold, aquiline nose. But her wide, plush mouth softened her—he could almost see her welcoming smile and the sparkle in her eyes when she did so, eyes that would never again light.

Had she been unbending or pliable? Both, perhaps. Yes, a woman firm in her viewpoints. Stubborn, even. Yet she'd laugh easily and embrace others with warmth. Her curls might be frozen, but he imagined them springy and soft.

The *Fates*. He was a practical man, pragmatic even. What was he doing, spinning stories about a dead woman?

He leaned back and pumped up the heat. After a couple swigs of warming troff, Rafe fell asleep as the hover took him home.

Kit opened her eyes. Leaden weights of exhaustion dragged at her lids, melted her muscles. Movement felt near impossible. Someone had wrapped a shearling coat around her. She was dry, and the chill was leaving her bones, her brain slowly coming back online.

Everything felt strange. Even the air smelled odd with a scent she couldn't identify.

Where was she?

Fuzzy memories of being in a pool, climbing to a cliff top, then…nothing.

Heat pumped from somewhere, warming her. Soft leather cushioned the fingers of one hand. Cool glass chilled her cheek. Except the window was convex, the world outside blurred by a raging snowstorm.

Absurd. She feared moving as if she'd shatter the spell enthralling her. But snow? In August? Winter came early in Maine. But not *that* early.

The dense pine forest slipped by, yet even through the storm, she glimpsed huge peaked mountains rearing in the distance, far larger than the ones of Acadia.

Fine. She was in a strange place that most definitely wasn't Maine. In winter. In a car. Ergo, she wasn't alone.

She inched her head far enough left so she could spy on the driver.

He was a large man with muscles bulging beneath a long-sleeved t-shirt. Thirtyish, perhaps. The blowing heat blew wisps of tawny hair that had loosened from his braid. The smile lines fanning from his eyes softened his hawkish nose and the bladed cheeks carving his tanned and weathered face. A striking man.

Who was he and where was he taking her?

He leaned against the opposite door, hands in his lap. Sleeping.

Tingles skimmed her body. He wasn't driving. *No one* was driving.

She would not panic. She never panicked. *Think.*

Of course. The car must be a Tesla. They drove themselves, didn't they? Horses she knew. Cars, not so much.

She remained statue still, but let her eyes survey the dashboard, the steering wheel, the seats.

What an alien-looking car.

Aliens had *not* kidnapped her, even if Bree would say exactly that. She chuffed a laugh, imagining her sister's reaction.

The man's eyes snapped open, then widened. "You!"

Words caught in her parched throat. She swallowed, or tried to.

He paled, a typical reaction to her mangled face, and then reached for her.

Kit pressed back against the car door.

"You're *alive,*" he said, his bewilderment obvious. He touched her hand, his fingers warm. "They must have put you in stasis. They knew, yet they didn't tell me." His voice trailed off, his eyes bright with wonder. "Are you warm enough?"

She nodded. Though he'd thought her dead, he'd wrapped her in his coat.

The hand he swiped across his face shook. "Water?"

Again, Kit nodded.

He retrieved a glass bottle from the console, unscrewed the top, and went to place it to her lips. "Yes?"

She tried to say "yes," but coughed instead.

The bottle he pressed to her lips contained cool, soothing water. She drank it down. Heaven.

She wanted to ask a million questions. Best to wait, to see what he offered about who he was and where they were going. The world was off-kilter, the car, the snowstorm—even *she* felt odd, like inside her an indefinable change had occurred.

"Better?" he said.

"Yes."

"I'm Radulfr. Rafe." He squeezed his thumb and forefinger to the bridge of his nose, then his light honey eyes sharpened. "You're... Safe. You are *safe*."

Sure she was. As safe as if surfing a hurricane. She remained silent.

"I'm here to help you," he said.

Ted Bundy had probably said the same. Her lips twitched. Sybi would claim she was being far more jocular than the situation called for. *Lucky stars*, where were her sisters?

Corralling her mind wasn't easy, but first things first. Her circus years had taught her to read not just her beloved horses, but people as well. The man's eyes had warmed and his face, so harsh when asleep, had softened to welcoming. One callused finger trailed across the back of her hand that rested on the seat.

She snatched it away.

"You'll be okay," he said. "Rest assured." He pressed two buttons on the dash.

"Changing route to MedSurge," came the mechanical voice.

A doctor, they would see a doctor. She fisted her hands. With each medical visit, some new ailment or hurdle rose to thwart her. "I don't want to go."

His jaw hardened to implacability, yet his eyes gentled. "We must."

"But..."

"I can't take you home until you've been checked. I'm sorry."

"All right." Kit cleared her throat. "When you found me, did you see two other women?"

He shook his head. "Just you."

"Are you sure?"

"I am," he said, his concern palpable.

Where were Sybi and Bree? They needed her.

She gripped his arm. "Find them, please. You must find them."

"Who?"

"My *sisters*." Her eyes burned, and she was growing frantic. "They fell the same as I did."

His jaw bunched. "I wasn't made aware of them. Let me find out. I'll make a call."

He pressed a series of buttons on the dash, tapped his earpiece, and spoke low, too low, so she couldn't hear. That terrible exhaustion was creeping over her again. She squeezed her eyes tight, then blinked fast. She had to stay awake to hear if there was any news. *Please, please, please.*

Kit startled when he punched the dash, tore out his earpiece, and flung it into the console bin.

She forced herself not to cringe. He was one scary-looking dude, his face taut with fury. If his anger erupted, and he hit her, she'd bite him and go for his eyes.

He clamped his hands to the wheel, knuckles white. "People are looking for them."

"Who?"

"Others are searching. That's the best I can tell you right now."

"We should look, too."

"They're not anywhere near here."

"But they must—"

"My information is accurate. They're nowhere in these mountains."

"But they…" Frustration seized her. "They'll keep looking?"

"They will. Until they're found."

She wanted to look, too. To find them. To make her world right.

He handed her another water bottle. "Try to finish it, to hydrate. Are you hungry?"

"No." So tired she could barely lift her hand, she clenched the bottle and sipped. Her hand. Her scarred hand. The one with the floral tattoo. Her scars and the tattoo were gone.

Stars alive, her brain had cracked.

Yet for being so tired, she felt fine. She reached for the visor to look in the mirror. There wasn't one. Nor a rearview mirror, either. "Do you have a mirror?"

"I don't." His big hand enveloped hers. "I know everything's strange. Please. You're in a different place, one you're not familiar

13

with. We're going to the MedSurge to have you checked out. I know it's hard, but try to relax. I swear to the Fates, you are safe."

Her lids dragged downward. *Safe?* Her lips twitched. Oh, the irony of that word. She tumbled into sleep.

Rafe watched the rise and fall of her chest as she dozed. He couldn't believe she was alive. Breathing. Talking.

The Alchemics must have triggered her stasis from a distance, which meant they knew exactly where she was, his search for the woman yet another one of their foul experiments.

The Made One rested her head against the doorframe, soft puffs of breath exhaled through her parted lips, his coat snugged around her as if for protection as much as for warmth.

He didn't know what to say or how to advise her, something his packmates would find as astonishing as the woman beside him. More than seventy years had passed since the Wolf Clan included a Made One—those rare women from parallel worlds whom the Alchemics remade and were prone to produce female children.

The phone buzzed. His Alpha, his *father*, kept calling. He sent it to voicemail along with all the others. Duty called him home. But *she* was his duty now, and he wouldn't awaken her. At the best of times his father was abrasive and high-handed. The Made One would learn soon enough. Though it would add another hour to their trip, he was right to change their route from The Keep to the MedSurge. By the time they arrived home, his father would be fully cooked and ready to blister him. How could he when Rafe returned a hero, having found the Made One? Quite the conundrum for his dear Alpha.

The Alchemics said she was from Earth. Rafe tried to imagine being ripped from Eleutia to land on a different world. He couldn't.

Sketches he'd seen another Made One draw of Earth disturbed him—hard highways and glass-and-metal towers, streets crawling with people and cars, and few open spaces for their humans and animals to roam free. How could they stand it?

He leaned back, watching her, waiting for her to again awaken, to prove she truly was real and alive.

The blizzard gave way to rain as they descended the mountain, the clouds clearing to leave sun-dappled prisms of beaded water on the pines. When they pulled into the MedSurge entrance, the still-wet grass blanketed the lawn. Once parked, he settled the hovercraft. She still didn't waken, and his patience ran out.

"We're here," he said, trying to gentle his voice's rasp so as not to startle her.

She leaned forward. "I fell asleep."

"You did." Her deep green eyes held all the forest colors within them. They also held confusion and panic. His chest tightened, squeezed by his deep need to erase her fear.

When she learned the truth, he'd be there to help her through it. "We're at the outlying MedSurge. They're an emergency clinic, and they'll examine you to make sure you're uninjured."

Kit didn't feel injured, she felt... *How the hell did she feel?* She flexed her fingers. Even her scarred ones moved easily. Her joints no longer ached, her head didn't pound, and her bad side wasn't in pain. How odd. She tugged the shift up to her thighs.

"What are you doing?" he said.

"I want to see my legs." She felt good. *Too* good.

The light pouring in from the now-sunny sky confirmed her suspicions. The scars on her twisted left leg had disappeared, just like the ones on her hand. In fact, her leg looked straight and silken and fit. *Too* fit for a woman in her fifties.

She raised her hand to touch her face and its map of scars. She fisted it, bolts of fear stabbing her gut.

Could Bree be right, and aliens *had* abducted her? Rafe looked like a normal man, but... She tamped down her fear. "Let's go, shall we?"

He nodded and pressed a switch that opened the winged doors. "Stay there. I'll come around to help you out."

"No need."

Kit stepped from the car and fell flat on her face. *Ow.* A combination of dirt and gravel scraped her chin, but she managed to get to her knees. How mortifying. Silly. Her clumsiness was from the absurd long dress she wore, not to mention the enormous coat.

She got her feet under her and using the car for leverage, she stood on her good leg, easing her bad one down and putting some weight on it. More weight. The leg held. Other than her scraped knees, both legs felt fine. Strong, even. She hadn't felt that strength in thirty-plus years.

When she looked down, she understood why she'd fallen. She'd misjudged the step. The car hugged the ground as if it had no rims or tires. The tires must fold up or…

A flying car whooshed into the parking lot. The vehicle hung in the air for a moment, then murmured to the ground.

Oh. That was how. Flying cars. Brain freeze, like ice cream's piercing pain through her head.

The car she'd just traveled in must have been flying, too. The car. Flying. Where the hell was she, Roswell?

Rafe clasped her upper arm, eyes narrowed. "All right?"

"No, but not because I pancaked in the dirt."

His quizzical frown said she made little sense to him. She wasn't making much sense to herself, either.

"This is Tallylow," he said. "The nearest town down the top of the mountain. Since I found you encased in ice… *Fark.*" His face stiffened.

He hadn't meant to tell her that. Encased in ice. "Like a popsicle?"

There was that puzzled look again, poor man.

"Where am I?"

"Eleutia."

Not a country or even a world she'd ever heard of. The tattered threads holding her together began to pop. "So I was abducted?"

Fark. Rafe drowned in those deep green eyes, the truth burning the tip of his tongue. She'd straightened her spine, her head held high, demanding the truth.

He couldn't. It was one thing to disobey his Alpha, quite another to defy the Alchemics' order not to explain before *they* chose the moment. The Clan would be made to pay. "I can't. Not yet."

She crossed her arms. "Why not?"

"Others will suffer." Would that he had a better answer.

She looked away from him toward the woods that ringed the MedSurge, as if she wanted to bolt. That's what he would do. His wolves could corral her in an instant, but that would only increase her mental turmoil. "Please. You'll learn everything soon. I don't even know your name."

Her left eye twitched, and he wondered if that tell was for fury or fear.

"It's Kitlyn. Kit. Let's go see the doctor."

Whatever was going on, Kit would figure it out. She'd survive. The circus accident hadn't defeated her. Nor had the death of her husband. Not even the Huntington's. She hadn't faltered then, and she wouldn't now.

The man—Rafe—seemed sincerely troubled, but whether it was truth or a performance staged to ease her fears, she couldn't tell.

He cupped her elbow as he guided her up a brick path to the circular building, his hand warm and protective. A predator cloaked in kindness would do the same.

Majestic pines encircled the area, the soil sandy, the grass emerald green. Another flying car zipped into the parking lot, and yet a roan horse stood tied to a fence post munching on a feed bag.

Eleutia, huh? She'd tumbled into a strange drama where she didn't know her role. Perhaps her looming death had created a fantastical world in her head. Yet the pine scents, the man's firm grip, the heat of him said all she saw, smelled, and felt were utterly real.

Until she understood what game she was immersed in, best to play ball.

She pinned her eyes on the safety of the entryway's banal silver and glass doors, shiny and clean but for myriad vertical scratches on the metal frame's bottom half.

When the doors slid open, a man sitting behind a large, semi-circular counter walked over. He raised his hand in greeting, looking perfectly human, with eyes that tilted upward and a full mouth wearing a smile.

Rafe released her. "Are you good, Kit?"

"Yes. I need to use the ladies' room." She needed to look in a mirror.

"We'll be right back," Rafe said to the receptionist.

Kit didn't bother to protest his escort.

With the bathroom lock's satisfying snick, she leaned her fore-head against the warm wood and took a couple of deep breaths. It felt good to be alone.

She shrugged off the sheepskin coat, then ripped the damned dress over her head. Naked, eyes squished tight, she ran her hands across unnaturally firm flesh—unnatural for a fifty-eight-year-old woman, at least.

No middle-aged pooch. No cellulite dimples. No swollen left knee. She opened her eyes, the ceiling's glow filling the small room with ambient light. But she wasn't ready to look in the mirror.

The arm she held in front of her was long and lean, the skin pale and dotted with a few freckles. Her fingers traced her bicep and forearm muscles, slightly defined and strong. Her arm hadn't looked like that since her vaulting days with her beloved circus horses. Voltige demanded strength, discipline, and endurance to execute the tricks while riding the ring before an audience of thousands.

Her hand glided over her muscled thigh, her firm abdomen, and her round, upthrust breasts—the way they'd been in her twenties.

She had missed this body.

With deliberate steps, she moved in front of the silvered mirror that hung above the sink. Gathering her courage, as she'd done before that first leap onto the horse's back, she stilled. Paused. Breathed. Then she raised her face to the mirror.

She gasped. The woman staring back at her was in her prime. Maybe twenty-eight or thirty. She gripped the sink, afraid she'd topple over from shaking so badly.

Kit pressed her palm to the mirror.

All right.

She pinched the tip of her nipple hard, twisted.

"Damn!" Pain. Real pain.

"Are you all right in there?" came her rescuer's voice.

"I'm fine," she said back, though her voice wavered.

Hands pressing on the mirror, she leaned in close. The nose that once had a bump from a childhood soccer injury was now aquiline. No spiderwebs of red threaded her eyes, nor did the clouding of cataracts gray them, her irises darkened to their original green. Her forehead was clear of lines, and lips once distorted by the pull of age now bloomed with youthful fullness.

The scars mottling the left side of her face, the ridges and rills, the flesh hard and shiny since that disastrous day at the circus—*gone*, her face unblemished.

Her fingers trailed down her cheek seeking the familiar texture of her disfigurement only to brush across the cream of flawless skin.

The face of her youth stared back at her. She wasn't just whole again. She was *young* again.

Tears spilled over her lids and tracked down her rosy cheeks to hang suspended on her undamaged chin.

Kit whirled, putting her back to the mirror and crossing her arms around her waist.

Astonishing. Incredible.

But what about her Huntington's?

"Kit!" She'd been in there too long, and Rafe hadn't heard a sound. "Open the door."

She didn't answer, so he waited a few more minutes, then told the receptionist to get the key.

"Kitlyn!"

When the receptionist returned, he took the key and unlocked the door. "Kit?"

She stood before him wearing that Alchemic tunic, fists balled, shaking. "Am I losing my mind?"

He reached for her and she skittered back.

"No!" she said. "Answer me."

"You are sane. You are young and whole."

"How?"

"I can't tell you that. Not yet."

She gave him her back. "I don't like games."

He stepped forward, close enough to catch her soothing lily-of-the-valley scent. He froze. The Alchemics gave each Made One an individual scent. Too preoccupied to pick it up earlier, it enfolded him in sweet-painful memories of his mam.

Then he caught the additional hint of lilac.

Oh, they were clever, as if they'd purposely designed her scent for him. "Kit."

If possible, she straightened further. He should've protected her from this, never should have left her alone. She was traumatized, and who wouldn't be, wearing new flesh in a strange place?

"Hey there," he said. "You're out of danger. Everything you're seeing and hearing is real."

She whirled, her face taut, cheeks flushed, and jaw firm. She blazed like a fiery Wolf warrior, making his blood race. What courage she had.

"Real, eh?" Her eyes narrowed. "Then let's find the doctor and get this over with."

CHAPTER TWO

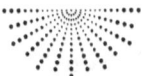

Kit stood in a decent-sized bathroom now shrunk to Lilliputian by a six-foot-three man looming over her. Though, to his credit, he was trying to appear inoffensive and conciliatory. Not happening.

How many sci-fi and fantasy books had Kit read over the years? Hundreds. None fit the situation in which she found herself.

A knock on the door, followed by a deep male voice. "Rafe? You coming out, my friend?"

If her sisters were here… The wild Bree would go with it as if it were a lark. Uber-serious Sybi? Lucky stars, she couldn't imagine that one. *Where* were her sisters?

"Just perfect," she muttered. "Too perfect."

"In a sec, Doc!" Rafe said.

Kit handed him his coat.

"Keep it," he said. "It's still cold outside. When we get to Wolf-Home, you'll have plenty of clothes."

"What's WolfHome?"

He squeezed the bridge of his nose. The man looked tired, dark smudges beneath his eyes, grooves of exhaustion carving his cheeks.

She hadn't noticed, and she felt awful. He'd been nothing but kind, something she prized above all else. "You're exhausted."

"It was a long hunt." His cocky smile sparked a warmth inside her. "But worth it. WolfHome encompasses the lands of our Clan, along with our keeps and towns."

"Why the name?"

He grinned. "Because we're wolves, of course."

"Wolves?" Her brain shorted out.

"Wolf Clan."

She exhaled a long, slow breath. "So, let's get this over with. Then you can rest, and I can find out what the heck is going on."

Tall, ebony-skinned, and dashing, the doctor seemed normal, though some of his instruments were strange. Rafe and the doctor knew each other, and though the doc was surprised about her being frozen, he breezed by it.

Rafe's injured arm was bleeding. She hadn't noticed that, either, and again chided herself for her self-absorption. The doctor had to insist before Rafe removed his shirt. He was beautiful, his broad bronzed chest sprinkled with honey-colored hair that trailed down to an admirable six pack. But half-a-dozen cruel scars marked his chest and arms. Sympathy for his pain fought with the awareness that he might be her enemy. A battle-scarred one. She knew no one, not even her circus performer pals, who bore scars like his.

Her fingers itched to touch him, surprising her.

When the doctor sealed Rafe's wound with a strange round disk, only a faint redness marred his skin. Magic, or so it seemed to Kit's eyes.

The doctor traced one of the uglier, raised wounds along Rafe's chest. "You understand I can erase these, correct?"

Rafe shook his head. "No."

The doctor shrugged. His tablet pinged, and when he read it, he smiled. "According to the Alchemics—"

"*Doc.*" Rafe's voice was almost a growl.

The doctor's lips thinned. "Because of MedSurge's isolation, they insist on a direct line to their lab." He turned back to Kit. "Your bloodwork is excellent."

"What about my Huntington's?"

"I'm afraid I don't know what that is."

"A genetic disease."

"Ah." The doctor opened his mouth, but Rafe cut him a sharp look. "What I can say is the lab performs deep DNA analysis. Your bloodwork came back clear of any disease or genetic disorders."

How could she believe him? That she might be free of the Huntington's made her lightheaded. "Who are the Alchemics?"

"I'm afraid that's not for me to say."

Her eyes narrowed on Rafe. "I see."

Outside the exam room, Kitlyn's brave face impressed Rafe as they walked toward the lobby. Tall for a woman, she was still a head shorter than he, an intimidating difference. Yet she strode with confidence, shoulders back, head erect. She had impeccable control, but he sensed her unease. The Fates, she had courage. Had he been transported to another world and given a new body, he'd be on edge too.

He hoped the Alchemics had done a better job with the other Made Ones, if in fact her sisters had also been transformed. They typically introduced Made Ones to Eleutia in more subtle and palatable ways. They hadn't just screwed up the coordinates with Kitlyn, but her introduction to their world.

It had been deliberate. He'd lay money on it. Yet another of the Alchemics' experiments, and didn't those twisted farkers love to tinker with lives and play the Fates.

Less than two hours earlier, she'd been frozen in a block of ice. Now, she was healthy as a mistral and thought herself deranged. And she mistrusted him. Damn them.

"Explain Huntington's," he said.

She laughed, and her bright smile drew him even as she was handing him some of his own medicine.

"I need to understand," he said.

Her fists curled.

"Please."

Angry eyes stared at him with insolence. "It's an inherited disease. Always fatal. It breaks down the brain's nerve cells. Your mental and physical abilities deteriorate. You lose your personality and your judgment. You can shake, have slurred speech, involuntary movements. Oh, and the pain is quite terrible. My sisters Bree and Sybi have it, as do I. Happy?"

Kit's narrowed eyes sparked fire. She looked like she wanted to geld him. *Happy?* No, he wasn't *farking* happy. Imagining her pain, her enfeeblement, gutted him. "I have to check something. Stay inside? Just for a minute."

"Why not?" she said, voice flippant.

Outside, the day had warmed, turning the sky a bold blue. He triggered his wolf senses to scan the parking lot and forests beyond. The hovers and the horses all bore the scent signature of WolfHome.

While this part of the mountain might be considered Wolf territory, Rafe trusted neither the Bears, nor the Cats—sneaky farkers—not to spy.

But the area was clear of danger, though he caught the signatures of several nearby Timberwolves, including their coywolf Alpha, Paulo, all part of the WolfHome pack. Cats weren't the only ones with rampant curiosity. Normally he'd greet his brothers and sisters and spend some time. Not today.

The fact that his Alpha had given him an untenable job where he couldn't speak forthrightly made the situation abhorrent. His gut boiled. The woman needed to know the *truth*.

Kit was watching from the glass doors, and he waved her outside. "Let's get you to the hover."

She nodded.

Rafe had almost blurted out the word "home." Was she missing hers? He'd always been curious about the parallel worlds, especially Earth. He was even more curious about her. He'd learn and discover everything he could about this arresting Made One named Kit.

The hover's full stop brought Kit awake. "Sorry I fell asleep."

She stretched, aware of every ache in her body. But these pains differed from those caused by her accident. They felt normal and right.

Rafe looked like he could use a nap, too. Though exhaustion tightened his mouth, his eyes warmed. "You needed the rest."

"How long was I out?"

"About three hours. I stopped here to show you WolfHome."

The cliff where they'd parked overlooked an enormous lush valley surrounded by a high wall. Circular houses with conical roofs dotted the landscape, and what looked like a town lay at the valley's center. A village green sat in the middle, and to the right stood an immense round stone structure speckled with windows and connected to outbuildings, the large building surrounding acres of green space.

"WolfHome," Rafe said, with obvious pride and affection.

"Beautiful." She pointed. "And that big round building?"

His eyes smiled. "That's The Keep, the heart. WolfHome is all that you see."

Verdant hills rolled across the valley, crisscrossed by roads. A few vehicles like their hoverthing traveled them, along with people on foot and carts pulled by shaggy beasts reminiscent of oxen. Dozens rode horseback, their seats excellent, with a few cantering, though most walked at a relaxed pace. *All those horses!* Her heart thrilled, then fluttered in fear.

The scene was pastoral, so different from the Earth she knew, yet similar. Too similar. Too bucolic. Too alluring. Her mouth dried, her thoughts dripping with sarcasm. In a way, that was a relief. Though she looked different, she was still the same skeptical Kit. She chugged the water bottle and returned it half-empty to the console.

Beyond the town lay a chain of hills, and farther off a large cove with a protective breakwater that held back a darkened turquoise sea, the antithesis of the wild, gray Atlantic near where she'd fallen.

She breathed in the fresh salt air, both calming and invigorating. The scenery reminded her far more of the English countryside than the New England she had "left." Her heart sped up. The surreality of her situation made her brain hurt.

"You're quiet," Rafe said

"Just contemplative."

He put the hover in gear.

She rubbed a fist across her heart. *Sybi and Bree, where are you?* Were they alive or dead? Sheltered or in harm's way? Tears threatened, a hot poker stabbing her with pain.

She *would* find them. As their big sister, she *always* found them.

Movement to her left. "What is—"

"Hush," Rafe hissed.

Though he remained face forward, his right arm snaked into the back. "Bend down."

She almost blurted, "Why?" but did as requested.

Something whooshed over her head, then a humongous unsheathed sword rested between them. A beautiful thing with sigils carved on the blade and pommel. "I'm going out to deal with… If anything goes awry, press this." He pointed to a red button. "The hover will enter safety mode and take you home."

"What about you? What's wrong? How can I help?"

"You are to *stay* in the hover under all circumstances."

Not if he was in trouble, she wouldn't. Damn him for not telling her anything.

A flash out her window near that large rounded rock. She rubbed her throat, the tension thick enough to steal her breath.

"I need a weapon." She scraped her hands across the loathsome dress. "Preferably a knife."

"You are to *stay* in the hover."

"You're a broken record. I get it. But holding a weapon will make me feel better." That should placate him. He saw her as a poor helpless girl. Right. The circus' Fighting Blade, Reggie, had taught her both throwing and blade-to-blade combat. She'd practiced long after her circus days ended. "Knife?" She arched a brow and held out her hand.

Though obviously reluctant, he drew a little beauty from his boot and slapped it on her palm. Her fingers closed around the hilt. Plain, well balanced. A sweet little mini-Bowie. "Thank you."

His gull-wing door snapped open. "Stay in the hover." He burst from the vehicle, sword in hand.

Two men gripping comparable swords appeared, dressed in black, balaclava masks covering their faces. Rafe drew his belt knife, and he blocked, parried, twisted, scoring a deep hit to one man's shoulder. The injured man fell back while the other pressed forward.

This was *real*! There was blood. Holy *shit*!

She reached for the door handle to go help Rafe.

A thud.

Outside, a black-garbed man smashed a rock against her window. He was short and bulky, his muscles straining when he hefted the huge rock and thudded it down again.

Fuck! She gripped the knife, a focused, icy chill cloaking her as it had when she'd performed.

Smash!

The window spidered but didn't break.

"Let me in, Made One," barked the rock wielder.

Of course she would. A deep breath, and she unlatched the door. If she pressed the handle and kicked out the door, that should give her enough time and leverage to surprise him. Reggie had taught her how to stab and slice, go in low and move high.

All she might have skewered was a straw dummy, but she could cut a man. She was sure she could. Probably.

One. Two. Thr—

A snick behind her. Kit twirled.

Rafe slid into the driver's seat, ignoring the man attacking the hover with a rock.

"There's a…" She pointed to the man out her window.

Rafe drew his kerchief down the blooded blade with meticulous care, as if they had infinite amounts of time.

"But..." Her words died when she pointed to her attacker. He lay on his back, shirt ripped and bloody, while an immense wolf stood beside him, the wolf's forepaws atop the man's chest. His eyes were open, and he stared at her with more fury than fear.

Beyond Rafe's door, the two men he'd fought lay on the ground, one rolling around, groaning, while a pair of wolves the size of ponies loomed over them.

"The wolves, won't they kill them?" she said.

"No." Rafe pressed a button, and the hover rose and slid forward.

"But the men," she said. "You're just going to leave them there?"

"Their Clansmen will eventually be along. Until then, our wolves will remain on guard and make sure all leave our territory."

"So you have trained wolves?"

"Fates, no," he said. "They're *our wolves*."

Kit didn't get it.

A cut scored Rafe's cheek, and sweat, blood, and dirt covered his clothes. "Do you have a first aid kit? I can—"

"No need. We're almost home." He flicked a switch, and the car's smooth motor changed to an amped-up hum. The vehicle tipped forward and went vertical, its nose facing the precipice bottom hundreds of feet below. She grabbed the "Oh shit!" handle.

Air blasted from the front vents, pressing her against the seat back as they skimmed vertically downward inches from the cliff face. At the valley floor, the car smoothly righted itself to a horizontal position, and the blasts of air eased off.

She pried her fingers from the roof handle. That was...interesting. Silly her, getting all squirrely about a little vertical flying.

"What *was* that back there?" She balled her fists to get the shaking to stop. "Why did they attack us?"

"Happens."

"Not in my world. The Wild West ended a long time ago."

"Wild West?"

"Never mind. What was going on back there?"

"Clan skirmishes occur."

"Would they have killed us?"

His smile wasn't the warm and friendly kind. "No. They wanted you."

"Me? Why?"

"Soon. You'll understand soon."

She doubted she'd like what she'd hear.

They drove through the yawning gates in the immense wall circling the valley, then passed fields bounded by low stone walls and crops that looked like corn and wheat and plants she found unrecognizable, those round houses peppering the land.

"Why are your houses round?"

He shrugged. "I never thought about it, really. They're poetry, I guess."

The poetry of form, like the circus' big tent. Some houses were clustered and connected, while others dotted the hills now cutting off her view of the sea. She and the girls would love to swim in that ocean. "Any word on my sisters?"

He checked his phone, then shook his head. "None so far."

If she didn't stop worrying about her sisters, she'd go mad. She must find them *soon.* "WolfHome reminds me of the English countryside. It's lovely."

"That it is," Rafe said, with obvious pride.

After another thirty minutes, they turned onto a hard-packed dirt road that rose up a small hill, and then down toward a second walled entrance near the town. "Do you get many ocean storms?"

"In the winter season a few batter us, though we've the occasional wild weather in spring and fall. But because of that breakwater around the cove and those hills, we're buffered some."

"You're farmers, but you must be fishermen, too."

"That we are. And hunters. And traders. And warriors." He gave her a grin. "We are a busy people. What do your people do?"

She had no idea how to describe her world or its people—the chaos and cement of the cities, the crush of cars and humans. Even where she lived in Down East Maine, wires threaded overhead. Fast-food joints and steel high rises. The drone of helicopters and planes. Pavement everywhere.

"I…"

"It's a lot. I know." Rafe reached out and brushed his hand across her hair. "Forgive me."

His tawny eyes had warmed to caramel, and she saw a kindness there, a gentle regard.

Was it real or fake? Artifice or truth?

They eventually came to a second set of gates that opened automatically when their car-hover-thing approached, then wended their way through the narrow streets, twilight turning the town molten with streams of gold. The verdant scents of honeysuckle and lavender filled the air, the landscape dotted with flowers and fruit trees and conifers. Several large and smaller round buildings flowed by as they headed for the large keep she'd seen earlier.

A few people walked the streets—all men—wearing jeans and long-sleeved t-shirts, with several dressed in tunics of varying colors over matching flowy pants. One man wearing a skirt, far longer than a kilt, hung laundry on the line beside a small home.

Where were the women?

"That's Jake." Rafe shook his head. "He insists on hanging out his wash, rather than using a dryall. Says it smells better. Do you have… Sorry, I didn't mean to—"

"Yes, we have dryers and washers and all sorts of appliances."

They didn't have horses in such prolific numbers, though, nor were they used any longer for transportation. Several clopped by— what looked like a massive Belgian and a sweet Appaloosa—while a smaller hover-thing passed them going the opposite way. The driver waved, and Rafe returned it.

What a strange dichotomy of animal and high-tech transportation. "You have many horses."

"That we do. You like them?"

"I *love* them." An image of her riding that Appie flashed in her head. But then the image changed to her Nessie, who could dance and leap and… Pain. Endless pain subsumed her flesh. She bit her lip hard and tasted the warm copper that brought her back to the now. Sweat greased her palms. As inconspicuously as possible, she wiped her hands on her dress.

"I need to know things, Rafe. What are we doing at the Keep? Why am I here? How long before you explain?"

"We'll be going to rooms in the Keep we've put aside for you. You're here to keep you protected."

"From what?"

He chuffed out a breath. "I promise you will get a full explanation."

"As I mentioned earlier, I dislike games. And secrets. Especially when it concerns my life. You're asking me to take a lot on faith."

"I am." His face hardened to a steely grimness. "But by the Fates, I swear you *will* know all soon."

The not knowing was intolerable. Rafe seemed sincere, as if he wanted to tell her what was going on. Comforting, but this strange reality was turning her nerves jagged. She could scream and rant, demand he tell her, but she suspected that would get her nowhere. He seemed a man who, once he determined his path, wouldn't stray.

Rafe took a right and headed for a building with multiple door bays. He garaged the hover, and as soon as he turned off the engine, Kit scrambled out of the darkened garage and into the dying day's light.

Her body felt good, *so* good, but what had happened to her… Its vastness swamped her like a tsunami.

A hand pressed the small of her back. "Kit."

"What?" she barked.

Lines bracketed his mouth as he frowned. "You're white as a dove."

Her heart beat a rapid tattoo. "Maybe because this is so screwed up."

"It'll get sorted. You're not alone, Kit. Promise."

Not alone? Different planet. Different body. Different reality. She snorted.

They wove through the circular keep. Up stairs, then down

another staircase to a first-floor hall where, thankfully, the stone walls bowing outward didn't make her freak.

Alice survived her Wonderland. So would she.

Along the way, they passed men of all ages, most going in the opposite direction. Many nodded to Rafe, a few saluted, fisted hands to their chests, and all stared at her as if she had grown a second head.

If she'd landed on an alien planet, then why did everyone look so human? Even the horses looked normal. And another thing—how could she understand their language? Rafe's speech was comprehensible but for a few words.

Nothing jibed. Not even a little.

So she'd wait, watch, listen, learn. She shoved her hands into the pockets of Rafe's jacket, squeezing them until her nails bit into flesh.

Rafe halted beside a meandering woman wearing jeans and a tunic, her nose in a book. "Hey, Tilde."

Tilde looked up. "Huh?" She had a tousle of bright red curls and lovely Asian features, with round glasses surrounding her deep brown eyes. She flung herself at Rafe, and they hugged.

"Reading in the halls again?" he said.

She tucked the book beneath her arm. "Rafe! Um, I'm reviewing the biology of mistrals for a class." She poked a finger to the bridge of her glasses and took in Kit. Her eyes widened. "Who's this?"

"Ah," Rafe turned to Kit, and with a wink said, "Kit meet Tilde, and vice versa."

Tilde leaned forward, stuck her nose near Kit's throat, and sniffed. "Oh!" She clasped her hands together.

Did she smell? Was it a custom? Was she supposed to sniff Tilde back? She moved closer and drew in Tilde's scent. "Rosemary. Nice."

"I was working in the herb garden. I am so glad to meet you." Tilde's smile beamed.

Impossible not to smile back. "It's lovely to meet you, too."

Tilde bounced like a pogo stick, as if she couldn't contain her energy. "There's a story here, isn't there, Rafe?"

"Perhaps." He chuckled.

"I need all the details!"

"Later."

Tilde rolled her eyes. "You always say that."

"He does," Kit chimed in.

The two laughed while Rafe stood there looking stoic. "You two done?"

Tilde wiped her eyes. "Did you hear the Cats were at it again?"

"I did. It's being addressed." Rafe cleared his throat. "Time?"

"Oh, no! I'll be late." Tilde took off.

He squinted, eyes sparking as he followed the redhead's progress. She'd slowed and had gone back to reading.

"Tilde!" he shouted.

"Oops!" She broke into a run again and disappeared around the bend.

"Tilde's precious to us, and she's highly distractible." He pressed a hand to Kit's back and steered her down the hall. "Almost there."

"Was it Cats who attacked us?"

"Yes. They're another Clan. A vicious one. We're here."

Rafe opened the carved door to reveal an inviting suite made up of an outer living room, partially opened pocket doors, and beyond them an expansive bedroom. Small balls of ambient light hovered near the ceiling. She swallowed hard, then stepped onto the mellow wood floor that glowed in the twilight. The boards were cool beneath her bare feet as she crossed the living room to the bowed picture windows that overlooked the green space she'd spotted from the cliff.

Pretty. And alien. And confined. "Do the windows open?"

"They do." Rafe pressed a button on the wall and the three lower windows louvered outward.

Her stomach muscles relaxed. If she needed to escape, she could fit out those. Just.

On the wall opposite the black leather sofa hung a large, curved flatscreen. "TV?"

His eyebrow rose. "VidScreen."

The room was large, yet cozy, with plump chairs, a kitchenette, and small welcoming touches—a vase of fresh flowers, a clear bowl filled with sea glass, an inlaid box set on the wooden raw-edged coffee table. She smelled the flowers—strong floral, with a hint of spice. They'd prettied up her jail cell.

She glanced at Rafe, who smiled at her. All except his eyes. He seemed on edge. Not jittery. More like he was holding his breath above a yawning precipice. Did he wish to jump or flee?

Kit entered the bedroom dominated by a huge bed and dresser, above which hung an artful landscape painting, and to its right a large convex louvered window. On the opposite wall was an Impressionist-style mural depicting a forest of pine and birch with several wolves barely discernible in shadow.

Perhaps she'd stepped into one of those novels she loved to read about shapeshifters. Did Rafe turn into a wolf?

Her eyes snapped to his. He was tall, with a powerful build and a raptor's stare, and he'd been tracking her every move.

Stars alive, did he shapeshift?

"To your liking?" he said.

"Yes." *Hey, fella, do you turn into a wolf?* "The suite is lovely. Are there any books here?" With books to read, she could survive almost anything.

He pointed to a tall, narrow armoire. "Several shelves of them."

They returned to the sitting area, and Rafe gestured to a door off the living area. "The bath's through there. Put your clothes in the bin. The cleaners come every three days, and they'll take your dirty laundry."

Perfect timing. "I need to use the bathroom."

Both the good-sized shower and pedestal sink were made of river stones. No shower doors, but the toilet looked much like hers at home. Hooray for toilets. A charming wrought-iron shelving unit held fragrant soaps, washcloths, and hand towels, but no bath towels. A shower should prove interesting. Once she'd taken care of business, she turned the shower faucets on and off. Oh, to be clean again. Soon.

She held her arm out straight. Rock steady. No sign of her Huntington's shakes. Was the MedSurge doctor right?

Returning to the living room, Kit found Rafe had piled clothes on the sofa—a pair of jeans, a rust-orange t-shirt, socks, boots, and… She rifled through the clothes. Soft bras and panties with an elasticized waistband and a teensy V of cloth in front and back. No grannie undies for the Wolf Clan, she guessed.

"There are more clothes in the bedroom closet," Rafe said.

"You seem well prepared for my arrival." How had they known her size?

Just the slightest widening of his eyes, then gone. "I phoned ahead."

Right. There was more to it than that, secrets she wasn't being told.

The place and Rafe were perfect. Too perfect. She hesitated, running her hands along the top of the windowsill, tracing the couch's buttery leather beneath her fingertips. "Am I a prisoner?"

He reared back. "No."

"So I can leave?"

"The suite? Of course."

"What about WolfHome?"

He rubbed the back of his neck. "Why would you want to leave? You're protected here. You saw how those Cats attacked us."

Said the jailer. "I did."

Arthur had jailed her, too. Oh, not at first. Her husband had been too smart for that. He was the most handsome man she'd ever seen —coal black hair, a cleft in his chin, and a smile to die for. On the outside. And decades after Art's death, not having been with a man for almost as many years, she stood with a wolf far more compelling than her late husband.

Rafe might be kinder, but he'd still imprisoned her.

The irony. She laughed. She couldn't help it. It started as a giggle and grew, her laughter blooming around the impeccable suite. She crouched in front of the mini fridge, trolling inside while cool air brushed her cheeks to hide the burn of tears.

She controlled them, dammed them. As always. Composure in place, she stood.

"Thank you," she said.

He turned to leave. The pull of him, a band stretched too taut, unnerved her. She willed him to stay, yet she was desperate to be alone. "Will you be back?"

"Not today." He stepped close. "But I'll send someone to stay with you."

"No. I'd prefer to be alone."

The sympathy in his eyes hurt.

"You're sure you'll be all right?" he said.

"I am, Rafe." She smiled. Did he see her desperation? "Have you any word on my sisters?"

"I'm sorry, no. Rest assured we'll keep looking. You'll hear as soon as we do." He took her hand. His was calloused, with scars sprinkled across the back, and warm. Its heat climbed up her arm as if seeking her very heart.

"Be well, Kit."

"Well" hadn't been in her lexicon for decades. She squeezed, then released his hand. "Thank you. For everything."

His eyes burrowed into hers as if uttering a silent a vow.

CHAPTER THREE

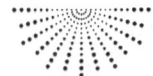

Once Rafe was gone, a vast aloneness settled around her, unfamiliar and unwelcome. If she chewed on the sum of her thoughts, she'd choke.

Kit doffed Rafe's coat, and as she went to hang it up, she pressed it to her, inhaling his scent of leather and pine and musk.

She placed his coat on a hook, since hangers apparently didn't exist, then ripped off the hated floor-length dress and tossed it into a corner.

In the shower, she soaped her body and hair, the warm spray pounding her. Exhaustion spread from her toes to the top of her head. She turned off the shower spray, only to be blasted by warm air from two wall vents, like a giant hand dryer. In seconds, her body and hair were bone dry, which explained the lack of towels.

Instead of dressing, Kit stepped before the large mirror above the sink. She froze, then touched her left cheek, her breasts, skimmed her hands down her ribs, her waist, her hips. She was...unbroken. Unblemished. Unscarred.

Yet familiar. So familiar.

She leaned forward, tilting her face to the left, and examined the right side of her skull. Long, thick hair glowing with vitality had replaced the accident's bald patches.

Was she Lazarus or Frankenstein's monster?

She threw a roundhouse kick, overbalanced, and landed on her ass. Laughing, she hauled herself up and massaged her sore butt. Time to practice.

After executing a series of katas in the living room, she bent in half, wheezing. And grinned. She'd completed all thirty-six.

Kit shoved the furniture back in place and flopped onto the couch.

Her new muscles and joints might not remember, but the discipline of how to move, of the forms, rested soul-deep within her. She'd improve.

How many got a second chance at life?

At home when she was this contemplative, her orange cat Buddy would leap onto her lap. He always knew.

But Buddy wasn't here. Nobody was here. She rubbed her hands up and down her thighs. She missed him, missed her dog, Charm, and her horses, oh, how she missed them—the ancient Ellipsis, shy Covert, proud Sassyass, and crazy Blitz. Snapshots in her mind were all she had left of them.

Her breath stuttered.

They'd be fine, safe, well cared for. Her helpers at her riding school would see to that.

Thinking about her assistants—Jane, Jules, and Jenny—she got all maudlin. The trio of 8-year-olds had begged, whined, and cajoled her for riding lessons. As kids, they'd driven her crazy, made her laugh, and dragged her from that hateful self-absorption. Watching the three Js grow into fine equestrians and lovely young women had been a pleasure.

The girls would make wonderful caretakers, as they'd done when her Huntington's had flared. Trustworthy, smart, and kind, the girls adored Kit's animals. So why was she blubbering like a baby?

Because she wasn't dead. Or was she? Perhaps her flesh had died on Earth or maybe she'd simply disappeared. Either way, the Js would mourn. At least her gifting them the farm would temper their sorrow.

But she was *alive*.

Not to them.

Lucky stars, this was all so confusing.

Kit scoured the room for tissues, but ended up sitting on the toilet seat, pulling paper from the roll.

How were her critters doing? It hurt to think of them. She honked into the toilet paper and rinsed her face. She yearned for her animals fiercely, so how come she couldn't think of a single person she missed? She didn't long for her house, either. Not really. What was wrong with her, that she felt nothing but emptiness for her home and those she'd left behind?

Kit blamed herself for creating that void. *She'd* been the one to cut ties with her circus family, and she'd hurt them. How could she have done that? When other friends mouthed expressions of pity or sorrow, she'd cut them off, too, instead of treasuring those friendships.

Hard to admit how she'd distanced herself. What a fool she'd been. What a stupid fool.

She hugged a pillow. *Face it, kiddo, your sisters and the Js were the only friends you had left on Earth.*

The self-indulgence ended right here, right now. Any new friends she made, she'd cherish. A smile lifted her lips. And she'd find Sybi and Bree. That was non-negotiable.

Kit kneeled on the couch to close the curtains, her eyes tracking the acres of grass, flowers, rocks, and trees. Easy enough to slip into the courtyard and escape.

She dressed in loose gray pants and a tangerine t-shirt, then plucked a hardback from the armoire's shelf. A couple danced on the bright green-and-gold cover, but was missing both title and author. When she opened the book, she groaned.

The writing was a gobbledygook of hieroglyphics and strange backward-slanting letters. She couldn't read a word.

Frantic, she pulled books from the shelves. All bore the same, indecipherable writing. *Gaaak.*

Kit sank onto the bed. Everyone she'd met spoke the same language. *Her* language. English.

So they'd developed a different written language, which made sense. *Damnit!* The thought of not being able to read…

The book she threw smashed against the mural with a thud. She whammed another. And another.

Squeezing her eyes tight, she rubbed her temples. Then she retrieved the books scattered on the floor. Thankfully, most were undamaged, though one book's binding had separated from the spine. She straightened its corners.

It could be fixed. It *had* to be fixed. She didn't even have a phone to call Rafe and ask where to get it fixed, to apologize for damaging the book, to…

A computer. With a computer she'd search the internet for signs of Bree and Sybi. The doctor's tablet and the hovercar were high tech. So was Rafe's phone. They *had* to have computers, the internet. Her frantic search of her rooms found nothing resembling a computer.

Maybe it was part of the television. Though she scoured the suite, she couldn't find the remote, and the stupid T.V. had no buttons at all. How was she supposed to turn the thing on?

So frustrating. Well, she'd find answers. How to turn on the T.V. Where they'd hidden the computer. Why she understood their language but couldn't read.

Kit slumped on the bed and plucked at the coverlet. The dresser top was pristine, virginal. At home, hers had been filled with photos. All she wanted now was one photo, one single photo of her sisters.

Sybi and Bree, where are you? Where am I? Why am I here?

Kit awakened starving.

She peered around her bedroom. No, not her bedroom, but one with a curved wall, strange art, and…

Memory slapped her.

Given her love of sci-fi and fantasy, she was now living the dream. "Fuck!"

More like a nightmare. If it were a dream, she'd be able to read.

She stretched, touching her palms to the floor. How many years since she'd done that? Nothing hurt, not her leg nor her shoulder, and she'd slept well, deep and refreshing. Through the open window, a soft breeze carried the scent of lilacs. She should get up. Leaning back against the soft pillows, she closed her eyes and just breathed.

A knock at her door had her scrambling off the bed. "One second!"

Kit smoothed her t-shirt and threw back her shoulders. Wearing only the soft bra, she hoped her abundant breasts wouldn't jiggle. She snorted. Of all her problems that was seriously low on the totem pole.

Another knock.

"Coming!"

When she opened the door, a male with the face of Adonis, honey skin, and sloe eyes that glimmered with humor stood before her. "Hello, Ma'am Kitlyn. I'm Max. Some call me Ferret though only my best pals."

"Um, for now I'll stick with 'Max,' okay? And please, I'm Kit."

He grinned. "Deal. Rafe was worried since you missed dinner and breakfast this morning. His patience wore thin." He wiggled his eyebrows. "Longer than usual though."

A small spurt of annoyance prompted her to say, "Rafe's been patient with me."

"Is that so?" Max's smile was slow and suggestive.

She rolled her eyes. "Yes, Max, it is."

"In any event, the Commander's patience has now flown, and he wants to make sure you get to mid-day meal. Rafe said you call mid-day, 'lunch.' He's on duty, and I'm the designated retriever."

So Rafe was a Commander. That made so much sense. Her stomach growled. "Yes to food."

"Lots."

"I have no money."

"Meals in the dining hall cost nothing."

"Oh, swell. I'm starved." She zoomed through her ablutions and returned to Max. Once he'd closed the door behind them, he demonstrated how to lock and unlock it with her palm. Sure enough, it worked. She shook her head as Max escorted her down the branching corridor.

"Rafe's being all secretive," he said. "So you're a friend of his?"

"We met yesterday, um… I guess we're friends."

"The Alpha's son makes friends easily. The Commander's a good man."

Alpha's son. If she was such a big deal why hadn't she met the Alpha? She lengthened her stride to keep up with the tall, lean male who wore his long black hair in a queue and looked to be in his late twenties. When they rounded a curve—and there were curves every-where—they approached a set of double doors with wolves and trees carved into their face. Carvings were on her door, too, but these were exceptional, made of some dark wood burl that showed wolves playing and howling, with one wolf pup peeking from behind the trunk of a tree.

Any minute this Max would change into a wolf. A part of her thrilled at the idea of shapeshifters. Wish fulfillment, much?

Kit swayed, seeing double—both the doors in front of her *and* the barn doors at home on Earth. Both were real, as if she was literally in two different places. Nausea spiraled up from her belly.

"Ma'am Kitlyn?"

A snap. "Oh." The wolf doors had coalesced into a singular real-ity. She reached out and pressed her fingers across the smooth letters marching across the carved door. She took a couple steps back.

The words were unintelligible, but the letter shapes were crisp and clear. Her eyes. On Earth, even in her prime she'd been near-sighted, worn glasses or contacts, and then her cataracts clouded her vision further. Her *eyes*. Glorious. "What does that say?"

"Enter All Who Wish the Clan to Prosper," Max said.

"A good sentiment." Earlier, she'd found a pad and pencils in a side table drawer, and she resolved to come back and sketch the words. It would help her learn to read the letters and glyphs.

That was practical. If she stuck to practical things, she'd be okay.

Max held one of the doors open to reveal an attractive dining hall with arched beams crossing its ubiquitous curved roof.

"The Hall," Max said. "We eat here. Celebrate here. Vote here."

Light flooded The Hall's many large windows that let in the warm sun. Noisy, with people eating and talking and laughing.

Food scents tickled her nose, and her mouth watered. Where was... The noise died to silence. She swallowed. Every eye in the room arrowed toward her.

Her palms grew sweaty. After her accident, people would either stare at her or avoid eye contact. She was maimed, a grotesque broken in body, her face riddled with hideous shiny scars.

And the diners were all staring, hundreds of wide eyes peering at her, some leaning forward, others rising to stand, as if she were still the freak, the gargoyle.

She had to run.

Rafe was royally pissed. Off shift, he'd entered The Hall right after Kit and Max, and over the top of Kit's head he saw the Clan acting like a bunch of curious pups. He'd warned them about that, but they just couldn't resist the impulse to gawk, which must be making Kit feel awkward and strange. *Idiot wolves.* That look on her face. Her remarkable control had slipped—she was horrified.

He wasn't having it, not with this unusual woman who'd obviously suffered and didn't have her bearings.

Where was his father? Ulfr would fix things in a heartbeat. He scanned The Hall. It was the Alpha's place to correct Clan behavior, but as was typical, his father was nowhere to be seen. *Fark.*

Tilde sat in her usual place. Good. His friend never fit the mold, but Tilde was filled with a love and kindness often unnoticed by some of his Clansmen. Her fortuitous meeting with Kit earlier would serve them both well. He'd seat Kit beside her, and he'd include Max, too. Max and Tilde would be welcoming, and they wouldn't make her feel like a party favor.

Would someone prank her? They'd better not dare. That initiation rite would send her running. His wolf's protective nature rose, and he had to bite back a growl. He'd rip them apart if they did anything to frighten Kit.

Kit froze, the world around her a blur, her heart thudding.

Cowardly. She was such a damned coward. To run. To hide. At home, her world consisted of her animals, her two sisters and the three Js. Bree had never married though she'd had long-term boyfriends. Sybi was all about work. And Kit's marriage, no children of course, to the uber-controlling Arthur… Inside her micro-world, she'd gotten groceries online or ordered take out. Shopped on Amazon. Even had her meds delivered. Her coping might have been chicken-hearted, but it had gotten her through the days.

She touched her face, a reassurance that her flesh really was altered, even if her mind remained that of a gimpy, scarred, antisocial woman.

What if she'd stood tall and proud and unapologetic for her infirmities? If she'd been brave enough to open herself to others, would they have accepted her? Perhaps not all, but many would have done so. If only she'd given them a chance.

Before the accident, she'd been ballsy and brave. That woman *had* to be inside her somewhere, buried beneath the cowering creature she'd become.

She wiped her sweaty palms on her pants, straightened her bowed back, and stared with intention at the crowd. Here, now, she had a choice. To run rabbit-scared from the room or to give these strangers a chance.

Kit dug deep, focusing on kindness and caring, and forced her lips up into a smile.

Most people in the room were men. Fair-skinned and black and Asian, and a combination of all three. Each smiling back. At her.

A hand gripped her shoulder. She whirled.

"Hello, Kit," said Rafe, his voice that smoky timbre burning with anger. He wasn't looking at her but surveying the crowd with a stare blistering enough to melt granite.

"Hi." Her stomach rumbled. "I could eat a horse."

He stared at her with revulsion. "You *ate* horses?"

She couldn't help smiling. "No. It's just an old saying about being hungry."

"Whew, that's a relief." He made a point of stepping beside her, clasping her hand in his big one, and running the thumb of his other hand down her cheek.

A dizzying wave roiled through her, beginning where he'd touched her and spreading outward to her extremities. She swayed, woozy with prickles running up and down her body. His large hand moved from her face to her waist, making sure she stayed upright.

The sensations hadn't been an imaginary swoon out of a romance novel. That feeling, the aftermath tingling her flesh, was real. She raised her eyes to his. "What did you do, Rafe?"

"You're hungry. Let's go."

She dug in her boots. "No. What did you do?"

His smile was slow, his honey eyes warm. "Just the blessing of the Clan."

How woo-woo was that? "Are you a wolf in sheep's clothing?"

He laughed. "I'm a Wolf all right."

"A wolf. Literally, like do you shapeshift?"

"Shapeshift?" Rafe's eyes widened, his grin broad. "You mean become a wolf? Wish I could. No, but as a member of the Wolf Clan, we're connected to the wolves. They're our brothers and sisters."

"Oh, I see." She didn't, but it sounded cool.

His eyes darkened. "It'll be fine. Come on, let's eat."

"Lead on, Macduff."

"Who's Macduff?" he said.

"Shakespeare."

"Who?"

Lucky stars, no Shakespeare. Sinful. "Just a joke."

He arched an eyebrow, but kept her hand in his as he led her into the dining hall.

The cafeteria-style service looked familiar and the food appealing. Since Kit was starved, she piled her plate with bread and slabs of what appeared to be meat and cheese, added a drink, a salad, and a cookie that smelled like walnut cinnamon.

Rafe went directly to the table after getting his meal, but she paused at the condiment station where she put together a sandwich, then followed Rafe to where he sat.

Someone pulled out a chair for her between Rafe and Tilde, and she put down her tray and sat.

Rafe stared at her plate. "What's that?"

"What's what?"

"*That.*" He pointed. "You put the meat and cheese inside your bread?"

"It's a sandwich. I put stuff on it, too. Mayonnaise and a little mustard." At least she hoped that's what they were.

"New to me," Rafe said.

"Hello Kit!" Tilde said with great exuberance.

"Hi." She was glad to see the redhead seated beside her with Max across from them.

"That's funny-looking, that thing with the bread," Tilde said.

Kit took her knife and cut her sandwich in half, then cut a half into pieces. She held one up. "Anyone want a try?"

Max snatched it out of her hand and chomped. "It's good!"

Tilde, Rafe, and another tablemate each took a piece. They chewed with deliberation and nods.

"Sandwich," she said brightly, then focused on her plate. Her tablemates—all eleven men and Tilde—were staring at her.

Inside, she reminded herself, she had to own it. She ducked her head. She had to fix the inside while she playacted the outside. Not an easy thing.

Rafe cleared his throat, and the others dropped their eyes and began to eat again. So did she, and after cleaning her plate except for the cookie, she laid her napkin on the table. The meal had been outstanding, with both familiar and unusual tastes and scents.

The first bite of the cookie melted in her mouth, like a cinnamon-chip-and-walnut cookie, but with a floral flavor she couldn't name.

During lunch, mid-day as they called it, there'd been comings and goings, which told her that not everyone ate at the same time. The Hall's atmosphere felt casual and relaxed and normal. Normal was good.

"Food okay?" Rafe said.

She waved a hand across her empty plate. "Delicious."

"Good." He leaned closer. "You've had a long sleep, and I wondered… How are you feeling?"

Weird as hell. Another lie to mouth. "Great! But I have a few questions."

"We haven't found your sisters. I promise the minute I hear anything, you will, too."

"I couldn't find the remote for the T.V., um, VidScreen."

"Remote? I don't know what that is."

Oh. "How do you turn it on?"

"Just tell it to."

Tell it. Right. "Why can't I read when I can speak your language?"

He rubbed the back of his neck. "I don't know. You should be able to do so."

Not a help. "I need a computer. Like the tablet the doctor used."

"Why would you want a medica tablet?"

"No, no. Like an all-around one that connects to the internet."

Max looked down, but she'd caught the pity in his eyes. In fact, everyone at the table was looking at her that way but for Rafe and Tilde.

Kit smiled as she imagined a queen would, then rose. "I'm going to get another cookie. Anyone want anything?"

No one did. Rafe followed her to the counter and watched her sniff cookies until she chose a peanut butter one.

He moved closer and peered down at her with intensity. "They will get used to you."

"I'm the shiny new toy, aren't I? And this toy wants an explanation of how and why I got here."

"I…"

"Paulo!" shouted an older man a few tables over.

Others took up the call.

Rafe chuckled as they returned to the table. Once they were seated, he leaned back, crossed his arms, and stretched out his legs. "We've been graced."

Tilde snorted. "You can be such a cynic, Rafe."

"Paulo wants something," he said.

Max poked Rafe across the table. "You are totally cynical when you're not being overly optimistic. Face it, you're a contradiction."

"Aren't we all?" he said.

Kit craned her neck to see what the fuss was about and choked on a bite of cookie.

A black-and-tan…coyote? Wolf?… was trotting through the dining hall. Once again, her brain was having trouble keeping up with what she was seeing. The creature had spots and was bigger than any Earthly wolf. It bounced as it jogged, its black tongue lolling from its open muzzle.

Rafe said they weren't shapeshifters. That the wolves were their brothers and sisters. So they joined WolfHome at meals? The Hall's din had elevated since the canid's appearance. She loved all critters, especially horses and dogs, but everything was tinged with the surreality of a dream. The handsome Commander. The quirky Tilde. The jokester Max. Wolves in the dining hall…

She needed to leave, get her act together, and figure out the next move to make.

"I've got to get going." She started to rise. "Back to my rooms."

"Wait, don't leave yet," Rafe said.

"But—"

"Watch Paulo. He's pretty entertaining." He paused. "Please?"

His eyes asked a question she couldn't refuse, and she sat back down.

"Thank you." Rafe inclined his head, "Our resident coywolf brother. He and our Timberwolf brothers and sisters are often at WolfHome rather than in their mountain dens. Paulo imagines himself their Alpha, though I'm not sure all the wolves agree."

"But he's so big."

"Not at big as some coyotes."

"Where I'm from, coyotes are smaller than wolves, who sometimes kill them."

"Coyotes are rare on Eleutia, which is why Paulo lords it over his wolf pack. When the pack's here, they're always looking for handouts. They get them, too."

It sounded normal. *Their* normal. "You're good friends, um, brothers with the wolves then?"

"More like…symbionts. We draw from them, and they from us."

"Draw what?"

"It's complicated. Traits. Power. Aid."

"How?"

For no sane reason, his soft laugh warmed her. "I've never had to explain it before. It's… We're connected. We pull power, skills, energy, strength from the wolves, and they from us."

How strange and fascinating. "Is it a conscious pull?"

"Mostly no, though occasionally it's proactive."

Symbionts. How magical and amazing. "Paulo's handsome."

"He knows it, too. As well as arrogant, a know-it-all, and a trickster."

"Coyote in our American mythology was tricksy, too."

A little boy, maybe five or six, crawled onto Rafe's lap. Brown haired, blue eyed, and espresso skinned, he cupped his small hand around Rafe's ear and whispered.

Rafe's laugh boomed, then he gave Kit a sly glance. "Vantha here wants to meet you."

Kit leaned toward the boy and smiled. "Hi, Vantha. I'm Kit. It's nice to meet you." She held out her hand to shake his, but his arms went wide and he leapt into her lap. Kit clutched him close before he could fall, and he wrapped his arms tight around her neck. He was warm and cuddly and totally adorable.

He sniffed her. "You smell funny," he said in his child's voice.

She frowned. "Funny good? Or funny bad?"

Vantha sniffed her again. "I think good." His grin was minus a front tooth. "Like a Wolf. Sort of. But you're not exactly a Wolf."

"No, I'm not."

He pressed a finger to his lips as if thinking deep thoughts. "But you smell like Clan." He nodded, so serious. "That's good. What are you?"

At that point, Rafe hauled the boy off her lap and blew a raspberry on his belly. "Off with you."

The child scampered away to a bearded, red-faced male who was slapping his thighs with laughter. When the boy neared, the man opened his arms wide, and the child flew onto the big man's lap.

"Our children are curious sorts," Rafe said with a fond smile.

"What a sweetie."

"That he is, and full of much mischief."

The child jabbered away to the big man, who was smiling and nodding as he listened intently. "Mischief is good in kids."

Rafe's eyes sparked. "And in some adults, too."

A bald man across the table cleared his throat. "Ma'am Kitlyn, do you know what you are?"

Rafe cut him a fierce look.

She was about to say, "No, do you?" when a man at the next table shouted, "Ma'am Kit, go say hi to Paulo." Another one echoed, "Yeah, go say hi." And another.

Paulo must be friendly though she wouldn't dare pet him. Interacting with animals felt uncomplicated and safe. She dashed off.

"Kit!" Rafe barked. "Don't touch him!"

She hadn't planned to. When she neared the coywolf, she slid into an empty chair so they'd be eye to eye, and then lay her hands on her thighs. She hoped he'd come to her. "Paulo, hello boy."

The coywolf's head turned her way, then he trotted over and sat directly in front of her. And stuck his nose in her crotch.

"Paulo!" she said, aghast. Except the humor of the universal gesture made her laugh. Men, dogs, wolves. Geesh.

He snorted, then raised his head to hers. His eyes were ice-blue, laughing eyes. Yet more. Deep as the ocean and clear as the sky. Fathomless and far seeing. As if he knew her yearnings and truths. As if he saw the many pieces of her—the conflicts and the calm, the sorrow and the joy, the pain and the love.

Desperate to stroke him, she curled her fingers into her thighs.

Paulo blinked, and his cold, damp nose nudged her left hand again and again. She raised her hand to touch his pelt.

When she stroked, he wuffled a sigh. His fur was silky-rough beneath her fingers. She petted him again and then scratched behind his ears. He made a growl-purr sound, his head drooping, and he rested it in her lap. Those ice-blue eyes closed. He sighed.

Kit wanted to sigh, too.

Which is when she realized the dining hall had gone silent. She lifted her gaze from Paulo and looked around.

Jaws were dropped and eyes bugged.

A cold damp nose nuzzled her, and then Paulo sat back on his haunches, blue eyes open, jaws wide, tongue lolling as if he thought the whole thing a riot.

She scratched beneath his chin. "You're a smart boy, aren't you? I don't really know how to talk to you, but I very much appreciate you visiting with me."

Paulo's black tongue curled out, and he licked across the spot on her face where Rafe had pressed his thumb. He lapped her opposite cheek, too, gave her chin a swipe, then moved away. His head swiveled back and forth across the dining hall, as if he were surveying the Clan. *His* Clan.

Wolf whistles and thumbs-up sprinkled the hall.

Paulo's pale eyes danced with humor, and he yipped and trotted off.

Oh, my. Wasn't that something.

CHAPTER FOUR

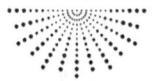

R afe appeared and straddled a chair across from her. "That was...surprising."

"Paulo is..." She shook her head. "I don't have the words."

His expression hovered between annoyance and awe. "Few do. He's the most complex, ornery, brilliant, pain-in-the-ass canid in the pack. Yet you had him in the palm of your hand. The wolves are yours now, too."

"Mine?"

"What Paulo sees, they see. Most non-Clan remain shadows to the pack." He chuffed a breath. "Neff telling you to say hi was meant to be a prank."

"A prank?"

"Normally, Paulo would have growled and snapped at you. He wouldn't have touched you or hurt you, but he can be scary. It's sort of an initiation rite, meeting Paulo. Befriending a stranger? That's never happened."

"I guess the joke backfired, eh? He has very big teeth. So I figure I'm lucky."

Rafe grinned. "Oh? I doubt luck had anything to do with it."

Back at their table, she gave the perpetrators of the prank a wink. Her tablemates grinned back and applauded.

"Want to go for a swim after lunch, Kit?" Tilde said. "It's just a short hike to the ocean. The water's heavenly."

"Your appointment?" Rafe said. "In ten minutes?"

Rafe had insisted she be checked by the pack's doc, and he'd made the appointment. "Raincheck, Tilde?"

Tilde's forehead scrunched. "Um? I don't understand."

"Sorry. Would you ask me again another time, for the swim I mean?"

Tilde brightened. "Of course!"

"I'd better go." Kit returned her tray and dishes, then threaded through the tables toward the dining room entrance.

Rafe was waiting for her. "I'll accompany you."

"That's okay. You gave me directions to her office."

He nodded. "Yes, but I'd like to go with you. For company."

No one ever went with her to the doctor, not even Sybi or Bree. She preferred to swallow any bad medicine alone. "No, I'll—"

"I insist, Kit." He pressed a hand to the small of her back.

He looked so damned savage—face taut, brows beetled, eyes iced with cold fire—and he towered above her as if his sheer presence would bend her to his will. But she was learning the many facets of Rafe and none of them scared her. He saw himself as her protector, which was sweet. She'd acquiesce. This time. "All right."

Kit insisted Rafe stay in the waiting room while she met with the doc—Kicks, a spike-haired, bubblegum-chewing woman. Kicks performed the same tests as the MedSurge doctor, with a few more added for "good measure."

Kicks made no mention of how different Kit was from Clan members, though she said in an offhand way that she'd been instructed to perform several unusual genetic tests. When Kit had asked what they were and who'd instructed her, Kicks said in usual doctor speak, "Let's wait and see."

"Let's not," Kit said as she dressed. "How about you tell me now, hm?"

Just like every Earthly doctor Kit had ever met, Kicks refused. Fine. She'd plant herself in the waiting room until she understood.

"All set?" Rafe said when she returned to the waiting room.

"Kicks said my blood tests should take a half hour. I'm going to stay until the results are in. You needn't wait with me."

If the test showed her Huntington's was viable, she wanted to be alone.

He slipped his hands into the pockets of his jeans. "I'll stay."

Damn. But he was trying to be kind. "All right. I wish I had a deck of cards. We could play to pass the time."

"What is a deck of cards?"

"Playing cards. For card games?" She described them, and he remained puzzled.

"We play dice, minjo, checkers," he said. "But card games? No."

If she made some decks, she could teach them. But how long would she be here? She didn't trust this world, her reconstituted body, any of it. She crossed her legs. Uncrossed them. Scratched an earlobe, which was oddly still pierced. Rested her hands in her lap.

Rafe reached over and squeezed her hands. "It will be all right."

Sure it would. On that thought, Kicks appeared, blowing a bubble, then sucked the gum back into her mouth.

Kit notched her chin, steeling herself for the worst.

"Your blood work's fine, Kit. So are the scans. No genetic disorders—"

"You're sure?"

Kicks blew a bubble, popped it, and smiled. "I talked to the doc at MedSurge. He said you were concerned about genetic disorders, so I had them double screen your blood. All clear. And no disease, I might add."

Chills shivered through her. Gone. The Huntington's, her death sentence, truly was gone. "I appreciate it." Her mind understood, though her heart hadn't quite accepted.

Rafe walked her back to her rooms. "You're healthy, Kit. It's real."

"You had me see Kicks for reassurance, didn't you?"

He shrugged. "Seemed to me you needed it."

"Thank you." Exhaustion crept through her like a stalker. Being out in public, plus a visit to a doctor could do that. Or perhaps her illness… Kit jammed the breaks on that thought.

"See you later. If you need anything, call." Rafe handed her a silver phone, bigger than the old flip phones, but similar. When she unfolded it, the screen looked like a hinged iPhone with a keypad. And she couldn't read any of the letters or numbers on the keypad or screen.

"I've programed a bunch of people into it for you. Me, Tilde, and Max, the dining hall, Kicks, and the Alpha."

"Why haven't I met the Alpha, Rafe?"

His eyes shuttered. "Only Ulfr knows the answer to that, I'm afraid."

"Oh, well I…" She stared at the screen. "I… I can't read any of it."

He took the phone from her hand and said, "Rafe."

Gobbledygook rose on the screen.

"That's my number, but you can also say, 'Call Rafe,' and the phone will do so."

"Great. Terrific." She was desperate to escape.

"I know I'm repeating myself," he said, his eyes softening. "But we'll get things worked out. I can't imagine what you're feeling, not very well at least. But you're managing better than anyone antici-pated. You're strong and capable. I swear to the Fates all will be well, Kit."

She should say something, but she couldn't find the words, so she palmed her door open and scooted inside.

Pressing back against the door, she squeezed her eyes, trying to erase the bombardment of overwhelming sensations.

Her doctors in the "real" world always found something. Maybe Kicks was wrong and would later find evidence of her genetic disor-der. Or maybe Kicks was the precursor to her being institutional-ized. Or maybe… "Damn."

Physically she felt fine, her body de-aged back to her circus days. What middle-aged woman wouldn't want that? Except inside she remained fifty-eight years old and dying.

If only she could find her sisters. The three of them would figure things out. They always had. Hearing their familiar voices would mean everything.

Kit had been here, what, three days?

The urge to go home, back to the familiar exploded through her. She raced into the bedroom and shoved the comforter off the bed, then began tossing clothes onto the sheet. In the bath, she gathered her toothbrush and soap and threw them onto the pile. What else?

These people hadn't given her a choice, just dragged her here and changed her without her permission. Now, she *chose* to leave.

Four books went onto the pile, but with a sigh, she put back three. Ridiculous idea, bringing books she couldn't read. Yet she kept one, for company.

Once she'd loosened the sheet from the bed, she tied the ends into a sack. There. When she hefted the bundle onto her shoulder, she swore. Too heavy.

She began untying the sack, but the knot fought her. "Fuck!"

What the hell was she doing?

Her plan to "escape" made no logic or sense. She sat on the bed, the sack tumbling to the floor, the knot untying, clothes and toiletries spilling out. It seemed the knot was done fighting. She laughed at the absurdity of it all.

A knock at the door jerked her upright.

Whoever it was, she'd get rid of them. She closed the bedroom doors behind her. "Coming!"

Rafe loomed in the door, hands on hips, face dour and threatening.

No. She was not up for bad news, not right now. "I was about to take a nap."

"You're flushed." Rafe squeezed her upper arm. "Are you well?"

"I'm fine." Kit shook off his hand.

Rafe stormed by her like a man on a mission. He seemed to have grown, expanded, eyes volcanic with fury, eating up the living room's ample space until it felt confining and small.

Oddly enough, this imposing Rafe sent a thrill up her spine. Though it took much of her depleted energy, she held her ground.

"Sit," he said, taking the chair for himself.

"Something's wrong."

"No."

"My sisters?"

"Still missing." He swiped a hand across his face, his eyes bleak.

She swallowed and sat on the couch across from him. She missed his usual smile. A darkness hovered around his formidable presence, and his focused purpose made her skin pebble.

"Is it about the doctor's visit?" she said.

"No."

"How about something to drink?"

His answer was slow in coming. "All right."

She opened the mini fridge. "Water or this green stuff?" She held up a pear-shaped glass bottle.

He muttered the word "kevitt," then said, "The drass, the green one."

She grabbed a second bottle. "Glasses?"

"Just the bottle."

Back on the couch, she popped the top on the fizzy green drink and sipped from the bottle, tasting cinnamon, honey, clover blossoms, and alcohol. Lovely as it was, she wished it were bourbon.

Rafe downed his in one long pull, his face somber, his eyes tight. "My father has been Alpha of our Clan for many years." He threaded his hands together. "He insisted I wait. I'm done waiting, no matter what my Alpha commands."

"But you said others would suffer if you told me anything."

"True. But the Alchemics finally gave me the go-ahead, so my Alpha will have to accept that. You may have noticed in the dining hall very few women were present."

"I did."

Rafe retrieved two more bottles of drass and set them on the table. "For the past two-hundred-and-fifty years, for no reason we have discovered, female birth rates have dramatically declined.

Today, only about twenty percent of those born on Eleutia are female."

Twenty percent. "No one knows why?"

"No. The falling rates didn't start with a dramatic drop, but rather as a trickle. At first the ratio was forty-eight percent female to fifty-two percent male. No one paid much attention until the birthrate for males rose to sixty percent and females dropped to forty percent. The Alchemic Clan is desperate—"

"Wait," she said. "Explain these Alchemics."

"Men, and a few women, who control all technology on our world."

"Control it?"

His nostrils flared. "Yes. For centuries their Clan has developed and ruled science and technology. If our tech breaks, the Alchemics retrieve it and replace it, if they're so inclined. We are forbidden to create tech. We have no access to science. No books, no one to train us, to teach us. They dole out their tech to us as if we are children."

"But that's awful and so strange. On our world, many people develop—"

"Eleutia isn't your world." He banged the bottle so hard on the table, it broke. "Shote."

Blood dripped from his hand onto the table. "I'll get the first aid kit." Seconds later, she'd retrieved it from the linen closet. Rafe had washed the injury, and he pointed out the salve to use on the nasty cut that crossed through scars and the callused heel. When she'd butterflied it, she said, "You might need stitches."

"This will do." Rafe clasped her hand. "You have a light touch. I'm used to Kicks brand of healing."

Though his hold was gentle, his was a rough strong hand. Like the man himself. "It will scar."

He grinned. "I'll add it to the collection."

The sting of phantom pain bit her and she reached for her face, only to drop her hand at her side when she remembered. "I wonder what you would have thought of my scars."

After binding and taping his hand in gauze, she cleaned up the mess, then handed him another bottle of drass. "Here, please continue."

He leaned forward and cupped her chin. "I would have wished to see your scars, Kit. They would have told your stories."

"You wouldn't have liked what you saw."

"Don't be so sure." He sipped the drass.

"Tell me about these Alchemics, please."

"I'm not overly fond of them."

From his dark expression, it sounded like a gross understatement. "Why haven't you rebelled at their highhanded tactics?"

His bitter chuckle gave her chills. "They'd laseblast us out of existence." He leaned back in the chair, the drass in one hand, and sighed. "We need to discover why female births have declined, not that understanding will necessarily solve the problem. All the sentient symbiotic Eleutian Clans have been affected—the Cats, Bears, Eagles and Falcons, right down to the Deer and Ferret Clans."

"What about the animal symbionts like the wolves?"

"This...*thing* has impacted some of our animal symbionts, too, but for them it remains an anomaly, all while we humanoid Eleutians are dying."

"What a tragedy."

Rafe continued. "About one-hundred-and-fifty years ago, in the pursuit of answers, two of our Alchemic Clan discovered several parallel worlds. These worlds occupy the same space as ours." His smile was sheepish. "I still have trouble getting my mind around that."

Parallel worlds. Some physicists on Earth claimed they existed, and that those worlds, in fact, interacted with Earth and were detectable on the quantum level. She was no scientist and trying to understand the quantum mechanics of the thing made her head hurt.

"So I'm not on another planet, but a parallel world to my Earth?"

"Correct. It was the Alchemics who told us your measurements for clothes." Rafe scraped a hand through his unbound hair, his tension so tight she expected any minute he'd snap.

The symbiont nature of the Clans, the pastoral-techno nature of the world, the Clan culture. "Eleutia is very different from my world."

"Is it? I'd like to hear. But I need to finish this. The Council of Clans..." He snorted. "They're useless. When the Alchemics suggested a plan, of course the Council went along with it. Several of our Alchemics developed a way to virtually explore these other worlds and even interact with them, your world included. They hunt for female candidates of all ages who they believe might be suitable to Eleutia and Eleutian way of life. For strict ethical reasons, each candidate must be dying or near death, so as not to rob her of her natural life. The Alchemics then bring the chosen ones here, to Eleutia."

"They can really do that?"

"They *did*. With you, a Made One."

"They must have brought my sisters here, too."

"We don't know that. We can't find them."

The anger inside her sparked. "You must."

"We're trying. *I'm* trying. Usually rumors abound. We've heard nothing."

"What right have they to pluck us from our lives without asking? To take anyone's life from them?"

His jaw tightened. "None."

"What do they think they are, gods?"

His face turned granite. "I suspect so."

"How dare they?"

Years ago, Rafe had determined to end the Alchemics stranglehold on Eleutia. He could feel their scrawny necks beneath his fingers. He'd squeeze the life out of them. For what they did. For what they *do*. "The Clans, us, we are culpable, too."

Kit nodded, her lips thin, her color high. She, who smiled easily, had grown solemn. "They remade you, in the sense they acquired your DNA and used it to recreate your flesh as a young woman and…"

"How?" she said, her voice taut with anger.

"No idea. Once recreated, they extracted your mind, your consciousness, your memories and personality, some say your soul, from your physical form on Earth. They brought what they call your 'Essence' here, simultaneously ending your life in the other world."

"So I'm dead on Earth."

"Yes."

"Once here, they infuse that Essence into your recreated flesh. I'm sorry about those you left behind."

"That's not the point. What matters is the invasive nature of it all. Without permission. Without choice."

Kit appeared calm, almost poised. But with his Wolf senses activated, he smelled her fury. But it was the scent of her grief that wrenched his soul.

Most Wolf Clan freely expressed their emotions. Unlike him. Then again, he was different from most Wolves. As was Kit, making him want to peel back her layers of control, one by one. To see her unleashed.

"I know," he said. "And I'm sorry. But Eleutians are desperate. We Wolves are desperate." Which is why the self-serving Alchemics acted with impunity. He longed to tell her of his real leanings, of Compass True, the group he'd organized across Eleutia made up of those equally opposed to the Alchemics and meant to fight them and frustrate their more outlandish projects. How the Anti-Made Ones mistakenly thwarted his efforts. How he'd spent years planting spies in the Alchemic ranks, two of whom had paid the ultimate price. So he'd keep his silence, for her sake as much as for his, and let her think he was onboard, even if it made her despise him.

"I understand your perspective, Rafe. I can. I do. But it's wrong."

His jaw tightened. "I *see* that it's wrong, but it means our world's survival."

"I've always believed the individual matters. That each person deserves a say-so. If I'd been asked to come here, to get a new body, a second chance, I would have said yes."

"I expect most dying people would respond that way."

"But I should have been asked. No one has the right to choose my destiny. The Eleutians have left their ethics and morality at the door."

His gut cramped. "Yes. For the good of the species."

"Hitler said the same thing. Oh, I know you don't know who that is. Be glad. He was a monster."

Maybe they were monsters, too. "Your body was...perfected, all the Made Ones' bodies are."

"*What?*" she said, eyes wide.

"No scars. No deformities. The ideal weight and musculature. All done on a cellular level, so I've been told, and created at the optimum age of mid-20s. You were also enhanced. You'll seldom get ill, your bones are stronger, and you'll be prone to having our much-needed girl children."

Her hands curled into white-knuckled fists. "What makes an Alchemic?"

Assholery. "They are born with a scientific bent, a strong one. Once indoctrinated, they become secretive and strange, and they are the single Clan not symbiotic with another living creature. Some members are born into it, while children with a scientific bent from the animal Clans are conscripted."

"Children conscripted? They sound like monsters, despots. What kind of oversight—"

"Little to none." No one would dare overtly oppose them, not in any way that mattered. Until he could predict where their floating city would land, all he could use were spies and stop-gaps. For success, he needed to beard them in their den.

She grew quiet, those mysterious eyes of hers turned to some far distant land he couldn't imagine. She laughed. "None of this feels even a little bit real."

"It is, though."

"Not my reality."

"You were brought here and placed where your makers intended for you to be discovered."

"On a desolate mountain top? If you hadn't found me, would I ever have been unfrozen, or would I have died?"

His fury boiled over, his words clipped. "Apparently they erred. An unusual misstep, as they are perfectionists. They meant to place you near the MedSurge we visited."

"They erred?" She was shaking now. "I wonder what other *errors* they made. Did they err where they placed my sisters? *If* they placed my sisters."

He moved beside her on the couch and rubbed his thumb across the back of her neck. "Please, Kit. When I found you, I was searching for you. They acknowledged their coordinates were off."

She had that faraway look in her eyes again. Was she feeling lost? Abandoned? Kit might not accept it, but she wasn't alone. He would protect her, keep her safe, help her adjust. From the moment he'd found her, that directive was prime.

"Why didn't they send dozens to search? Hundreds?"

He quirked an eyebrow. "And reveal their screwup to so many? Never."

"Arrogant, prideful creeps."

"That they are."

"So from what you've said, I'm breeding stock. Revolting. What if I want to return home?"

He shook his head, pained for her lost life. "Your former body is a husk, Kitlyn."

A shiver wracked her, but she nodded. "The odd thing is that part of this gives me hope. That Bree and Sybi were transformed, too, and they're here somewhere, and I'll find them. I'll simply ask the Alchemics."

"Don't you think I've tried?" His bitter laugh made her stare. "They refused to answer, and the Alchemics cleverly remain hidden in a floating city that moves, for Fates' sake."

"A floating city? With so many people aboard? Impossible."

His brows rose. "Yet true. Their incredible tech enables them to do just that."

"You *must* be able to contact them."

"Sometimes," he said with derision.

"Your father is Alpha. Surely *he* can."

"They fail to respond to my father, as well, and when they do respond, they often compel him to secrecy."

"Is that why I haven't met your father?"

Though he couldn't tell her how sick he was of keeping secrets, he wouldn't turn away. "I expect so."

"I'll find them." Her eyes burned, her determination worrisome.

"No."

She jumped to her feet and paced, her hands fisted. "Who are you to tell me no? What rights do I have here? Or am I your prisoner?"

What a fiery woman. He rose to clamp his hands on her shoulders, stilling her movement. "You are *not* our prisoner."

She glared at him. "Don't you see the irony of saying that and holding me still?"

He released her immediately. "It's for your safety."

"Safety, Rafe? It's overrated."

How to make her understand? "Those who have tried to find the Alchemics have failed. Most have disappeared. Even the majority of the Alchemics don't know where their city is from day to day. It's not possible." Though his Compass True team worked to achieve exactly that.

Kit must feel trapped, alone, missing those she loved. But she didn't comprehend the dangers Eleutia posed to her. The deadly creatures, the Alchemics viciousness, the warring Clans, and the Anti-Made Ones, comprised of betrayers disguised as friends. *Shote.* That Cat. He'd cut him from his heart, but it seemed the poison remained. "I'm sorry."

CHAPTER FIVE

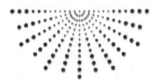

K it was so pissed she was near blind with it. "*Are* you sorry, Rafe?"

Rafe walked to stare out the window. Outside, the sun blazed across the green space alive with colorful blooms and wildness, the light illuming the blond streaks in his hair. He dug his hands into his back pockets.

Damn. None of this was his fault. "I shouldn't be snapping at you."

He looked over his shoulder. "It's fine." He winked. "My hide's tough."

Two steps, and he faced her, close enough to touch. Her fingers itched to do just that. "Will your father be angry you told me all this?"

He grinned and cupped her cheek. "Da will be furious. That's always fun. Ah, Kit, I'm sorry to lay this on you now, but I couldn't wait any longer. You deserved to know."

A frisson of something stirred where he touched her. He'd put himself on the line. For her. No one beside her sisters had done that, drawn a line in the sand and tugged her close.

Mordecai. The trapeze catcher who'd dated Bree. After Kit's accident, he'd threatened to quit if the circus didn't agree to sell her the horses she'd raised and trained for her act. Others in the circus had stood by her, too. They'd all been good friends, the memory as distant as a dream. And Mordecai, he'd died so young.

Though she feared it, she gave in to an urge she hadn't felt since forever and leaned into Rafe's hand.

His warmth spread through her, a soothing balm.

Long moments later, she straightened. "If I could have a computer, I could learn about Eleutia and the Clans."

"I'll make sure you get a tablet."

"Thank you. Having the internet will give me something to do while I search for my sisters online."

"You mentioned that before, this 'internet.'" he said, tilting his head.

"The web. What connects computers around the world." Rafe's confused expression hollowed her belly. "You know, so if I wanted to research the mountains where I appeared, it would show me pictures, have descriptions, yes?"

He shook his head. "Our library—"

"No, I don't mean like that." Other words. She needed other words. "From across the globe, I could buy something online or watch a show or listen to a song."

"Eleutia has nothing like you describe. WolfHome's library is online. You can explore and contact others within WolfHome. But there is no way to connect to other Clans."

No internet. If she couldn't physically leave WolfHome, how would she find Sybi and Bree? "You have this amazing technology. Hasn't anyone tried to connect the individual Clan networks? To share knowledge, for communication?" As the words left her mouth, she got it.

The Alchemics controlled all technology. Perhaps they hadn't developed an internet, or, more likely, they had, but they'd not shared it with the Clans. "Never mind. I understand, and I'd still like a tablet."

"Of course. Be well, Ma'am Kitlyn." Muscles bunched tight, he shook his head, as if unable or unwilling to unleash any remaining words. He strode out the door, the swing of his long, tawny hair hiding his face from view.

Kit closed the door. She ached. Though it had been only a few days, her past was starting to feel like a dream.

The next few days were a blur of activity and contemplation. After her talk with Rafe, she had so much to process. It was hard letting go of the middle-aged woman whose impending death still felt real. Her headspace was crowded with thoughts and emotions. And she'd never been very good at boxing up any of those. The rigorous physical activity helped. As did her strategy for finding her sisters.

She'd used her new phone to call the Alpha. Dozens of times, in fact. He never picked up, so she left message after message, finally stopping when she learned he'd left to attend a treaty meeting in the Falcons' territory.

The idea that the Alchemics had a floating city that moved was right out of a sci-fi novel. Hard to comprehend. Easier to imagine them as ruthless, deadly, and prone to hiding information They sounded like despots whose desires steered the course of Eleutia.

To find her sisters, she reasoned her best bet was to search the Alpha's office. He had to know something. Even if he'd been forbidden to tell her, he might have paperwork or images of them.

But finding the time was near impossible. Someone had slipped a schedule beneath her door. It was all timed and quite precise, consisting of physical training, weapons training, and studies on Eleutian history and life.

Physical and weapons training were a must, according to Tilde. While all Wolves might not be warriors, they all trained. At the outdoor practice ground, after demonstrating her skills with knives, she was initiated into sword training, bow-and-arrow combat, and claw training. She'd rather have done gymnastics, those skills rusty, but then, she wasn't given a choice. The positive thing was that training honed her physically, giving vigor and strength to her "new" body.

The claw training was, simply put, odd. She was to become wolf, so a set of claws hugged the palms of her hands, strapped to the backs. The rig was jointed and clever, and allowed her fingers to move in a natural motion. The claws themselves were six inches of lethality made up of some hard material she didn't recognize. Of course, her instructor didn't let her practice with the real claws, but rather stiff, curve-shaped pads which would do no harm. But they taught her how and where to strike. The throat was prime, and she pictured blood gushing as her enemy clutched his neck in a vain attempt to live. She hadn't realized she was so blood-thirsty.

Her enemies? According to her claw instructor, Eevon, the Wolf Clan had many.

One thing she didn't do was reveal her martial arts skills. At the training grounds, the Wolves boxed and wrestled, but that was it. She'd seen no one using anything like Taekwondo, Krav Maga, Karate, or any of the other fighting arts with which she was familiar. After she'd left the circus, she'd studied many, in part as physical therapy and in part to not feel so helpless. She might be at sea with most of life here, but her one secret made her feel a tiny bit in control. Yet assumptions could kill, and she would dig further into the Eleutians' knowledge of Earth's martial arts.

In between her schedule, she ate. Did she ever. Her new "improved" body not only was getting quite a workout, but she suspected the Alchemics had upped her metabolism. She downed food like a lumberjack.

The dining room meals were excellent, though often made with strange spices and unusual ingredients. They didn't have mac and cheese—a sin!—and she still didn't like green peppers, which was oddly reassuring.

Strange dissonances occurred daily. Her clothes, for example—jeans and dresses, t-shirts and such—replicated her Earthly ones, yet with subtle changes that told her she wasn't in Kansas any longer.

The TVs were curved, and hers floated against the wall on a

cushion of air, much like the cars and the cart she'd seen a man pushing down the hall. Except when the cart had first passed her, she'd seen double, given it legs and wheels, too, as if she were literally being pulled in two directions. That had happened twice, and each time she'd grown nauseated and woozy, her mind picturing Earth's reality overlaying this new world's truth.

Other than her sisters, the three Js, and her critters, she didn't miss Earth much. She longed to read, of course, and when her boot lace had snapped, she'd immediately thought to order another one on Amazon. She didn't care for the scented face cream, a minor irritation quickly solved with Tilde's help, yet she longed for certain comforts she was used to at home. But as Rafe had said, Eleutia was now her home.

The part of Eleutia where she lived was filled with beauty, both natural and Eleutian-made. The quiet soothed her, the Wolf Clan's lack of hustle-bustle welcome, their rhythms in tune with her senses.

There were shops and movies and money, the latter of which she had aplenty. Max explained how a large sum was settled upon each Made One, and he'd shown her how to access and use it. The town was charming and pristine and reminded her of Holland when she'd performed there with the circus.

Part of her felt like she was on some exotic vacation and eventually everything would go back to normal.

On the third day after Rafe's revelations, she opened her door to find three items on her stone-paved stoop. A bouquet of wildflowers tied with red string, a glass jar of cookies bound with green ribbon, and a small picture of a picnic with a blue band around it. Though she found no cards or notes, they seemed like gifts. When she picked them up, she buried her face in the bouquet, inhaling the delicate scents. She put the cookie jar and photo on her dresser, then put the multicolored flowers in a tall water glass when she couldn't find a vase. She set the flowers on the round end table in her bedroom. If they were gifts, who'd left them? Perhaps Rafe, others, welcoming her to the Clan?

She hadn't seen Rafe since he'd revealed all. Though only three days had passed, she felt bereft, as if part of her was missing. Perhaps now that he'd told her the truth, he had fulfilled his obligation and was done with her.

No. She refused to accept that. She'd find Rafe and discover why he'd been avoiding her.

The hard bench hurt Rafe's sore ass. Men milled around him, his cadre of Peacekeepers having just returned from a days-long mission. Once a month, at minimum, he'd venture out with one cadre or other. It kept him close to his troops, giving him the opportunity to assess their weak points and their strengths, their rivalries and friendships. He might be their First Commander, but he wasn't so different from the rank and file soldiers who made WolfHome strong.

They'd gotten into muck chasing those farking Cats who'd dared infiltrate their land. Playing games. Idiot felines loved games.

Except when they'd come for the Made One. For Kit. No game there, but a kidnapping attempt. Next time, they wouldn't be as cavalier. Or send a mere three warriors.

Covered in swamp filth, his leather brigandine stunk. He double-checked the closures, making sure they were solid, then washed the muck off with a soft cloth and mild soap. He swiped his leather conditioner from the bench. The others teased him, but he preferred vinegar and linseed oil to the "magic" brush supplied by the Alchemics. Trusting them was like befriending a goddart.

After working the mixture across every inch of leather, he set his brigandine aside and started on his boots.

"The Commander's after the Made One."

Laughter.

Rafe's smooth, measured strokes continued, though that shote Damian was talking trash about him.

"She's hot," Gard said.

"Oh yeah, sizzling," Damian said.

"Of course he's after her," Gard said. "So are half the males in WolfHome."

Did they think Rafe was deaf?

"Give you fifty that he doesn't land her," Damian said.

"I'll take that bet."

Max! His best friend. Curse him for joining in on this ridiculous betting about a woman who deserved only respect and honor.

"I'll put seventy-five on Neff winning her." That was big-mouth Borne. "Neff's face is so pretty."

Farking... He surged to his feet. "Enough!"

He surveyed his men, half of whom were bent double with laughter.

Max winked. "Gotcha."

Kit hadn't found Rafe, having learned he was off with some troops hunting Cats. For some reason, the knowledge that he was away made her feel better, lighter.

The following morning, dressed for sparring practice, she discovered more goodies outside her door. A lucky rock striped with iridescent red crystal. A picture frame tied with blue. A small frosted cake with a green bow atop it.

Again, no attached notes, so she'd call them Mr. Red, Mr. Green, and Mr. Blue.

She scooped them up, set them on the coffee table, then stepped into the hall. A petite blonde with a bee-stung mouth and corn-flower-blue eyes walked across the hall toward Kit.

"Hello. I'm Kit."

The blonde sneered. "Don't bother with nice. I don't care about the other two males, but stay away from Rafe."

Kit rested a hand on her hip. "Why should I?"

"At least you're not as mealy mouthed as I was told," the blonde said with a snort.

Kit went to brush past the blonde.

The woman's hands flashed toward Kit wearing those clawed

braces. She stiffened. Easy enough to deal with this fool, but she didn't want to escalate things.

"Stay away from him or I'll do this." The blonde made a swiping motion with the claws.

Kit smiled. "Bite me."

"What?" The blonde's head tilted.

"Don't mess with me."

The blonde laughed and sauntered off. Over her shoulders, she said, "You've been warned."

Leaning against the wall kept her vertical. Her martial arts gave her confidence, but as those deadly claws had neared, she'd felt her face crack, breaking apart as it had once done. Her fingers roved down her smooth cheek, feeling the old caverns, the shiny plastic skin, the drooping eye. Well, fine, she hadn't lost it in front of the woman.

She supposed it was good to know your enemies.

Kit was on fire during her workout. She didn't like being bullied, the blonde's actions discordant, as if out of character for the Wolves. Toweling off after her claws training, she wandered over to the cage to watch the next sparring match.

A minute later, a Viking entered the ring, with white-blond hair, easily six-six or -seven, and a heavy Dwayne Johnson frame. The day was chilly, but he wore only a leather loincloth and held a sword in each hand, long curved things that she'd bet could split a man in two.

The second man entered at the far end of the cage. She sucked in a breath—Rafe. Her eyes drank in his broad shoulders, massive thighs, and carved muscles rivalling Michelangelo's David. His bronze skin glowed in the late morning light, his loincloth much as the Viking's, but he held a short sword in one hand, a long knife in the other. Rafe might be tall, but the Viking topped him by a good three inches.

As Rafe prowled toward the center of the ring, his muscles flowed in a spellbinding poetry of motion. He spotted her and smiled.

She flushed but gave him a smile and a thumbs up back.

The men circled one another, and the empathetic and kind man she knew as Rafe disappeared beneath a blank face with dead eyes.

Both growling, the men engaged, moving so fast they blurred. Squinting, she tried to make out their movements, but it was impossible. She'd seen others spar, but nothing like this.

Only the clash of steel and the scrape of feet on dirt broke the silence.

Murmurs from the crowd, shouts urging on the combatants, with Kit hollering, "Yes. Yes! No!" A blade swipe, Rafe's shoulder bleeding. She bit her cheek, the coppery taste filling her mouth.

The Viking flew backward, Rafe leapt, bouncing off the cage wall with a grunt, sweat and blood flying like banners through the air. A droplet landed on her cheek, and she smeared it away.

Her fingers curled through the fence. "Yes, no. Oh, yes!"

The crowd around her pressed close, shouting, screaming, and her eyes darted this way and that trying to track the men's movements.

Rafe and the Viking battled—grunting, groaning, swords crossed, teeth bared, bodies slick with blood and sweat.

A bell chimed. The men sprang apart, chests heaving as they inhaled gasps of air.

Kit ran a shaky hand through her hair, telling herself Rafe wasn't seriously hurt, though his body was scraped and bruised and slashed with cuts.

The fighters turned to the judge, who sat on a tall platform like those at a tennis match. Rafe's eyes might be ablaze, but he still wore that awful dead-man mask.

"Rafe, Thorn," the judge said. "Well done."

"And...?" the Viking said.

The judge's lips twitched. "A tie."

Both men groaned. Then a laugh burst from Rafe's bloody lips, his teeth ghoulishly red.

He held out his arm to Thorn, and they clasped forearms.

"One of these days," Rafe said.

"In your dreams, Commander." The Viking grinned.

Rafe turned her way, and his eyes lit when he found her in the crowd of onlookers. He stalked toward her, and for a moment, her eyes widened in fear. Then he gave her this red-toothed cocky grin that said he was glad she was here, had seen him fight, and...more.

He hung his fingers on the chain link, leaned his forehead against the mesh. "Well?"

Standing on tiptoe, she leaned forward, hands clinging to the mesh. His face was bruised, a nasty one purpling his temple. Mean and dark, it must hurt. She lifted her chin, pressed her face to the mesh, and kissed him.

Oh, shit. She fled.

Kit couldn't believe she'd kissed Rafe. And in front of all those Wolves, too. So out of character for her. She'd better step up, or those prankster Clansmen would have a field day with their jokes, not to mention how she'd react when she saw Rafe himself. *Oh, boy.*

She took extra care with her clothes for mid-day, eager to see Rafe and nervous as hell.

Rafe never appeared and no one said a word about their kiss. Except for Tilde.

"So how was it?" Tilde said with a conspiratorial whisper.

"Bloody." He'd tasted of blood and sweat and Rafe, pure Rafe, his warm lips on hers making her tingle all over.

That afternoon's lesson in all things Eleutian settled her right down. Her teacher, a shaggy-haired older woman with a pale wrinkled face, bright blue eyes, and freckles sat in a wheelchair that hovered two inches off the floor. Her name was Yuan and she spoke to Kit with a near-painful deference. She suspected Yuan had gotten her assignment because Kit couldn't read, and she doubted this was her usual gig. The poor woman must have drawn the short straw.

Lessons. She could do today's lesson, even with the taste of Rafe lingering on her lips.

Eleutian society was multifaceted, heavily agrarian, yet possessed of amazing technological advances, too. Clean air and water were essential to them, as were healthy foods, and respecting the earth, the waters, and the sky. There was a reverence in Yuan's voice when she talked about nature and the animals of the fields, forests, and skies, of the plants and the waters, and of the planet herself.

"Do Eleutians worship the planet?" Kit asked.

Yuan nodded. "Though the Fates steer our course, in one sense we do, yes."

"Perhaps because of your symbiotic nature with animals?"

"Most definitely," she said. "We attribute much to our relationship with our brother and sister animals. Our Mother is perfection. She must be cherished."

"You think of Eleutia as a woman?"

Her eyes widened. "Of course."

Easy enough to contrast bucolic Eleutia with the mess that was Earth, but everything wasn't all rainbows and unicorns.

When Yuan pushed an encyclopedic tome toward her, she talked about the Clans—the Wolves, the Cats, the Bears, many others— their myriad wars, and how often they were at odds. Yes, they traded goods and services, but leaving Wolf territory could turn deadly in an instant.

"Dangerous, is it?" Kit said with a wink. "Maybe they should watch out for me."

Yuan slapped her knees, her grin infectious. "Just so, Ma'am Kit. Made Ones are always full of surprises. Our last Made One, though she arrived more than seventy years ago, was memorable."

Kit found herself leaning forward, eager to hear. "In what way?"

"During The Challenge we call on our animal symbionts for strength, endurance, and speed. All the Clans do."

"I just saw Rafe and this Viking spar. Do they draw on their animals then, too?"

Yuan chuckled. "The *Viking*? I don't know what that is, but you must have watched Rafe sparring with Thorn. An old and lively rivalry."

"It was pretty intense."

Yuan tilted her head. "And who won?"

"A tie." Kit grinned. "Neither man was pleased."

"I suspect not. As to your question, we are trained in the draw as children. Only in carefully moderated training bouts are we allowed the draw, to teach its use in battle, you see."

"Ah. Go on, please. The Challenge?"

"That fateful day, the Cats were winning. There was but one bout left, when one of our own entered, at the last minute mind you, to call Final Challenge!" Her eyes sparkled. "I can see it as if it were just a blink of time away. Our Wolf eliminated the Bear, fast. Then he went after the Cat. He won! He defeated that damnable Cat!"

"What was she like, the Made One?"

"Elegant. Regal. Kind."

Maybe Kit wasn't elegant or regal, but she'd like to think she was kind. "Tell me more."

Yuan wagged a finger. "For another day. We must continue with the lesson."

She hid her disappointment, unwilling to hurt Yuan's feelings. "Of course."

"We are a disorganized society, our packs often in conflict."

"Haven't the Clans organized with the Central Council? Can't they make peace?"

"Ah. The Council is impotent, puppets who do their Alphas and Clans bidding. How is your world organized?"

She explained about different countries. "But wars exist on Earth, too."

"I see. As we now stand, war is often necessary."

Was it? Wars might break out on Earth all the time, but she hadn't seen any up close and personal. What was it like to live in constant fear of conflict, of dying, of loved ones deaths? She couldn't feel it, that ever-present sense of danger. Perhaps it was like watching Bree's high-flyer act. Prickles all over her skin. Holding her breath. Biting her lip so she wouldn't scream "Careful!" aloud.

"I don't like the idea of being afraid all the time," she said.

Yuan reared back. "Afraid? We're not afraid. It's our way of life. It's your way of life now, too, Ma'am Kit."

A half hour later, she interrupted one of Yuan's endless text readings. "Do you like teaching?"

Her chagrinned smile charmed Kit.

"I didn't mean anything bad, Yuan. I think you're wonderful, but I sense you don't love working with me."

"How wrong you are." Her emphatic voice remained soft. "I delight in you. But I'm no teacher. I was the chief arms maker until my hands failed." She held them up—knobby and rheumatic, they must hurt terribly. "Talos helped for a while."

"Talos?"

"He now heads the Armorer's Guild." She shook her head. "My chief assistant, he'd help when I ran into trouble with the forge or a particularly intricate design. When I began dropping implements, the old cretin had enough. So he made a bet with me. How that man loves a bet, mostly because he seldom loses. Nor did he this time, and so, to my sorrow, I retired. My legs, well, that came later."

Kit took Yuan's gnarled hands in hers. "What I like best, what you do so well, is tell stories. Just like that one. When you tell tales, you bring this world alive for me."

Her blue eyes brightened. "Do I?"

"Yes." Kit made a cross-the-heart motion. "That means I promise or swear."

"Ah ha!" Her light laughter filled the room. "Good. To continue with our lesson. You must beware of the Battle Beetles." She wagged a finger. "They are plentiful, seasonal insects that approach two feet in length." Her lips thinned. "They fly and their bite can kill."

She shivered. Other deadly predators flew, walked the land, and swam the seas, and Yuan passed her a list with their descriptions and pictures. A long list.

"Study up, hear, Ma'am Kit? The Keep and the town are safe, but lethal creatures prowl our wildlands."

"Snakes?" She made a motion with her hand like a snake slithering across the grass.

Yuan tilted her head to the side, pursing her lips. "What an odd mode of locomotion. Except for the swimming creatures of the sea, of course."

Kit could live happily in a world without snakes. True, that was before she read Yuan's list of lethal creatures, any one of which could take her out in a heartbeat.

Rafe's seat was empty throughout dinner that evening, and she learned the Alpha wasn't due back for days. The following day Rafe was again a no-show, and none of her tablemates knew his whereabouts, though they spoke easily enough of the bout between Rafe and Thorn. No one expressed concern.

She shouldn't be worried. Except he hadn't been at breakfast, either. Was he avoiding her because she'd kissed him? Maybe his injuries had been more severe than they'd appeared? Tilde or Max would know if that were true, and they hadn't said a thing.

Back from training, and after she performed her katas and showered, she held the silver phone in her hand and said, "Call Rafe." A buzz, buzz, buzz came through the speaker.

Frustrated, she left a voicemail saying she was checking in and asked if all was well, then disconnected.

The silver phone gleamed in her hand.

With Rafe gone, she felt very much alone.

Perhaps she'd call Max or Tilde. But what would she say? How's it hangin'? Kit knew little about their lives. Less about their thoughts and feelings.

She'd been so sure she'd find leads to Sybi and Bree. But not a single Clansman she'd asked knew how to contact the Alchemics. Leaving WolfHome would be lethal from what Yuan and others said, and she believed them. Given the abundance of wilderness and the Cats' attack on her way here, she wasn't ready to risk it. What if she never found her sisters?

Of course she'd find them.

Kit dressed in clean clothes, then called Rafe again. And again it went to voicemail. This time, she didn't leave a message.

Why had she kissed him? Instead of going to mid-day, she walked outside to a shady grove with a bench and small rock water feature. She pressed her hand to the bench as she sat and closed her eyes, the water's song calming her.

She'd kissed Rafe because...

When he walked into a room, pleasure burst inside her. She got nervous when he looked at her with those deceptively sleepy eyes. Her heart sped up when he smiled.

Simple chemistry. She couldn't recall when she'd last felt that pull. Was that why when he'd appeared all bloody and grinning, she'd kissed him?

"Hello!"

Kit's eyes flew open just as Tilde stepped from the path wearing a smile, the ubiquitous book tucked beneath her arm. "There you are! Rafe sent us to look for you."

Rafe had sent Tilde, which pleased her enormously. A wolfie head poked out from a tree. Paulo. Kit slid her phone into the jeans' pocket and stood. "What's up?"

"Rafe was concerned that you hadn't come to mid-day."

Concerned? *She'd* been worried about *him* for days. "He's okay?"

Tilde's eyes gentled. "He is."

Though the tightness in her chest eased, she was more than a little ticked. He couldn't return her call? Text a message? Come find her himself?

"Kit?" Tilde said.

"Oh! Sorry. I was woolgathering."

The redhead giggled.

"What's so funny?"

"I once met a Made One of the Bear Clan. She used that expression, too."

She could learn so much from another like herself. They'd also share a bond. "So you've met other Made Ones."

"Just Susannah. Many years ago."

"I'd love to meet her."

"I'm sorry, Kit, she's dead."

"Dead?"

"In the war between the Bears and the Falcons." Tilde held out a hand, and her book fell to the ground. "Oops. I'm always doing that, dropping things, losing things."

"Because you're such a deep thinker, Tilde. No biggie."

"Biggie?"

Kit laughed as she scooped up Tilde's book, then stared at the woman's outstretched hand. The touch of another. She slid her hand into Tilde's and squeezed, maybe too hard, maybe with too much emotion. Tilde tugged her forward, her grin mischievous. "Come on. Like I said, Rafe is waiting for you. It's never a good thing to test the Commander's patience."

Oh, she was tempted. "Then let's go."

CHAPTER SIX

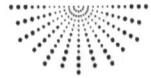

Her tablemates had held her seat, a kind thing to do. Rafe was
there, and though Tilde had told her he was fine, relief
soaked into her soul. She was starved, but she hungered more to
hear how he was. He pulled out her chair, and butterflies tickled her
stomach when he flashed that broad smile of his.

When she sat, Rafe leaned close. "I missed you."

"I've missed you, too," she said.

He paused, and his eyes heated, mouth tightening, almost as if he
longed to touch her.

Or maybe she was projecting her own wishes onto him. She'd be
mortified if he saw her desire, so she looked around for the coywolf.
"Paulo followed us inside. Where did he go?"

"I suspect," Rafe said, "he's on secret coywolf business."

"Of course he is."

"Now that you're here, he'll put in an appearance soon." He
winked.

Max snorted. "Oh, yeah."

"Enough, Ferret," Rafe said.

"Watch it, Whitey."

Rafe whispered, "Only Max would dare call me that childhood nickname."

Max leaned toward Eevon, her bald, burly claw trainer. It was as if her tablemates were collectively holding their breaths, their eyes focused not on her, but on the table in front of her. Kit looked down.

A large crystal sat tied with a red bow in the middle of her otherwise empty plate. Much like watermelon tourmaline with its bands of pink, white, and green, with the crystals pointed like amethysts. It fit in the palm of her hand and sparkled in the light. Mr. Red somehow knew of her love of rocks and crystals.

On the left, a gold bracelet lay wrapped in a green bow, and on the right, Mr. Blue had gifted her a photo of a snowy mountain peak. Both lovely, but the crystal was a treasure.

Eevon's striking face split with a grin.

"What?" she said.

"Three someones are courting you."

"Courting me?"

He pointed to the gifts. "Yes. We leave gifts for those we are courting. It is our way. The first pass allows for only the first three applicants. If all three are rejected, then six are allowed to court, and onward."

Did it mean she had to marry one of them? "But there are no notes or cards to tell me who they are."

Tilde laughed. "That's part of the fun. You have to guess."

Oh, swell. How? She laughed. It was all too absurd. Yet she was charmed. Lightening her heart after that morning's dark thoughts and her distasteful encounter with that blonde. Speaking of which…

When Kit got in line for food, she scanned the dining hall's three-hundred-plus Clansmen. There she was, the witchy bitch preening amidst the men at a far table. She memorized her face.

Kit could handle bullies, but she never underestimated them.

Midway through the meal, something warm and heavy pressed against her leg. Paulo moved his head to her lap, and she reached out to scratch behind his ears, then picked up her fork to finish her meal.

The coywolf nudged her.

"Yes, Paulo, but I'm eating. I see you."

I see you too, mistress.

Her fork clattered to her plate, her eyes snapping to Paulo's innocent ones.

"Something the matter, Kit?" Eevon said.

"No, I'm fine." She most definitely wasn't.

Rafe was shoveling in food, while between bites he casually talked to the man on his left. No help there.

She leaned down and whispered in Paulo's ear. "Did you just say something?

Of course. I responded to your greeting.

She jerked upright. "Rafe, could I speak with you for a minute?"

He tilted his head in that wolfish way. "Sure."

"Privately." She rose from her seat. "It's somewhat delicate." Then she walked toward the dining hall doors hoping he followed. Given the click of nails on the stone floor, Paulo was coming as well.

Outside, she climbed a small hill to a large birch and slipped beneath the branches for privacy. She leaned against the tree's silvery bark, simply enjoying the soft breeze that played through the dusky pink leaves. But it wasn't quite enough to take her mind off of a coywolf, the one sitting at her feet who'd talked in her head.

Rafe provided a distraction as he walked toward her with his fluid, graceful stride, his long hair flowing in the breeze. He was moving poetry, and he felt so beyond her reach. She might have a 20-something-year-old's body, but her soul was that of a crippled, frumpy 58-year-old.

When he stood inches away, he leaned forward and clasped her shoulders. "What's wrong? You know you can tell me anything."

Even if he'd think she'd lost her mind? She gnawed her lip. It sounded ridiculous.

She looked back and forth between Paulo and Rafe. "Um. I think, um... I would swear that Paulo spoke in my head. Twice."

Rafe's brows pulled together. "Did he say anything he shouldn't have?"

Paulo yipped, and Rafe laughed.

"This isn't funny." She crossed her arms. "Where I come from, people who hear animals talking in their heads are considered crazy."

A slow smile stretched Rafe's lips "Really? We have those who are out of balance, too, but talking to our canids isn't one of the causes."

"Does he talk in your head?"

"Occasionally."

"Do the other timberwolves?"

He nodded.

"You could've warned me!"

He spread his arms wide. "How would I know that the coyotes and wolves in your world don't talk to their Clanmates?"

Ack! "You should've, that's all." She raked her hands through her hair. Okay. On Eleutia, canids could talk to people. "What about the dogs? Can they talk to people, too?"

"Dogs? What are those?"

"You know…dogs." She wasn't explaining. "They look like wolves, sort of. With the breeding help from humans, they evolved down from gray wolves to domesticated pets on Earth. Companions. Guardians. Man's best friend."

Rafe's eyes sparked. "*Bred* them? *Domesticate* them? We would never do such to our brother and sister wolves."

Paulo growled.

"Or a coywolf, either."

Of course not, given their symbiotic relationship. But she loved dogs—she'd swear her pups had saved her after her accident, been her pals, offered her unquestioning love. They didn't care what she'd looked like, that she couldn't walk right. That Eleutia had no dogs saddened her. Paulo was wonderful, but it wasn't the same. "Can other animals talk to people?"

"The Felidae—"

"I don't know that word."

"Cougars, leopards, tigers, jaguars—the Cats. They talk to the Cat Clans. Ferrets to the Ferret Clans. Bears to the—"

"But why can *I* hear Paulo? I'm not a symbiont."

He brushed his thumb down her cheek. "But in a sense you are. I gave you the touch the other morning."

The touch. Her flesh goosebumped. Sounded like magic to her.

"You're cold," Rafe said. "We can go inside."

"I'm not cold!" She gave him her back. "It's just all weird. Don't worry, I get the drift."

"The drift?"

Why was everything so damned hard? "I see your point. I comprehend. I get it. I…"

His hands clasped her waist, and he turned her to face him. "It's all right. I'm sorry I don't always understand. This is new to me, too. We've only had one other Made One in our Clan. She died many years ago."

"A Made One. That's me, all right," she said, her sarcasm bitter on her tongue.

She brought a shaky hand to her throat. It was too much.

Paulo leapt up and rested a paw on her chest. He leaned forward and licked her nose. *I am sorry, too. I did not mean to frighten you.*

She nuzzled his fur. He was so huge, far taller than she when standing on his back legs. "It wasn't your fault. It wasn't anyone's fault." She straightened.

The coywolf yipped and trotted off.

"I…" She hesitated saying the words. "I thought I was going crazy, hearing voices."

"You're not crazy," Rafe said, drawing her into his arms.

Rafe's warmth and comfort surrounded her, making her want to melt into the embrace. But she couldn't. Any minute that surcease from pain could be stolen away. "I'll think I get what's going on, how to deal with your world, and then something flattens me. I'll be fine."

"You don't have to be fine. It's okay if you don't understand everything right away. You will. You're pale as ice." He smoothed a hand over her curls. "The Fates, I wish for you peace, Kit."

Peace. When had she last known the luxury of peace?

He leaned down, inhaled deeply, then his warm lips touched her cheek. "Kit."

Her name sounded like a prayer, the squeeze of her heart unfamiliar. She wanted to turn her cheek so her lips would brush his, feel their warmth, know their tenderness.

Rafe filled her with hope and reassurance and desire. In that indecisive moment he drew away, straightening to his full height, his eyes burning, with what she wasn't sure.

"So you're good?" he said.

No, she wasn't good. She was in a state of confusion. Rafe drew her like honey drew flies. He was all she esteemed—kind and caring, intelligent and ethical, and possessing a sharp sense of humor that spiced up the pot. He'd risked his father's wrath by telling her the truth.

She had to admit it was more than chemistry. At least for her. He made her want things. Like touching him. Talking with him. Sharing with him.

His face could have been chiseled from stone, his eyes probing. Did he want her? He may not have any romantic feelings for her. Was she too much of a coward to find out?

Well, *damn*. She'd kissed him once, hadn't she? She rested her hands on his shoulders, and he was so tall she had to stand on tiptoe to reach those sensual lips. She tilted her face upward. His half-lidded eyes burned. Their breaths mingled, and she could almost taste their mutual desire. He leaned forward.

"Rafe!" called a man's voice from nearby.

His eyes never left hers. "What?"

Footsteps. Her hands slid from Rafe's shoulders, and she stepped back.

Eevon ducked beneath the canopy of trees. "We've got a council meeting in ten minutes. Did you forget?"

A flash of annoyance, then, "No, let's go." Rafe returned his attention to her and took her hand. "Go back to dinner, Kit. Enjoy your meal."

Then he was gone.

. . .

Outside the council chamber, Ulfr dismissed Eevon with the notch of his head and pulled Rafe into the shadows as other council members streamed into the chamber.

"As I understand it, you engaged the Cats while out with the cadre."

"We did, Alpha. It was unexpected, but we succeeded in routing them with little trouble. The cadre was in excellent form."

"The Cats have stepped up their raiding," Ulfr said.

"So it appears." His Wolves would deal with it, as always.

"*She* is the cause."

Kitlyn was a treasure, but he couldn't disagree. "The Cats are working up to something."

"I fear war."

"When have you ever *feared* war?"

"Since I've spent decades orchestrating treaties with the other Clans."

The man *loved* a good fight. Ulfr was just baiting him.

"*You* are the one who requested a Made One in the first place," Rafe said.

"Don't remind me of my folly."

"Folly? We are fading, Da."

Inga passed by to enter the chamber, her sultry look almost making him wince. Would the woman never leave off?

"Rafe," his father said. "We're being harried from all sides. The Cats, the Alchemics, the Anti-Made Ones."

Nothing new there. "We will handle it, as we always do."

"Easy to say. The Alchemics are threatening to appropriate two of our mistrals for revealing all to the Made One." His face soured as if he'd eaten a lemon.

"Our *mistrals*? Not on my life will they get their greedy hands on even one. They'll kill them for their bones and try to replicate them. You know it to be true."

Most Clansmen would flee like rabbits at Ulfr's sneer. "I did not say I would allow it, just that they were threatening."

"They can bluster all they want. As I informed you, I gained their permission to tell her. They have no cause for threats."

Ulfr rolled his eyes and barked an unpleasant laugh. "You did gain permission, my son, but *not* by one of the Eleven."

"The Cabal of Eleven can go fark themselves. Kit's mental and emotional torment was taking its toll. She needed the truth."

A bell clanged, signaling the meeting's five-minute warning.

"Have you told her about Juliette?" Ulfr stumbled over her name, as he always did, the pain seeming never to fade.

"I have not."

"Coward."

Rafe stayed silent, knowing his father was correct.

"The Cat Alpha has made overtures. I've agreed to meet with him."

That was it then, the bomb he'd been waiting to explode. "You should not." Gato was a deceiver and a liar. Nothing good would come from such a meeting.

"I will consider your thoughts, Commander."

A dismissal. Ulfr straightened his tunic, smoothed a hand over his unbound hair, and stepped from the shadows to greet an elderly councilor.

The two Alchemics peered down at the blonde on the table, who twitched. She lay in the transparent pod filled with a gaseous mixture designed to keep her flesh in perfect health, yet naked and unprotected, as all the females were while the Alchemics created the Made Ones.

Per usual, both men ignored Calix, who stood to the side, working unnecessarily on a distillate so he could be close to her. His lowly apprentice status assured him that neither Gabin nor Fukkes would pay him any notice. Which helped, since he had committed his life to destroying the Alchemics.

They'd conscripted both he and his little sister, sweet Hyla, an innocent who was only six when they took the both of them from their parents and FalconNest. He recalled those heady days of being cosseted as children by the Alchemics. Early on, he'd thought the Alchemics walked on air, so impressive, so mighty, so gentle and kind. Until his sister took sick. They'd had many Aspirants back then, and they'd tossed her away as if she were detritus. Little Hyla. He bit back a sigh. At least she'd died in their mother's arms. Now Calix was spying on the scumbags.

"This one is strong," Gabin said, pointing to the woman in the pod.

"Yes," Fukkes said. "An unexpected surprise. When we observed her on Earth, her Essence appeared weak."

Gabin snorted. "As they say on Earth, looks can be deceiving."

Beneath lowered lids, Calix glanced at the two men. He worried for this Made One whose beauty had stilled his heart. A ridiculous thought for an Alchemic. But his Falcon Clan blood ran strong and he wasn't such a fool as to deny his truth.

Gabin pressed a button, and the domed lid whooshed open, though the gasses still clung and flowed around her. Gabin lifted her hand and began testing her fingers' flexibility. "We need to win this game, so we must move forward and activate her."

"No. We wait." Fukkes stared at the woman as if she were a bug beneath his microscope lens. "That Kitlyn concerns me. She is not behaving as anticipated—she is less fearful, more proactive, and I suspect less controllable, which wasn't our intention. She has gained advocates since her arrival, also. The wolf Radulfr made her a Clan member, and I suspect the damned coywolf communicated with her mind-to-mind. I don't like it. It's too much, too fast. She has the potential to influence the Wolves in a direction we do not wish. She must be seen as the destruction of the Clans."

"Agreed." Gabin scratched his beard. "She's proving somewhat unpredictable."

Fukkes scowled. "She is deeply irritating. Kitlyn at first was properly awed and fearful. No longer. We observed her extensively on Earth, yet it's concerning. The one on this table may be full of surprises, too." Fukkes lips curled. "She may prove too dangerous to awaken."

"After all our work these months?" Gabin said. "You would let her die?"

"I would." Fukkes said.

The beaker in Calix's hands shattered. *Fark.*

Gabin turned to stare at the mess. "Problem?"

"No, sir." Calix scooped up the shards, the vial of which fortunately hadn't contained any of the precious distillate. "A hairline crack in the tube. Better to shatter now, before I poured the liquid."

Gabin's lips thinned. "Take more care."

"Of course," Calix said. Care, yes. They didn't know the meaning of the word. They'd stolen the blonde from Earth, thus they had an imperative to revive her according to the Alchemic covenant.

Fukkes toyed with the gaseous mixture, wafting it this way and that—almost, but not quite—letting it expose the Made One to the air. She would begin to decompose almost instantly if that happened. She wasn't a *plaything.* "Let's wait a week or so to see how the Made One fares."

"Time is getting short," Gabin said in a neutral voice. "This one will begin to deteriorate if we don't Make her."

"I'm aware of that." Fukkes words were clipped. "But it's worth the risk rather than have her tip the scales in the wrong direction."

Shote. Calix couldn't believe they might let her die.

"Agreed. We wait." Gabin pressed another button, and the lid closed and sealed. The pod was but a meager stopgap to her deterioration.

Calix battled the urge to slide his knife across their throats. He could easily do it. Few Alchemics were physical creatures. Ah, the temptation.

He finally won the fight with his inner animal, and the two Alchemics departed unharmed while he continued filling the beakers. *Farkers.* If he must, he could revive the Made One himself.

Months earlier, he'd memorized the complex Making procedure, thankful he remained an inconsequential and overlooked apprentice. Prejudiced pricks, all because he was born a Falcon. Only those born to the Clan gained swift Alchemic status, the pinnacle being the Cabal of Eleven. In all the years he'd been with them, not a single Alchemic had ascended. His lowly status worked in his favor—if any discovered his real truth, his life would be forfeit—but it still rankled.

If they did not unleash her Made One potential, he would Make her himself, his mission be damned.

At that afternoon's lesson, Kit asked Yuan, "Why can't I read?"

The older woman shrugged. That was it.

"Who would know?"

"Those blasted Alchemics."

"Yuan, is there no way to contact them?"

Her bitter laugh gave Kit the answer. She'd find a way. Somehow. "You talked about those hovercars the other day."

"Hovercraft."

"Right. Can they travel long distances, or do you use airplanes or something else?"

"What is an airplane?"

"A metal flying thing." She made a flapping motion.

Yuan shook her head. "The only things that fly are the birds of the sky, bugs, dakos, and mistrals."

"Mistrals? Tilde mentioned them, too."

"They are sacred. Here." She tapped her tablet, and a diagram appeared of what looked like a horse. "See the long, curling feathers on their hooves? Those hooves are stone hard and filed to sharpness in battle mistrals. Note the knobs behind their ears. During a fight, they come in handy. Plenty a Peacekeeper has clung to them when in the saddle."

The picture showed a horse looking much like the warmbloods she'd owned, lighter than a Clydesdale, but stockier than a thoroughbred, its wings outstretched. Still… "They really fly?"

Her blue eyes sparkled. "Oh, yes. Swifter than wind."

"How is that possible?"

"A fine question. You see, a mistral's bones are hollow like a bird's, making their bodies far lighter than a horse's. But the bones are composed of unbreakable organic matter stronger than our finest metals. In the old history, men would kill mistrals for their bones. But the creatures are sacred and rare, and the Clans now have laws in place where is illegal to kill a mistral for any reason. If you are found with a mistral bone and it's proven you harmed or killed the animal, you are sentenced to death."

Kit couldn't imagine anyone harming such an amazing creature. But greed was a vicious human motivator. She tried to imagine the creatures. Horses with wings. Pegasus in flesh. "Are they wild? Symbionts? Domesticated?"

"A little of all three," she said with a grin. "We Wolves are privileged to have several. You see, the mistrals are the embodiment of magic. The Alchemics hate magic."

She had to see one. Ride one.

To ride... Would she ever ride again? After that last performance...

The world of the circus unspooled in her head. The sawdust arena. The hushed crowd. The saddle's warmth beneath her thighs. A headliner. She'd been a headliner, and her chest swelled. But the rhythm... A misstep. A stumble. A glitch. Something was wrong. Very wrong.

"Ma'am Kit?" Yuan's bushy eyebrows squished together. "Ma'am Kit!"

"Oh! Oh, yes, Yuan. Apologies."

"Of course." A kind smile warmed her face, but her eyes were sad, as if she knew her truth.

A fresh breeze blew near the crest of the hill, cooling her on a day that had to be near ninety degrees. A riot of wildflowers were in bloom, the wind making the grasses hum. The scent of horse greeted her when she inhaled, and her lips widened into a smile.

Yuan told her the horses and some mistrals were housed in

several large circular structures less than two miles from The Keep. Up ahead were the massive barns.

She jogged, picturing her work with her horses at home, a combination of sweat and bliss. Perhaps she could do that here.

Neither of her sisters was so inclined, but following in her parents' footsteps, they'd all worked at the circus, Bree as an aerialist and Sybi as bookkeeper. How she'd adored performing voltige before an audience, her five horses clever and responsive beauties she'd cared for and trained. When she'd danced on horseback, those moments were immaculate and pure and perfect. Until…

She squeezed her eyes tight, opened them, and ran the remaining distance to the stables.

When she stepped through those big barn doors, it felt like coming home, the space cool and redolent with hay and musky horse smells.

Two practice rings took up much of the center inside the circular barn, with dozens and dozens of stalls lining the barn's curved walls. The place was pristine, the wood and brass gleaming. High above, fans circulated air, and the barn's thick stone walls served as a coolant. Passages led from the central barn to the smaller circular structures she'd seen from outside. What did they keep in those smaller structures? Tack rooms, for sure. The mistrals? She'd bet on it. Yuan had said they were sacred.

A few horses nickered as she approached, but before she could pet any, a short, burly, middle-aged man emerged from one of the passageways. He was diddling with his phone, which he slipped into a pocket before he approached her.

"How can I help you, ma'am?" He came to her chin, the top of his bald head beaded with sweat. He might be short, but his muscles bulged and he bristled with authority.

She tucked her hands into her back pockets. "I'm Kit. I'd like to see the horses."

"Because…?" he said,

"I love horses."

His eyes narrowed. "Who doesn't?"

"I'm good at working with them, too."

He tugged the lobe of his ear. "I'm Arne, the stable master. You're the Made One, are you not?"

A flush warmed her cheeks. She didn't much like the label, but it was obvious he saw her as something apart, so she smiled. "Yes, I am."

He waved her forward. "Come along, then, and I'll show you my beasties."

For the next hour, they toured the barn. She saw horses of all types—Clydesdales and Morgans, Percherons and Thoroughbreds, Quarter Horses and Arabians—names that came to mind when she saw sizes and builds similar to Earthly ones. When they reached the opposite side of the barn, a breezeway led to a smaller one.

"More?" She pointed to the closed doors where she'd bet they'd housed the mistrals.

"Not for today, I'm afraid. Not without Hisself's permission."

"Hisself?"

Arne grimaced. "The Alpha, of course!"

"Of course."

They continued the tour, and the stablemaster's generosity of time surprised her, as if he were protracting her visit. Worrisome.

While they petted and talked to the various horses, several teenaged stableboys tended to them, freshening hay, cleaning stalls, and watering.

Once they'd circled the entire barn, Arne asked, "Do you ride?"

"Not for many years, but I'm good with horses, and I've trained them, fed them, doctored them, and bred them, not to mention cleaned stalls. Many, many stalls."

"You mucked them out, eh? As any horse person should. Good. Good." Though he didn't smile, his sharp brown eyes softened. "I'll find you the perfect mount. We can work with that."

An ideal opening. "Speaking of…"

At first, Arne wasn't keen on her working in the stables, but after a half hour of bartering, they agreed that Kit would come to the barns three afternoons a week to clean six stalls and feed and groom the same number of horses. She would be paid. Not much, but she was pleased to be *earning* money, instead of having it given to her.

They shook on it. Which was when Rafe jogged toward them from that mysterious breezeway. She'd bet dollars Arne had called him when she first arrived. Why?

Rafe slapped a hand on the stablemaster's shoulder. "Thanks for showing Kit the horses, Arne."

The older man nodded to Rafe, then gave Kit a long look. "See you tomorrow."

"I'll be here." Working with horses again. The normalcy of it thrilled her.

Rafe turned to her, his expression impassive. "You felt you needed a job?"

"I have to do something useful, and I love horses. It seemed perfect."

"You're bored."

She wanted him to understand. "Not exactly. It's not boredom, really, but even with all that's happened, I need some way to help out. A purpose."

"You have a purpose."

Her jagged laugh startled a nearby horse. "You mean being a babymaker? In my world, a woman's body is her own."

He stiffened. "The Fates, Kit, of course it is. I wasn't implying—"

"No? It's how I feel."

His face tightened. "That's not how it's supposed to be."

"Perhaps not, but—"

"I'll fix it."

"You can't, Rafe."

"I don't want you feeling that way."

She softened. "I appreciate that, but I doubt you can change my feelings."

"You'll see. I can't fix things right now, but I bet a ride would help."

Oh, no. A tremor rippled through her, and she laid her hand on a stall door to steady herself. "I'd love one."

"Good. I'll check with Arne to find you a suitable mount."

"Super." When Rafe disappeared, she wiped her forearm across her sweaty forehead. With a calm she wasn't feeling, she walked toward the door to the breezeway. *Why had she said yes?* She hadn't ridden in thirty years.

Inside the breezeway, the nickers and neighs came from the other side of the smaller barn's closed door, the barn forbidden by the Alpha. Yeah, she didn't care about his rules so much.

"Kit?" Rafe, calling from the arena. Then he called again. Closer.

"Coming!" She'd tell him how she hadn't ridden in ages. That since she was rusty, she'd like to put it off today. She was already sweating like a dockworker.

When she stepped onto the sawdust floor, a nasty surprise awaited her.

CHAPTER SEVEN

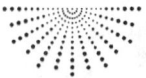

Rafe stood by one of the stalls surrounded by tack. The woman standing beside him holding a bay horse's lead was the blonde who'd threatened her.

Show her vulnerability to that woman? Not in this lifetime.

Kit pasted on her best smile. "Hey."

Rafe paused stroking the big bay's neck and smiled back. "Inga says Blackie here will suit you fine."

"I'm sure he will," she said, closing the distance between them.

"Have you two met?" he asked.

The damned blonde was smirking.

"We have," she said with enthusiasm. She felt like biting the woman's smile right off her pretty face.

Rafe walked off to saddle a 16-plus-hand piebald with fiery eyes.

"I'll saddle Blackie for you," Inga said.

"No need," Kit said lightly. As if she'd trust that woman to do anything for her. She reached for the bay's lead.

Inga held the rope a moment too long, then handed it to Kit.

"Thanks," she said to Inga. The big bay gelding was the size of Rafe's horse, a handsome boy, with large liquid eyes and a blaze on his forehead. He nudged her shoulder, and she laughed, giving him a scratch. "Blackie? He's a bay."

Inga shrugged. "You'll like him." Her eyes looked sincere, her smile appearing genuine.

It seemed acting came naturally to Inga. A reckoning was coming. Soon. Kit was eager for it.

They saddled up, and she found Eleutian tack wasn't much different from Earthly ones. The Wolf Clan didn't appear to use bits, but rather hackamores, nosebands that directed a horse through pressure points on the face, nose, and chin. The reins were one-handed Western style, rather than English. She could work with either, but liked the freedom the Western gave her.

As she cinched Blackie's saddle, she made sure Inga hadn't sabotaged her by cutting part of her cinch or stirrup leather. The hackamore was untouched, too.

Rafe checked her saddle and bridle. "Well done."

"Thank you. When do I get to meet a mistral?"

Rafe's shook his head and chuckled. "Of course you found out."

"I did. So when?"

"They're breeding Ulfr's stallion. My father's funny about that. No visitors."

"Soon, I hope."

"Soon." He nodded for her to mount.

She'd been atop horses for thousands of hours, yet when she took the reins, her hands trembled. Blackie would instantly sense her fear. She went to put her foot in the stirrup and froze.

Her gut clenched. Inga had thankfully disappeared. "Um, Rafe... Would you wait outside for me?"

He didn't even blink. "Sure."

Once he'd left, she leaned against Blackie's flank. There was a good reason she hadn't ridden for thirty years. Or so she'd told herself. Yet here she was. Karma? Good for the soul, right?

Blackie turned his head and nuzzled her. "You're a good boy." She blew in his nostrils. "We'll get along fine."

Why was this so damned hard?

She'd begun sweating, hands shaking, body stiff. She pressed against Blackie's neck and inhaled deeply. His scent transported her home, to their old barn with its tin roof and weathered beams and wood floor. Where swallows nested in the eaves and pine boughs sighed in the chill wind.

"Kit?" Rafe's call brought her back to the now and the task in front of her.

Blackie dipped his huge head to her shoulder and began to delicately nibble her shirt.

She reared back, grinning. "Oh, you're one of those, eh?"

Home was *then*. Now was Kit 2.0, a new body, a new world. Except her headspace hadn't quite caught up with her physical changes.

Having battled that demon on Earth, he was an old friend. Time to drag her old self into mindset 2.0. As if that would be easy. Seemed some tough love was in order.

She lifted her foot and placed it in the stirrup. Blackness ate the edges of her sanity. *Fuck you, flashback.* She swung her leg over the bay, but her anxiety translated to Blackie, whose prancing made her settling in the saddle awkward.

Awkward or not, she'd done it.

Why now? Why could she get on a horse now? What had changed? Irony pinched her, and she began to laugh, slightly hysterical, but it felt so fine.

Rafe reappeared atop the piebald. "I heard you laughing. It sounded good." He slipped on his sunglasses, pulled a bill cap from his pocket, then walked the piebald over to a cabinet and retrieved a cap.

"Ready?" he said when he'd brought his horse to stand beside hers.

"I am."

He handed her the cap. "Thanks." Helmets weren't an option, apparently. Twenty-six bones. Phalanges, metatarsals, tarsals, fibulas, tibias, femurs...

Stop.

"My pleasure." Rafe's voice was a deep, reassuring purr.

He knew. He saw her fear. Yet he wasn't blathering on about how it would be okay, as so many others had done.

As much as her past haunted her, she was eager for Rafe to see her skills even knowing she could fall out of the saddle if her PTSD struck. So strange, wanting to impress him. Her late husband was un-impressible when he wasn't trying to control her.

A tremor shivered through her. The circus arena began to take shape.

She bit her cheek hard, throttling her fear.

Rafe walked them up a trail that passed through grassy meadows filled with wildflowers. He figured Kit would love that. Her mysterious fear in the barn had struck him like a blow. But she'd mastered it, determined creature that she was. Though she remained nervous, she sat Blackie like a pro, graceful and in tune with the gelding. The Fates, he admired her.

Pastured horses whinnied as they walked by. The horse, Blaze, was a good mare, and though he'd rather be on Nightfall, no mistrals should be taken out while he was breeding Moonrise to Ulfr's Mistralys.

His Kit looked good on a horse. No, she wasn't "his" yet. But she would be. Two others were competing for her hand, good men. He suspected his rank concerned the other hopefuls. Fools. From what he'd observed, rank mattered little to Kit. Only the man beneath would hold her attention. His hands clenched the reins, and Blaze danced.

"Sorry, ma'am." He patted the horse's neck.

He would be the one to win Kit's heart. He must. When she'd awakened in the hover, those mysterious forest-green eyes hit him like an anvil, saying, "I know you." In that instant, he knew her, too. While the feeling had passed, he remembered that strange awareness. Coupled with her lovely face and fine body, she drew him in.

Her resilience and the inner core of strength he sensed from the first made her impossible to resist.

Rafe hadn't told her Made Ones could wither if they were unable or unwilling to accept the changes wrought by the Alchemics. Few knew of that withering, yet another reason to end the Alchemics' conscription of Made Ones. He'd seen it firsthand with Fujiko, a lovely flower of a woman whose tragic end nearly crippled the Falcon Clan.

That Kit thought of herself as a breeder troubled him. Fujiko had thought the same. When Compass True ended the Alchemics death grip on Eleutia, Kit would understand. But outside of his group, no one, not even Kit, could know of his unsanctioned activities.

"How many horses does the Clan own?" Kit asked him.

He thought for a minute. "Four hundred? More? Hard to say. Many more are privately owned."

"Do you have horses?"

"I do."

"And mistrals?"

"Yes."

He wasn't ready for Kit to meet his small herd, so he'd been terse, and she'd lapsed into silence. Yet it was a comfortable one. He liked that, too, how she didn't feel a constant need to fill the quiet with talk. Though when she had something to say... He chuckled to himself.

The reading thing bothered her. He didn't know if the Alchemics had purposefully altered her translator disk or if it was malfunctioning. Either way, he could help her learn to read their language and was pleased she was attempting it on her own. Resilient *and* determined.

She'd cajoled a job out of Arne, who'd had no intention of giving her one. After overhearing their conversation, he wasn't surprised when the old stablemaster folded. He would have, too. Kit had a way about her that made people want to please her. She also hadn't taken Arne's "no" as a dead end, but cleverly talked him around to her point of view. When he'd spoken with Arne, the man couldn't believe he'd relented. After all, she was the Made One. Imagine if a horse kicked or bit her. She was a precious… he'd almost thought "commodity." Fates above, never let him fall into that way of thinking.

Riding alongside him, her face flushed, pleasure lighting her eyes, a thrill of anticipation arced through him. Her body swayed with a natural, pleasing rhythm, her legs strong but relaxed. He imagined her on Nightfall, her strong legs wrapped around the mistral as he took flight. The image shocked him. No one but he rode his mistrals. But wouldn't she be glorious?

A picture of those long supple legs wrapped around him, while he entered her slowly, carefully, joyfully burst in his mind.

"Rafe, what's that tree called?"

He cleared his throat. "Um, a madronis. Feel like a canter?" He waited long seconds. Though shadowed by the cap she wore, her eyes glistened in the light. He'd swear he saw fear.

"Let's!" Kit said.

But he'd caught her brief clench of a fist. She was lying, though he didn't know why. She rode brilliantly. "You sure?"

"Yes."

He broke Blaze into an easy canter as Kit squeezed Blackie's flank, leaned forward a bit, and took off.

Rafe kept an eye on her, caught her brief moment of panic, where she stiffened. Never a good thing to do in the saddle. *Shote.*

Then she loosened and found the rhythm. The woman could have been born riding. A huge smile broke across those plush lips, and she laughed aloud. But were those tears on her cheeks?

Such a strange, yet oddly beautiful, sight.

He ached for her, bewitched by her own unique brand of magic.

The distance between them widened as he watched the bay's large stride eat up the ground. Until that moment, he hadn't realized how badly he wanted Kit, unlike his feelings for the three female Clan members who doggedly pursued him. Of those, two failed to catch his interest, and Inga was a good friend whose mating ambitions made things awkward between them. But Kit. From the strange moment when she'd awakened, and then at the MedSurge when she'd exited the hover, fallen flat on her face, picked herself up and carried on, he'd felt in tune with her. An inexplicable sensation. When he'd begun courting her, he hoped she'd return his interest. She hadn't responded…yet.

She would. He watched her like a wolf on the hunt, gaining a good notion of what she liked, what she treasured. An idea popped into his head, and he smiled.

Blackie's sides were heaving by the time Kit reined him in atop a rise. They stood overlooking a verdant valley cut by a sparkling stream and bordered by low stone walls. Birds swooped here and there, diving for bugs. It wasn't Battle Beetle season, thankfully.

She scrubbed her face, trying to wipe away the tear tracks before Rafe arrived, then leaned forward and hugged Blackie's neck. It came back. Her rhythm and ease in the saddle. How she felt a part of the animal, as if they were born to do this singular thing together.

In seconds, Rafe reached her on the rise. That grin. The way his eyes crinkled. Here was a man filled with sunshine. "Why are you smiling?"

"The air. The horse. You." He winked.

They cantered down the hill into the next valley, Rafe riding beside her, and eventually reined in to a walk. She patted Blackie. "We did it, boy. We did it!"

"Did what?"

The words she wanted to say stuck in her throat, so she muddied the waters. "When can I see the mistrals, Rafe?"

He chuckled and shook his head. "Where did that come from?"

"I'm curious." She gave him a look from beneath lowered lashes. "We don't have flying horses on Earth."

"No?" His slow smile did funny things to her belly. "A shame."

"So when?"

"When the Alpha says so. But be sure I'll remind him of his duties toward you."

His utter seriousness made her lips twitch, especially when she saw him trying not to smile. "You're awful."

"Awful, am I?"

"Yes. I'm bursting with curiosity, and you're being all secretive."

"Not me. My father."

She waved a hand, determined to keep a straight face. "Incorrigible." But she burst out laughing, which ruined the whole effect. "I may just have to sneak in and find out on my own."

"I didn't hear that."

"Hear what?" She took off. "Catch me!" The big bay stretched out, his stride lengthening, and they flew across the world as if floating on a dream.

When he caught up with her, she was so happy, she laughed aloud. She'd done it. How glorious. Utterly familiar, yet new, too, with a body that wasn't hers, yet was.

"Having fun?" Rafe said.

"Deliriously so." She nodded and gave herself over to the ride.

An hour later, she was hot, sweaty, and content as they made their way back to the stables at a walk.

The ride had been the most fun she'd had in…forever. Yes, forever. Rafe rode as if he were one with the horse, and it was like watching a symphony of muscle and movement. Earlier, when they'd stopped to rest the horses, Rafe and she had talked about Earth and Eleutia and his duties as the Alpha's First Commander. He'd asked about her life and career, and she'd carefully sidestepped her circus days by telling a joke, which led to another, until they were trading jokes, both Eleutian and Earthly ones. They'd laughed hard and often as they'd woven through the pines.

Now the day was waning, the sun dipping low.

"Do you ever ride beside the sea?" she said.

"Sometimes."

"I'd like to do that."

He was about to answer when a flock of birds with long fluttery tails started dive-bombing for food. They didn't come too close, but one must have seen a goodie near Blackie because it dove right in front of him.

The bay reared, and Kit tried to retain her seat, but she was out of practice. She flew off his back, managing a backward somersault that was second nature to land on her feet.

Except this wasn't the ring, she hadn't done this in years, and her left foot hit a loose rock on landing. Down she went, right on her butt, her leg twisting.

She was embarrassed. Winded. But she didn't re-experience, didn't disassociate, didn't relive the accident.

A shadow, then Rafe was beside her. "Kit!"

"I'm fine." She hadn't freaked, either, and she was near euphoric. All those years when riding a horse had been a trigger. Oh, she'd tried. How she'd tried. But each time she'd re-experience the accident. Her sisters had finally convinced her to keep her horses but to stop trying to ride them.

"I'll get a doctor," he said.

Arne was running toward them.

"I don't need a doctor, just a hand up." She went to move and her left leg protested with a shot of pain. "Well, hell."

"Wait," Rafe said.

Arne took Blackie's reins, then walked over. "Foolish horse gets spooked by those birds every *shoting* time. The pesky things come same time every day, and if Blackie sees them…"

Rafe's face froze into an impassive mask.

The birds. The timing. Inga.

And there she was, hovering in the shadows by the barn doors.

Kit's hands fisted.

Except a soft ray of afternoon light splashed across Inga's face. Her eyes were focused on Rafe, her face one of longing and sorrow.

Kit had once longed for someone, too. For Finn, Bree's aerialist partner. He'd never seen her, his eyes only for her sister, who wouldn't give him the time of day.

Eons ago, Finn had faded from memory. But she understood.

"I'll be right back." Rafe stepped toward the barn, though Inga had disappeared.

"Let it be. Okay?"

His eyes narrowed.

"Let it lie, Rafe," she said.

He snapped her a nod, though he didn't look happy about it.

She shifted, finally able to straighten her leg. It was achy, but didn't feel broken or sprained.

"Broken?" Rafe said.

"I don't think so. Not sprained, either."

He rubbed her leg, and though it hurt, the massage loosened her abused muscles. "I'll be sore tomorrow." She smiled as he wrapped an arm around her waist and helped her stand. "Thanks."

Arne scowled. "You sure the stable's the right place for you?"

"Even more now that I've landed on my ass. That's my quota, right? Good to get it out of the way."

The following morning, Kit's aches were tolerable. Even so, she took a pass on her arms training. Her head was muzzy from dreams where she'd relived her accident, so used to them she barely reacted. Barely.

She wrapped her arms around her waist and sat. The dreams were the first she'd had since coming to Eleutia. As much as they hurt, they were but a small price to pay for what she'd done—ridden on horseback. A thrill skated up her spine. She wanted Rafe to know about her accident, unsure why that mattered, yet it did. She'd tell him, right after she punched Inga in the mouth.

No, no, she wouldn't do that, but she wanted to. A lesser rider could have been killed. She'd ridden Blackie, fallen, yet she hadn't died. Maybe she should thank Inga instead. A laugh bubbled out. Self-awareness was a funny thing.

A surprise awaited her when she opened her door to leave for breakfast. A small sculpture of a wolf sat on the doorstep with Mr.

Red's bow around its neck. Beside it was a gold box wrapped in green, and Mr. Blue's photo of a lagoon.

She lifted Mr. Green's gold box and opened it to reveal what looked like soft candies. She sniffed, the smell delicious. Not chocolate, but spicy and sweet. A lovely gift, though the photos confused her. Was Mr. Blue planning on taking her to these places?

Now the carving... With care, she set the wolf in her palm. Carved strokes delineated its tan fur, decorated with black spots. Paulo—sitting on his bum, mouth open, black tongue lolling in a happy smile. She curled her hand around the little coywolf, but not so tight that she might break him. She'd always said a gift of the hand was the most precious, for it held a piece of the giver's spirit within.

Did Mr. Red's spirit reside within? She wanted to meet him, her secret hope being that he was Rafe.

But now wasn't the time for courting. How could she form a relationship when she should be out hunting for her sisters?

Tempted to take the wolf with her, she instead set it on her bedside table where the flowers she'd been given still bloomed, then she placed the gold box and picture on her dresser.

No viperous blonde awaited her as she set off for the dining hall. Tilde joined her, and they speculated on what Cook had concocted that morning.

The green sautéed potatoes at breakfast reminded her of St. Patrick's Day and how everyone dyed stuff green.

Did they have Saints in this strange land? Religion? Many religions? At today's history lesson, she'd ask Yuan.

She was halfway through her meal, and Rafe still hadn't appeared. "Rafe isn't joining us?"

"He's dealing with a border skirmish," Garth said through a mouthful of food.

Tilde shot him an angry look.

"Border skirmish?"

Garth looked everywhere but at her.

"Tilde?"

"I don't think Rafe wanted you to know." She pointed to Garth. "That bigmouth over there."

If Rafe were injured… "What kind of skirmish?"

"The wolf's out of the den now." Max snorted.

"It sure is." Tilde's eyes grew serious.

"I want to hear all of it," Kit said.

Tilde poked her glasses to the bridge of her nose. "I'd rather—"

"Please," Kit said.

"The Cat Clan has objected to you being here. Several times. They've made a point of it."

Rafe said it was Cats who'd attacked them on their way to Wolf-Home. The blood. The Cats' injuries. Those could have been *Rafe's* blood, *his* injuries. The Clans slipped so swiftly into armed combat. "*Why?*"

"It's complicated," Max said. "Yesterday, they slit the throats of five of our sheep and left them in the field. An affront and a message. Rafe wasn't having it and chose to ignore his Alpha's wishes by going after the perpetrators. We're setting traps for the interlopers, as well as upping patrols."

Eevon bristled. "Useless. It'll take more manpower than we possess to apprehend everyone who enters our borders."

Paulo yipped. He'd joined them earlier, his head resting on her lap a comforting weight.

"Yes, Paulo." Tilde gave his head a scratch. "Our wolf and coyote brothers and sisters are helping too. But if the Cats want to harry us, they have ample opportunity."

"Why?" Kit said. "What objections have they made about me?"

Tilde wouldn't meet her eyes. "That's not for me to say, Kit."

A simmer of temper burned her gut, but she kept her voice even and calm. "Who can I ask?"

"Rafe, when he returns."

"Which is…?"

"Two or three days, at the least. Our territory is vast. The Alpha—"

"I haven't even met the Alpha." Which bugged her. Everything circled back to him—her sisters, the Cat Clan's objections, the mistrals.

If the Alpha wasn't going to come to her, she'd go to him.

Kit might think it was time she met the Alpha, but evidently the Alpha disagreed. She was done with waiting. Directly after breakfast, she beelined it to his office and was turned away by an imperious espresso-skinned woman named Meela. She'd been told the Alpha's gatekeeper was actually a Cat, though mated to a Wolf. A warrior, in fact, and quite lethal.

Yes, Meela told her, the Alpha *had* returned from the Falcons, but he was "on a conference call."

Was he hiding? Exactly what did the Wolves' leader have to conceal from her?

Three hours later, mid-day in full swing, book in hand as camouflage, Kit purposefully strolled to the Alpha's office, which she'd learned was attached to his den, as they called it.

How could she get in? She didn't have his palm print. And she made a U-turn when she spotted the dragon lady who guarded the entrance. Now what? She couldn't scale the walls to the half-open windows.

Could she?

Beneath the canopy of a large tree, Kit strapped on the claws with rock-steady hands. Five steps, and she'd stand beside The Keep's wall directly beneath the Alpha's office, with its soft glow of light. He was inside. She would finally meet him, demand that he tell her about Bree and Sybi.

Darkness shrouded the night but for a spangling of stars, a quarter moon, and a pale light cast from an open window.

Those stars. She dropped to her knees, drilled to her core. There was Orion, the Hunter, and there, Ursa Major, the Great Bear, and Ursa Minor, too, the Little Bear or Little Dipper. Her breath stuttered. Since arriving on Eleutia, why had she never noticed the stars? They were identical to those above *her* Earth.

A soft breeze rustled the leaves and played with a loose strand of her bound hair. Her brain cooled, and she recalled her mission. She pulled the hood of her black sweatshirt up to hide her face, standing as she did so.

Was she really going to do this?

Whistle a happy tune and all that. Kit took a running start, landing three feet up the wall, gripping it with her sneakers and her claws. *Ouch.* She'd forgotten her sore ankle. She paused, slowing her heartbeat and breaths. *Push on.* Powering through the ache, she forced her hand up and into the next indentation, lifted her foot and did the same, and she climbed the wall one handhold and foothold at a time.

By the time she neared the open window, her hands, arms, and shoulders screamed that her strength was badly waning.

A rustle on the ground. Kit froze.

Stars alive, if she fell…

She flashed to her accident, awash with pain.

Dammit, no. Not now. Not *ever*.

She pressed herself tighter to the wall, hands straining, until her panting subsided. If she entered that fugue state where memory was more real than reality, she'd careen from the wall to die on the ground below.

But she held it back, again, thank the lucky stars.

So be it if someone was down below watching her progress.

With her left hand, she gripped the left frame of the window, dug in her claws and peeked inside. Empty. She could climb back down, or she could look around. Her right hand followed on the right frame, and she clenched her core, her arms raising her, curling her legs upward to slide through the window, tucking her head, and performing a perfect roll into the office.

Her landing made more noise than she'd hoped, but no other lights flicked on, no voice asked what she was doing. For a moment, Kit lay quiescent, catching her breath and letting her quivering muscles relax, then she sprang to her feet, shaking out her weary arms and legs. In seconds, her eyes had adjusted to the dim light.

Was she really burgling the Alpha's office? "Shit."

Kit froze. She'd just said that aloud. Listening almost hurt, but no sound came from the outer door. She wiped her hands on her pants and got to it.

CHAPTER EIGHT

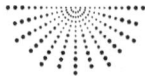

K it began with the papers scattered across the Alpha's desk. She might not be able to read their language, but she searched for names—hers or Sybi's or Bree's.

After several minutes, it was clear nothing of the sort was on the desk. She started on the drawers, finding few papers, though she found it interesting he kept a bottle of drass, a laser pistol, and a single claw in the bottom drawer.

She rested her hands on the desk, a bead of sweat dropping onto the surface. She swiped her sleeve across her forehead. Tempting to push back her hood, but her face would be a beacon to anyone.

Where would the Alpha hide important papers from curious eyes?

The office was austere in the extreme. No file cabinets, no secret drawers, no family photos, no...

Above the fireplace, the painting of men and wolves battling some hideous winged monsters had potential. Kit walked closer. She'd swear that was Rafe on a giant black flying horse, sword bloody, the dragon-lizard thing shooting green flame.

She carried over one of the chairs that faced the desk and stood on it, balancing on the edges, and raised her hand to the painting. She pulled. It didn't move.

Obviously her burglary skills needed work.

She twisted her torso and tugged with both hands firmly gripping the painting's frame.

The thing didn't budge. It must be bolted to the wall, and if he hid papers behind it, she didn't see how he'd get to them.

Hopping down, she repositioned the chair in its original spot, making sure its feet rested on the indentations in the rug.

Was this all for nothing?

Voices outside the office door.

The ping of a palm print's acceptance.

Clamping down her nerves, her eyes skimmed the moonlit room. Two doors. Closets? A bathroom? One to the Alpha's den? Either way, she'd better move it.

She glided to the left-hand door, opened it as quietly as possible, and waited until the sound of the outer door's click would mask the opening of her escape route…or the dead end she feared.

There went the click, and she scooted inside and pressed against the door to listen. Except the thumping of her heart was like a bass drum. She managed to quiet her breathing, soothing the adrenaline shooting through her. Okay.

Kit turned. The bathroom's double sink and the facing door had to mean she was connected to the Alpha's suite of rooms, his den. She rubbed her temples. Why was she doing this again? Oh, she knew, all right. And the bathroom—what a perfect place to hide important papers. Easy enough to scour the ten-by-ten room, so she looked beneath the sink, through the linen closet, along with the medicine cabinet, all while listening for sounds from the office. When she ran her hands across the bleached pine walls hoping to find a secret door, a spider literally crawled out of the woodwork. A huge, hairy, eight-legged spider with big, fat banded red-and-black legs and four bulbous red eyes that stared straight at her.

She jumped. *Oh, shit.*

Nope, not afraid of spiders. Even ones the size of her hand. Of course she wasn't. She took a cautious step closer. Where had the thing come from?

How did you get on this paneling, you little beastie?

It opened its mouth. Jaws like lobster claws, four of them, the creature swayed back and forth, as if to mesmerize her. *Lucky stars.*

She jumped back just as it spat at her.

A glob hit her throat, instantly numbing the spot. She tried to swallow but her throat felt twice the normal size.

The spider scuttled away, and through her panic, Kit watched it slip into what looked like an open knot in the paneling.

Her breath came in pants, the spot where the venom had landed now burning. She didn't dare turn on the water, but it felt like someone was stabbing a hot poker into her throat.

She swiped a towel and rounded the corner to the private toilet keeping her eyes on the hole where the spider had gone. Crouching down and gross as it seemed, she dipped the towel into the toilet bowl, then slid it over the burn.

Ahhh. Cooling relief. She still couldn't swallow, but her breathing felt more natural. Back in the main bathroom, she peered at the hole, its knot missing. No way was she looking in there.

She should leave, anxious that the spider's venom might damage her further. But where would she go? If she entered the Alpha's bedroom, he or his wife might be there.

Back to the office only meant she'd run into whoever had entered. And she'd still found nothing about her sisters. She *had* to find something, anything about her sisters, dammit. She sure wasn't scaling walls and confronting spiders again.

Kit gnawed her lip. She could breathe. She wouldn't die.

The knothole might just be that. But if it was a door behind which they'd hid something important, she had to look.

Pressing her fingers to the wall, she felt for a seam. Nothing. She'd have to poke her fingers into the knothole and pull to see if it was a hidden door. And wasn't that a tempting idea?

Her neck started to itch. Before she scratched it, she leaned sideways to peer into the mirror. Dozens of tiny blisters covered her blotchy red neck. Stars alive, it was driving her...

The outer bathroom door clicked.

Kit slipped inside the toilet enclosure so she was screened from the intruder. Unless they had to use the toilet.

Footsteps on the tile.

What fantastical tale could she tell? *See, I was here looking for the Alpha's private papers.*

She sat atop the closed toilet seat, feet up, arms banding her legs.

Perhaps she'd been searching for medication, an aspirin. Lame. Maybe her curiosity got the better of her, and she just had to see the Alpha's office. Right.

Noises of someone moving around the room. She closed her eyes. She opened her eyes. She bit her lip.

Crap. Crap. Crap.

If he discovered her, the Alpha might... She had no idea what the Alpha would do.

A shadow fell across the tile floor.

"I see you found the facilities."

Meela—tall, lean, elegant—looked like a Wakandan warrior as she stared straight at Kit, her mouth tight, her eyes narrowed. All she needed was a spear for the image to be complete.

"I did."

"Might I ask the obvious—what are you doing in the Alpha's private quarters?"

"Would you believe—"

"No." Meela leaned back against the vanity counter and crossed her arms. Right by the hole. What if the spider crawled out and attacked her.

"Move, Meela. There's a giant spider—"

Meela waved a hand. "Yes, yes. So? Answer my question."

Kit stood, now face-to-face with the woman, and squared her shoulders.

Meela blinked. "And...?"

"I was going to lie," Kit said.

"I see."

A fire bloomed in Kit, one of pride. She notched her chin. "But I won't. I was searching for papers, anything, that related to my sisters. I didn't find them in the office, so I came in here and realized the bathroom is the perfect place to hide stuff."

"You dare much, foolish woman." Meela gave her teeth.

"Foolish, am I? Perhaps, but a person acts in crazy ways when no answers are forthcoming. Do you have sisters? Or brothers? Do you know what it's like to have lost them? Would *you* do anything and everything to find them?"

The woman's shrug pricked her.

"Please move away from there," Kit said. "There's this huge spider. Look what he did to my neck. He spat at me, and…"

Meela began to laugh. She pulled on the knot in the wall, opened a door, and inserted her hand.

"Don't!" Kit said.

Out came Meela's hand with the spider standing on the back of it.

"Holy shit." Kit backed away.

Her eyes still sparking with humor, Meela petted the spider's back with one finger. "This is Percy. He's a pet."

"A pet. He spat at me."

"What did you expect? You must have scared him. He's harmless."

"Not harmless."

"Here."

The next thing she knew, Meela thrust the spider at her. It was either put out her hand or Meela would lay Percy on her chest or shoulder or somewhere. Jaw tightening, nostrils flaring, she glared at Meela as she held out her hand. Then feathers brushed her palm as he climbed aboard. *Stars alive.* There he sat, a ginormous fuzzy spider covering, no, overlapping her entire palm, his four red eyes observing her with what she'd swear was some sort of sentience. Percy's jaws opened. Oh no, he was going to hock another loogie, maybe hit her face this time.

Easy enough to toss him away. But he might get hurt.

Percy's jaws widened further.

She swallowed. At least her throat was working again. Kit had to make friends. She knew animals. She loved animals. "Hey, Percy. I can be a friend, too, big guy."

Percy stared at her. One of his legs moved back and forth. Those pointed hairy things by his mouth twitched. Then his jaws closed.

Kit forced a smile. Please don't let him move or jump or spit. "You're a clever fellow, I can tell."

The spider folded himself down so his hairy belly rested on the flat of her hand. He closed his eyes, then one red eye popped open to stare at her.

"Yes, I see you, Percy."

"Problem solved," Meela said. "He's decided not to spit at you. Good. Poor thing gets scared so easily."

Poor thing? What about me? She'd seen Meela do it, so why the hell not? With her index finger, she stroked Percy's back. "Hey, fella." His open red eye drooped closed.

When she looked up, Meela held a green folder, eyes dancing with laughter. "Point of fact, we do keep important papers in here. This folder has your name on it. Perhaps it's the one you want?"

"Perhaps it is, Meela." Kit waited. And waited.

Then Meela scooped up Percy, replacing him in his hidey-hole, and held out the folder. "I had a sister."

Kit took the folder. She was dying to open it. "Had?"

"She was malformed. She was sent to the CastOuts and lost to me."

"The CastOuts?"

"The Alchemics tolerate no imperfections."

"How awful. I'm sorry." Even as Kit said the words, she felt their inadequacy in her bones.

"I am old. It was long ago. But I remember."

Kit nodded. She understood that terrible pain but had no words to fill that aching space. Kit opened the folder. Though she couldn't read the text, her name appeared on several pages. Then another page, and the name "Breena" stood out. She froze. Took a deep breath and found the page beneath containing Sybelle's name. Her heart thundered. "Would you read the text for me?"

"I will." Meela reached for the folder, then her head shot up. "He comes. He will not be pleased. Go. Take the papers and go."

Meela pointed to a door at the opposite end of the bathroom. "That leads to his den. The mate and child are in the dining hall. Go now!"

Kit hugged the papers to her. "Thank you." She dashed out the door.

At the following afternoon's lesson, though she was dying to ask Yuan to read the papers, she didn't dare. Instead, she sat through a grilling on the Cats, since they had reopened hostilities with the Wolves.

The imperious and lethal Cat Clan tended toward savagery first and discussion later, which was why their "peace" with the Wolves was always shaky. Deadly fighters, with far larger numbers than the Wolves, the Cat Clan was thought by many to be the strongest of all the Clans on Eleutia.

Just great.

Back in her rooms, after staring for minutes at the indecipherable papers with her sisters' names on them, she slid her fingers across the letters that spelled them out. Rafe was away, so he couldn't read them for her. Tilde might without giving her away, "might" being the operative word. Stars alive, she was dying to know what the papers said. Maybe Max? No. If she wasn't cautious, whoever she chose could go running to the Alpha.

She wasn't ready to poke that dragon.

A ping reminded her of her new stable job. *Oh, hell,* she was about to be late. She slid the folder beneath the couch cushions and ran.

· · ·

Sweat coated Kit by the time she'd cleaned her six stalls and curried all six horses, the exercise having eased her aching body from the wall climb. Satisfyingly exhausted, she was thrilled with her new charges, especially the elder bay stallion, Drofus, who nickered and neighed as she talked to him, as if they were having a two-way conversation. She freshened their hay, then reviewed the feeding chart Arne had made for her detailing how much grain, vitamins, and minerals each of her six horses should get. As soon as she was done, she'd go find Tilde.

After preparing each horse's specific feed bucket, she distributed them, as well as fresh water. She hung the last water and feed buckets for Izka, the chestnut mare who nuzzled her with enthusiasm. Dust tickled her nose, and she swiped it away with the edge of her t-shirt now covered in sweat and grime. Lucky stars, she was filthy, and she loved it. Time to call it quits.

Even with the cooling fans whirring, she stank from sweat, her hair a greasy mess. Oh, for a refreshing swim. She'd taken several with Tilde. Today, she'd take a quick shower, grab the papers and hunt down her friend for the translation.

Kit patted the mare and closed the stall door behind her.

When she turned, Inga stood in front of her, hands on hips, wearing a contemptuous smile. Great. She'd like to slap that smile off her face. Instead, Kit brushed on by.

Inga grabbed the back of her shirt and whipped her around. "Where are you going?"

"I'm finished for the day." Her temper was rising, and she struggled to leash it.

Inga shoved her. "You have three more horses to do."

"I'm afraid I don't. Arne gave me the six, and I just finished up. It's not your purview to give me orders."

"Well, aren't you the fancy one." Inga circled her. "Purview is it? The Fates, what does Rafe see in you? I have to leave, so you will feed and water my three remaining horses."

Kit leaned back against the stall door and crossed one booted foot over the other. "You know, Inga, if you'd asked me nicely, I would've been happy to help you out. But now there's not a chance in hell I'm taking care of the horses you were assigned."

"Yes, you are, or…" Inga whipped out a six-inch knife and thrust it beneath Kit's chin. "Or I will cut you."

A firecracker exploded in Kit's brain. She gripped Inga's knife hand in a hyperflexing wrist lock, pressing it into her *hard*. Inga shrieked, struggling, but Kit pressed even harder inward. Inga screamed, and Kit's other arm went in for a "hug," her right leg moving behind Inga's and sweeping her downward onto her back.

She went with the shrieking woman, and they landed with an oomph, her knee on Inga's belly. The knife gleamed long and lethal, and Kit plucked it from Inga's lax grip and tossed it far away, her other hand clamped on Inga's other wrist.

Inga's eyes were wide as she desperately tried to suck in a breath.

"Don't *ever* pull a knife on me again," Kit said. "Or I'll do more than simply plant you on the ground. Understood? You can't command Rafe's affections."

In one fluid move, Kit sprang to her feet.

Rubbing one shoulder, Inga pushed herself to stand. "How did you do that?"

"Magic."

Inga sneered. "The Alchemics forbid High Magics."

"I'll take my chances." Kit laughed, not about to disclose her martial arts training, especially to this viper. "You're an interesting and capable woman, and I would have liked us to be friends. Obviously, that isn't going to happen. Your call, not mine. I'm leaving. Have a good night." Curious what Inga would do, Kit deliberately gave the woman her back and walked away.

Inga's arm snaked around Kit's throat. "I asked you a question."

So predictable. Kit dropped her shoulder and flipped the woman's body over hers, slamming her hard onto her back.

Inga struggled for breath.

Kit wiggled her fingers. "Magic, remember?" Kit left the dark barn for the warmth of late-afternoon's copper sun.

. . .

Kit finally got Tilde alone. The past three days had been uneventful, though she'd spent another satisfying afternoon in the stables, no Inga in sight. She'd also received two more gifts on her doorstep. It seemed Mr. Blue had withdrawn before she'd even met him.

Maybe she *had* met him, and he didn't much like her.

One gift was a jar of opalescent pink balls wrapped with a green ribbon, either bath beads or candy. Unable to read the label, she'd sniffed. She still couldn't tell. Tied together with red string, the second gift thrilled her—a green leather-bound journal and an elegant quill pen made of the longest blond feather she'd ever seen. On the journal's first page, the giver had sketched an amusing scene of wolf pups playing. This man, whoever he was, got her. But the spark in her heart had dimmed. Rafe was still away, and perhaps he'd asked someone to leave it for her, but that didn't feel like his style, not at all.

Missing Rafe was almost painful, and it was such a strange feeling, that hunger for another. While she missed Sybi and Bree, that feeling was...different.

Today, she'd gone for a tidal pool swim with Tilde, Max, and several of their tablemates.

"Tilde," she said when the two of them sat alone atop a rock. "I need you to read something for me."

"Sure." Though her friend spoke to her, Tilde's eyes followed Max as his elegant strokes cut through the pool's waters. "What is it?"

"I'll have to show you."

Tilde's eyes shifted to her. "Why can't you tell me?"

"Um, it's about my sisters."

"Really? Do you know where they are? Have you found them? Are they here?"

Kit laughed at Tilde's flurry of questions. Proto Tilde, she was coming to realize. "Like I said, I'll have to show you." She paused, hesitant, but plunged on. "Um, what are your thoughts on Made Ones?"

Tilde's brow scrunched. "How do you mean?"

"I was brought here without my permission to become a brood-mare. Does that bother you?"

"It's not like that. We need you!"

"What if you were torn from Eleutia and brought to a strange place without your permission?"

"Well, when you put it that way... I've never really thought about it like that. I'd hate it, losing my connection with the Clan and our brother and sister wolves, with the land, with home."

"Exactly."

"Are you unhappy here?"

Was she? "No. In fact, I like Eleutia and the Wolves very much. But I wasn't given a choice."

Tilde hooked her arms around one knee. "Have you ever seen how sometimes chimney smoke can hover low, just above the rooftops? That's sort of what life here is like. We're a positive-thinking people, I believe."

"I'd agree."

"Yet like that smoke, death hovers just above us. Eleutians are dying and desperate, so desperate we don't think about the moral cost of bringing over Made Ones." She shrugged. "At least, most of us don't."

"Do you?"

Tilde's attention was snared by a woman swimming through the water toward Max. Her friend's eyes narrowed, then she dove off the rock into the pool.

She reached Max just as the brunette wrapped her arms around him. Tilde did a flip-turn, swam to the pool's edge, and stalked off.

Max disentangled himself from the brunette and watched Tilde until she disappeared. The way she'd moved, both purposeful and sensual, made Kit envy her friend's beautiful body. Then she remembered her new body was pretty fine, too.

Though Kit pursued Tilde, she failed to find her, and on the hike home she felt old. Maybe not in biological years, but in spirit.

The age change remained startling, her mind bouncing from her concept of middle-age to sudden youth and back again. The polarity would pounce when least expected. Earlier at the tidal pools, when Neff had flirted with her, she'd thought, *Why is this handsome young man making eyes at a middle-aged woman?* Then she'd remembered. Yet young or old, here or on Earth, she was Kit, and she'd contemplate "age" and its meanings on an infinite loop.

Contemplation fell by the wayside when she'd learned of tomorrow's Clan party. Her first. And she had no idea what to wear. No joy when she'd called Tilde, and she tried to find Meela, but she was out of luck there, too.

The party was to celebrate a Clanmate's advancement to Peacekeeper. She almost stayed in her suite. But that little beastie on her shoulder said she'd be an ass if she didn't attend.

When she stepped into The Hall wearing jeans and a floufy shirt, she searched for Rafe, Tilde, and Max. All three were MIA. Damn. Tilde's failure to show trumped her disappointment about Rafe. She hadn't seen Tilde since she'd left the pools, and all of Kit's phone calls had gone to voicemail. Tilde had gone to ground. Because of Max? Tomorrow she'd find her friend. Period. She could be a good hunter, too.

The few women present at the party wore either Empire-waist dresses or swirly skirts, with half the men wearing those long kilts she'd seen that first day with Rafe. When the men whirled in a dance, what did they wear beneath their kilts? *Shame on her*, but she'd look anyway.

If anyone cared about Kit's clothes, they didn't show it, and the Wolves welcomed her with enthusiasm.

Drinking, great music by a band using instruments both familiar and strange, and dancing between men and women, men and men, and women and women kept her busy. By the time The Clan began their pattern dances, her spirits were so high she gladly joined in. Her favorite pattern dance was a spiral that began loose and wound tighter and tighter, ending with the Wolves clustered together, raising their arms, and roaring "Huzzah!"

She danced every single dance, and the years fell away. No, more like the decades. Had Rafe been there, the evening would have been perfect.

When Eevon walked her home—which she found sweet—her preoccupation with Tilde consumed her. So she was unprepared when Eevon asked to kiss her.

"May I?" His deep gray eyes peered into hers with longing and...desperation?

"Um..."

He moved closer, a big man penning her in, making her claustrophobic. "Kit?"

"I guess." *Why had she said yes?*

He leaned in, tucked her hair behind her ear, his breath sweet with the scent of drass. "As you wish, Made One."

When his lips brushed hers, he kindled no desire. He deepened the kiss. Tongue was about to be involved. She pivoted away and pressed her palm to her door. "Thank you for walking me home, Eevon. Good night."

She didn't turn back to see his reaction.

CHAPTER NINE

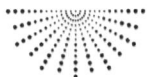

Tilde again proved elusive the following day. That evening, Kit sat in the library comparing Ulfr's stolen papers to the Eleutian alphabet she already knew.

"Hey."

"Tilde!" Kit rose. "Are you okay? I've been worried and trying to reach you for days."

Her eyes widened. "You have?" She pulled out her phone and flipped it open. "Oops. Sorry. I forgot to charge it and then I got so busy I didn't look at it and...I'm fine."

"You, Max, the pools?"

"It was nothing."

It hadn't looked like nothing to Kit.

"Forget it," Tilde said.

"I'm only trying—"

"Please."

Kit smiled. "Of course." Waving Tilde over to the table, she opened the folder. "Read these for me?"

"Sure." Tilde lifted the top sheet, the one with Bree's name on it.

Please, please let it be something good. Something Kit could work with to find her sibs.

"Where did you get these?" Tilde said.

"Um, well…"

Tilde's face paled, and she pointed to the watermark— μ. "You do realize that's the Alchemics' mark."

"No. No, I hadn't."

"You got these from the Alpha."

She wasn't about to tattle on Meela. "I stole them."

Tilde's eyes widened, then she giggled hard enough for her red curls to shake.

"What?"

"Oh, Ulfr's going to be furious when he finds out."

"Then why are you laughing?"

"Because he has these fits of fury, and they're pretty scary. But they're funny, too." Her face froze. "Fates, never tell him I said that."

"I won't."

"Be right back." Tilde left the table and walked deeper into the stacks, returning with two iced drinks. She handed one to Kit.

"Thanks." The drink was light and minty. Delicious, but… "What I wouldn't give for a cup of coffee and a bar of chocolate."

"I know what chocolate is. It's is rare here in the north continent."

"Have you ever tried it?"

Tilde shook her head. "No, but I've always wished to go to the southern continent. It's quite different from here. So many species to study." Her eyes unfocused.

Kit was itching with impatience. "What do the *papers* say, Tilde?"

"Oh, right, the papers." She hunched over the table, peering closely at the document and running her finger just above the lines of text.

Holding her breath, Kit waited. And waited. "Tilde?"

Her friend jerked up, eyes wide, glasses askew.

Kit straightened Tilde's glasses. "The papers?"

"Yes, well." Her lips compressed. "It's in code."

"Can you break it?"

Tilde shook her head, sending her red curls flying. "Max maybe can."

Max. The best scenario would end with her having the translations. The worst? "Would he tell Rafe?"

"Absolutely."

No biggie. She would've told Rafe herself. "What about the Alpha?"

"Maybe."

Stickier. Was she up to facing the Alpha's fury? Kit sipped her drink. "I'll ask Max."

"Would you like me to?"

That would be great. Except. "It will make you complicit in my thievery."

"I know." A flush stole from Tilde's neck up to her cheeks. "I'd like to ask him."

She'd suspected Tilde was sweet on Max, and her friend's flush confirmed it. He'd better not break Tilde's heart. Kit put the precious paper with Bree's name back into the folder and slid it in front of Tilde. "Do it."

It was the oddest feeling, the waiting. For the papers' translation. For Rafe's return. For something else she couldn't define. Like she was about to soar. Or plummet. Kit wasn't sure which.

Most nights, she went to the library and read the children's books, making progress with the written language, though her efforts were snail paced. The dozen times she'd asked Tilde about the papers, she'd received the same answer: Max was working on them.

That morning was the final straw.

"Does he know how much it matters to me?" Kit sat quietly in her suite across from Tilde, binding her emotions into a tight, tiny ball.

"I made a point of it," Tilde said.

"The cypher is that complicated?"

"He says it's the most complex and frustrating one he's ever dealt with." Tilde poked her glasses up her nose. "I think he's loving it."

"The Alpha would know what the papers said, wouldn't he?" She'd go to Mr. Invisible Alpha and demand he tell her.

"That's the interesting part. Ulfr may *not* know. We don't know if the papers were stolen or not intended for translation. In truth, Max has concluded that's exactly it. That Ulfr knows they're important but has no idea what they contain."

"What if I asked the other Clans about my sisters?" Kit said. "Maybe they have them or have seen them."

"First, that's not done, except through diplomatic channels." She held up a hand. "I know what you're going to say, Kit—forget those channels. But again, and I agree with Max on this, no other Clan has seen them or knows, either. Or if they do, they're deliberately hiding them from the other Clans, which would be on order from the Alchemics."

Kit opened her mouth.

"I'm not done. Why would I say this? Because *all* the Clans on Eleutia know about you. Since we've heard nothing about your sisters, I suspect a Clan is deliberately hiding them. *That* would be on order from the Alchemics. Given you and your sisters fell together—even that's unusual, bringing more than a single Made One over—I suspect they made the same mistake with Breena and Sybelle. Think about it. Look at the Cats. Didn't you tell me they attacked you and Rafe on your way here?"

"Yes, they did."

"Once a Made One arrives, word travels. We have heard no word on either of them. Nothing."

What Tilde wasn't saying was that she believed them dead. "I see. What you say makes sense. Excuse me." She went into the bathroom, turned on the shower, stepped under the spray, and screamed.

Thursday night, or as Eleutians called it, *Thordi*, Tilde convinced Kit to go to a movie, which was why she was walking across the town green to meet up with her friend.

What were movies here like? She'd always been a huge fan, but if she went by WolfHome's TV programs—nature or battle films or stories where lots of women lusted after men—she'd be bored to tears.

That dearth of women permeated everything. Over the last two-hundred-plus years, the imbalance must have profoundly shaped all the Eleutian Clans. While the Made Ones helped, they were but a stopgap. Given the Alchemics technological advancements, they should have learned to shape genes to produce female children. Or create clones, for that matter. Or at the very least discovered *why* the female birthrate had plummeted. It smacked of manipulation. But if that were true, she failed to see the endgame, other than an entire species dying out.

No one knew. That the Alchemics could bring her across worlds, yet fail to find a solution for the gender disparity signaled Will Robinson warnings. Both Rafe and Max had talked about the Alchemics choke-hold on their society. The Alchemics didn't share their knowledge, and she'd been horrified to learn they conscripted children with a scientific bent from symbiont Clans.

It made her wonder if the Alchemics were manipulating the male-female ratio, too. But who would want to do that, engineer an entire race out of existence?

Up ahead, Tilde waved with her usual enthusiasm. Except the bubbly redhead wore a disgruntled look.

"What's wrong?" Kit said when she approached.

Tilde poked her glasses to the bridge of her nose. "Max has left to help Rafe. He was supposed to come tonight."

So, he'd had to pause his deciphering. Tilde might be invested in Kit's quest, but her unhappy look spoke to a deeper upset. "You care about Max. Is he—?"

"Courting me?" She shook her head. "No, the gifts left for me, no... He's not."

"But you wish he were."

Tilde dropped her eyes and nodded. "He's all about Inga, at least I think so, not that he stands a chance with her. She's set her sights higher." Tilde hooked her arm through Kit's. "C'mon, we don't want to be late."

After buying their tickets, Kit's mouth began to water for popcorn. Except there was none, just a stall with homemade muffins, warm troff, and some cold drinks. Horrified, she determined to introduce that delicacy to Eleutia. Popcorn and the movies were an essential combo.

Inside, the village movie theater reminded Kit of the old-fashioned kind back home, with plush velvet seats, gilding, and carvings that graced the walls and ceiling. Here, the carvings were of wolves in various positions, of male and female warriors in battle and of romantic poses, ones she'd never seen at any Earthly movie theater, including men with men and women with women.

The theater was beginning to fill up, and Tilde offered Kit the aisle seat. Once settled, Kit leaned close so she could whisper. "Is it common for men to pair up with men here and women with women?"

"You mean romantically, sexually?"

Kit nodded.

"Sure. Why not?"

Why not, indeed? She was glad Eleutian society wasn't as splintered about same-sex parings as existed on Earth. "I also see women warriors on the ceiling."

"Oh, that was long ago," Tilde said, frowning. "We're no longer allowed to fight. Or leave the domain without special permission. Or take on tasks that might threaten our wellbeing." She sighed.

"It sounds awfully restrictive," Kit said.

"Of course it is. Historically, we were the equals of men. But we women have become rare, and we're treated as such."

Halfway through the rather surreal film that was a combination of *The Shape of Water* and *War of the Worlds*, someone slipped into the seat behind her. Who joins a movie midway through?

During a loud battle scene, a pair of hands rested lightly on her shoulders, pricks telling her the hands were clawed. And way too close to her skin.

Inga. With those claw pricks, it had to be.

Her stalker's breath blew hot on her ear. Kit wanted to turn to see the woman's face, but resisted the urge. She wasn't up for having her flesh ripped.

"You will be mine," the male voice hissed into her ear. "Know this. You will be mine." Claws or no she whipped around only to see a dark figure loping up the aisle, laughing. She scrambled after him and ran. But he was yards ahead of her. He flung open the gilded doors and disappeared into the night.

She followed, catching glimpses of him beneath the spill of streetglows. He wore dark jeans and boots and a hoodie, though the hood wasn't raised. The man was fast, lean as a whip, with a long dark braid that flapped as he ran.

He flew around a bend, and she pumped her legs, and... Gone, the treed paths branching off every which way.

She braced hands on her knees, sucking in air. The area was deserted, and it took her a few seconds to get her bearings before she trotted back to the theater, for the first time aware of the sting across her shoulders.

Tilde stood in the lobby, eyes wide. "What happened?"

Kit told her, and her eyes widened further. "Gorm! You're bleeding!"

Her fingers felt for the warm stickiness of blood and she peeked beneath her shirt. Fortunately, the cuts weren't deep.

Tilde pushed aside Kit's shirt to see the marks. She paled.

"What?" Kit looked at her left shoulder. Five pinpricks oozed blood. Five.

She'd worn the wolf-clawed hand braces enough times to know that they had four claws, not five.

"What Clan has five claws, Tilde?"

Tilde's soft eyes hardened. "Cat."

. . .

Rafe had yet to return, producing in Kit an ache that refused to die. That morning, she'd learned the Alpha was back from his latest travels. Time to go hunting. Hard to do when Tilde clung to her like an octopus's sucker. Much as she cared for her friend, she'd begun feeling a little suffocated, so she was grateful when Tilde was called to a small town across WolfHome's valley to consult on a project.

Kit renewed her determination to meet the Alpha, to find out once and for all if he knew the meaning of the cyphered pages. How strange that he'd made a point of avoiding her. When Rafe returned, she'd ask if he knew why.

At mid-day, Eevon said he'd seen the Alpha heading toward the horse barns. She'd be late for Yuan's lesson, so be it. She made a beeline for the large circular buildings.

The jog was pleasant, the day crystalline, with fluffy white clouds drifting across the bright blue sky. The breeze fluttered her hair, smelling of the sea and its infinite possibilities, much like the hike to the top of Cadillac Mountain. That life-changing hike in Maine.

The nickers and whinnies of horses greeted her as she approached the main barn. Except for that one time with Inga, the barn always buzzed with stable boys performing chores, so she hadn't explored the "mystery" barn which she was sure housed the mistrals. Even if she failed to find the Alpha, today she'd find the mistrals.

She stepped into the cool space, her feet making shushing sounds on the packed earth, the smells of horse and hay delighting her. She hadn't ridden since that day with Rafe, not trusting herself to ride alone. At some point, she needed to overcome that hurdle. Much of the Wolves transportation was on horseback, and she didn't like being without a mode of transportation other than her two legs.

Greeting each of the six horses she cared for as she passed its stall, Kit scratched their heads and behind their ears, while her eyes searched for any sign of the Alpha. She encountered several grooms she'd met in the course of her work, most young men in their teens, but she didn't mention the object of her quest. No point in alerting the Alpha to her search.

Around one row, then the next, her steps taking her into several smaller buildings that held tack, more horses, and Arne's office.

Kit had purposefully left the mystery barn to last, hoping that's where she'd beard the elusive man. She strode through the breezeway and entered the smaller circular barn, which was empty of humans. No Alpha. Well, damn. She slapped a board. "Ow!"

Several horses nickered. She shook out her hand and took in the circular stable. Perhaps a dozen horses were stalled there, including a fiery stallion. The stalls were immense, each easily many feet larger than those in the main barn, with the stallion's stall set away from the others. Of the horses she could clearly see, they reminded her of Friesians, even more than those in the large barn. Heavier boned, with proud curved necks, shortish ears, and curly feathers on their hooves, just as Yuan had said. Unlike the black Friesians she was familiar with, their colors were striking—pure white and midnight black, silver gray and red chestnut, with contrasting manes and tails, which were also curly. There was no branching in this barn and the scents were slightly different, though if pressed to describe how, she couldn't.

The horses were alert and exceptionally attentive, their eyes following her as she progressed around the barn to pause at each stall. She petted them, talked to them, not that they answered back like Paulo. If only.

These couldn't be mistrals, they had no wings.

She was halfway around the circle, hoping to discover the Alpha in one of the stalls, when a shadow darkened the far entryway.

"Hello," came a small voice by the outer barn doors.

"Hi." Kit crossed the ring toward the little girl who wore jeans and a long-sleeved t-shirt with frills on the shoulders.

The girl skipped closer, with seemingly little fear given that Kit was a stranger. She was a beautiful child, with eyes a light golden brown and tawny hair to her waist tied back with a violet bow.

"Who are you?" the child asked.

"I'm Kit." She dropped to her haunches. "And who might you be?"

"Mimi." Big grin. "I love horses. But I especially love mistrals."

"But these aren't mistrals, they have no wings."

The child giggled. "Of course they do." Mimi's chin punched out. "You really don't know anything, do you? They're in their bodies, silly. They only come out when they fly."

"Oh." She had nothing else, her mind having gone blank.

"You're being funny about the wings, right?"

Kit made her smile a reassuring one, not that she was feeling it. Wings inside their bodies? "I really haven't ever seen one."

"Everyone's seen the mistrals fly. How come you haven't?"

"I'm not from around here. Not originally."

The child's eyes widened and her mouth formed an "O." Mimi took her hand and led Kit around the circle of mistrals, naming each one.

"This is Moonrise. She's not normal. That's what my mam says. She's weird and ugly and an anomie."

"An anomaly?" Kit said.

Mimi's eyes lit up. "Yes!"

Kit gasped when she peered into the stall. Staring back at her was a huge mistral with a silver curly coat, like a sheep's fleece, so different from the glossy coats of the others. Her mane and tail were black as night and poker straight, her nose pink with black freckles.

Moonrise's blue eyes glared at Kit. Anger swirled in their depths, as did arrogance and a defiance that said, *I'm even better than the others.*

What an intriguing creature. Kit unlatched the stall door.

"No!" Mimi said. "She'll bite you."

She'd been around bitey horses before, and she knew how to avoid those big, square teeth. Moonrise couldn't be worse than her nippy Ellipsis, who was her smartest, most talented horse. Most loving, too, once she accepted Kit. Gone now, all gone. She reached to pet Moonrise's fuzzy neck. The mistral swiveled her head around and chomped.

"Don't you dare!" Kit had been ready for it, moving her hand away in time. But she didn't back off.

Moonrise's nostrils flared, and she blew out a fierce breath, stomping hooves that looked like silver metal.

"I mean it," Kit told Moonrise, then tapped the mistral's nose twice. "I see you're different. So am I. Get over it, sweet girl."

Another fiery breath, another stomp of hooves—Kit making sure to keep eye contact with the imperious creature—then Moonrise snorted and settled. Kit's heart squeezed, and her eyes watered. This, *this* she knew. The hesitant acceptance. The possibility of friendship. The potential for love and devotion between creatures of two species. The mistral rested her muzzle on Kit's shoulder and wuffled a sigh, as if to say "achievement won." And started chewing on Kit's shirt.

Kit laughed and extracted her garment from Moonrise's teeth. "Mine, dear one. No chewing my stuff." She nuzzled her cheek against the mistral's, so the mare could get a good sniff of her. All wonderfully familiar, yet Moonrise was different. She sensed the creature's feelings, could almost taste her emotions.

She raised her arms to hug Moonrise's neck. The mistral's curls were soft, as if Kit nestled against an angora.

"Wow." Mimi peered over the stall door. "Da says she is a nasty one. She never lets anyone pet her except Rafe sometimes. She's his, but she's here for breeding."

Kit stood for a few more moments, soaking in Moonrise's scent and weaving her fingers through the mistral's fleece. She squeaked when Moonrise lipped her ear, tickling her.

"C'mere," Mimi said. "I want to show you more stuff."

She whispered in Moonrise's ear. "I will be back to visit. Promise." When she closed the stall door behind her, she glanced over her shoulder for a final look at the shaggy silver creature. Moonrise nodded. Perhaps she'd understood.

Since the wolves were sentient, maybe the mistrals were, too. She still couldn't picture wings emerging from that body.

Mimi took her hand again as they toured the ring.

"Does your da work here in the stables?" Kit asked.

More giggles. "No, silly, he's the Alpha."

Rafe's little sister? There must be at least twenty years between the two. "Do you know where your father is?"

She shook her head. "He might be in some meeting or other. He's always in a meeting or other." Mimi frowned, the light in her eyes dimming.

Kit squeezed her hand. "That must be hard for you. My dad was always busy, too, running the circus. Yours has an important job watching over all of his Clan, and I bet that makes you proud."

Mimi nodded but remained quiet as they continued their stroll.

"You're Rafe's sister, which I'm guessing is lots of fun."

"I am." Mimi's face lit up. "Rafee is the most fun brother ever."

"I don't doubt it for a minute."

"But he's away, and I miss him." She bounced on the balls of her feet. "He's promised next week, when I turn ten, he'll teach me to use the Claws. He'd better be back for my birthday."

"I'm sure he will be. He wouldn't miss a big day like that. So he's going to teach you the Claws, eh?" Hard to imagine beginning arms training so young.

"He taught me to ride, too," Mimi said. "But he won't let me ride Nightfall yet."

"Nightfall?"

"That's one of his mistrals." Her eyes got huge. "He's got three, more than anyone but my da."

"Perhaps Rafe will let you ride Nightfall when you're bigger."

"Maybe." She drew out the word. "But he's all worried I'll fly off and tumble down all the way to the earth and go splat. Isn't that dumb? I'm a *good* rider." The child's expressive hands went to work, making swooping motions. "They go this way and that, and if a rider isn't careful, they fall out of the sky and die. Then the mistral flies off if it's bonded, and it's never seen again. It's bad." Her head popped up, snagging Kit's eyes. "But I won't fall. I won't!"

Kit blew out a slow breath. "You'd best wait until Rafe gives you the go-ahead, don't you think?"

"I guess so. Another thing about Rafee." Mimi sounded like a 40-

year-old ticking off Rafe's various infractions. "He won't tell me anything about the new lady he's courting, which I think is mean."

Courting? Hope blossomed. Maybe Rafe *was* courting her. Oh, she liked that idea. Very much. Except she had to find Sybi and Bree. *Ack!*

Mimi pointed to the immense black stallion who stomped and snorted as they neared. His coat glistened, yet his mane, tail, and hoof feathers were curly. "This is Mistralys. He's the leader of the herd. He's Da's, and he's mean. Meaner than Moonrise." Her brows snapped together and she frowned. "Really mean."

The closer they got to Mistralys, the more noise he made kicking the stall door, his eyes rolling in fury that they'd dared invade his territory. And there, as if coalescing out of the ether, wings began to emerge from his body. Attached to his shoulders, they gleamed with feathers black as night, one overlapping the other. The mistral arched his neck and rose on his hind legs.

Oh, dear heavens. She had never, *ever* seen anything more magnificent.

"You're bad." Mimi shook her finger at the huge animal. "Put them away! Not in the barn!"

His neck snaked out, teeth bared, and Mimi danced backward.

A shattering pain in Kit's back took her to her knees, fire emanating from just beneath her right shoulder. Her left hand slapped onto the floor to stop her collapse, while her shoulder began to go numb.

CHAPTER TEN

W*hat...?* Her eyes lifted to Mimi's face, which had turned
chalk white.

"You're shot," Mimi said.

"Run," she hissed at the child. "Run fast away from here." Kit
shook her head, trying the clear her mind.

Mimi stared at Kit, lips wobbling, tears rimming her eyes. Kit
saw terror there, and anger, too. The fierce little thing was frozen.
"Mimi, goddamnit, run *now*!"

The child looked rooted to the stable floor. "You're bleeding."

Kit croaked out, "Go, Mimi!"

Mimi came alive and took off at an astounding speed.

Without Mimi around, Kit was an even easier target. She
suspected the shooter was waiting for Mimi's departure to finish her
off. She turned. The shooter stood at the opposite end of the ring in
shadow. Kit gave them the finger, even if the Wolves had no idea
what that meant.

The shadow took a step forward, though the darkness still hid
most of their body, as did the cloak and the hood, which concealed
the person's face. But there was enough light for Kit to make out the
longbow held in the archer's right hand.

Kit pressed against the stalls, trying to make herself a smaller target. She'd enter Mistralys' stall, but that would be suicide. All she could do was inch her way back to Moonrise's stall, where she'd be safe.

What was the shooter waiting for?

The numbness was seeping from her right side to her left, and still the archer hadn't raised the bow again. The shooter seemed as frozen as Kit was becoming. A breeze lifted the archer's cloak, and Kit glimpsed a pointed-toe pink boot.

She shut out thoughts of the archer, about whom she could do nothing, and inched toward Moonrise's stall. The neighs and nickers of the horses grew muffled, as if penetrating cotton. Kit's right leg had gone fully numb, but she might yet reach the stall and safety. It wasn't that far. Just a few feet away.

The archer took a step toward her. Kit still couldn't see the archer's face, but the sun glinted off a long knife held in their hand.

Moonrise would protect her. She crawled.

The archer stalked closer.

Ignore that wicked-looking knife. Just crawl.

Waves of pain slowed Kit, yet she finally made it to Moonrise's stall. The archer stood ten feet away. Why wait? Why not just kill her and have done with it?

Kit's hand crawled up the wood to open the stall door. Except she couldn't quite reach it from her position on all fours. She had to rise.

Dammit, try.

A shout, someone calling her name from far, far away.

Then a curse, followed by the swirl of a cloak.

She went to shout, "I'm here!" Only a croak came out.

Her knees failed, and she pitched forward onto the earthen floor, the world dimming to black.

Kit swam through sludgy, debris-filled water, aching for that first breath of air. A milk carton with Mimi's face bumped her nose. She pushed it away, along with a Pez dispenser and a paper container of popcorn. Her sisters' faces moved toward her, then receded, the thick oily water distorting their features. She kicked with her legs, pulled with her arms, and rose higher. An old-fashioned tube TV tumbled by, then a Red Sox bobblehead.

Nessie surged toward her, daring her to clamber on. She almost reached for her, but she couldn't bring herself to mount the horse who'd almost killed her.

She had to get away, couldn't breathe, must get out of the water. With one powerful scissor kick, her face broke the surface. She gasped a breath, and her eyes flew open.

She was on her belly surrounded by darkness. Where was she? Her hands patted the surface. She felt the softness of sheets beneath her, a pillow under her head. On a bed, but where was Charm's heavy weight pressing against her hip? Her hand searched for her pup who always slept with her.

Light leaked from the bedroom door, and she inhaled the soothing scent of lavender.

"Kit?"

A man's voice.

The snap of a match, the clink of glass against metal, the scent of bergamot.

"Kit, are you awake?"

That voice… She recognized the deep timbre. But who…?

She moved toward the voice, but pain radiated in waves from her right shoulder, down her back, and across her buttocks. When she stilled, it softened. Unpleasant, but bearable.

Light flared from an oil lamp. A large hand placed a lantern on her bedside table beside the carving of a wolf and a wilted bouquet of flowers. The man neared, and his scent twined with the bergamot, musky and pleasing, one that she knew, one that made her happy. She reached out a hand to pick up the little wolf. Someone had made it for her. A gift. A courting gift.

The dam of memory broke, thoughts cascading into her mind.

She'd been shot. "Who's there?"

The man sat in a chair by her bedside.

A smile blossomed on her face, though her lips cracked when she did so. "Rafe."

"How are you feeling?" he said.

"Alive."

In a calm, almost serene voice, he told her of Tilde's worry and Max's anger, and that the Alpha was livid. "Mimi told me what happened before she ran from the barn. Do you recall anything more?"

She described what she remembered, though much was fuzzy, but something was wrong, very wrong. His pose was relaxed, his eyes missing their usual fire. He looked tired, with fresh lines bracketing his mouth, but he'd been gone for days on a mission. He must be exhausted.

"I really need to sit up," she said.

Rafe rolled her to her back with a startling gentleness.

"Ready?"

He sounded detached. She had to be imagining that. Rafe was never detached. "Yes." She girded herself, and it was a good thing.

As he lifted her to a sitting position, pain sizzled up her back into her brain, making her lightheaded. He added two more pillows, and she was panting by the time he settled a light blanket atop her. She closed her eyes to collect herself.

Worth it.

When she lifted her lids, he again sat beside her bed holding a glass of something cloudy that smelled of honey and lemon.

"Drink this down. It'll help with the pain."

"Will it make me sleepy?" She eyed the glass with trepidation.

He nodded.

"Put it on the table, please. I feel like I've slept an eternity."

He set the glass down and resumed his relaxed pose.

Before she could ask a question, he reassured her she would heal and that the Peacekeepers were hunting the perpetrator, all in that calm, deep voice lacking emotion.

She searched for any signs of worry or concern for her—his lips thinning, his hands fisting, his eyes burning. Nothing. He was like the perfect host at a party, making chatter, but with his attention elsewhere.

Nor had he touched her. Well, he'd touched her to move her, much like a nurse would help a sick person adjust their position—helpful, but impartial. She hungered for his hand stroking her brow, his fingers sifting through her hair, his lips brushing hers. She longed for the tactile reassurance that he cared, yet his hands remained resting on his thighs.

All her imaginings about Rafe's feelings had been just that, imaginings.

But he'd embraced her, offered her warmth and comfort, supported and reassured her. That time she'd kissed him, and later when Eevon had interrupted, she'd swear she'd felt his burning desire, the same as hers, a desire that was more than chemistry, more than simple hunger. A longing for a true connection.

Rafe was one of those rare people who she'd known instantly—what would make him smile or frown, what troubled or pleased him. That mysterious tie that occurs in a moment, yet endures.

But now, when she thirsted for his touch, she only felt distance between them.

Reason said he cared. He'd been at her bedside when she'd awakened, hadn't he? But emotion said his being here was a shallow thing he'd do for any injured Clanmate.

She wanted quite desperately for him to care. "What's wrong, Rafe?"

"Pardon?"

"Is there anything wrong?"

The lamplight cast a shadow across his face. "Other than you taking an arrow? I'll go and send in the healers."

"Stay?"

He rose, paused on the balls of his feet, then snatched the carved Paulo off her bedside table and crushed it beneath his fist.

"No!"

His hand unfurled, the carving in pieces, broken beyond repair.

"Rafe, why?" She curled her fingers around his.

He scooped her up and buried his face in the crook of her neck, his body trembling.

"The healers said I wasn't to stress you, wasn't to upset you with my fury at what's been done to you. I was doing fine. But just now you looked so lost. So sad. I..."

"Oh, Rafe." Though her right shoulder throbbed, she raised her arm to smooth her hand across his back.

"I'm caught between fear and fury. I can't breathe. I can't think."

"Lay on the bed with me? Hold me?"

He set her back down, crawled onto the bed, and folded her into his arms. "Is this comfortable? Am I hurting you? I hurt you picking you up, didn't I?"

Roiling pain filled his voice, a storm breaking against the shore.

She pressed his hand to her cheek, and he shivered. "I'm all right. It will be all right."

"How much pain are you in?"

"I feel like I've been pummeled by Thor's hammer."

"I take it this Thor isn't a nice guy."

His voice sounded more normal, more Rafe-ish. Good. "No, he's a hero, but he's got a really big hammer."

Rafe chuckled.

"She tried, but she didn't kill me. I'll be fine." And Kit's attacker *had* been a woman. The way she'd moved, the pink boots. It wasn't a leap to suspect who'd shot her.

He brushed a curl from her cheek, his eyes soft.

"What happened after I passed out?"

"I was just back. We'd dismounted and were on our way to the barns to unsaddle the horses. I was about to go hunt you down." His jaw bunched. "If I'd been a few minutes later, you'd—"

"But you were on time. I survived."

He chuffed a breath. "Mimi came tearing toward us screaming, 'Kit's shot. She's shot.' We raced up the hill, all of us, Mimi clinging to my back like a monkey. The mistral barn was empty except for you with a farking arrow sticking out of your back."

His nostrils flared, and he went silent for long moments. Finally, he said, "I was sure you were dead. The arrow had pierced your heart."

"No, it didn't."

"I saw it. I still don't understand how you lived."

She pulled down her thin nightgown, exposing the unblemished spot above her heart.

"What are you doing?" he said.

"See? The arrow came nowhere near my heart. She missed."

He shook his head, his soft chuckle a beautiful thing to hear.

"What's so funny?" she said.

He pressed her palm to the right side of his chest. "Here. Here is where our Eleutian hearts beat."

It hurt to laugh, but she couldn't help it. Their hearts were on the opposite side of their bodies from Earthly ones, from hers. Poor killer didn't know where the human heart lay. "Apparently your scientists kept my body's innards where they'd been on Earth. Including my heart."

He cupped her face, leaned down, and kissed her.

This was what she wanted. The touch of his lips on hers, their pressure soft yet insistent. His insistence grew, as did her desire. He combed his hands through her hair, cradling the back of her head, bringing them even closer, his chest brushing breasts sensitive with desire.

A creak signaled the doors parting, but Rafe didn't stop, didn't even pause as he ate her up.

Someone cleared their throat.

Rafe took his time, ending his kiss with a final lick across her lips. He clasped her face, lips smiling, eyes warm.

When he stood, she sighed, feeling bereft.

He squeezed her hand, silently mouthing one word: *Later.*

Drunk on emotion, she nodded. Rafe had just kissed her senseless. He'd burned, the bulge in his jeans telling her exactly how he was feeling. But it had been more. An opening, a beginning, an adventure unfolding. If not for the intrusion…

Her eyes drifted to the tall man who stood glowering at the foot of the bed. A stranger, but she knew who he was.

"Don't you believe in knocking?" she said.

He stepped beside Rafe and peered down at her. "Alphas don't need to knock."

Her teeth snapped together.

Rafe pressed a finger and thumb to the bridge of his nose. "Da, really?"

Kit knew she should be respectful, but the man had been eluding her forever. Purposefully. She reached for the glass of painkiller Rafe had poured and raised it to her lips.

The Alpha stilled her hand.

Rafe slapped his father's hand away.

The Alpha growled.

Rafe growled back.

Command filled the dark look the Alpha shot Rafe, who continued to growl.

Bad form to smile, except they looked like two dogs posturing over a bone. She replaced the glass on the table. "Fine. Since you obviously don't want me to drink this, I'll wait. Rafe, help me sit up again."

Once that was accomplished, she stared at the two men who were a matched pair. The Alpha was older, true, a man nearing the end of his prime, and though his voice was lighter than Rafe's, they could be twins but for the wings of white brushing back from his long, unbound mane.

"Now isn't the time, Da." Rafe leaned toward his father, face taut. "Kit just regained consciousness."

"I have been priming you for years, boy. Years. And you blow my hard work out of the water by telling the Made One how she came here and what she is before I gave you permission."

Rafe shook his head. "Everyone knows what Kit is. How could we keep that a secret from her? The not knowing was stressful."

"So?" Through gritted teeth, he said, "The Alchemics forbid it."

"I got their permission."

Ulfr scoffed. "Not from one of the Eleven, you didn't. Consequently, they've made threats, which I've dealt with, no thanks to you."

"Fark them," Rafe said with hooded eyes and enough snark to make her cringe.

Oh, shit.

The Alpha's face reddened, and he gave Rafe teeth. "We used to fight tooth and claw for Alpha. I remember those days well. I won five challenges. *Five.* Wolves died. I survived. Now we vote, each Clan member having a say."

"I got honors in history, Da. What is your point?"

The Alpha frothed, while Rafe calmly let the man's fury break over him like waves crashing against the shore.

"Don't you see?" the Alpha continued. "The Alchemics can subvert the election. *Your* election. We all know they have spies in WolfHome."

"Spies which I have suggested we root out."

"We're playing the long game, as I've explained. If you keep sabotaging your candidacy, you will fail."

A vein throbbed at Rafe's temple. "I am who I am, Da."

The Alpha gave him teeth. "Intractable."

"Not true. I'm simply not the political animal you are." Rafe balanced on the balls of his feet. "I will become Alpha on my terms, or not at all."

Kit swallowed. Any minute fists would fly. "Could someone pour me a glass of water?"

Both men jerked, as if they'd forgotten her presence. Rafe poured and winked when he handed her the glass.

The Alpha deflated. "I know, son." He rested a hand on Rafe's shoulder. "And you will lose, which is why I've hung on so long."

"Old fool."

"Young reprobate."

They hugged, and when they broke apart, Rafe was grinning. "Have a little more faith in the Clan, Da. I'll win Alpha whether the Alchemics have taken a dislike to me or not. Plus, you've many more years left leading the Clan. Do not hasten your departure."

"I'd like to," his father said, gesturing to Kit. "Especially after playing hide-and-seek with this one all week while you've been checking out our sources."

"Sources?" she said. "What sources?"

"Later, Da." Rafe said.

"Now. I came to talk about your sisters," the Alpha said.

She sat up straighter, the pull at her back overridden by the enormity of what he implied. "My sisters. Alpha, what have you learned?"

"Call me Ulfr."

His eyes were dark and secretive. Could she trust him? "And...?"

"I've learned much," he said. "Including your wall-climbing to my office. Heard you met Percy and that you took the papers."

"What the fark, Kit?" Rafe said. "You climbed the outer wall. You could have fallen and died."

His face had gone white. She slid her hand into his and squeezed. "But I made it."

"*Shote*." He squeezed the bridge of his nose.

The Alpha's eyes pinned her. "But you couldn't read the papers, could you?"

She clamped her lips tight, but she wouldn't lower her eyes, though the Alpha's were burrowing into her soul.

"Stop, Da," Rafe said. "She might be Clan, but she won't drop her eyes, not for you, not for anyone."

The Alpha laughed. "Good. She's strong. She needs to be strong."

"Rafe?" she said.

His eyes met hers, and they held sorrow.

"It's my place to tell," Ulfr said. "As her Making should have been. Your sisters are dead."

"Da! Fark."

"Dead?" Her voice was a whisper, her throat tight. "You can't know that."

"I do." The Alpha pulled over a chair beside Rafe's, reversed it, then slung one leg across the seat as if he were mounting a horse. He rested his forearms on the chair back. His brown eyes—far darker than Rafe's—held no sorrow or pain, only determination. "Because while Radulfr gallivanted off to pursue those farking Cats, he took it upon himself to make a side trip I didn't sanction. He met with the Alchemics who brought you to Eleutia."

So that was the reason behind the Alpha's disappearing act. He was waiting for Rafe's return. To learn her sisters were dead. But they couldn't be. She would feel it, know it in her bones.

She shot Rafe a dark look. "You said nothing."

"You'd just woken. It wasn't the appropriate time."

"Tell me, Alpha."

"Watch your tone, woman," Ulfr said.

She gave him the finger.

His face scrunched in apparent confusion. Then he shook his head and continued. "The Alchemics told Radulfr that they brought across only one woman. You."

"But my sisters came, too. I watched them tumble into the abyss along with me." Kit hadn't screamed, nor had Bree, Sybi making up for it by howling like a banshee. She'd watched them whirl and twirl until she'd lost sight of them in the chasm's abyss. Though she'd awakened alone, she was sure since she had survived, they had, too.

"It's obvious you don't trust these Alchemics," she said. "Why should I believe them now?"

Rafe whooshed out a breath. "The male I spoke to, Gabin, could have deliberately misdirected me. But a former Falcon, an Apprentice Alchemic and a friend, corroborated what Gabin said. They're processing one other Made One, who's blonde. Didn't you tell me your sisters had black and brown hair?"

Sybi's was a soft brown, while Bree's… She'd said black because Bree had dyed it forever, and she'd forgotten. Bree's hair was redder than hers, almost strawberry. "Neither is blonde."

"It's possible they lied, but I can't see any point to it. I suspect your sisters are gone, Kit. I am sorry."

Pain ripped through her far worse than any physical injuries she'd sustained. But then her mind caught up with her emotions. She refused to believe it, at least not because those puppeteers of Eleutia said it was so. "Do you have any hard evidence?"

Rafe shook his head.

"What about the papers with Sybi and Bree's names on them?"

Ulfr snorted. "Perhaps they intended to bring them across along with you, and they failed." Ulfr stood and snapped her a bow. He left room with the parting words, "To my office, Radulfr. Now."

"Go," she said to Rafe, her voice a hoarse whisper.

"No."

She looked straight ahead, unable to turn to him. Whether they were alive, dead, or somewhere "other," she needed to weep for her beloved sisters. She couldn't cry in front of Rafe. He would want to take her tears, and those belonged to Sybi and Bree. "Go, please."

His voice was soft with worry. "I would not leave you now, Kitlyn."

"I'm not angry with you. Not angry with your father, but I need to be alone."

Perhaps it was the wobble in her voice or the stiffness of her face, but he bent, kissed the top of her head, and left, shutting the pocket doors quietly behind him.

Rafe strode to the Alpha's den, frustration beating about his head like crows' wings. That shattered look on Kit's face had nearly unmanned him. She was suffering and alone. Though it wasn't the Wolves way, he understood. *Fark*, he wished Kit had allowed him to comfort her. The need to care for her hammered him, especially after sharing that kiss. She'd tasted lovely, glorious, her enthusiasm sparking his soul with delight. It confirmed everything he'd learned and felt about Kit since she'd opened her eyes on Eleutia. She was for him, and he for her.

If she hadn't been injured. If Ulfr hadn't entered at just the wrong time. But time's twists could prove beneficial. His patience would win the day. Even with the loss of her kin, Kit would heal and thrive. They'd find their time, their place.

When they'd given him the coordinates to Alchemic City and allowed him to visit, the one Alchemic, Gabin, was lying at the very least about not bringing Kit's sisters to Eleutia. He could smell the lie before the man uttered it. The women might nonetheless be dead, given the evidence of their near-disastrous mistake with Kit and Calix's confirmation. He doubted Calix knew the total truth, yet he might know some part of it, some crumb that would ease Kit's aching heart. He'd left Alchemic City frustrated, unable to talk privately with Calix. The man had been bursting with some information, but to meet with his concealed operative was too risky. He'd send a message through their usual channels and wait until Calix replied.

More important than her sisters absence was who would dare to shoot Kit, a Made One. The Anti-Made Ones were an obvious choice. He scraped a hand across stubble grown too long since Kit's injury. Eevon had put forth the CastOuts as the perpetrators, which was irrational. Eevon blamed those poor souls for everything, and he wished his friend would get over that grudge. No, the Anti-Made Ones made sense, though that meant they'd escalated from protest to assault. His certainty that a few lived among the Wolves chilled him.

He reached his father's door. Right now, Ulfr wanted him for something he was sure would go against the grain. His father delighted in pushing him, testing him, expecting of him things which were anathema.

If Ulfr ever discovered Rafe's covert war against the Alchemics… He doubted that "discussion" would end well.

He squared his shoulders and breezed through the door of the den that had once been his home.

CHAPTER ELEVEN

K it pulled out one of the pillows and pressed it to her face. The tears burned her eyes, and she let them fall.

Sybi and Bree were *not* gone.

She was the eldest, had known them since the moment of their birth. They had played, fought, laughed, and loved each other infinitely. They had shared secrets and wondered at mysteries, and they'd wept together over everything from their mother's death to puppy videos. Her sisters were the only ones to ever see her cry.

The three of them were each so different. She was the most serious. Breena was a huge mischief maker, while Sybi worried about everything and everyone. Kit had once secretly sewn a heart on the arm of Sybi's jean jacket, and Syb had stomped her foot, demanding to know why Kit had done it. Bree had been the one to tell her. "Because you wear your heart on your sleeve, Sis."

Prankster Breena drove Sybi and Kit up the wall. Kit hated those awful tricks. Well, maybe she didn't, but she'd never tell her sister that. Now she wondered who would put a fake lizard in her bed or plastic wrap on her toilet seat? Sybi and Bree had laughed their heads off at both, and eventually, so had she.

Gone.

She had hoped, *believed*, that they'd been given a second chance at life, too.

Why was *she* special? Why should she survive and not them? It should have been them. She was flawed inside, the accident breaking her into a thousand twisted pieces.

Kit vowed to track down those scientists and to find out why her, why only her?

After she was spent, she fell into a troubled sleep filled with nightmares of Breena and Sybelle riding around and around the circus ring...

Someone lifted her, pain jarring her awake. Her eyes flew open. Rafe was stretched out beside her on the bed, an arm around her shoulders.

Kit stiffened.

"You are not alone, Kit," he said.

The tears burned. This was new, this welling up all the time. Lucky stars, they would *not* fall. "Stop. Go."

"I can't leave you like this, Kit. I can't."

Her heart splintered, but her voice was rock steady. She needed him to understand. "My sisters are gone forever, and I am a stranger in a strange land. With no past, no profession, no family. My friends are few. I'm a 58-year-old woman in a 28-year-old body that feels strange, like it doesn't belong to me and someone's going to take it back. Like I'm hallucinating. Nothing is familiar. Nothing is right. My biggest connection? I've managed to piss off someone so much they want to kill me. And my beloved sisters are gone. I had such hope." A bitter laugh burst from her lips. "Please, go. I'll be okay. My pity party will end. I'm not the falling apart kind."

"No, you're not," Rafe said. "But I won't leave you alone, either. Sleep, Kit. You've been injured, both physically and in your heart. I know this feeling, how much it hurts. I will be here when you awaken."

His force of will was like a towering wave, yet he was warm and comforting. Weary, she rested her cheek on his chest, the thrum of his heart making her lids heavy. He stroked her hair.

In her mind, she held out her hands to Sybi and Bree, and they joined together and formed their circle. Once connected, nothing could touch them. Nothing.

Calix dug his nails into his palm, hard enough so his face retained its mask of disinterest. He could not believe what he'd just heard Gabin spout to that toady, Effexx.

Gabin had *orchestrated* a Made One be shot by the Anti-Made Ones' faction. Yet another damnable experiment. *Un-farking-believable.* Though Gabin belonged to the Cabinet of Eleven, Calix bet Gabin had done this particular "test" behind Fukkes and the other nine members' backs. He'd almost queried Gabin as to which Made One, but that would be so out of character for an Apprentice as to be suspect.

What if the Made One had been killed? Gabin seemed unconcerned about that "minor" possibility. Thankfully, she lived, and Calix wished Gabin had named the Anti, so he could pass the information onto Rafe.

Perhaps if he...

"What are you doing, boy, hovering around? Have you no work to accomplish?"

Calix blinked, rounding his eyes. "Me, sir? I... yes, I do, of course. I've been pondering my latest cytosine DNA comparisons and lost in thought."

Gabin's hand wave was dismissive. "Then get back to it."

"Immediately." Calix bowed, but he didn't miss the narrowing of Gabin's eyes. He escaped down the corridor.

For a few days he'd have to be a model Alchemic so as not to draw unwanted eyes in his direction. He'd have to wait days, perhaps longer, before informing Rafe.

Kit awakened cocooned in Rafe's arms, cozy and warm and cared for. She yawned. Better. She felt better. Those dreams she'd had of her sisters gave her hope. Maybe it was self-delusional, but she refused to believe what those Alchemics had told Rafe, not without proof or talking to them herself.

Rafe was awake, and the pulse of his heart thrummed beneath her cheek. She pushed to a sitting position, and he stared at her with intensity. Those sleepy eyes and that tousled hair said he'd dozed, too. She nuzzled the crook of his shoulder. Lucky stars, she loved that he was here and holding her. "You're a kind man, Rafe."

He barked a laugh and tightened his arms around her. "Seems I have much work to do if you think all I'm feeling is kindness."

And how was she supposed to interpret *that*? She was definitely *not* a ball to be tossed between paternalistic men. "The guy in the movie theater sounded the same way. Do all men on Eleutia—"

"I've been meaning to talk to you about that." He sat up, too, nostrils flaring, then his face went blank, those dead eyes of the killer she'd seen when he'd fought the Viking staring back at her. *Oh, dear.*

"Tilde and I think it was a Cat," she said.

"So I heard. He could have ripped your throat out."

"Why would he want to do that?"

He chuffed a breath. "Oh, I don't know. Maybe because someone just shot you with an arrow."

"That was a stealth attack. This was different. I'd swear he was playing some game, like tag."

"I suspect you're right. What did he look like?"

"I never saw his face, even when I chased after him."

In a growly whisper, he said, "You *chased* him. I hadn't heard *that*." With exaggerated care, he placed her back on the bed and stalked out the door. "I'll be back later."

She rubbed her arms. *Oops.*

Rafe didn't return that day, nor the following one.

Yes, she'd chased her movie-theater stalker, and maybe her reaction had been knee-jerk, but he wouldn't have harmed her, either. If he'd wanted to, he could have done so in the theater. She hated games, at least that kind. She almost phoned Rafe but decided the wisest course was to let him cool off. Still, she was antsy stuck in bed all day. That was until a whirlwind blew into her bedroom.

"I heard about your sisters." Tilde stood for a moment, her eyes welling up. "I'm sorry, Kit. I would have liked to meet them. Oh, maybe I shouldn't have said that."

Kit smiled. "You would have liked them. You *will* like them, because I'm not convinced they're dead."

Tilde sniffled, her eyes gleaming with pity. "You should be wearing your sling."

"I forgot." Tilde might think she was delusional. Everyone might. Tough. She reached beside the bed for the stupid sling.

"Here." Tilde leaned over her and fixed it around Kit's neck and shoulder.

"When can I get out of this suite, Tilde?"

She shrugged. "Talk to Kicks. Sorry."

Her friend stayed for about an hour, chatting about this and that, then whirlwinded out with a smile and the words, "Back later!"

Tilde was such a good soul. She blew out a breath. What she'd said to Rafe earlier... She regretted her "nothing was right" here comment. There were good things on Eleutia, too, Tilde being one. Rafe, Max, Yuan, even Paulo. Her tablemates, too—they'd welcomed her. Whether they saw her as a babymaker or not, they'd shown her warmth and caring.

What to do about Rafe?

He'd been furious. At her? At the guy at the movies? Both?

But Rafe had also implied deeper feelings. Hadn't he?

On Earth, where she'd been in her 50s and dying, she certainly hadn't been in the dating game. It was like she was 14 years old again and trying to figure out boys and girls.

Where had he gone? He could be tracking down that Cat or hunting the archer. According to Tilde, the pack's forensic people were examining the arrow, had photographed her wound, and the Wolfe Peacemakers were searching for the shooter.

She was restless, but each time she moved, her wound pulled. Lucky stars, she wanted out of this bed. *Now.* She pushed to her feet, waited until the wobbles ended, and staggered to the bathroom. Time for a shower.

Kit was seldom left on her own, which was driving her crazy. Sybi and Bree understood her need for alone time. The Wolf Clansmen most definitely did not. They were only trying to help, but *damn.* Hordes of people popped in at random times. Though she became ambulatory pretty quickly, meals were still brought to her suite by a *very* chatty young Wolf. Outside her door, Paulo and his wolves had stationed themselves twenty-four/seven. They, thankfully, remained silent.

The following day, the healers allowed Kit to leave her rooms. She wasn't stupid, so she remained within the Clan environs, and she suspected she was safer than Fort Knox's gold bullion. If she and Tilde went to another movie, she'd bet half the Clan would join them, not to mention Paulo and his buddies.

The courting resumed. For the next three days, she was gifted more flowers—roses, sort of. With petals of green, their purple stems and square-shaped leaves surreal, yet when she put her nose to them, their scent was the same. They were bound with a red bow.

Since the courting had been winnowed down to Mr. Red, whose gifts were those that touched her heart the most, she couldn't figure out why the elusive "he" didn't approach her. Kit suspected Rafe was Mr. Red. But she didn't *know*, and it was driving her batty.

The following day she received a crystal jar of honey, with a note that said "Bee my honey." She grinned.

Yet Rafe had done a vanishing act since he'd stormed from her room. She missed him. Was he missing her?

That evening, Rafe reappeared at dinner and sat beside Kit as if he hadn't played the Invisible Man for days. Confounding Wolf. He chatted with her and Max but didn't speak to Tilde, she guessed because he was still ticked about the movie thing. Tilde didn't seem to care one bit.

Midway through the meal, a crash of plates, and two Clan members began to fight, using teeth, knives, and anything they could get their hands on. Blood began to flow.

Rafe and Eevon leapt to their feet and quickly broke up the fight, with Eevon escorting the perpetrators from The Hall, while Rafe resumed his seat cool and calm as could be.

"That was handled efficiently," Kit said. "Looks like you might have a black eye."

"Part of the territory as a Peacekeeper," Rafe said.

"Like police or soldiers?"

"Both. We keep the peace and we fight the wars. Eevon and I are on duty. Too much testosterone, a result of our male-female imbalance, and not enough sense. Rage is easily come by. Fights are expected, and we keep a lid on them."

So many repercussions from the disparity between men and women. "Finding the cause of the imbalance might be the key."

"I agree. We'll find it."

"Soon, I hope."

Rafe's smile was one of irony. "Yes. Or we'll die out like James Dinkmore said."

"Who?"

"A hundred-plus years ago, Dinkmore wrote *Source of the Species*. 'Survival of the fittest,' and all that."

"Whoa. On Earth, Charles Darwin wrote a book called *Origin of the Species*. Maybe a hundred-and-fifty years ago. He said the same thing. It's uncanny."

"I'm not surprised. We are parallel, after all."

"But so different in many ways."

"That, too."

After dinner, Rafe walked her to her suite. "Want to come in?" she said. "I have a treat."

There was that grin. "You?"

Kit's fingers itched to touch him. "Coffee."

"And that's…?"

She pressed her palm to the door, unlocking it, and tossed Rafe a come-hither look. At least, she *hoped* that's what it was, being woefully out of practice. "You'll see."

Much to her joy, Tilde had researched coffee, scored some beans, and had them ground for her. Kit put water on to boil, portioned out the grounds into the paper towel she'd cut into a filter, and set the filter atop the rounded glass carafe Tilde had found.

Rafe watched her with a single-minded focus. "You're making this…coffee?"

"You'll see." She soon set two steaming mugs on the sofa table. "Here you go."

Rafe reached for one and inhaled. "Ah, bunno, by the smell of it."

She retrieved the milk and honey. "I prefer mine with these. Bunno?"

After he swirled in some milk and honey, his eyes twinkled over his mug when he sipped. "Delicious! In my travels down south, it was all those barbarian Tiger Clansmen drank."

"It's ubiquitous on Earth. Let me get some cookies to go with it."

His hand reached for hers, and a shiver rippled through her.

"No need," he said. "I've got a surprise, too."

He looked like a mischievous little boy as he withdrew something from his shirt pocket and laid the oblong package on the table. "Go on. Open it."

She bit her lower lip as she carefully untied the string, then unwrapped the tan paper and lifted the lid. Large, dark squares sat inside. Her mouth watered. "Chocolate?"

His grin was infectious. "For you. Tilde couldn't find any, but I managed. Try it."

She separated a square and bit down. Chocolate melted across her tongue. Bliss. "I've officially ascended to the lucky stars."

"It tastes like yours?"

"Yes. Oh, how I've missed chocolate. Thank you!"

"I'm sorry about the carving I crushed. I'll get you another."

"No, it's okay. You were...upset. I understand. Do you know who made it?"

He shrugged. "I'll investigate."

Another bite. She paused, savoring the flavor. Then took another sip of coffee. "Heaven."

"What else?" he said. "What other food do you miss most?"

She grinned. "Popcorn, which I'm going to remedy."

He shook his head, smiling. "You realize I have no idea what that is."

"Yeah, I sorta do."

His smile died, and he leaned forward, expression intense. "I'd like to know all your likes and dislikes, the things you miss from Earth, the things you think about."

"Rafe, what I said the other day... I didn't mean to sound ungrateful or unkind. Eleutians have been lovely to me, excepting the arrow in my back."

He didn't smile at her joke. "I'd like to know all of you, Kit."

She bit her lip. "I miss my sisters. You know how I feel about them. My critters, so much. My friends... I'd distanced myself from them. I was expecting to die"

"I'm glad you didn't." His eyes grew distant, and she wondered if he was thinking of family or friends he'd lost. "But you miss something more." He moved to sit beside her, wrapping an arm around her. "I sense a loneliness inside you."

His shirt was soft beneath her cheek, his muscled shoulder firm. A comfort. "Not more, but different. I have no backstory with anyone here."

"Backstory?"

"If I refer to things or events of my Earth world, no one gets it. Shared connections and experiences, you know?"

He stroked her hair. "I never thought of it that way. It's such a casual thing that we have with others."

"I'd never thought of it before, either. If I said how much I loved *Lord of the Rings*, you'd look at me with a blank stare. If I referred to President Obama's election, you'd say, 'Who?' You might even say

'What's a president?' Those tiny shared moments are so woven into the cloth of our lives, especially when two people shared the same experience, like gone to the same party or worked at the same office. I have shared little with anyone here. No one knows my backstory. And I've found that hard. It makes me feel as if I never existed before I arrived on Eleutia. That the rich, full life I led never happened."

He clasped Kit tight and kissed her forehead. "I understand, and I'm sorry."

"Me, too, but the only person who can wrestle this particular demon is me."

"Not true." He threw the words out like a gauntlet. "First, you'll weave new stories, new fibers that will connect you here until they're rich with memory and promise. Also, you can tell me tales of your world. Tilde and Max would be eager listeners, too. It won't be the same, but it could help you bear the loneliness. I can record them, have them transcribed. We'll have a book of Kit and her history to share with others of the Clan. If you'd like."

She slid her arms around him and paused, breathing in the goodness of him, the gifts he gave her. "Rafe, that's lovely. The other day... I was a mess. It wasn't true, not all of it. There's much I like about your world. Its natural beauty. Your Clan's relationship with the wolves. The way you care for the land. You."

His eyes sparked with heat. "I like you, too." His mouth closed on hers, and she exploded with desire as he explored, delved inside, then nipped her lips.

She wanted more. Much more. To touch him everywhere. To feel his skin beneath her palms. To undo his braid and card her fingers through his hair.

He kissed her cheeks, her eyelids, returning to her mouth like a man starved.

When they came up for air, he straightened, his eyes hot, the bulge beneath his pants evidence of his desire.

She wished he hadn't stopped.

"I look forward to your stories," he said.

She chuckled. "I hope they don't bore you to pieces. I did not live an epic life."

He nuzzled her neck and whispered, "You're a Made One. Carefully chosen. Even better, you're Kit. You won't bore me."

"You never know."

"I know. So begin."

She ran a hand down his cheek, her heart full. The temptation to tell him about her accident rode her hard. Instead she began the story of the circus horse who ate her straw hat while she was wearing it.

Kit was still cloud-floating a day later. Tilde had come back to her suite after mid-day for a taste of the precious chocolate. As Tilde took her first bite, something rustled outside her door. She lunged for it, hoping to catch her admirer in the act. Please let it be Rafe.

She thought it was, hoped it was. But she had no proof it was.

A single turquoise box, maybe five by five, sat before her door wrapped in a silky red ribbon.

Paulo, lying to the left of the door, gave her the side eye.

"Who was it?"

The coywolf remained silent, as she knew he would. Clan tradition forbade telling the court-ee who the court-or was. Unfortunately, Paulo had gotten that memo.

"Thanks," she said, grumbling. "Not." She gave the coywolf a scratch behind the ears, then walked back inside to show Tilde.

Her friend's bouncing excitement knocked her glasses askew. "What is it?"

"I'll look in a minute."

"Hurry up!" Tilde waved her hands.

Kit slumped into the chair and placed the box on the table. "I just don't get it."

"Get what?" Tilde's eyes remained glued to the box.

"I had three suitors. Now, there's one, Mr. Red. He's left me many marvelous gifts, and yet I have no clue who he is. How am I supposed to figure this out?"

Tilde tipped her head much as Paulo had done. "That's definitely odd. He should've left hints by now. Maybe your responses haven't convinced him of your interest."

Whoa. "My responses?"

Tilde's eyes widened. "You *have* been responding, right?"

"Why did I not know about this?"

A flush raced across her friend's cheeks. "Um, we discussed it. Didn't we?"

"Not a word."

Tilde bit her lip, then straightened her glasses. "I, um, maybe I forgot to—"

"Forgot?" Kit hadn't meant to sound so sharp, but Tilde had squeezed her eyes tight. "Tilde, please explain."

Her friend rested her chin in her hands. "Because it's not allowed, you *must* not ask someone if they're courting you. Instead, when the person being courted decides they're interested in a particular someone courting them, they leave them a note or gift outside the door as a response. The note or gift could be funny or sweet or mysterious. That signals your interest, and the clues start coming."

"I'm confused. If there were several gifts left, how would they know which gift I was responding to?"

"You tie the same color ribbon the giver has used around your note or gift. See? It's easy."

Kit groaned. "Easy? Sure, if I'd known about it. All this time I should've been leaving notes or gifts. I had no idea."

"Oops," Tilde said.

"Oops?" If it was Rafe, he must think she was playing some stupid game by not responding.

But what if it wasn't Rafe?

She picked up the turquoise box and tugged. The red ribbon fell to the floor, and she opened the lid and pushed aside the silver tissue. "Oh."

Her heart seized as she lifted out the carving. A silver horse, its coat carved with curled swirls, and with a black mane and tail. She rested the carving in the palm of her hand. It was perfection, right down to the freckled pink blush on the horse's nose and the straight black feathers above her hooves. Moonrise.

Tilde's eyes were big as saucers. "Wow."

After Tilde left, Kit fetched paper and pen, then sat for long minutes, finally writing something funny, except it sounded flat when she read it back. Then she went for mysterious, except everyone in the Clan seemed to know her business. How mysterious could a girl be in that situation?

Finally, she simply wrote: *I'm interested. Please tell me who you are.*

Boring, but she couldn't think of anything else. She started to fold the note when her hands froze. *Yes.*

She folded the paper into a Cootie Catcher, making sure the reverse, unwritten side was what showed, then she drew smiley faces and question marks and the words "tell me" on the catcher's sides. Finally, she used the same red ribbon he'd used to loosely tie it to the Catcher.

True, it might be a little childish, but it was not boring. She placed it outside her door near a snoring Paulo. When she looked up, Max was racing up the hall. He took her hand and tugged.

"Come on! The Cats are coming."

Inside the great hall, the frenzy of activity hit her like an anvil. Shouts of orders, growls and anger, and tables scraping, while Clansmen rearranged the dining tables into a huge circle with empty space in the center. Mid-day was approaching, but instead of the usual buffet setup, a bunch of musicians stood in its place, tuning their instruments and adding to the cacophony. Though not identical, the instruments were similar to an Earthen violin, several drums, symbols, and...was that a bagpipe? The Wolf pressed his lips to the mouthpiece and, oh, it sure was. Garlands were being hung, tapers lit, and tablecloths spread. And she'd swear she saw black-garbed Peacekeepers stowing weapons around the hall. Several wolves appeared, Paulo at their head, their necks circled by collars studded with gems.

"Did you say the Cats, Max?"

He blew out a breath. "Yes. A celebration, mainly to point out our magnificence."

"Why are they coming?"

"Hard to say.

She chuffed. "Max."

"They're coming for you."

CHAPTER TWELVE

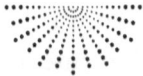

K it sat between Tilde and Max, Rafe and his father seated at the head table two tables beyond. Threaded through the Wolf diners, some three dozen Cat Clan members talked, laughed, and engaged with their Wolf counterparts without a sign of hostility. As with the Wolves, most of the Cats were men, with only three females in evidence, two seated among the general diners, while a striking female Cat, along with an analogous male, sat at the head table. Both had sharp, handsome features reminiscent of Latino and American Indian, with skin a warm latte. Siblings by the look of them. The male was Rafe's height, but leaner, while the woman beside him was nearly as tall and slim as a willow. His long jet hair flowed down his back, and while hers did the same, it was pure white.

She'd expected tension. Instead everyone acted as if the Cats hadn't slaughtered the Wolves' sheep or been harrying them for weeks. She assumed they practiced guest rights, like on Earth of old.

The meal was lavish, servers presenting bountiful dish after dish, finishing off with flaming towers of dessert that seemed to be a signal. The crowd quieted.

Drums sounded—*boom, boom, boom*. Around the tables, black-clad Peacekeepers rose, Rafe and Eevon included.

The drums beat a slow, heavy tattoo as the men flowed onto the empty floor encircled by the diners. And flow they did, in an almost choreographed glide.

Once at the center of the circle, they formed a line. The drums ceased, the men bowed, and with a blast of sound, they began to dance. She'd never seen anything like it, but it recalled a Scottish reel combined with a Cossack dance she'd watched on T.V. with her grandfather. Memories of the time she's spent with her mother's father hit her, a sweet spike to the heart.

The dancers whirled and twirled in perfect unison, their rhythmic feet pounding the floor as the hall rippled with sound. The Timberwolves appeared, threading through the dancers. The beat sped up. Men broke the line to jump and spin in exquisite acrobatic feats. Certain flips and leaps she knew, some she had performed, while others were strange, and her mind deconstructed the movements so she could replicate them.

The men stopped. The line reformed. The peal of a bagpipe. Rafe stepped from the group bearing two swords that he placed on the ground, crosswise. He raised his arms and began to dance around the swords faster and faster, until he was a near blur of speed and grace, his feet never touching the swords, his long, unbound hair flying. She sipped her wine, her throat dust dry, utterly entranced by his beauty.

He performed the Highland sword dance, but this version included jumps and squats, too.

The music abruptly halted. Rafe stood holding the two swords, grinning, looking right at her. He bowed and blew her a kiss.

The kiss might be Rafe yanking the Cats' chain, but it still sent a thrill through her. Hard to be blasé with her pulse racing.

Seated beside Ulfr, the male Cat grew red in the face, his jaw working.

Oh, Rafe, you devil.

Rafe stepped back into the line of Peacekeepers while others performed solo dances, the Highland Fling and more Cossack acrobatics, as the crowd clapped and stomped in time to the music.

When the music segued into thumps of a drum, the Peacekeepers linked their arms across shoulders and performed in unison, with individuals leaving the line to execute some acrobatic leap or twirl, all as if they were improvising. Her training told her it was anything but. Kit's heart beat faster and faster as if she were one of the dancers, too.

She wanted to be out there, wanted to see if this new body of hers could perform those jumps and kicks and whirls.

Boom.

The music silenced, the dancers stomped three times, the hall stomping with them, then they froze into a long line, arms at their sides. They bowed to thunderous applause.

When the hall finally quieted, she expected Ulfr to rise and give a speech. Instead, a violin trilled to whistles and shouts of "Yes!"

She recognized the notes, the beginnings of a waltz, as diners rose and made their way to the dance floor. Rafe moved toward her with sinuous grace, a wolf stalking its prey. And she was trapped. She couldn't. Couldn't.

Her body failing, her bad leg collapsing, her mind flashing to that awful day.

"May I?"

The voice was sinuous and low, with a faint accent unlike the Wolves. It cut through her PTSD, and she found a man standing before wearing black leathers with graceful silver tooling that curled up from his breast up and over his shoulders.

"Not today, old friend," Rafe said, his posture relaxed. "She is mine."

The Cat's green eyes heated. "Is it not for the Made One to choose, *old friend?*"

Oh, great. "Thank you, gentlemen, but I'll pass on this dance."

The Cat scowled.

Rafe took her hand and kissed it.

Yup, the man was upping the ante. Priming the Cat Alpha like a pump.

"I'm afraid, Kit," Rafe said, "that only you can open the dancing."

Beyond Rafe, every eye in the hall was turned to her. She smiled. "But I don't know the dance, Rafe."

"It's simple," he said, his voice low and sensuous.

She almost shook herself like a dog. This wasn't about her, but rather the obvious rivalry between the two men.

The smirk on the Cat Alpha's lips was at odds with the fury in his eyes. "Am I, Gato, not the honored guest who should open the dance?"

Kit rose, legs wobbly. She wanted so badly to dance with Rafe. And yet she was afraid. Thankfully, the men were too wrapped up in themselves to notice.

"You are our honored guest, Alpha." Deep in Rafe's sleepy eyes lay a deadly threat. "But only Wolves can open the dance."

"The Made One is not a Wolf," Gato said.

A thump against her thigh. Paulo.

"Ah." Rafe grinned. "But you see, she is."

Paulo yipped.

"What have you done?" the Alpha spat.

Rafe's face grew serious. "The same thing you would have were she found by the Cats."

The two men stared at one another for long moments, almost as if they were having a silent conversation, one they'd had many times.

The Cat's eyes fell first and landed on her. He snapped a bow, took her hand, and kissed her palm, his lips lingering, his eyes demanding. "We will dance next, Made One."

Not if she could help it.

Rafe held out his hand.

She uncurled her fist, hoping hers wouldn't shake.

Once Rafe clasped her hand in his larger one, he said, "Your hand is cold."

Her whole body felt cold. She smiled. "The dancing will warm me up."

Rafe led her to the center of the dance floor, the musicians struck up a waltz, and off they went. Though she wanted to ask a thousand questions, Kit kept her silence. In part because the strange waltz included unfamiliar stomps and kick, but mostly because he was wearing that appealing half smile that sent her senses into overdrive.

One of his hands clasped her with a firm confidence, while the other steered her with assurance through the steps. His warmth washed over her, his musky scent making her dizzy with desire. When the dance ended, the room whirled momentarily.

The Wolf Alpha stood. "We must depart. Enjoy the dancing. Remember, you have training tomorrow."

Laughter and shouts of "Huzzah!" shook the hall, while Rafe guided her, not to her table, but through the dining hall to enter a much smaller room off the main hall. Inside, the male and female Cats from the head table, along with three other Cats, stood on one side of the room, while Ulfr, Max, and several Wolves stood on the other.

"Please be seated." Ulfr gestured to a small circular table set with drinks and data pads. Once seated, she found herself between Rafe and the Alpha.

"What's going on, Rafe?" she said.

"Wait."

Conversation careened around the table, the tension ratcheting up to nuclear levels, yet no one mentioned the Cats' attack on their way to WolfHome or the raid on the Wolves' sheep. This had to be some orchestrated palaver under their peace accords due to the Cats disapproval of her being with the Wolves.

Rafe kept frowning and sliding her glances, the Alpha ignored her, while the lead Cat blatantly cast heated glances her way. Once the after-dinner wine had been served, the Cat Alpha clinked a glass.

Kit raised hers, expecting a toast.

The Cat Alpha stood, his eyes fixed on Kit. "As many of you know, I am Náshdóítsoh, Alpha of the Cat Clan. Call me Gato, Made One." He grinned, giving her a nod, then turned his attention to Ulfr and Rafe. "Release her to us, and we will offer your Clan a

169

fine and fair trade of goods and a continuance of our peaceful coexistence."

Dammit, she was not a piece of goods to be bartered. Her eyes snapped to Rafe. His warrior face was back, eyes dead, face blank.

She leaned close. "I'm not a *thing*, Rafe."

"They're assholes," he said, loud enough for the entire room to hear.

Ulfr shot Rafe an angry glance and rose, his bearing calm and measured. "The Made One was found by the Wolf Clan, as you know. Thus, I am afraid we must decline."

"She is a beauty," the Cat male said. "Unfair to keep her all to yourselves. She would be a fine breeder."

Like an electric current, fury rushed through her veins seeking an outlet. With effort, she wrenched it under control.

Rafe sipped his wine, his pose relaxed. "You underestimate the Made One. She is far more than a breeder. In any case, you will never get your hands on her."

The female Cat ignored Rafe, nodding to Ulfr. "Be that as it may, I see your point, Wolf Alpha, though I don't agree with it. We plan to initiate The Challenge for those who wish to claim her."

"A familiar ploy, Dona Arina," Rafe said. "One you've used to your advantage in the past. She belongs with the Wolves."

The Cat Alpha smiled. "Only if you can keep her."

Rafe winked.

Arina snorted, while two spots of color dotted Gato's cheeks. He rose, followed by the other Cats. "I believe it's time for us to take our leave, sadly without Ma'am Kitlyn." The Cat Alpha and Arina nodded to Ulfr, then walked toward the exit, followed by their Clanmates. At the door, Gato turned. "As you know, this isn't over. We will have our due. Farewell, lovely Kitlyn. Until we meet again."

Once the Cats were out of earshot, Rafe turned to Kit. "We would never release you to the Cats."

Was she a "thing," to be kept or bargained away? Talking around her, not one of them had asked about her choice, her needs, or her desires. She might not know Eleutia well or understand its conventions, but...

Kit's temper spiked. She was done. With fierce care, she placed her napkin down and stood. "Though none of you seem interested, I merit a say in my own destiny. Excuse me."

She strode from the room, willing herself not to run. Once outdoors, she sucked down a lungful of fresh air.

Clouds hid the moon, and the night was thick with the promise of rain. A pressure on her thigh told her that Paulo had followed her, and she ran a hand across his rich fur.

As she climbed the rise to the horse barns, its fecund, familiar scents dampened her raging emotions. She was tired of being tossed around on some tsunami of others' wants and needs.

Nature might have made Kit a pleaser, but this reconstituted "her" was finding nooks and crannies that she hadn't plumbed in her Earthly life.

She wanted things, too. Needed them. Things that didn't seem to be on anyone else's agenda. A place. A purpose, along with finding her sisters, that quest like a bee buzzing endlessly inside her head.

Were they here? Were they alive? Were they safe?

She gulped the clear air, stopping those burning tears of anger and frustration from falling.

Rafe. He pulled her in another direction, one of shelter and caring and love.

Kit longed to touch him, taste him. To learn him and all his secrets. To feel his heavy weight atop her when they made love. A consuming desire she fought, yet longed for.

She felt entombed by wants and needs she had no way of fulfilling.

Paulo kept pace with her as she raced through the large barn, across the courtyard, and into the mistral barn. Her eyes sought Moonrise, but when she neared her stall, it sat empty. Her heart deflated. She had promised to visit the mistral and wondered where she was, concerned that something had happened to her.

"She's safe."

She whirled. Rafe stood before her, hands on hips, face rigid with tension. "I moved her last night to the private barn behind my home."

Words about that stupid scene with the Cats threatened to spill out. She clamped her jaws. He'd been nothing but caring since he'd pulled her from the ice.

Yet she was still furious.

His eyes narrowed, as if he were gauging her mood. He stepped forward into her personal space.

She took a step back. "Not now, Rafe."

"Why not?"

Boom. "I'm not a thing to be bartered away. Or kept close because I was a found prize, like in some treasure hunt. A possession. An object. A piece of baggage."

"You're none of those." His fists clenched. "And you know I don't feel that way."

He was too close, too large, too compelling. She wouldn't let his siren song of kindness leech away her fury. She gave Rafe her back and walked toward the exit, Paulo hugging her side.

"Would you like to see her?" came that husky, spellbinding voice.

She stopped and wheeled to face him. "A bribe? One that will get me to do your bidding without word or protest?"

"No, simply a question." Rafe approached slowly, his expression wary as if expecting her to explode. "Nor do I want you acting like some puppet, Kit."

Too much. It was all too much. She inhaled deeply, intending to rail at him, to make him *see*. Except his scent of leather, pine, and musk washed over her, and she clasped his face with her hands and kissed him.

His arms banded her waist, and he snugged her to him, tight, answering her passion, tongues dueling, her body turning liquid in his embrace.

Not what she'd intended.

Oh, but it felt so fine. Perfect.

No. No. No.

She thrust herself away, both of them gasping, and searched for stable footing on the deck of her storm-tossed emotions.

"Yes," she said. "I'd very much like to see her."

Were his lips twitching? He found her funny, did he? But behind that spark of laughter, she glimpsed a quieter joy.

Rafe took her hand, and she let him.

Tanned, scarred, roughly calloused—well-used hands that spoke of a hard active life. Those hands tingled her senses, an electric rush she disguised by walking briskly. Unable to look at the face that gave her a thrill and scrambled her brains, Kit instead fantasized herself atop Moonrise as they flew across the skies.

They walked across the thick grass damp with the surrounding mist, down the hill and across the town green that held The Hall, its lights glittering a welcome in the darkness. Rafe led her up a path she hadn't seen before. More like a goat track, it zig-zagged until it poured them out onto a small rise above The Keep.

Silence accompanied them, yet conversations went on in her head about where they were going, what they would see... and *him*. They halted at a small, round house with an amber light in one window. "Home."

A smooth flagstone path led to the front door, and flowerbeds encircled what she could see of the house. Three tall cypress stood guard on the lawn's left side and in its center a huge weeping birch's limbs cascaded toward the ground, its white bark and black markings silvery in the moonlight.

The front window light beckoned, and Kit tried to imagine what his home looked like inside. Was it simple or ornate? Had he used dark wood or light? Was it one large room, or were there several? He led her around back, up a gently sloping hill toward a tall oval building with yet another conical roof.

Once through the human-sized door beside the larger barn sliders, the horsey smells drained away much of her anger.

Rafe swooshed his palm across a wall panel. A mellow string of lights traveled around the oval to illuminate the barn's glowing oaken beams, brass fittings, and six immense stalls. She spotted Moonrise three stalls in.

"Those two, Baloo and Barron." Rafe pointed to a smallish black and a large gray in the first stall. "They're horses. No knobs behind their ears, though those are sometimes hidden beneath a mistral's mane. The other three are my mistrals."

She greeted the horses first, crooning and petting, and when she neared Moonrise's stall, the silver mistral nickered a hello. The stall across the ring from Moonrise's held a liver chestnut at least nineteen hands with a curly mane the silver of Moonrise's coat. It perked its ears and nickered.

"Hello, boy," Rafe said.

Just beyond the chestnut's stall, an immense golden mistral echoed the greetings.

Rafe laughed. "You, too, old fella."

Tack hung in a corner of the barn, with saddles a combination of English and Western sitting on saddle trees. A few of them had large vertical projections in front and back, similar to a Western saddle's pommel, though taller by a good eight inches.

But Kit's eyes were drawn back to the silver mistral, who tossed her head and pranced.

Rafe chuckled. "Go visit."

She hurried down the aisle to greet the mare, who poked her head out of the half-open stall door. Willing to suffer the inevitable ache in her shoulder, Kit stood on tiptoe and wrapped her arms around Moonrise's curly coated neck, breathing in her rich, earthy scent.

The mistral felt like home, just as Rafe did.

Oh, no way. Her pragmatism had seemingly fled with her old flesh.

Moonrise chuffed a warm breath across her back as if to say, "Good."

Again and again, she ran her hand over the mistral's fuzzy coat, while wondering if it could be knit. The wool would be as soft as cashmere. "Hello, girl. Sorry it's been so long since my last visit."

Rafe opened the chestnut's stall door and began brushing the mistral's already gleaming coat. He was giving Kit time, as he knew how to do so well. He might pressure her on some things, but he also sensed when she needed space.

The curry comb sounds stopped, and Rafe lifted the chestnut's leg and began clearing debris from his hoof with a pick much like an Earthly one.

He set down the first hoof and went onto the next. "Feeling any better, Kit?"

"Yes."

"Good. Want to talk?"

She smiled inside. He was treating her like he would a skittish foal. "Do you have another pick?"

"A minute." In the tack area, he found what he was looking for, walked over, and handed her a pick.

Rafe's fingers whispered across hers, and Kit's mouth dried, then he reentered the chestnut's stall and lifted another hoof to clean.

Time slid by with Moonrise snuffling and lipping her shoulder, while she cleaned her hooves, the motion tugging her back, not to Maine, but to the circus, where she'd cared for her act's horses. All had passed on except for Ellipsis, but she'd taken them with her after the accident forced her to leave the circus, even Nessie who'd... She took a deep breath.

She braced herself, unable to halt the steamroller speeding toward her.

The cheering begins when Kit's name is announced. She's a headliner, after all. She's grinning as Pi, Nessie, and Ellipsis follow her into the ring. She signals the trio to trot, then canter around. She runs beside them and vaults onto Nessie's back, Ellipsis and Pi moving up to parallel each side. Applause. The rhythm is perfect. The four of them are one. She does the Flag, the Mill, the Scissors, then stands. Applause. Ellipsis moves closer, and she waits until the perfect moment when both horses are in sync, balances on her left leg and stretches her right onto Ellipsis back. They thunder around the ring to wild applause. She leaps off, signals the trio to halt, and all four of them bow in concert. Her loves are always in concert with her.

When they're standing again, she gestures Nessie to move up, while Ellipsis and Pi back away. She begins to shake. Why is she shaking?

She vaults onto Nessie's back, slips her feet into the stirrups, and...

"Kit! Kit!" Rafe was squeezing her shoulders, but she wasn't reacting. *Shote.* She was somewhere else, arms limp at her sides, eyes wide with fear, but sightless.

"No, no, no," she whispered.

"Kit, beauty, wake up." He folded his arms around her, her back to his chest, and she slumped against him, eyes closed, whimpering, and shivering as if it were ten degrees outside.

"What is it?" He began to rock her, crooning low in his throat as he would to a wolf pup. "Beauty, please, how can I help?"

Kit's hands climb up to wrap around his forearms. "Oh. Is that you, Reggie?"

Who was Reggie? "You're on Eleutia, Kit. In the stable. With me, Rafe. You're safe."

She breathed a long, tired sigh. "Yes. Yes, I am."

They stood like that for long minutes, just breathing, him holding her as tight as he could until her trembling ceased and her muscles relaxed.

He didn't know how to help her, though he was desperate to do so.

"I was back in the circus, my final performance."

He held his breath, lest he break the spell.

She rested her cheek on his bicep. "I did what's called voltige, vaulting and tricks on horseback. My grandfather was a Cossack, and he taught me their tricks, too."

As much as he wanted to hear, what he didn't want was Kit to suffer another flashback. "You don't have to explain."

"Don't worry. I won't. Not now. I was top-billed in the circus."

She told him about the circus, and though they had none on

Eleutia, her act sounded much like the games they held at WolfHome.

"That last day, I'd mounted Nessie. I did a few tricks, the ones I did every day of the week, then…"

Her voice trailed off. Moonrise was nuzzling her, and Kit had begun absently stroking the mistral's forehead. He was pleased the two had bonded. He wondered if she knew how special that was. The fractious mare had finally found a partner she'd accept.

His wish to take Kit's pain was a foolish one. But he could support her, help draw her poisonous torment out. "Please, continue."

"Yes, I should, shouldn't I?" she said in a sing-song voice. "We were cantering around the ring. With my left stirrup around my ankle and my right foot in the stirrup, I hung from Nessie and opened my body wide, my hand trailing just above the ground. Very dramatic, but easy. I'd done the trick hundreds of times. That day…that day, I overbalanced regaining my seat and flew over Nessie's opposite side, except my left ankle was still caught in the stirrup."

She paused, as if catching her breath before the pain hit.

Farking Fates. He pictured his beautiful Kit being dragged around that arena, his horror making him almost wish he'd never begun his campaign against the Alchemics. He was *glad* they'd Made her. To live her life enfeebled, without her grace and athleticism, was anathema to him. On Eleutia, she'd been given a second chance. Thank the Fates.

But she hadn't been given a choice, which was wrong, which was one of the reasons he fought those imperious monsters.

"I went round and round," she continued. "The pain of my leg breaking, my arm, too, my head slamming over and over…" In a small voice, she said, "That's all I remember."

"Dear Fates, Kit. But you survived."

"Barely. Nessie must have been terrified. It took forever for them to stop her, or so I was told. I broke twenty-six bones, was in a coma for weeks, then physical therapy for a year. My body was crippled."

Her laugh was high pitched. "So was my mind. My career, my life over."

"Easy, beauty. You didn't stay with the circus?"

"I tried. I *wanted* to. They were my family. But I couldn't handle the pity and sorrow. The man I'd been dating looked at me with horror. My best friend still loved me, but every time she saw me she'd start to cry.

"I had flashbacks, negative thoughts and feelings, even after I left. I startled easily, too. Sometimes I couldn't sleep or concentrate. But it got better. Over the years, with therapy, though I never rode a horse again, not on Earth. Riding Blackie the other day, that was the first time."

"A brave move, Kitlyn."

"Brave? No. I have to get on with my life, don't I?"

He squeezed her tighter, resting his chin atop her head. "Yes, you do."

"It's happened here, too, the flashbacks, the fear. You see, it's all an illusion, this Made One appearing whole. I'm nothing special."

He turned her so she faced him. "You are *everything* special. You rode Blackie as if you were born in the saddle. You've confronted things here that have broken others. Don't make less of who you've become. When I first saw you, I knew your spirit would be as beautiful as your face. You amaze me."

For one moment, his heart soared. Kit looked at him as if he hung the stars. But then she turned back to Moonrise and bent to lift another hoof for the pick.

CHAPTER THIRTEEN

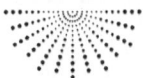

Kit brushed Moonrise's mane until it gleamed, then moved on to her tail. Rafe was now currying the giant golden mistral, so she walked to the sink at the end of the barn and washed up, then hung over the half-opened stall door watching him work on the golden mistral, an epic creature.

Rafe left the stall door open when he went to the tack area, and the golden stallion walked out. Kit peered up, way up. He was the largest horse—mistral—she'd ever seen. Bigger than Moonrise, who was a solid nineteen hands, he had to be at least twenty-one hands tall, his conformation exceptional. He was perfectly balanced, his structure and bone well aligned, his muscles evenly distributed. He awed her.

Yet for all his huge size and fierce golden eyes, the only word that came to mind was "enchanting."

His coat shimmered with iridescence, his hooves were crystal, his mane sparking with every color of the rainbow. A transcendent creature.

Though he towered over her, she and the golden were almost nose to nose before he halted, dipped his head, and rubbed it against her chest. She stumbled backward, laughing. He blew on her, and she'd swear he was laughing, too. He knew his worth. His scent was much like Moonrise's but thicker, deeper.

"He's the founder of my stock," Rafe said from down the aisle. "A rare golden mistral."

Kit petted him with reverence, and the mistral had to lower his head again for her to scratch him behind his ears."How did you get him?"

Rafe strode down the aisle, grinning. "Lucky break."

"I suspect more like a wise choice."

"Perhaps. We have trading days, when breeders will bring a mistral foal to trade or sell. He was born black, a common mistral color. Underweight. Small." He barked a laugh. "Of the Wolves, my father naturally has first dibs. He passed, expecting me to pass, too. Even a small mistral costs a fortune. Daybreak was a bargain, but that's not why I bought him. My Da winced when I bid on him."

"You didn't bid because he was cheaper, did you?"

He chuckled. "No. That perfect conformation was a plus, but I saw something in those eyes, as if he were telling me he would be exceptional, even if others couldn't see it. And when his coat began to change…" He laughed again, his eyes softening as he scratched the knobs behind the huge golden's ears. "Da's fury at being bested was a beautiful thing to see. Daybreak is Moonrise and Nightfall's sire."

"What a coup," she said.

His phone buzzed, and he murmured a curse when he looked at the screen.

"Problems?" she said.

He shook his head and smiled. "No."

Daybreak nudged her to keep scratching. "Sorry, boy." Her hand roved over the scars that crisscrossed the golden's neck and upper chest, reminiscent of the scars she'd seen on Rafe that first day in the doctor's office. Her finger trailed across one. The cut must've been deep and mean, and she couldn't imagine who would hurt this shining creature.

Years earlier, when she'd been giving riding lessons, she learned her local competitor beat his horses. Once she verified the truth for herself, she cut her prices so low, struggling as she did so, but she put him out of business and bought his string of horses at auction. Going all out against him had been worth it. She knew he'd start over, another place, another time, and again beat horses or dogs or some other unfortunate creature. But she'd saved those five horses and had never regretted it. "Why is Daybreak scarred this way?"

"He was my battle horse when we fought the dakos."

The image of Rafe flying atop Daybreak in battle seared her. "Dakos?"

"They're vicious creatures. They seldom fly our skies anymore. The mistrals defeated them, but not without cost."

"Your battle horse."

"Yes." He waved a hand at the stallion who nodded and returned to his stall.

Daybreak's scars looked old. "When did this take place?"

He scratched his chin. "About forty years ago. Mistrals live long lives."

Forty years ago. Rafe was in his early thirties. "How old are you?"

"Seventy-two years."

Her hand gripped the stall door. The Clan members she'd met. Tilde. Max. The Alpha. "How old is your father?"

His chagrinned smile made his eyes dance. "Now that's a good question. He lies about it. I think he's about two-hundred-and-seventy. But only a few oldsters know the truth, and on pain of death they're not telling."

"Oldsters?"

"Those over three-fifty."

"Tilde?"

"My age."

"Max?"

"Around the same."

"Seventy-two?" Her voice came out a squeak.

"Does that bother you?" he asked.

It rearranged everything she knew about the Eleutians. Perhaps not. Maybe they calculated the days and years differently. No, the days were the same, twenty-four hours. "How many days are in your year?"

"Give or take, 365."

"Humans live much shorter lives than Eleutians. Since we're parallel, I don't understand why. It's shocking to me."

"Perhaps it's the way we evolved, going back to James Dinkmore and his *Source of the Species*."

"Could be, though I wonder if your wolves, your symbionts, play a part."

He raised his shoulders as if to say, *Who knows?*

The upside smacked her, and she grinned. "You're seventy-two? That means you're older than I am."

His smile was slow and warm. "I guess it does."

Yet her joy dimmed. "I need to know about the Cats, Rafe."

"Go on to the living room," Rafe said, after they'd removed their boots in his mudroom. "I'll bring us something to drink."

Rafe's home was the first she'd entered, though she'd visited Tilde's and Max's suites in The Keep. So much could be learned from someone's nest—the stories of their lives and tales told. What they read and the art they liked. Their favorite colors and shapes. What held deep meaning for them. She wanted to learn these things about Rafe.

A spectacular bronze mistral—wings revealed but furled—dominated the living room, with the conical ceiling soaring above multi-windowed cream walls hung with landscape paintings, swords, and masks. Atop an overflowing bookcase sat a battered, Roman-style helmet complete with cheek plates and horsehair crest. She'd love to try it on but didn't dare.

The burbling of a water feature drew her to the opposite corner. A cascade of river rock larger than those in her friends' rooms, with the water flowing down to a basin carved with symbols and glyphs. The mantle atop it held a small altar with a stone, an empty bowl, a blue cloth swatch, and a pulsing crystal. Yuan had told her the altars honored The Fates, representing Sky, Earth, Air, Water, and a fifth element, Sorcere. The cluster of photos beside the stone were irresistible. Kit lifted a frame holding a smiling blonde woman who hugged a boy with his arms stretched to the sky. Standing beside them, Rafe beamed at the woman, his eyes soft. She'd seen that look on his face, and it melted her.

No, not Rafe, but Ulfr, with the child Rafe and his mother. By all accounts, theirs had been a happy family. Lifetimes ago, when her parents had been alive, their family had been close, wild and turbulent and fun.

Where was Rafe's mother now? He seldom mentioned her.

Kit set the down photo, lured by the sculpture of Daybreak, the artist's strokes reminiscent of the carved mistral she'd been given. A gorgeous piece. A deep, soothing comfort settled into her bones. His cottage was an intimate one, well used and well loved, like her first home. The one-story she'd later built was more house than home, each object placed for ease of movement.

A cocktail of disgust and shame took her to the sofa, where she pressed her hands between her knees. Being on Eleutia showed her how she'd squandered her life on Earth, wasting it on anger and bitterness. She had been self-focused, but certainly not self-aware.

Once, she'd grabbed life by the throat and *lived*. She wanted to be that woman again, wanted it desperately.

"Are you good?" Rafe strode into the living room carrying two bottles and a pair of rounded steins with handles, a platter of cheese, what looked like dates, and some crackers.

"I am." She smiled. "Your home is lovely."

"Thank you. It suits me." He set their drinks on the table and slipped into the chair across from her.

"Daybreak's sculpture is incredible." She gestured toward the bronze. "Whose work is it?"

He poured them each a frothing glass of blue liquid, eyes laughing. "Mine. I call it my ego piece."

Oh, that smile. Had he carved the tiny mistral for her, too?

"Growing up," he continued, "every Clansman learns an art.

Some take to it, others discard their art as adults, and an exceptional few can create art with their minds."

"Wow. With their *minds*?"

He nodded. "A very few. I'm not one of them."

She surveyed the room and raised her glass. "To home and hearth."

"To home and hearth."

When she sipped, the effervescence tickled her nose, and the sharp, dark taste held hints of honey and clover. "Delicious."

"Fafner Ale. We make it here at WolfHome. Lots of brewery competitions on Eleutia."

"Lots of competitions, period."

He grinned. "To impress you, I'll win against all comers. Then you'll do anything and everything I desire."

"Of course I will," she deadpanned. If he only knew how much she'd welcome his desires.

His rich laugh flip-flopped her insides, a warmth remembered from long, long ago. But Arthur's warmth had begun to smother. This feeling, it was sharper, more piquant. Different. Because Rafe was different. He was more than she'd ever imagined. Her mouth dried, and she took another sip. "So why did the Cats storm in thinking they could simply appropriate me?"

He finished his drink and poured another. "The Cats will never have you, so it's pretty immaterial."

It *was* material. To her. "Rafe."

"It will upset you."

Thinking of all that had happened, a laugh bubbled out. "I'll handle it. You're being overprotective, like you are with all your women. Did Ulfr order you not to tell me?"

Drink in hand, he walked to the altar and fingered the stone sitting atop it. "No, he did not."

"Please."

He tossed the stone back onto the altar, where it bounced off and flew to the ground. He caught it before it hit. "Fark." He laid the stone down with care.

"Come." She patted the sofa. "Sit. Tell me."

Crossing his arms, he paced. "The Cat Clan is perhaps the strongest Clan on Eleutia. When a Made One is brought over from another world, the Cats sponsor a competition called The Challenge. The winner receives the Made One as his prize."

She *was* upset. "His *prize?*"

He waved a hand. "Don't go crazy on me, Kitlyn. The Alchemics, not the Clans, created The Challenge along with their first Made One."

"The Clans could have refused!"

"And risk the Alchemics' ire? But in truth, history tells us the Clans were thrilled with the hope Made Ones offered."

More and more she saw this world as being controlled by dictators posing as benefactors.

"Whether through skill, guile, or outright cheating, the Cats frequently win. Thus, their Clan has grown in strength and number. It's simple really. More births, more Clan members, more strength. A cycle that's been repeated many times."

"So, the Cats almost always win."

"In recent memory, often, though other Clans have won The Challenge."

As if she would stand for being a prize in a contest. "Yuan said the Wolf Clan won a Made One."

"We did." He leaned back in his chair. "My mam was a Made One, won by Ulfr. She passed away many years ago."

His face didn't give away the sorrow she glimpsed in his eyes.

The mother he obviously loved was dead, and he was... "You're half Earthling."

He froze, a smile twitching his lips. "I guess... I am. I never thought of it that way."

"Mimi...?"

"Mimi's mother is of the Clan."

From the way he said "Mimi's mother," she suspected he wasn't a fan. "You don't like her."

"Heard that, did you?" He chuffed. "I need to learn circumspection. She flaunts her superiority of having a girl child, yet she resents my mam, whom Ulfr loved very much. The same can't be said for Mimi's mother. Somehow my sister remains untainted by that woman's sense of entitlement."

"Mimi's lovable. Funny and bright. Quick witted, too."

"That she is." He nodded, staring into his glass as if it held the secrets of the world.

"The contest?"

"Basic. Elemental. We battle until the last man standing receives his prize."

"Not exactly a chess match," she said, unable to keep the bite from her words.

"Chess?" Rafe asked.

"An Earthly war game of intellect and strategy, one that uses carved pieces on a board."

"You'll have to show me."

"Aye, aye, Commander." She should just reach over, frame his face with her hands, and kiss him. "I will, though I'm not awfully good at it. To say the least, I'm underwhelmed that the guy with the biggest muscles wins me."

"The Alchemics sent *me*, a Wolf, to find you. No one else has any claim on you."

"Ah, I see. I'm a possession. Finders keepers, and all that?"

"No! You're free to leave at any time, though I'd try to convince you otherwise. But you're a precious treasure."

"My ovaries, you mean."

Laughter burst from his lips.

She bottled her own urge to laugh with him. "Why you—"

"Apologies! No, not simply your ovaries, Kit. But you have to admit the image was funny."

She crossed her arms.

"Look, you're a member of Clan Wolf." He held up his hands. "Making you Clan wasn't a trick or a way to secure you. If I'm honest, I simply reacted, and I don't usually do that. You were willing or the magics wouldn't have worked."

Those "magics" sure sounded interesting. "The Cats don't see me as belonging to you."

He thunked his stein on the table. "We will not release you to them. We'd go to war and farking fight to our last man."

"You're serious."

"I am."

The thought horrified her. A war over *her*? One person? Idiotic.

The Wolf Clan was vicious and strong. The Cats sounded stronger. She could picture hundreds, maybe thousands, wounded and dying.

She was no Helen of Troy, and look how that conflict had ended, nor was she anyone's pawn. Not going to happen. That veered into *I'd rather die* territory. "If your scientists could create me—something far beyond Earth's capabilities—why can't they figure out what's causing the decline?"

"We've asked the farking Alchemics that question many times and always get the same answer. 'We are working on it.'"

Kit scowled. "A good way to put someone off, if you ask me."

"No argument here."

She wondered why the Clans didn't rebel. Deep waters she currently wouldn't swim. "If you were a tree, what would you be?"

"What?"

The startled look on his face was almost comical. "Nothing. Just a silly question to learn more about you."

"I'd rather hear more about your Earthly life and *you*. I wish I'd seen you perform."

So did she. "My parents owned the circus. They were aerialists, and Bree became one, too. She was incredible. Sybi has a heart as big as the world. She's amazing with growing things and numbers, so she was our bookkeeper. Marie, our youngest sister, died when she was ten."

"I'm sorry."

"Thank you. It was long, long ago."

"I want more."

She wanted more, too, to know him, to make love with him, to be with him. But what if he wasn't the one courting her? What if she'd misread the gifts? "My favorite foods are lobster and chocolate. I don't like green peppers."

"Why not?"

"I don't know!" She laughed. "You're being ridiculous."

"You're the one who asked about the tree!" He sat beside her, wrapped his arms around her, and pulled her close.

Her back was to his chest, and Kit melted into him. He held her in such a peaceful way, resting his chin atop her head.

"Moonrise is yours, you know," he said.

"I can't accept such a gift, Rafe."

"She's not *my* gift. You're the only one she's ever accepted. That mare is an impossible creature, contrary at the best of times, yet an element within your spirit resonates with her. Mistrals are like that. Some wolves, too. Mistralys adopted my father in the same way. No, she's yours, whether you accept her gift or not."

"Put that way, I'd be honored." A huge gift of trust and a responsibility, too, one she'd gladly take on. "Words are inadequate, but thank you."

"Her first foal is yours, also."

"But you bred her."

"Tradition. The next foal she gets will be mine."

"Oh, Rafe, I'm... I don't know what to say."

He chuckled. "Many an Eleutian has been stymied when the mistral they own chooses another. Whereas Moonrise's choice brings me joy."

Words failed her, then his breath brushed her neck, and he dropped kisses there, light, airy ones that made her shiver. She relaxed further, the back of her head resting beneath his chin.

"I got your message," he said in that husky-low voice of his.

Message? She couldn't think with him touching her like that. She tried to turn in his arms, but he held her firm.

"Did I read it right?" he said.

Read it right? *Oh!* "The Cootie Catcher. Childish, but different, Unexpected, I figured."

"Hmmm?" He kissed the spot just below her ear.

Her body ached in all the right places. "Yes. You read it right."

"Dance with me?"

She grinned, though he couldn't see it. "Didn't we already do that once?"

"Teasing me, Ma'am Kitlyn?"

"Perhaps."

"I can barely breathe with wanting you."

Lucky stars, to hear him say those words. "Me, too."

He turned her, his lips crashing down hard and hungry on hers. Her arms twined around his neck, and she pressed tight against him. Still kissing her, he lifted her and walked, opened a door, and laid her on a large bed.

"Just let me look for a minute." He stepped back, eyes near glowing, and he ate her up. "My beauty. My Kitlyn."

Heat blossomed everywhere, though a different kind warmed her belly and lower. She held out her arms. "You're too far away."

Then he was on her, covering her, his erection pressing into her cleft. It felt so good to be touched and to touch his smooth muscles, his dear face. And their clothes were horrible, just too much. She began to rip at his shirt and he pulled it over his head, then did the same for hers, taking her bra along with it. His skin felt like fire, so smooth, yet crinkly where his chest hair rubbed her breasts. His mouth plundered hers, and she plundered right back, touching him everywhere, wanting him inside her, filling her.

"Sshh, love, we have time."

And a demon possessed her. "We may have time, but I have no patience."

He chuckled "I thought that was *my* shortcoming"

There was that smile that turned her night to day.

"You're right." She raised a hand and brushed it across his forehead, then moved to touch his brows, dark gold and thick. The laugh lines that scored his tanned skin were irresistible, too, reminding her how often he smiled. His nose, with its slight bump, his cheeks, now brushed with stubble, and finally those lips. The golden eyes watched as she whispered the pad of one finger over his lower lip, and then traced the upper. "You are beautiful."

One eyebrow arced, and he mock-scowled. "Beautiful? As commander, I'm supposed to be fierce."

"You are, just not to me. Not anymore." It seemed she couldn't stop touching him, so she brushed her hands across his bare shoulders.

His eyes flared. "I want to kiss you."

"Isn't that what you've been doing?"

"Not there." He nipped her lower lip and began to crawl down her body, dropping kisses as he went.

She grew warm, very warm, anticipation thrumming through her. Of her few lovers, none had relished the nether kiss, though she recalled liking the act enormously. But what if she screamed? Or moaned too loud? It was just all so… "Oh!"

Her flesh burned where he'd just kissed, her thigh now on fire.

Burrowing her fingers through his hair, she found his braid tie and slipped it off. Her throat closed when his tongue laved. She hissed. Then he touched her bud, and the world grew dark and muffled as she gave over to pleasure.

"Oh, Rafe. Rafe!"

For long moments she floated as the sweet storm of bliss rocked her.

He climbed up her flesh, nuzzling and licking only to take her in a wild kiss that tasted of herself and Rafe, the tip of his cock nudging her entrance.

Kit pressed a hand to his backside, desperate to have him fill her.

A slam, followed by, "Open the farking door, Rafe!" just outside the bedroom.

CHAPTER FOURTEEN

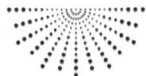

Shote! Who the fark had just blown into his house?

Kit had frozen, and he kissed her lightly until he had to deepen it, couldn't stop because she'd shaken his world to its core.

"Rafe!" Max hollered.

He scowled and ran a finger down her cheek. "Back in a sec, beauty."

Abandoning her warmth hurt. He didn't want to leave her. Never wanted to leave her.

"Rafe!" Max hollered again.

Kit's eyes mirrored his frustration, but the languid smile she gave him stiffened his cock further. *Fark!* He leapt off the bed, tugged on his jeans, and stalked out the door, closing it softly behind him.

He stormed down the hall. "What the fark, Ferret? You don't even knock?" He braced his hands on his hips. If he didn't, he'd throttle his friend.

Max snorted. "You mean like every other day when I just walk in?"

He was about to wipe that smirk off Max's face.

"Sorry to interrupt, man." Max's grin said he was about to wise off.

"Don't."

Max burst out laughing. "Wouldn't think of it. We've got patrol in ten minutes. I texted you about Borne's broken wrist."

Rafe froze. *Shote*. He'd forgotten. A first. "Give me five."

Back in the bedroom, he put a knee on the bed and leaned down to kiss Kit. Her body was lax with pleasure, her eyes lambent with desire. All he wanted was to bury himself inside her. Feel the warmth of her embrace and ardent passion. Tasting her hadn't been enough. He covered her body with his, fingers threading through her thick russet hair.

"Rafe!" hollered Max.

"In a farking minute!" he shouted back.

"You swear a lot more when you're agitated." Kit smiled.

"I've got patrol. Four hours' worth."

She stroked his cheek. "It's all right, Rafe. Actually, it's not all right, but I understand. The Commander cannot shirk his duty."

His brain fizzed at her slow smile. How could he leave her? "We have time, beauty. Lots of it. I'm hungry for you. This was just the appetizer. I want to feast on you for days." He nuzzled her neck, inhaling her delicious scent. "You are my heartsong."

Her eyes misted. "Rafe." She drew up to kiss him long and slow, then watched him with hungry eyes as he tugged on his shirt and gathered his weapons. She was here, in his bed. He stole one more kiss, a too-brief one, before returning to Max.

"Let's go." Max followed as he went to saddle Nightfall.

For all of his annoyance, he was filled with elation. Kit was open to his courtship. Now to make sure he won her heart.

In search of Yuan, Kit jogged through The Keep, still wobbly from the memory of Rafe's hands on her body, how his eyes had softened when he'd stared at her, how his sweet words and even sweeter lips had taken her places she only recalled in dreams.

How he'd filled her to the brim with a chaos of emotions long dormant and so very welcome.

Her chest tightened. He'd called her his heartsong. He was hers, too, the melody so beautiful her eyes teared. *He* was the one courting her. The thought made her giddy.

Down the hall, the sounds of children's voices made her pause. There were so few children in WolfHome. She stopped before an open door and peeked inside. A dozen kids sat on couches and in chairs, while a youngish man darted around the room, helping one child, then another. Two girls and ten boys danced their fingers across large tablets. The group looked to be set up in teams, sharing their work with their partners.

The teacher spotted her and waved her inside. "Welcome, Made One."

"Kit, please."

"Would you like to join us?"

She really had to find Yuan.

"Please!" said a little boy with a cap of brown hair. Vantha, the child she'd met in the dining hall.

"I would love to."

An hour later, after she'd feasted on the children's joy while they'd read aloud the stories they'd written, her worries about war nagged her into leaving. She wanted to linger longer, much longer, but resumed her search for Yuan.

She'd been pondering ways to eradicate *any* idea of war, and she'd come up with a plan. Two, actually. Her first was easiest—though it revolted her feminist sensibilities—which is why she was looking for Yuan. She found her in the library, Yuan's chair hovering beside a table, where her teacher made notes as she studied a book.

Yuan was glad to see her.

"You're well?" Kit said.

"I am, Made One. Sit. Sit. Refreshments?"

"No, thank you." She pulled out the nearest chair. "Rafe told me about The Challenge.

"Ah. That explains your fierce look. It upsets you?"

"That, and the idea of war."

A small, sad smile touched her lips. "Both are facts of life."

Not to Kit, they weren't. "On Earth, historically, if a woman wasn't a virgin that caused all sorts of problems with regards to marriage, social mores, men's perceptions, and such."

Yuan tapped her lips with one gnarled finger. "I'm afraid I don't know this...virgin."

"Oh." She dove back into high school bio. "A virgin is a woman whose hymen, a bit of flesh across her vaginal opening, is generally intact until her first sexual intercourse."

"How strange." Her berry-black eyes lit with curiosity. "Our women and symbionts do not have that flesh you described. What was its purpose?"

"No one knows. It doesn't do anything."

"Then why would anyone care about it?"

This should be interesting. "On Earth, women used to be prized for their virginity, an intact hymen. In some Earthly cultures, that's still so. Historically, the fact that they were untouched signified that the child of the union belonged to the man who had taken the woman's virginity. I thought, since I'm not a virgin, that might affect how Cats and other Eleutian men regarded me?"

Yuan cackled. "That's so absurd I can scarcely believe you." She leaned back in her chair. "I'm afraid I must get back to my studies."

"Of course, but one more question." She should probably ask Tilde, but she'd already trolled these waters, so... "I haven't had my period on Eleutia yet. Where would I find pads or cotton tubes for my menses?"

"Your period?"

"Monthly flow? Menses?"

"Do you mean coming into season?"

"Not exactly. We used that term for horses or cats on Earth when they ovulate."

She smiled. "Yes, just like that."

"But it's sort of the opposite. That's how I've always looked at it, anyway. When horses are in season, they *can* get pregnant. When women menstruate, they *can't*."

"How inconvenient and strange. Our women come into season

just as horses and mistrals do. As you will soon. Since it's spring, you'll ovulate any day now."

That rocked her back. "You're saying that when I'm in season, I *can* get pregnant, but when I'm not, I can't?"

Yuan nodded. "Correct. Forgive me, but I must resume my work."

"Of course. Thank you."

Wasn't that something? Wait'll she told Sybi and... Damn.

Since her virginity or lack thereof made no difference, she headed to the armory. *Of course* the easy route hadn't worked.

She'd begun devising Plan B once Rafe explained the possibility of war between the Cats and Wolves, all because of her. A plan she hoped would cut through the insanity.

The thought of war was horrific, the death and devastation it would wreak terrifying. She'd found happiness on Eleutia, and joy, too. She'd found Rafe.

No. She would not let it happen.

Pulling out her tablet, she began a checklist of what she had to accomplish to effect her plan. Learn more about the Cats. Practice her riding, gymnastic skills, and martial arts. Learn routines of Peacekeepers, Rafe, Alpha, etc. She chewed a nail. A lot to accomplish, but doable.

The armory was a large round building attached to The Keep by an enclosed walkway, where the Clan crafted arms and protective gear for both Eleutians and horses in battle. The button she pressed beside the heavily carved double doors was answered by an older teen who invited her inside a warm alcove redolent with the smells of metal and sweat and leather.

"Please don't wander, Ma'am Kitlyn. The armory is a dangerous place."

They walked through two large rooms where men sewed leather on large machines, sanded odd-looking saddles, and shaped metal into what looked like swords. Her steps slowed, fascinated by a man crafting a crossbow.

A touch on her elbow by the teen.

"Sorry." She waved him on.

Heavier air hit her when they entered a large circular room at the heart of the building, the cacophony making her cover her ears. Men on ladders stirred two immense bubbling cauldrons, pounded several anvils, and worked huge braziers. A sense of urgency filled the air. Sparks flew, and many of the workers wore face shields and headphones. Heads turned as she crossed the circular room, some men wearing smiles on their faces, while a few nodded.

The intensity of the place made her breathless. Passing through another set of doors, the teen led her down a flagstone hall to a closed door. He knocked.

"In!" barked a gravelly voice full of aggravation.

The boy waved her into an office that was a jumble of papers, discarded arms, and leather samples. A middle-aged, white-haired man with massive tattooed arms sat behind a desk rearranging the detritus. When he looked up, his look of annoyance transformed to delight. "Sit, Made One, sit!"

She hefted an axe off the chair across from the desk, wobbling a little at its weight, and sat.

"You're Talos, yes?" she said.

"That I am." The man picked up a small gold-handled knife and began threading it through his fingers. "How can I be of service, Ma'am Kit?"

She'd thought about what to ask for, knew it was an outrageous request, and did it anyway. "I need a sword and a set of fighting leathers with a hooded mask. Some knives would be good, too. And a long stick that folds."

His sparse gray eyebrows inched to his hairline. "Do you? And why is that?" His voice might be mild, but his eyes had sharpened. And he kept playing with that damned knife.

Thankfully, she'd prepared. "It's a surprise." She smiled, trying to project innocence.

"Ah! A gift?" But his eyes remained dark with questions.

"No, they're for me. Oh, and the chest leathers have to flatten my breasts, too. It's a masquerade, a surprise for my friend."

He shook his head. "I'm afraid not without the Alpha's permission. That isn't done."

She tried to emulate Bree, and put as much snark into her smile as possible. "It is, now."

His hand moved with blurring speed. The knife he'd been toying with thunked into the wall behind her head beside half a dozen of its brethren.

Lucky stars. He was fast, maybe the equal of Reggie and his circus act.

"I'm afraid no, Ma'am Kit," he said.

"I see." She rose, as if to leave.

"Do wait. I'd like you to see some of our work here."

"I'd love that. But I have to go find someone else to make the suit for me."

"You can't." He pressed his hands to the desk and rose. A huge man, intimidating and powerful.

"No? Why can't I?"

"It's not done." His agitation grew. "We do finer work than any private armorer."

"Do you?" Thank the heavens for Yuan. "Then riddle me this."

His eyes gleamed. "A riddle? You've been talking to my old friend." He burst out laughing and sat.

She returned to the chair and crossed her legs, feigning a relaxation she was far from feeling. "If you solve my riddle, I'll leave without the armor. If you can't, you'll craft my requests and keep them secret. Beware, it's a hard riddle." That last bit, too much icing on the cake? Damn.

His lips twitched. "I know thousands of riddles, and I always win, my dear." He picked up another knife and again began his finger dance. "And when *I* win, the prize?"

"I'll forget my request."

"That's not a prize." The knife moved faster, threading through his fingers with lightning speed.

"I suppose not." She tapped her lips, sure she had him.

He leaned forward. "You allow me to purchase Moonrise's first foal."

How had he known Moonrise was hers? Rafe might not be pleased if he heard this bargain, but he'd said the first foal was Kit's, plus she was certain she'd win. And wasn't that every gambler's downfall?

"The foal," she said. "Do you care about the gender?"

"I do not."

"Deal." She held out her hand.

He slid his hand across the desk to hers, and they clasped forearms.

Victory was sweet. Kit had asked Talos the old honey bees in the lion riddle and won. What she did not do was a happy dance. Talos was too furious for that. He was also suspicious. Nothing for it.

But he'd assured her she'd have the leathers, a sword, knives, and that "shoting pole," as he called it, within seven days. He'd also sworn to keep her secret.

One more request. She hoped he didn't stick her with that knife he always played with. "Can you make the leathers white?"

Talos brow crinkled. "That's not very wise. Perhaps green or—"

"I want them white." Kit smiled. "Please."

"As you wish."

She'd gotten what she wanted. Now let's hope she didn't have to use them.

Two weeks had flown by, ones of delight and frustration. With rumbles from the Cats, Rafe had been forced to send many of his men on three-day patrols, including himself. Her arms training had stepped up, too, but she cut back on her history lessons, displeasing Yuan. She had other things she needed to focus on.

Though constrained by her stable work, she practiced both her gymnastics and martial arts daily. During the days Rafe was away, she used his barn's arena, always bringing treats for the horses and mistrals. When he was home, she performed her gymnastics in the green space, while practicing katas in her suite.

One special day, she'd watched Rafe shear Moonrise under the hawk eyes of a Clan spinner, Kit pressing Moonrise's curls into the spinner's eager hands as if she were passing off the crown jewels. When spun, she'd have yarn to accompany the cherrywood knitting needles Rafe had made her, a courting gift that had appeared on her doorstep once she'd explained knitting to him. A gift she'd responded to with enthusiastic kisses, much to both of their delight.

One evening, with Tilde's help, she'd made several decks of playing cards, ones she used to teach her dinner-mates Spite and Malice. At Rafe's request she drew a chess set on paper, and she'd also made time to again visit the children.

It had been a good two weeks, though they'd had almost no alone time. That was starting to grate since her libido seemed to be in overdrive, her hunger for Rafe ever-present.

That morning, Kit sprang out of bed, eager to take a ride with Rafe. They'd be away from the Clan. Today they'd make love with no one knowing where they were. No one would interrupt. No one would pester Rafe or herself. Her body was so primed, she hoped she didn't come riding Moonrise.

While the sun shone bright, the air held enough chill for her to don a barn jacket before saddling Moonrise. As Rafe tended to Nightfall, saddling, then strapping on their picnic packs, his jeans cupped his fine ass. Oh, she had it bad.

When he slid his sword into its saddle sheath, she said, "You think there might be trouble?"

"No. We'll be deep in WolfHome territory, but caution rules. Do you have your daggers?"

"Yes, but only because you suggested it. I'm not used to strapping on weapons when I go for a picnic."

"No one on Earth wears weapons?"

"Some do. And some places are very dangerous, but not where I'm from."

"I'd feel naked without mine."

The picture she conjured made her lick her lips.

How would her sisters feel about wearing weapons? Picturing Sybi wielding one proved impossible. Bree? She'd be lethal, especially with those nails. Her heart hitched. Her middle sister always wore those ridiculous fake nails with glitter and designs on them, calling them her "weapons of disguise." Highly tease-worthy.

"Let's go!" Rafe said.

Once off, riding Moonrise was silk on four legs. She'd ridden Blackie five times since, but the bond she felt with Moonrise gave her a special kind of confidence. Not a hint of a flashback in sight.

"Why is her coat like a sheep's fleece?" she asked, following Rafe up the steep trail behind his barn.

"It's one of those mysteries. A rare occurrence in some mistrals."

"Moonrise knows she's different."

"That she does." He shot her a warm look. "I like different, in case you hadn't noticed."

She blushed, basking in the heat of Rafe's desire. "Soon we'll fly?"

"Promise. Just a few more rides."

Having watched Rafe fly Nightfall, the idea of soaring on the back of a mistral fired her blood and terrified her at the same time. Why not break one more barrier? If she thought about it too much… "Let's test it out. Let's fly now."

"Soon, Kit."

"How soon? Tomorrow soon?"

"Not tomorrow. Soon. Period." He shook his head, but his eyes laughed.

"So, I'm funny, am I?"

"You're like a wolf with a bone."

She waved a hand. "La, la, la. Old news."

They cantered across the rise, walking through one of the many inner wall's gates, then rode up and down forested hills and into a valley of lush meadows and burbling streams sprinkled with stands of birch and aspen. The valley was wide and long, the vista gorgeous, and Kit breathed deep of the fragrant air. Hard to believe the entirety of the Wolves' domain was encircled by the vast outer wall she'd seen weeks ago. Ahead, a larger hill led to the foothills of the mountains where Rafe had found her.

Her stomach rumbled. She was more than ready for their picnic. They trotted over to an aspen grove beside a small grassy glen banded by a larger stand of pine and unloaded the packs. Rafe gathered the food and drink he'd brought, as did she—sandwiches and brownies she'd made herself. With walnuts, of course.

As he spread a blanket on the soft grass beneath the aspens, the mistrals began to fuss, stomping their hooves, flicking their tails, and nickering.

"Fine. Go!" He snapped his arm straight up, and the pair rose into the sky.

Magnificent. "Just like kids, they want to go off and play."

"Yes. They are children. Young in mistral years."

Kit handed him a sandwich. "I think you'll like it."

"You made it?"

"I did."

With a wary grace, he lifted the top of the baguette-style sandwich and eyeballed the innards. He sniffed.

She bit her lip so as not to laugh. "It's turkey, cheese, and slices of apple."

"That's…strange."

"It's yummy."

"What kind of cheese? It'd better not be goat cheese."

Her laugh burst out. Impossible not to with that frown on his face and a touch of fear in his eyes. "I don't know the name, but I tasted it. It's like cheddar. I don't know your word."

His face cleared, his eyes softening. "My mam, she called our farmhouse cheese 'cheddar.'" He took a huge bite, closed his eyes, and smiled.

"Good?"

"Good."

Rafe had brought meat pies, with flaky crusts and savory with spices. They drank a dry red wine, and when a drop lingered on the corner of his mouth, she had to lick it off.

His smoky laughter filled her with a sense of rightness, and she kissed him hard and fast. "You taste good."

"And you continually surprise me."

"I'm glad."

He nuzzled her neck. "You smell good, too."

"Wait. We have to have dessert. I made brownies."

His half-lidded eyes heated, and he opened his mouth to speak. He clamped it shut, held up a hand, and smiled. "Don't move fast. Act natural. Unload the brownies. We're being watched. Cats, possibly, though the scents are confusing. At least three individuals."

She forced her muscles to relax. Her free hand patted one of the three knives she'd brought, the ones she trained with. Not that she'd ever used them on actual people. Her throat tightened. She'd never been in an actual fight, and though she'd been training, she prayed she'd keep a cool head. The aspens partly obscured them, which she supposed was good. Rafe's muscles remained relaxed, but tension rolled off him in waves. He would fight. Get all protective. He could be injured. Killed.

Rafe reached into the picnic basket and drew out half a dozen metal disks, each no bigger than his thumb.

"The brownies, Kit," he said. "Our movements should look natural, as if we're still picnicking."

Kit did as asked, while Rafe straightened the blanket, scattering the metal disks in front of them.

"What do they do?" she whispered.

"Smoke. For cover." Reaching for her, he pulled her close, as if they were going to become intimate.

"What should I do?" she said.

"I've got this." What looked like a black clicker rested in one hand. With his other, he brushed the hair back from her face. "Much as I'd like to engage, retreat is sometimes the best course." He emitted a high-pitched whistle. "Keep your eyes on me."

"Why?"

"The mistrals are coming. Pack up the basket, as if everything was normal."

As she packed, she glanced skyward. Two specks grew into Moonrise and Nightfall diving rocket fast.

A red light darted across Rafe's shoulders. Kit threw herself on him, flattening them both as a laser scorched an aspen directly behind him.

"Are you hurt?" he said.

"No."

A different-toned whistle from Rafe, and as the mistrals landed three men ran toward them from the trees.

"Mount and fly." He pressed the clicker and smoke burst from the metal disks, shielding them from their attackers.

They vaulted into their saddles, except Moonrise was on the move before she fully settled. She started to slide, saw double, reality and the circus arena. Tightening her thighs, she bit her lip hard and the double vision coalesced to the here and now. Then she was upright, grabbing the reins and flying.

As they rocketed into the sky, Rafe fell behind on Nightfall, drew out a laseblaster, and strafed the men, who returned fire. Seconds later, wolves led by Paulo poured into their campsite. The attackers dashed to the wood, the wolves in pursuit. A hover lifted from amidst the scrim of trees and fled.

As the wolves gave chase, the hover disappeared over a rise.

She and Rafe beelined for the inner wall, landing just outside the main entrance, then thundered through WolfHome's open gates.

Safe. She was panting, sweaty, and exhilarated as the gates closed behind them.

She'd *flown!*

A glint of light from the tower high above. Rafe slammed into her, tumbling them both toward the ground.

Bursts of laser fire, shouts, and screams.

She hit the earth hard, her breath stolen. Once she could breathe, she pushed to her hands and knees to find Rafe sprawled on his back, an arrow sticking from his shoulder.

"Rafe!"

She kneeled beside him. Blood covered his left shoulder, and he lay limp, his face pale. He couldn't be dead. She pressed a hand to his throat, felt the thready beat of his pulse. Alive.

Should she pull the arrow out? Leave it in? *Stars alive*, this was not in her wheelhouse.

His eyes fluttered open, and he ground out, "Pull it out."

"Just...pull?"

"Yes."

For a second, she thought about it, then reached into her pocket for her abandoned kerchief. Her nostrils flared when she wrapped her hands around the arrow's shaft. Thin, made of some kind of metal, she hoped the tip wasn't barbed. Rafe was staring at her, his tawny eyes calm.

"On the count of three," she said.

He nodded, his breathing labored, as if his lungs were filling.

Her hands shook. She wiped them on her pants and breathed deeply, trying to steady them. "One. Two." She ripped the thing from his flesh and pressed her kerchief to his seeping wound. "Rafe?"

"Did good," he panted, neck stretched, gasping air. "Get healer."

"I'm afraid to leave you. The bleeding. Your breathing."

"I'll die. Healer."

She brushed her lips over his. "Don't you dare die." She scrambled onto Moonrise and thundered down the road toward The Keep yelling "A healer to the gate!" over and over again. By the time she pulled in front of The Hall people were pouring out of the building. She screamed it again.

Tilde punched through the crowd and ran to her. "A healer's on the way. Take me there!"

She turned Moonrise, held out a hand, and Tilde sprang up behind her. Kit pressed her heels to the mistral's sides, and Moonrise leapt into a gallop. *Please let him be okay.*

CHAPTER FIFTEEN

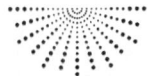

Hours later, Kit paced the outer room of the Alpha's den, her eyes glued to the closed pocket doors where three healers and Kicks worked on Rafe. He was fighting for his life, and she didn't understand. How could his shoulder wound be fatal, a wound that wasn't anywhere near his heart?

Blood covered her clothes, and though she'd washed her hands, the coppery scent nauseated her. She should go change, but she wouldn't leave Rafe, even if they had relegated her to the suite's expansive sitting area.

As an apprentice healer, Tilde was in the bedroom with them. The Alpha was inside, too, and she hoped he'd do more than glower at his son. Her gut roiled, her throat tight and raw.

Rafe would live. He simply must.

The hall door creaked, and Max slipped inside. She raised a hand but couldn't seem to stop her pacing.

"I thought you might need these." He held out a stack of clothes.

"Thank you. That was thoughtful." She reached for them, her eyes burning—they'd been doing that all day—and her tears spilled over.

Dismay rippled across Max's face, and he stepped toward her. "Kit?"

Her dam of tears breaking, she clutched the clothes and ran into the Alpha's bathroom, shut the door, and sat on the toilet lid, clothes falling to the floor as she pressed a hand to her mouth so no one would hear her sobs.

On Earth, death had been an old companion. Death here was different. *Rafe* was different.

Rafe could not die.

But what if he did?

She clenched the rim of the sink and looked into the mirror at that strange-familiar face.

If he died, she would survive. She always did. On Earth. Here. The loss of her sisters was like two of her limbs missing. If she lost Rafe, too…

It felt like she was being hollowed from the inside out. As if a part of her, an essential part, was being stripped away layer by layer, fundamentally altered in ways far more profound than what the Alchemics had done to her.

The eyes that mirrored back at her were puffy and red-rimmed, but they were clear. Naked. Truthful.

So many needed Rafe, none more than she. He deserved life, had so many years to come—to see Moonrise's foal born and Mimi become a teen. And their relationship, it had just blossomed into a beautiful thing.

A heart pain, so sharp she lost her breath, staggered her.

She shucked her blood-soaked clothes, scrubbed her face, hands, and neck, and donned the jeans and t-shirt Max had brought.

To keep Rafe safe, she must learn who had shot him. The Cats? A traitorous Wolf? Who? And why? She kicked her dirty clothes into a corner and rejoined Max, who lounged in a chair, worry clouding his blue eyes. He jumped to a stand. "Are you—"

"I'm fine. I'm okay, Max. It's just been a lot. Right before Rafe passed out, he told me if I didn't find a healer, he would die. I don't understand. He was hit in the shoulder, so why would that kill him?"

Max's face darkened. "Because he was shot with a goddart's sting. Their arrows are poison."

She sat on the sofa arm. "Who would do this? Why?"

"I don't know." But he wouldn't meet her eyes.

"Who and why, Max? It's obvious you're hiding something."

He spread his hands. "I'm not."

He was. "Tell me about the arrow."

"Goddarts tip them with a distilled poison made from plants that only grow high in the Pellopine mountains. The method and plants used are secret. Because of the distillation, the poison flows through the body at a shocking speed. It can either paralyze or suffocate, usually both. Our Council of Clans prohibits their use, not that the goddarts pay that any attention. They stay in the mountains, but they're like vermin."

"In other words, someone had to steal one of these arrows or the poison itself."

"Yes. Which isn't easy." He slumped back into the chair. "They won't let me in to see him."

"Nor me. Before Rafe was shot, we were on a picnic, and three men attacked us whose scents Rafe couldn't identify. Cats?"

He shook his head. "The Cats are high handed, but they don't tend to use assassins. With their numbers, they'd rather wage war."

"But it's possible."

"Sure. They could disguise their scent." He shook his head. "I just don't see the Cats attacking or trying to assassinate."

That gave her pause. "Someone from the Wolf Clan?"

His eyes met hers. "That's what I think."

"But who, why?"

He raked a hand through his close-cropped hair. "Don't you see, Kit? They were aiming for you."

Had *she* been their target? Rafe had barreled into her. "It's possible, I guess."

He threw up his hands. "Possible? You were already shot once."

Kit believed that to be Inga. "I know, but—"

"To some fringe groups and individuals, Made Ones are anathema."

"Anathema? Your female population has dramatically decreased. Which is why I was brought here."

"True, as far as it goes, but…" Max started to tap his foot. "I don't like talking about this."

"That's just too bad. I'm tired of people keeping things from me."

The pocket door to Rafe's room opened, and Tilde's head poked out. She and Max stared at each other for a long moment.

"Tilde?" Kit said.

"He's going in and out of consciousness, asking for you," Tilde said.

She rushed to Tilde's side. "Is he better?"

"No, he's not."

Inside the Alpha's large bedroom, Rafe lay supine on the bed, eyes sunken, breathing labored. The tendons on his neck stood out, as if he were fighting some fierce battle. He had to be in terrible pain. Two IVs snaked into his left arm, one clear, the other a pale green.

Her vision blurred, the anger inside her coiling into a hot, tight ball.

She lifted one of his fisted hands. "Rafe?"

No response.

Rafe's father leaned against a wall, arms crossed, jaw tight enough to crack teeth. Tilde returned to the three healers surrounding Rafe's bedside, while Kicks leaned against the wall, empty-eyed.

"Kicks," Kit said.

The doctor shook her head and pushed away from the wall. "I'll come back, but only the High Magics can save—"

"No!" the Alpha said. "There must be another way."

Kicks cast him a dark look and left.

"How could the High Magics help?" Kit said.

Tilde snagged her gaze, her finger pressed to her lips. *Later*, she mouthed.

Later was too late.

Inga had referenced High Magics, too. "Ulfr, isn't Rafe's life worth their use?"

"The Alchemics," the healer in black said. "They forbid it."

She was about to speak when the healer held up his hand, his eyes on her. "We symbiotic Eleutians… Over time we have lost the High Magics through disuse. They are complicated and arduous, with extensive discipline, practice, and training needed. With the Alchemics disallowing them, far fewer have the skills, and they've faded with each generation. The magics we use to heal are Simple Magics that cure some bodily ills. Neither the soul nor the spirit is touched. I don't know a person alive who can perform the High Magics. Do you, Alpha?" The sharp look he cut Ulfr could have sliced marble.

"I do not." Ulfr flushed. "Don't you think if I had that ability, I would use it to save my son?"

Kit believed he would, the Alchemics be damned. She stepped closer to the bed. "Excuse me," she said, bumping one of the healers, who gave her a sour look.

"Manners, healer!" barked another healer in black.

Kit stroked Rafe's fisted hand. "Hey, fella."

After long minutes, he turned his head in what looked like a massive effort. The fist she held unfurled, and she saw how his short nails had scored deep moons across his palm. He clasped her hand, and she threaded her fingers through his. Though his eyes remained closed, he whispered, "Kit."

"How can I help?"

He raised their clasped hands and pressed them to his chest. "Stay."

"A swarm of Battle Beetles couldn't drive me off."

His lips twitched into the barest of smiles. "Good." His hand relaxed.

She stayed put, even when his father stepped forward and hissed in her ear, "He's unconscious again. Now, get out."

Kit's eyes narrowed. "Bite me. Rafe asked me to stay. I'm not going anywhere."

The Alpha rocked back on his heels and winked at her. Winked! "Well, well. The little Made One has teeth. Nice to know you're as tough as Rafe says. I personally didn't see it. Until now."

She dozed in a chair by Rafe's bedside, resting her head on the mattress, her hand still entwined with Rafe's. The healers and Tilde had gone, but Rafe's father remained. He'd fallen asleep in the other chair, legs sprawled, his head pressed to one hand, eyes closed. He looked so much like his son, yet they were so different. She got the feeling he wanted to like her but didn't. As long as his son did, that was okay with her.

The healers had put Rafe in some kind of stasis. They'd halted the progress of the poison but were unable to reverse its effects. If they removed the stasis and he was too exhausted to fight the poison, he'd die.

A screech sounded from the outer room. Then a shouted, "No!"

"What the...?" She squeezed Rafe's hand, then zoomed through the doors.

Mimi was struggling in a woman's arms, the child batting at the woman with her small fists, cheeks red, tears streaming down her face.

"Rafe is sick, Mimi," she said. "Hush, kiddo, so he can rest."

Mimi's eyes widened when she saw Kit, and she froze. "I know he's sick. I want to see him."

"No!" The woman holding the squirming Mimi frowned. "My child escaped our den."

Kit was in the Alpha's den. Why wasn't the Alpha out here, anyhow?

Ulfr's mate was tall and willowy, with a porcelain face, jet black curls, and bee-stung lips. Her forehead was pinched, her mouth pursed, her eyes bloodshot and weary.

"Who are you?" The woman's imperious voice was like nails on a chalkboard.

"I'm Kit."

The child held out her arms to Kit. Taking Mimi would only piss off her mother further.

"Stop now, Mimi!" the woman said and turned to Kit. "You are the cause of all this trouble."

"Not deliberately, I assure you."

"When the Cats attack, many of ours will die. Because of you and that arrogant son of his." The woman returned to battling Mimi's squirms.

"I won't let that happen," Kit said.

The woman snorted. "As if you'd have a say."

She tabled that little discussion. "I think it would be okay for Mimi to see her brother."

"Half-brother," she said as she marched for the door, a howling Mimi in her arms. "I'm afraid it's not okay with me."

Kit hadn't even gotten the woman's name.

She spent the next thirty-six hours in the Alpha's bedroom, watching Rafe fade. That was the only way to describe it. His skin had grown so hot, the hand she held burned, yet was desert dry.

The healers had returned hours previous, but nothing they did helped as his temperature rose higher and higher. Tilde and Kit sponged him down repeatedly, even gave him an ice bath, and if it helped at all she couldn't tell. Ulfr's face grew bleaker by the minute, until around one a.m. he pushed out of his chair and stalked from the room.

The eldest healer straightened, his face drawn with exhaustion. "We can do no more."

"Hold on," Kit said, trying not to shout at the man. "You can't give up."

Tilde looked as shocked at the healer's pronouncement as she was, but the three healers moved in concert toward the pocket doors. One turned back and signaled for Tilde to join them.

"I'm going to keep trying," Tilde said.

"Foolish apprentice, we can do no more," the eldest said.

The trio filed out, but she caught a glimmer of moisture in the eldest healer's eyes.

Kit rubbed her cheek across the back of Rafe's hand. "Isn't there something radical? The High Magics? Anything?"

Tilde shook her head, her lips wobbling. "The poison is consuming him."

Not for the first time, she wondered if anything on her Earth could save Rafe.

Their enemy, time, crawled onward. Kit was going loopy, so exhausted she could barely keep her eyes open. An hour earlier, Tilde had stretched out on the floor for a quick nap. Kit couldn't sleep. Rafe needed someone with him if he...left.

Her friend jackknifed to a sitting position. "Gotta go see Max. I've got an idea."

An hour later, Tilde returned. "I'll take over. Rest for a bit if you can."

Kit slumped into the chair and laid her head down on the bed, just for a moment.

Calix had followed Fukkes to the lab connected to the Made One's capsule on the pretext of renewing the chemicals for her elixir. Days of frustration, while Fukkes and the Controller argued about where next to set the Alchemics' movable city, made Calix's fuse as short as the increasing risks he took. If he didn't take more care, he'd be found out. He might be a spy, but he had a life in Alchemic City, friends, lovers, too, including Darva, a born-and-bred Alchemic. But were any to discover the true nature of his work, his death would be the result, his mission a failure.

He'd gleaned Fukkes was planning to go off-City, a rarity. Something powerful was compelling the Alchemic, but he'd yet to discover what.

While Calix worked inside the lab, a good dozen apprentices and Alchemics bustled around, several bent over their fluorescopps. He kept Fukkes in sight, and the Alchemic's behavior only got stranger. Fukkes was gathering a surfeit of equipment, which was unusual. The man seldom performed experiments himself, preferring to direct others. Calix sidled around another apprentice to retrieve a condenser, noting Fukkes adding a fusion tube to his kit.

Odd. He returned to his task. What was Fukkes planning? These people always had agendas, with Fukkes' particularly opaque and always self-serving.

The door slammed open and Gabin stormed in, hastening over to Fukkes. "Why are you going on this trek?"

"I've told you why," Fukkes said.

Calix held his breath. They were speaking in hisses and whispers, but the others had given them a wide berth. Several had left. Calix strained to hear their words.

Gabin pulled Fukkes around to face him. "We agreed you wouldn't go to the Wolves."

Fukkes knocked his hand away. "No, Gabin, only you agreed."

More people fled the lab. Calix tried to make himself small and to look industrious. Most would have no idea what Gabin was objecting to, but having seen the fusion tube, Calix understood Fukkes planned to perform a transfusion, a normally simple procedure. Calix had no idea why Fukkes would go to the Wolves or who he planned to treat. He needed to know.

"It will alter his blood," Gabin said.

"Of course it will."

What could alter an Eleutian's blood? Calix twisted a receptor into place.

"And, my good friend, if they discover the secret of the Made Ones' blood?"

The *secret*? Calix knew of none.

"Discover the blood's secret?" Fukkes said. "Don't be ridiculous.

They have neither the facilities nor the intelligence. As an extra precaution, I'm using the Lucanidae. To obfuscate."

Lucanidae were rare and precious. A single one cost a small fortune. Using one as a ruse was bizarre in the extreme.

"Let him die," Gabin said.

"We chose him," Fukkes said. "*She* chose him."

Gabin grunted. "And how do you know this about her?"

"I have better spies than you." A cruel smile rippled across his face.

Calix hoped never to see that particular expression aimed at him. Over the past five years, three wolven compounds had acquired Made Ones, two of which were in the Southern hemisphere, with only WolfHome in the Northern.

"Spies. Bah, worthless," Gabin said. "When he dies, she'll choose another."

"Not in this instance."

"And why not?" Gabin said.

"It is suspected she's fallen in love with him."

Calix was shocked. Kitlyn Balážová had fallen in love. With whom?

"You going is dangerous. It could ruin everything." Gabin shook his head, unfortunately catching Calix's eye. "What are you doing here?" He scanned the room, his eyes widening at the three remaining Alchemics. "Get out! Everyone, get out! Now!"

Kit awakened in a muddle, eyes scratchy-dry. She went to rub them, but she was holding someone's hand, a hand that burned. That snapped her back to a reality she refused to accept. She shook herself, then dunked a cloth in the water, squeezed out the excess, and began again to bathe Rafe. Across the bed from her, Tilde was doing the same.

Rafe's lips were cracked, his eyes crusted with gunk she carefully wiped away. She put aside the cloth and lifted the bowl with the ice chips. He'd been in stasis for hours. Rafe was dying.

Come back to me.

Tilde held his head up, and Kit slipped the ice into his mouth.

A ruckus at the outer door, and a roly-poly middle-aged man appeared, looking like a circus ringmaster with his impossibly huge mustache, striped pants, brocade vest, and black velvet jacket. He swanned into the room carrying a large square case he placed on the dresser.

Tilde bowed.

What the heck?

The man's piercing black eyes studied Kit for long minutes. "You."

"Yup, me," Kit said. "Who are *you?*"

Tilde's eyes warmed. "You're here for Rafe. Are you—"

"I am Fukkatsu. You may call me Fukkes for short. Now, shut up."

The arrogance. "How dare—"

"You shut up, too. My peace has been disturbed. I will fix this, then get back to my work." He pointed a finger at Kit. "You smell."

"Thank you. It's called Eau de Pain."

He snapped open his case, withdrew a pair of latex-like gloves, and tugged them on. Furling a white cloth across the dresser, Fukkes removed a package from his case, ripped it open, and pulled out a long, clear tube, which he lay on the white cloth.

"Roll up your shirt," he said to Kit.

"Why?" she said.

"Hmm." He pressed a finger to his lips. "Do you want me to save the Wolf's life or not?"

Not that she trusted him, but she did as asked. For all his clownish appearance, his eyes told a different story, one of intelligence, arrogance, and entitlement. She'd add a hint of deceit, too.

From another package, Fukkes extracted two glass vials with suction cups at their end and placed both on the white cloth. Something that looked way too much like spider legs fluttered at the ends of the cups.

"Ready?" Fukkes said.

"You'll safe Rafe's life?" she said.

"That I will."

"Okay, go."

"There will be a price."

"I suspect I've already paid."

He gave her close-lipped smirk, then lifted a vial and pressed its cup to her elbow's inner flesh. Horrible wriggling brushed her skin, then a sharp pinch. "Ow."

Fukkes nodded.

"What is this thing?" Kit said, wariness in her voice.

"If you must know, a Lucanidae Kabutomushi."

"But they're poisonous!" Tilde said.

"Only if used improperly."

Tilde bit her lip. "What if he's too weak for—"

"Madame, *you* contacted *me*, as did the Alpha. Perhaps you should take your issues up with…yourself."

"But—"

"Shut up, apprentice."

Kit's spine stiffened. "What exactly does it do? And don't tell Tilde to shut up again."

He leaned close, his breath smelling of cloves. "The bug secretes a venom that absorbs the goddart's poison as we transfuse your blood to his. Placing the Lucanidae in you, as well, prevents any of the blowback to you from the poison. You don't want to fall prey to it, correct?"

It sounded plausible, but… Kit looked at Tilde, who mouthed, *We must.*

"Do it," she said.

CHAPTER SIXTEEN

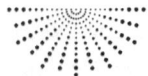

K itlyn watched Fukkes glide around the bed toward Rafe.

He was an *Alchemic*. He knew about her sisters. He must. Rafe didn't trust them. She didn't, either. But they were out of options.

While Fukkes talked, he attached a similar suction cupped vial to Rafe's inner elbow.

Kit hated seeing that bug-thing dig into Rafe, parting flesh already bruised and hurting. His lack of reaction made it worse.

Fukkes pushed one end of the clear tube into Rafe's glass vial, and the other end into hers. He lifted a small, oval device from his case and pressed a button.

Pain screeched as the creature burrowed deep beneath her skin. She gripped the chair arm, steadying herself. Stars alive, a bulbous lump *moved* beneath the skin above her forearm. Bile surged into her mouth. She swallowed hard as she watched her blood flow into the vial, then through the tube and into Rafe.

The pain was unrelenting, like the creature was biting her insides. She gritted her teeth, nostrils flaring.

Watching her, Fukkes professorial mask slipped, his eyes lit with pleasure. That prick!

Rafe began to thrash, threatening to rip the suction cup and IVs out of his arm.

"Hold him!" Fukkes ordered Tilde.

Tilde grabbed Rafe's shoulders and pressed down. He was such a big man and she was so petite, she couldn't completely stop his thrashing.

Kit looked at Fukkes. "Help her!"

"Me?" He posed, hand on hip, the other pointing to himself.

She reached with her untethered arm and pressed against Rafe's shoulder trying to help Tilde. Her movement amped up the pain, and she clenched her jaw.

She'd glimpsed the rot in this man, this pure scientist whose Clan espoused science above all else. *Science, her ass.* She suspected something far greater than the creation of Made Ones was at work here. Something more insidious and deadly.

The outer door banged open, and Rafe's father burst into the room. He shoved Tilde out of the way and pressed his upper body across Rafe's, stilling his movement.

Five minutes. Ten. Fifteen.

Tears streamed down Kit's cheeks, and the only thing keeping her present was focusing on Rafe's face. It had begun to lose its gray cast, a product of the poison's relentless quest. As Rafe's pain eased, the Alpha rose off his son's body, though he kept a grip on his shoulders.

"All cooked!" Fukkes clapped his hands, then pressed another button on the oval device.

Though the immediate pain ceased, torturous aftershocks sparked through her flesh.

Fukkes took hold of her used vial and, with surprising delicacy, pulled it from her arm. Along with the vial and suction cup, a huge, iridescent, spider-like bug emerged from the hole in her skin. The thing hung limp, dead.

Nauseated, Kit clamped her teeth tight.

"I told you they wouldn't die," Fukkes said to Tilde.

"Lucky you," Tilde said. "Or I'd have taken my claws to you."

Fukkes snorted a laugh as he dropped the device, including the dead bug, into an orange leather case, then cleaned, sewed, and bandaged her arm. He performed the same procedure on Rafe.

She stared down at Rafe, as still as death. The sheet had slipped lower, baring his chest, the scars he bore, the pain he'd endured, things Fukkes had no right to see. She drew the sheet up to his neck. She was thankful her hands didn't tremble. "Rafe... he'll live?"

"Of course." Fukkes rounded the bed, and Kit stood to face him. He gripped her chin and turned her head left, then right.

"What?" She could bite him. Easy enough to take a chunk out of the arrogant bastard.

"Word has it you can't read Eleutian. True?" He smiled, revealing a set of crystal teeth.

If those teeth weren't creepy, she didn't know what was. "Correct, I can't read."

He pursed his lips. "Your translator disk is malfunctioning. Hold still."

Before she could react, his scalpel flashed and pain spiked behind her ear. "You could have warned me!"

"Hold still, I said."

She froze. She didn't trust Fukkes, didn't like him breathing on her, mauling her. Plus, he gave her the willies.

Fukkes had known she couldn't read. He must have spies in WolfHome. She'd have to tell Rafe.

Fukkes delved into his case. When he approached, he held two small bags and some kind of instrument. At least there were no bugs. A pull behind her ear, then a push, and he raised the instrument. Its pinch made her wince. He swiped the area with a cloth.

"What is that thing?" She stabbed her finger at the now-bloody instrument. "What did you do?"

"This 'thing' is a miniaturized sealer."

Now that she got a good look, she saw it resembled the tool the doc at the MedSurge had used on Rafe, but a quarter of the size.

"I replaced your translator," Fukkes said. "Feel."

Smooth. Not a ripple or ridge. She lifted the book Tilde had been reading earlier. *Whisper of Love*, with a half-naked couple on the cover. She opened the book, found the first chapter. *She covered his supine body, shielding him...*

Hugging the book, Kit spun to face Fukkes. "Thank you."

"But of course. Can't have you misfiring."

He made her sound like a car. "No, of course not."

Fukkes gripped her chin again, his thumb stroking her cheek. "I do good work."

Humble, too.

"As comely as your siblings."

She clutched his wrist. "*Where* are Bree and Sybi?"

Red suffused his face. "She dares touch me."

Ulfr pulled her off Fukkes.

"No one touches an Alchemic," Ulfr hissed. "It's forbidden. There are penalties."

"*Where* are my sisters, Fukkes?" she said, struggling against Ulfr's hold.

The Alchemic nodded to Ulfr and walked toward the door.

"Don't you dare leave!" she shouted. "Where are they, Fukkes?"

Over his shoulder, he said, "Our debt is paid in full, Alpha." Fukkes wiggled his fingers in a wave and disappeared out the door.

Her sisters were *alive*, damnit, and he knew where they were. She tore from Ulfr and raced after Fukkes.

But she never found him.

Calix stood in the incinerator room. Fukkes had been gone for hours, but once he'd returned, Calix had followed his trail around the facility and caught him disposing of medkit materials. Now, after the Alchemic's departure, he had three minutes before the medtech turned on the incinerator. Calix poked around the disposal bin with a pencil. His laser light showed fusion tubing and... *Holy shote.* Fukkes had used *two* Lucanidae Kabutomushi. Calix pulled his tweezer from his tool case and took great care removing one, which he bagged up. Obfuscation, Fukkes had said. What in truth had saved the patient Fukkes had gone to treat?

The incinerator flared on.

Shote. He tried to retrieve the second, but it was impossible before the bin's contents combusted. One out of two would have to suffice. From the dead bug, he could recover enough blood to have proof of at least one person Fukkes had treated. Perhaps the sample would also lead him to a second patient.

Fukkes had been to see Kitlyn Balážová. He'd performed a transfusion. On whom, he couldn't guess. He doubted it was the Made One. Their blood was infused with organic chemicals that made them highly resistant to disease and infirmity. That much he knew. But perhaps their blood contained *more*—hidden properties known only to those in Fukkes' Alchemic cabal. Which was why he needed those rare spiders. A shell game that hid the fact that it was the Made One's blood doing the healing. It fit.

Fates! He rubbed his temples, a thundering migraine coming on.

Yes, that *could* be the case…or the bugs' purpose might have been quite different.

Calix had learned Fukkes had an agenda, one not necessarily aligned with the Alchemic Clan's. He'd already threatened not to animate the Made One here in the City, which breached the Alchemic Code.

Fukkes and Gabin would be in the Made One's room by now, at their daily meeting to discuss her health. Calix stored the dead bug in the hidden cubbyhole inside his locker, then retrieved some vials and added an innocuous liquid to a beaker. He stationed himself outside the Made One's door and attached the listening device he'd recently acquired to his ear. He was told it would work well even through the lab's thick steel. He leaned in, taking care with the vials he held, and pressed the listening device's "record" button.

"You performed the transfusion with a Made One and that creature." Gabin, his voice angry.

No one spoke that way to Fukkes without dire consequences.

"Of course I did, fool." Fukkes said in his most pompous voice.

"Now he has gained some of her Essence."

Who was "he?" Calix needed a name. He'd begun to sweat. Any minute, someone could round the corner.

"Obviously." Fukkes again. "But we stand no chance of our plan coming to fruition if she's distraught over the creature's death."

"Bah. There must have been another way."

"And what might that have been?" Fukkes' tone grew increasingly icy.

Gabin harrumphed. "It's done, but it leaves us open when they take his blood. The properties are so well camouflaged in the Made One. They won't be in the man you healed."

Name him, you shotes. Calix hoped the spider engorged by its "victim's" blood would be enough.

"Stop whining," Fukkes said. "So they take his blood. They'll have no idea what they're looking at or what we're doing."

Gabin scoffed. "They aren't as dumb as you believe them to be. Caution is everything."

Footsteps sounded down the hall, coming closer. Calix had no choice but to...

Calix palm-printed the lock and breezed into the lab, startling the two men.

"What are you doing here?" Fukkes barked.

He'd better sell his dumb routine. "Bringing the lab the requested samples, sir."

"We didn't request any samples." Fukkes' eyes pulsed with a calm fury that gave Calix chills.

Gabin laid a hand on Fukkes' shoulder. "It must've been Marley."

Fukkes gave Calix a long look. "Indeed."

Calix placed the fake samples in one of the open sample trays, bowed to each of the men, and left, pausing after the door slid shut behind him.

"I don't like him, and I don't trust him," Fukkes said.

"He's talented." Gabin.

"Many are. Set a Watcher on him."

"People will notice. A Watcher is a bit extreme."

"Extreme times," Fukkes said. "Extreme measures."

"You read that somewhere."

Fukkes laughed, a thin, watery sound that chilled Calix's blood. "Of course I did."

Calix pulled the listening device from his ear and fisted it. A Watcher. He was doomed.

Rafe was out of danger. As if a shroud had lifted, she could breathe again, smile again, hope again, the feeling euphoric. The healing was progressing at lightning speed after his infusion using the bug. She was shocked. Thrilled, but the bug thing was odd. Odder was Fukkes, whose eyes held a world of deceit and secrets, including the ones about her sisters.

His confirmation that he'd brought them to Eleutia heartened her. They had to be alive.

She'd asked Ulfr about what Fukkes had said, but he'd repeated that he had no idea where they were. She believed him. Maybe, like herself, they'd landed in terrible danger. Or perhaps they were still with the Alchemics. Or lost.

She badgered Ulfr until he begrudgingly agreed to try to contact Fukkes.

The Alpha was many things, both good and bad, but a bullshitter he wasn't. She had hope.

While Rafe recuperated, Kit and he talked about everything from mistrals to the Clan's tidal caves to life on her Earth. Sometimes, he'd get cranky at his own weakness, but she'd charm him into a better mood. Well, not charm exactly. More like kisses and lots of lusting and promised rendezvous. With each day that passed, he grew stronger, healthier.

One afternoon while Rafe was dozing, Ulfr barged in minus his usual blustery manner and suggested she get something to eat. Suspicious of his manner, she nonetheless admitted she was starved. But rather than eating in the dining hall, she'd grab a now-popular sandwich and hustle back to the room.

When she returned to the Alpha's bedchamber, the room was empty. Rafe had disappeared.

Kit stood before the door of the Alpha's den. Should she knock or just barge in?

Two days had passed since Kit had last seen Rafe. Since he'd vanished from the Alpha's bedchamber.

She'd called him, of course, to a repeated, "If you wish to leave a voicemail." She'd left them. Lots.

It felt as if she were playing hide-and-seek with a ghost. He wasn't at home, wasn't in the Alpha's suite. When she went to tend Moonrise, he was nowhere to be found, nor was he in the dining hall or anywhere anyone knew…or would admit to knowing. She'd asked Tilde and Max, Eevon and Thorn the Viking, others she didn't know as well, but who were under Rafe's command. Even Kicks.

No one else seemed concerned.

He'd been sick, near death, and now everyone acted like it was okay for him to vanish. What if he relapsed, was alone, without help?

"Rafe goes off sometimes," Tilde had said. "Alone time, he says."

But why now?

"Rafe can get moody," Max had said. "He's a deep thinker."

True, but he was also one of the most balanced people she knew.

Lucky stars! She was going mad, his absence consuming her. He'd called her his "heartsong." Well, he was *her* heartsong, too. What had changed?

The Alpha had to know, so she stalked him, bearding Ulfr in his den.

The Clan's drilling of troops had increased, as had the frenzy in the armory when she'd stopped by.

War was coming.

Her chest hurt, and she rubbed it, then raised a fisted hand to knock. *Gagh!* Instead, she barged through the unlocked door into the living room, where the Alpha sat on the sofa reading a book, calm as you please, wearing a sort of lounge attire of black silk pants and a t-shirt.

"Where's Rafe?"

He mumbled something, and a panicked thought crashed into her head. "Has he relapsed?"

"No."

"Then where is he?"

Ulfr put aside his book, his face creased with annoyance. "Sit down."

"Is this some kind of a game?" She sat in the chair across from the sofa. "Well?"

The Alpha rose, went to the kitchen, and returned with two glasses and a bottle of kevitt liquor. She'd been told this stuff was potent as hell. He poured her a finger of the frothing red liquor, then half-filled his own glass and belted it down.

He massaged his temple. "I was mated to one of your ilk. I was about to be Alpha, and I needed progeny, a lifemate. A girl child. What could be better than a Made One. So, I won her." Those bright eyes dimmed. "Damn if I didn't fall in love with her. When we Wolven love, it tends to be deep and true. We're wolves, after all. We may not look like it, but at heart, that's who we are. Wolves mate for life, you know. Juliette became my everything." He lifted the bottle and poured enough of the red fire into his glass to kill a mistral. His eyes watered as he drank it down.

"What happened to her?" She'd never asked Rafe.

Ulfr's jaw tightened. "One day… Rafe must've been about seven. Yes. Even then he was a top rider, and Ettie was so proud of him. He rode like the wind, was clever with numbers and machines. He laughed often, which he got from his mam, and he loved the mistrals to obsession. You've seen where that landed him. He was bright and brave and full of himself. Too full of himself. He got into mischief constantly, which she found amusing. Ettie…" He paused and took a long, deep breath.

He was working up to something, but what, Kit couldn't guess.

"She was from a place called Canada. She told me how cold it was there and how much she loved the deep snow. We don't get near as much snow as she described. She missed her home, but she grew to love it here, too." He swallowed hard. "She had midnight hair and dark blue eyes and was the loveliest creature I've ever seen. Late one afternoon, we were talking. Nothing important. We were here in the den, just having one of our usual conversations about... I can't recall what. Rafe was playing in the room. He'd lined up his Wolves, Cats, and Eagles and was staging a battle. Yes, that was it."

The hand he swiped across his face shook, his eyes unfocused and distant.

"Ulfr, are you well?"

He speared her with those Wolfie eyes of his. "Ettie died. She just keeled over and...was gone."

Kit leaned forward, hands clasped. "How? Why?"

His eyes warmed, growing distant again. "She was always fussing with her magnificent hair, which was curly. It annoyed the shote out of her, and, Fates, Ettie once took a scissor and hacked the whole thing off. We ended up laughing about it like a pair of hyenas. Another time she baked Rafe a cake." He smiled. "It was a terrible cake. Lopsided. Ugly. We joked about that, too, and then..."

Kit was stunned at Ulfr sharing such intimate memories. "Rafe saw her die?"

"Yes."

He must have been crushed. Traumatized. Unable to understand.

It was obvious Ulfr hadn't gotten over her death. She felt for him and suspected his current mate was a placeholder, a spouse he needed in his job as alpha, as breeding stock and little more. How sad.

"Why did she die?" Kit said.

He gave her teeth. "The Alchemics told me that it was a byproduct of her Making. They said sudden death sometimes occurs with your kind."

Her kind. A Made One. She was doomed, the clock ticking. Best to put that aside. For now. "Why did you never tell him before this?"

He straightened, donning the mantle of Alpha. "We have rules on

Eleutia, imposed by the Alchemics. They've multiplied over the years, and as much as possible, I obey them for the good of the Clan. I've seen firsthand their retaliation on rule breakers. I would have suffered telling him, yes. Worse, Radulfr would have also been drawn into their net. I couldn't have that."

She spread her palms. "But you're telling me."

"Fukkes 'happened' to call but an hour ago. For a chat. To clarify, he said." Ulfr slapped his knees. "They're more crooked than a wildewood tree. He thought to mention how they've improved the Making process. That Made Ones no longer end suddenly or run out of time."

"You're obviously wary. Are they telling the truth?"

"In this instance, I believe they are. Not that I trust them."

"I see. Juliette's death must have been devastating for both you and Rafe."

"Which is why I warned him to stay away from you."

"It was *you* who had Rafe search for me."

"No, it was those farking Alchemics who insisted on it, much to my dismay. Wouldn't you know my willful son would come to care deeply for you. He shouldn't suffer, not as I suffered."

She sighed. "At least now your attitude toward me makes sense."

He cleared his throat. "Apologies. That was not well done of me."

"I understand, at least about your point of view. I expect I'm a horrible reminder of your loss. But none of that explains why Rafe has disappeared."

His eyes sparked with anger. "I know!"

She took a sip of her drink, and fire lanced down her throat.

"When Rafe was young, as Alpha, I wasn't around much. Not enough. It was Ettie who raised him. He was her world. Rafe adored his mam. Her death...it changed him. He already had Alpha tendencies. His mother's death solidified them. He became obsessed with protecting everyone and everything he loved."

Yes, Rafe was protective, but Kit was missing a huge chunk of where Ulfr was going with this. His father might have warned him off, but Rafe often ignored his father's wishes. "He's known from the beginning that I'm a Made One. Why now?"

Ulfr growled. "Because I just told him, foolish woman!"

"Told him *what?*"

He sprang to his feet and paced, his hands clasped behind his back. "I just told him how and why his mam died. All these years, he believed her heart failed. A natural thing, unrelated to her Making. I let the lie stand." He stopped directly in front of her. "After he recovered from the goddart's poison, I told him how Ettie had really died, and I said that you would probably die the same way."

Oh.

When she started to speak, he held up a hand. "Let me finish. The boy has given me just about every white hair on my head. He's not an egoist or selfish or self-important. He's got more courage than is good for him. He's strong. A warrior. But your death…it would crush him because he felt he should protect you and he couldn't. Not from that." He shook his head. "Now he's eating himself away from the inside out. The conflict's within himself, see? It's killing him. He went off to ponder the divergent desire to love you and the fear of knowing you might die at any minute."

"But you just said the Alchemics had fixed those issues. Did you tell him that, too?"

He slumped back in his chair. "I've tried. He's not answering his phone. Worse, he hasn't responded to my Alpha's call. He's a planner, so I'm sure he's projecting a dozen scenarios about how and when you'll meet your end. It horrifies him. I made your death sound inevitable."

They both were silent for long moments, then the Alpha poured himself another drink.

She might be furious with Ulfr, but she got why he'd done it. "He's trying to resolve this inner battle himself. Or perhaps he's simply trying to forget me."

The Alpha laughed. "If only I knew. My boy—he's a great one for reaching out when others need help. When the pain is his? He goes all tortola."

"Tortola? Turtle dove?"

He sat back down, his brows beetled. "Of course not. It's a hard-shelled creature with scaly skin and claws. It draws into itself."

Ah, a turtle.

"Now what are you going to do about it?" he said.

A wisp of hope blossomed. Rafe had deep feelings for her, and he had the strength to care for her more than his fear of her death. She was sure of it. But perhaps he simply wished to erase her from his life, as if she'd never existed.

No, that wasn't Rafe.

It was a terrible thing, imagining your loved one could die in an instant, a death he saw as inescapable. She was intimate with that feeling, having watched Sybi and Bree be consumed by the Huntington's. Her heart had bled far more for them than it had for herself. "As you said, Rafe has courage. This doesn't sound at all like him."

His anger sparked. "It's not, which is why it will destroy him."

"You asked what I'm going to do about it?" Kit said. "It's pretty obvious how much I care for him."

"Good." He slapped his knees and stood. "I was wrong, you see. Wrong not to want you together. Wrong not to tell Rafe earlier about his mother's passing, so he could absorb it. It came to me only the other night that I wouldn't have missed a day with Juliette. Not a single day."

That she understood. "I'll find him."

He pressed a hand to her shoulder and squeezed. "It won't be hard. I had word he returned home this afternoon."

She peered up at that lined face, aged, yet so like Rafe's. "You realize, he's the one who will have to choose."

CHAPTER SEVENTEEN

K it's steps were slow as she walked the path to Rafe's house. It had taken her time to decide how to present herself. Flowy skirt or tight jeans? Red shoes or black boots?

She'd chosen the skirt, boots, and a button-down shirt, wearing her knives, but keeping her hair loose.

Perhaps all foolishness, but it mattered that he saw her as strong and competent, but also as feminine and alluring. She wasn't sure of her plan, nor had she any idea how he'd react.

He *got* her, so he must know how badly he was hurting her. And that ticked her off.

The late afternoon's pewter skies reflected her mood, with greenish storm clouds threatening. She could picture the sea churning with the angry colors of the Atlantic.

Her mouth dried. Her steps faltered. She stopped. Her plan might be a bad one when her emotions felt like a crazy tilt-a-whirl.

Fark that.

She trotted up the small rise, the gloomy day casting shadows across Rafe's home. Even the riot of flowers looked glum. She heard his commanding voice come from behind the barn, and she squeezed her fists, stiffened her spine, and strode forward.

Standing in the center of the ring, Rafe was working Moonrise and Nightfall, who raced around the fenced perimeter. She drank him in. He stood relaxed, his face wearing a hint of a smile. He waved an arm, and the mistrals turned, cantering in the opposite direction. She paused and simply watched the poetry of the mistrals and of the man she loved.

Lucky stars.

"Love" was such a small word, really. Four letters. Brief and to the point. Yet it made her heart clench, her pulse race, her mouth dry.

"Love" made her fear.

All it took was a glance at the broad-shouldered, tawny-haired man and feelings avalanched, freezing her, its power stealing her breath.

What if...? No what ifs. She forced one foot in front of the other and in too few steps reached the corral's fence and leaned her arms atop the crosspiece. Rafe knew she was there, but he failed to acknowledge her. She didn't wave because she didn't know if he'd wave back.

"Love" was also a knife.

Even in the gloom, he wore sunglasses. Perhaps his eyes had dulled when he'd gotten his first glimpse of her. Or maybe they'd brightened at seeing her here.

A heartbeat later, Kit squared her shoulders. For all the pain, "Love" was a treasure not to be squandered.

She climbed the fence and dropped inside as a dust devil swirled across the corral. Rafe's hand made a chopping motion and the mistrals froze, chests heaving from their exertion.

Though Rafe faced her, he didn't approach. "What's up?"

"I need some help."

He just stood in the center of the ring, hands on hips, and waited. A patient man was Rafe. She refused to have this conversation when ten yards separated them, so she walked forward until they were almost nose to nose. He must have released the mistrals because Moonrise came up behind her, rubbing her nose on Kit's back.

"Hello, girl."

Moonrise nickered.

Kit reached over her shoulder to scratch Moonrise's forehead. And...she was using the mistral as a distraction. "Like I said, I need your help Rafe."

"With what?" He tilted his head upward. "You'd best hurry. We've got bad weather coming."

Hurry, huh. "There's this guy I know, and he vanished. I need to understand why he didn't leave a note or say goodbye."

What she didn't say was, *I'm not going to keel over and die like your mom. I'm not going to run away. I'm not going to leave you.* But she believed all those things.

Rafe shrugged. "Sometimes people can't explain themselves."

She wished she could see his eyes. While his face wore that blank expression, his eyes always told her stories. She reached to remove his sunglasses.

He stepped back. "Don't." He returned his attention to Nightfall, made a rising hand motion with his palm, and the mistral reared, front legs pawing the air, tossing his head and whinnying.

"Rafe."

He paid no attention, setting Nightfall on a sidestepping path diagonally across the corral, and took one more look at the sky.

"Don't you see me anymore, Rafe?"

"I'm right here talking to you," he said in that horrible flat voice.

She wouldn't cry, wouldn't beg.

What to do? How to get him to open up to her? She could kiss him or take all her clothes off. But she wasn't sure she could handle him not reacting or pushing her away.

The wind picked up, scouring her cheek with dust. Clouds churned the darkening sky.

Rafe had move toward the opposite side of the corral, his back to her as he worked Nightfall.

Crack! Lightning scored the sky.

"Hurry!" Rafe shouted at her. "Barn! These storms are danger-ous." Rafe raced toward the corral's gate and flung it wide.

The mistrals tore through it. Another boom, a shriek of wind, and a snap. She'd heard that sound in Maine, just before a tree crashed to earth.

"Run, Kit!"

She ran.

A giant pine on the rise above began what looked like a slow descent to earth. But it wasn't slow. The tree would kill her.

Rafe raced toward her, and she moved, but somehow, the huge tree was faster than she, her heart flaring, mind frozen, the immense trunk picking up speed.

"Kit!" he shouted.

"Stop, Rafe! I've got this!"

Timing was everything, and she'd have to time this right. She backed up further and further. Wait. Wait. *Now.*

She ran, leapt, somersaulting over the now-vertical treetop's trunk as it crashed to the earth. Landing, she rolled to a stand.

Rafe scooped her over his shoulder and ran. Another strike, another snap, another pine toppling, its branches alight with flames, creaking and groaning as it descended toward them.

They made the barn, and he set her on her feet, then peered outside just as the second pine crashed atop the corral, flattening it.

The mistrals and horses were going crazy, Moonrise and Nightfall prancing, eyes rolling, the two horses squealing while Daybreak pounded his stall door with his forelegs.

The boom and crack of lightening split the air. The barn swayed with a terrible groan.

"The barn won't hold!" he shouted over the shrieks of the wind. "Let's get the animals out of here!"

He flung open Daybreak's stall door, while she ran first to the two horses, snapped leads onto their halters, and led them out. They fought her, Barron pawing the air in terror.

She dug in her heels, then Moonrise appeared, which calmed the horses enough for her to leap onto the mistral's back, wrapping the horse's leads around her hand.

Rafe took a running jump, flinging himself onto Daybreak,

Nightfall beside them. He whistled, and they charged out of the barn.

Rain pounded them, so much rain she couldn't make out where they were headed, so she let Moonrise follow her sire while Kit clung with her legs, one hand wrapped through the mistral's mane, gripping the two horses' leads with her other.

"Re-see the l—ds," Rafe barked.

The din of the rain stole his words. *What was he saying?*

Her arm holding the horses' leads jerked backward, but Moonrise kept moving forward. She flew off the mistral's back.

Lightning split the sky overhead as she twisted, hoping to stick a landing. Instead, she thudded onto the ground, breath stolen.

Horror consumed her. She'd be trampled, dragged by the ropes she'd...

A small, sane part of her uncurled her hand, freeing the leads, while Moonrise circled her, protecting her from the frantic horses' hooves.

A third snap cracked the air.

She rolled onto her belly, her skirts tangled about her, got to her knees, blinded by the pounding rain, deaf from the screech of the falling pine. Everything ached. Her back, her ribs, her neck. She shook her head to clear it and pressed against Moonrise. Hands digging into the mistral's curly coat, she pulled herself upward.

The immense pine—bigger than the rest—began to topple. It would flatten her, kill Moonrise.

"Go, Moonrise!"

The damned mistral kneeled! Kit managed to sling a leg up and onto her back, and Moonrise leapt into the air.

Kit clung to the mistral's mane as she peered at the earth below. Rafe, Daybreak, and Nightfall were out of the tree's path. *But the horses!*

The pine thundered to earth, its huge limbs scoring the ground and crushing Barron, his screams silenced.

Moonrise landed. Kit lay there, sprawled across the mistral's withers and neck, catching her breath.

The cold rain might be pounding them, but hot words scorched her ear as Rafe peered up at her. "You stupid, stupid woman."

She pushed herself up. "Don't you talk to me like that, Rafe."

"I'll talk to you any way I like. When we left the barn, I told you to release the leads."

"And I couldn't hear you over the rain! The horses were panicked."

"You... *Fark!*" He stomped away.

A patch of sun broke through the clouds, the pounding rain softening to a drizzle. She slid off the mistral in an ungainly fashion and when her feet hit the ground she kept going, so shaky she couldn't hold herself upright. Rafe's arm snaked around her waist, halting her collapse. His face was a blank mask, but his waves of anger scorched her.

Kit pushed away from him and wobbled toward the downed pine where the gray gelding lay, a crushed mass of blood and bone. She pressed her fist to her mouth so as not to cry out.

Baloo trotted round and round the downed tree, nickering and whinnying for her stablemate. Moonrise stepped forward, steam rising from her soggy coat, and nuzzled Kit.

She brushed her cheek across Moonrise's velvet nose, then stepped toward the bay. The mare tossed her head. "Hush, girl. Hush." Closer still, and with careful deliberation she reached out and gripped the bay's lead. "Hush." She walked to the black mare and stroked her neck. "Hush."

The corral was a total loss, but the three trees had thankfully missed the barn, and it had miraculously held. Without turning to face him, she said, "Is it safe to take them back?"

"Yes."

The rain had softened to a sprinkle as she led the bay to the barn, Moonrise following.

What was Rafe thinking? Feeling? Oh, he was pissed all right, that was obvious. They could have all died in that freak storm. Well, they hadn't. She wanted to scream, *See, Rafe, how easy it is to die?*

The sun parted the screen of clouds. Even so, a chill had seeped into her bones that even the sun's warmth couldn't fix.

Kit led Baloo to her stall, Moonrise nudging her shoulder every so often. She settled the black, dried her off, and freshened her grain and water. Rafe had returned Nightfall to his stall, and she brought Moonrise to hers, got more towels, and dried her as best she could. Water droplets made little plops when they hit the stall's straw floor.

A burn between her shoulder blades. Rafe was watching her. Somehow she got her icy fingers to continue rubbing Moonrise until she began to tremble. Nonetheless, she made sure Moonrise had a fresh bucket of oats and one of water before she closed the stall door behind her.

Something scratchy wrapped around her, and she was lifted off her feet and carried to the wooden bench against the wall at the end of the barn. Rafe sat, nestling her on his lap. Warmth had begun to seep into her from the blanket and the furnace that was Rafe.

"Why are you so angry with me?" she said. "It wasn't because I didn't release the leads."

"No." He ran a hand up and down her back. "You could have been killed, and I imagined the light fading from your eyes, a light that I can't live without. I've been a total ass and cruel, and I'm hating myself. For hiding away, for not dealing with my feelings, for hurting you."

He laid the back of his head against the stone wall, eyes closed, face stretched taut. "I'd no idea my father's words would turn me back into that seven-year-old boy. That's no excuse. But I'm sorry, Kit, so farking sorry." He opened his eyes, but they were unfocused, as if he were watching a faraway scene.

"When my mam died.. I can still see her falling—it seemed to take forever—and then she was gone. One minute, laughing, the next, empty. A husk. A memory. Her death altered me. Inside. I thought I'd addressed it. I thought I'd tempered the anger, the grief. Yet when Da told me the truth of how she died…" He swiped a hand across his face. "I kept seeing you, Kitlyn, you, falling. Empty. Gone."

She nuzzled closer. "Ulfr told me some of it. And I'm so sorry.

But tell me this, Rafe, would you have missed even a moment with her?"

Silence fell, and he squeezed his eyes tight. "Of course not. I admit I'm a despicable fool. I wanted time to think, with little concern of how I was hurting you. Forgive me. Please."

She thought of her crazy plan if war came. How it would be Rafe's turn to forgive her. Forgiveness was a treasure, and so often just out of reach. "I do, Rafe."

"What say you to a damaged man more fearful of your death than of a dakos' claws or a goddart's sting?"

"I'd say, yes, please."

Rafe didn't understand how she could forgive him. His heart had stopped when she'd tumbled to the ground in the path of that falling tree. When she'd escaped death, he'd been stomach-clenching, brain-scrambling furious for all the wrong reasons. Now she lay nestled in his arms, and she still wanted him. She shouldn't. He'd been a prick and a coward. He'd *hurt* her.

He'd been sure she'd storm out. Except when had his Kit ever done the expected? He almost laughed. She'd stayed. And she wanted him still, fool that he was.

She'd stopped shivering, and her lips had warmed from blue back to their blush pink. As he leaned forward to kiss her, her breath, sweet as honeysuckle on the vine, mingled with his. Her lips parted, and he devoured her. She let him inside, their tongues dueling in some frantic wish to meld the two of them into one. Wherever she touched him, sparks lit his flesh. He wanted all of her, everything.

"Here," she said. "Now, Rafe."

Kit slipped from his lap to kneel on the bench, her arms around his shoulders, her clit pressing against his cock, and he was going to farking explode. He craved her so bad he shook.

He steadied his fingers, but it seemed to take hours to undo the buttons and part the shirt hiding those lovely breasts. Once she was revealed, he drank her in. A scattering of freckles sprinkled the round beauties, their dusky pink tips tight with need. He pushed her shirt off her shoulders and cupped one breast, dipping his head low to suckle the other. His lips closed around her peaked nipple, and he slashed his tongue across that taut flesh. Her moan stiffened his cock to a white-hot poker. Her hands roamed his back, her lips kissing his chest, his neck, his ear, nipping and biting…he wasn't getting enough of her, not near enough.

He was out of time. He held her waist as he ripped off her panties, then his fingers explored her sweet folds, so wet and plush and warm. His groan mingled with hers.

"Kitlyn, love." His index finger slid over those swollen lips, and when he found that nubbin, his fingers danced.

"Rafe!" She zipped open his jeans and pulled out his cock, fingers tightening, stealing his words.

If he didn't get inside her soon, he'd die. "*Now*, beauty."

She lifted her bottom, her hand fisting his cock, and she slid down onto him, down and down and… *There.*

The Fates, he had to stop. He held her tight, panting so he wouldn't go off like some teenaged pup. "Time out."

"Not a chance." Her hot walls squeezed him tight.

Rafe was inside her. Oh, lucky stars, so good. His big hands lifted her by the waist and slammed her down onto him. And stopped. He was hard and pulsing, his cock huge, and she wanted him to move so badly, so badly. She licked his chest, his neck, bit his pectoral, and still he held her. "Rafe."

His face taut with pleasure, lips pulled tight. Her Rafe, her beautiful man. She shivered and rocked, so close, so close. With her knees resting on the bench, she pushed upward. He slid almost out of her, then she lowered herself back down. Up, down, he squeezed her breast, took her lips in a vicious kiss, teeth clanking, tongues fighting, daring each other to go higher. His hands clamped her tight, and he pistoned into her, over and over, and she was climbing to that stratosphere, pleasure aching her breasts, her clit, her flesh, his mouth devouring her. Her hands tightened on his shoulders and he sped up. And it felt so good. Beyond good. One of his hands worked its way between them, finding her clit. Oh *yes*. He squeezed.

Pleasure blasted from her curling toes to the tips of her fingers, her back bowed, hands digging into his shoulders, and she came and came and came. He pounded into her harder, faster, pumped again, again, his arms banded around her, and he stiffened, cock pulsing inside her, his groan quaking her with aftershock tingles.

Rafe bowed his head and pulled her to him, and she lay ragdoll limp against him, his musky scent perfume to her senses.

He chuckled, and she squeezed him tight, clasping him within, unwilling for him to leave.

"Something funny?" she said in a breathy voice that couldn't be hers.

"You wrecked me."

"I think we wrecked each other." She couldn't stop touching him, petting him. How many years had it been since she'd made love? Never. She'd *never* felt like this, so thoroughly loved, so wrung out and pleasured she might simply stay here forever. "We don't have to move, do we?"

He raised his head, a grin spreading across his lips. Her hand smoothed down his cheek, then carded his sweat-soaked hair. He stood, taking her with him, holding her bottom, an arm at her waist. "Of course we do." He strode from the barn, carrying her as if she were thistle down.

"We're naked, Rafe. Outside!"

"Yes, we are."

"Your jeans are around your ankles."

"That's true. Awkward."

"What if someone sees?"

"So?"

Oh, my.

He shuffled down the path to his home and went inside. "I'm looking for an encore."

"Really?"

"Maybe two." He nuzzled her neck.

She laughed, couldn't stop herself.

"You're a banquet, beauty. How could I stop with one course?"

He snared her eyes. And Kit saw passion and desire and care, yet fear's glimmer hid in their depths, too.

He put a knee on the bed and laid her down in one smooth movement.

"Boots off. Jeans, too," she said.

In seconds, they were both naked, and her eyes feasted. He was a banquet, too, from his strong calves and thick thighs to his jutting erection to his chest that, the longer she looked, the faster it heaved in and out. Kit curled to a sitting position and roved her hands across his broad shoulders, down his muscled chest, then further downward.

He trapped her hands with his. "Wait."

"Why?"

"I've imagined this moment. Planned it. I would have forever, Kit."

She froze. Did she want that? Rafe, forever? A dream transformed to reality. But… "I have to be sure about my sisters, to know what happened to them. Fukkes said something, and I… I must know."

He lifted his head, and his kiss was long and languorous. "Together, then?"

"You'd help me?"

"A partnership, love. And a promise."

She buried her head in his shoulder. "You knew I'd say that about them."

"Of course I did. I'm a planner, remember?"

"You're such a bad, bad man."

"True." His breath tickled her ear. "But am I enough? For you?"

"Oh, Rafe, more than, my love. You're everything."

"Together, then."

And the fierce joy in his eyes scorched her soul.

· · ·

They'd made love twice more, once in bed, slow and gentle, and again in the shower.

She held his face between her palms. "You are my Christmas, Thanksgiving, and New Year's all rolled into one."

He shook his head. "No idea."

"I know. You are the most unexpected gift."

"Are those tears?"

"We're in the shower, silly. How could they be?"

"Ah, my beauty, my Kit."

When they napped, Rafe curled around her, and she slept with an unremembered contentment.

The buzz of the phone startled her awake.

Rafe's arm reached across her. "Sorry, beauty." He flicked open the phone. "Yes?" Seconds later, he snapped it shut and took his time kissing her near senseless again. His eyes ate her up as he ran a hand down her body. "I've got to go."

"What's up?"

"That was Max. They've called an emergency council meeting."

"About what?"

His jaw tightened.

She knew. "I'm going."

"You won't be able to speak. At a formal meeting, only council members can do so. Are you sure you want to come, Kit?"

"Absolutely."

CHAPTER EIGHTEEN

When Kit entered the council chambers with Rafe, two dozen men and several women clustered about the circular room ringed with interconnected desks. Max was there, as were Tilde and Eevon. She recognized several others, including Yuan, Kicks, Gus, Talos, Arne, Yuma the librarian, and the Alpha's mate. Seated at the Alpha mate's right was Meela, the mocha-skinned dragon who guarded access to his offices. She nodded to the woman who had helped her find the encrypted papers that even Max had failed to decipher. Meela's lips bowed into an almost-smile, and she nodded, then rang the brass bell that sat in front of her. The doors swung closed, and the council members moved to their seats.

Rafe led her up three stairs to a gallery that held a few observers. Down below, at the far end of the circle, the Alpha entered through a carved door. The room hushed. He opened his mouth to speak, but the entry doors opened once again. In bustled Inga. Given the Alpha's hot look, Kit was glad they'd been on time.

Before Kit took her seat, Rafe clasped her upper arms and moved his lips over hers in a slow, sensuous kiss that lasted until someone cleared their throat.

He'd made a declaration for all to see.

Blushing, but pleased, Kit sat in the front row as Rafe circled the room and pulled out the chair to the right of his father.

Ulfr peered down at his son. "How gracious of you to join us, Radulfr."

"The pleasure is mine, Alpha."

Ulfr grunted and turned his attention to the council. "We have several items to discuss. First, the use of the goddart's sting on my son, Rafe."

Murmurs flew around the room.

Meela hit the bell, its full sound demanding everyone's attention. Silence.

The Alpha frowned. "You've heard of its recent use. How it almost killed our First Commander. Some of you are aware that the arrow was shot from within the walls of WolfHome."

Angry voices rose, and the Alpha let them play out. Ulfr's mate looked bored, while Inga was shouting at the council member seated next to her.

The bell pealed again. Silence.

"Inga?" the Alpha said.

The blonde stood and nodded to Ulfr. "Alpha. First Commander. Council members. We either harbor a traitor, or someone has infiltrated WolfHome from another Clan. The latter isn't hard to do, since our open-door policy allows visitors access to our towns and their environs. The Alpha has initiated a search comprising both Peacekeepers and our wolf brothers and sisters. We will find the perpetrator."

The day Rafe had been shot, hadn't Max said something about an Anti-Made One sentiment? It was hard to remember, her mind a fog of those events.

After Inga spoke, angry words and a few fist pumps circled the room. Yet Rafe sat with his arms crossed, sleepy-eyed, tilting his chair back on two legs. He watched Max, who shot him a questioning look. Rafe nodded.

What was that all about?

Again, the clang of the bell.

Silence.

"Our investigation is in motion," the Alpha said, "so we will table the talk of the goddart's sting for now. Onto our second bit of business and the reason we called this meeting. We have received a demand from the Cats. They insist The Challenge be held in four weeks at CatHome, the winner of which will claim Kitlyn, the Made One, as mate." He paused, his eyes snaring those of the council.

Rafe had warned her this might happen, but it still grated. She ground her teeth so she wouldn't yell, "How dare they?"

"The Cats," Ulfr continued, "give us three days to hand over Kitlyn. This isn't a bluff. Our scouts report hundreds of warriors on the move from CatHome. They say if we do not hand over the Made One, they declare war."

War!

A cacophony broke out across the hall amongst the council members, as well as those in the gallery, most shouting "War!" with enthusiasm.

She stood up and yelled, "I am not a piece of meat!"

No one paid the least bit of attention. *Idiots!*

She wasn't a bargaining chip. She wouldn't be bartered. Nor would she stand by while two Clans warred over her.

The idea was absurd.

Except neither the Cats nor the Wolves were joking.

These fools would go to war, and the Wolves would battle a Clan that outnumbered them two to one. Not that a Cat victory was a given. The Wolves were clever and strong and protected by mighty walls.

But how many on both sides would fall? How many would be wounded? How many mates would suffer? How many children would be left fatherless or motherless?

An image coalesced of the little boy, Vantha, with his bright smile and proud papa, losing that father to some Cat's blade. A chorus of weeping Vanthas deafened her.

At least she'd prepared.

The Alpha shouted "Stop!"

The room calmed, and a more civilized discussion broke out, with most of the council members embracing war. They needed her as a babymaker, not to mention the Wolves' pride. The Cats had gotten too big for their britches, and the Wolves could not risk becoming lesser in the hierarchy of packs.

Inga and a few others insisted on giving her to the Cats. The Wolves could enter the contest, they reasoned. They could fight for her.

Few agreed.

Finally, Rafe stood, arms crossed. Much as his father had done, his eyes snared the entire council. Then he looked at Kit and smiled. The Alpha glared, and Rafe laughed.

"Hear me," he said. "Kitlyn is right—she is not a piece of meat."

Rafe got it, he so got it.

"No, not a piece of meat," he continued. "Nor a bargaining chip. That is how the Cats see her. She is one of us. A woman we have brought into our Clan. A Wolf. I vote for war!"

What!

Meela chimed her bell.

"We vote!" the Alpha said.

The box Meela produced was the size of a cookie tin. The Alpha wrote on a piece of paper and slipped it into the box. Rafe voted next, and passed it on, each council member making their opinion known. When the box returned to Meela, she cast her vote, then stood, reached for the key on a chain around her neck, and unlocked the box.

Meela read each slip of paper—yea or nay for war—making a pile to the left and one to the right. When she closed the box's lid, one pile was far higher than the other. She whispered in the Alpha's ear and again chimed her bell.

The Alpha stood. "We go to war!"

"War!" echoed many voices.

Kit stood. "No!"

She was ignored. Big surprise.

She walked down the gallery steps, and as she crossed the hall toward Ulfr, murmurs replaced the shouts of war. Rafe was expressionless, arms crossed, chair tilted back. Ulfr was red-faced. "Return to your seat, Made One." She kept walking. Meela shook her head. That didn't stop her, either.

Kit swiped up the padded ringer and hit the bell.

Silence.

She turned to face the council, angling her body so Ulfr could see her, too.

"You have treated me well here on Eleutia, brought me into your Clan, and I have seen and learned many things. Your world is filled with intelligent, wise people. It's a beautiful world. So for the love of the Fates, how can you contemplate going to war over me, a single individual?"

Ulfr stood. "Please return to your seat, Made One. You have not been given permission to speak."

"Forgive my impertinence, Alpha, but I don't care. I am one. Hundreds may die, thousands may be injured, humans and wolves and cats. Widows will be created, along with fatherless and motherless children and pups."

"Women do not fight in wars, Made One!" someone shouted.

Most stared at her as if she were speaking Klingon. Except Inga, who smirked.

Ulfr signaled the guards, who marched toward her. It seemed she was to be ejected from the council chambers.

Rafe stood. "Halt!" he said, his words freezing the guards. "Let Ma'am Kitlyn speak."

"Have you gone mad?" Ulfr said.

She closed her eyes and sighed. Then she again raised her voice over the murmurs of the councilors. "I will do anything to stop this war. What can I do? Tell me, and I'll do it."

Rafe approached and took her hand. He spoke softly, just to her. "You can do nothing, Kit. War has been declared, and war it will be."

She didn't know what to say, so she crossed the council chamber and walked out the door.

. . .

She trudged back to Rafe's home, where they'd agreed to meet after the council meeting. Kit had never been more terrified in her life. Pacing, she calmed herself down. Once the meeting concluded, Rafe would be home, they'd make dinner and...

Was this really happening?

All along, she'd been practicing, not only the Eleutian skills, but her taekwondo and karate, her gymnastics and Nihon Jujutsu. She was in the best shape of her life, even better than her circus years. She had the leathers Talos had made for her and had been working on Tilde to bring her around to Kit's way of thinking. She would need help to bring her plan to fruition.

Only three days until they'd start killing each other. For all the movies she'd seen, the articles she'd read, the stories she'd been told, she had never been to war. Though she could picture what it was like, she suspected her imaginings were but a shadow of the real thing.

Throughout her life, when wars had broken out in various countries, and when the U.S. sent soldiers to places like Iraq and Afghanistan, she would wonder what the soldiers and the Native peoples felt. How did one live in constant fear? Of death. Of a loved one's death.

She might know of debilitating injuries and PTSD, but not the uncertainty of if and when the boom might fall. How did one deal with lost income, the absence of privacy, and the dearth of laughter? How did one survive war's aftermath, which rippled through the years?

Three days to war.

Funny how there were different flavors of fear. This felt unlike her fear of losing Rafe's love. Different again to the fear of death's inexorable march toward her and her sisters. She could picture the loss of love and its aftermath. She understood their disease, as well, with its markers of what to expect and when.

But war.... There was nothing predictable or comprehensible about it. How did one *do* war? She didn't know.

Kit would make certain that, with at least this particular conflict, she never found out.

That evening, Kit and Rafe cleared his dining table of the simple meal they'd prepared. They'd wanted to be alone after the meeting, not surrounded by others in the dining hall, so they'd made fresh venison, green beans, and rice the color of pansies. Cleaning the dishes could wait. Now, Rafe wanted to sit in front of the fireplace and talk.

She snuggled beside him, and it was the most exquisite sensation. His arms around her were firm, and every so often he'd kiss her cheek or nuzzle her neck, building her anticipation for lovemaking.

Resting in his arms, she felt she'd finally found home. She didn't want to be anywhere else or think of anything but existing in this moment.

Which was impossible.

In three days, all this would be vapor in the wind.

Rafe grew unsettled, his vibe scraping her skin. And though he tried to conceal it, he was failing dismally.

"Tell me what's bothering you," she said. "The war?"

"How could anything be bothering me with you in my arms?"

She ran her fingers across his scruff. "You're deflecting."

He chuffed out a laugh. "Perhaps."

"And...?" She took his palm and kissed it.

"If you keep doing that, I'll—"

"Rafe."

"I'm worried about my da."

"Your father? Why? Ulfr's strong and extremely competent."

He squeezed her arm, then rose and disappeared into the kitchen. Minutes later he returned with a bottle and two small glasses. He set them down on the floor, uncorked the bottle, and poured each glass half full with clear liquid. "Fruit of the ilaberry bush. It's found by the ocean and only produces fruit every three years. The wine is rare and fine." He handed her a glass and raised his to his mouth.

"Wait. Let's clink glasses and make a toast."

His eyes warmed to that caramel color she loved. "And what toast would you make, beauty?"

"To us. To..." She'd been about to say "forever." Oh, how she wished. "To all our tomorrows."

He tipped his glass forward and tapped hers.

When she sipped, a bouquet of flavors beguiled her mouth, both sweet and tart. "Please tell me what's concerning you about your father."

"He's not right. Something's up with him. I fear he will put himself in the kind of danger that will bring him to the Shade."

"The Shade?"

"That which is the journey unto death."

"It sounds like a quote."

"From *The Book of the Fates*."

"Which is?"

"The Heavens' guide to life." He kissed her nose, licking the tip. "It has much to say that is good, though the Alchemics claim it's drivel. I tend to rely on myself rather than Sky intervention, though I respect the Fates, as do most of Wolf Clan. We study the book from childhood, and every Clan member knows some passages by heart."

"Yuan never mentioned it."

"That's odd. Perhaps she didn't want to influence you. Sky is the Fates' Paladin."

"A defender?"

"Of a sort. More like a guide or a counselor. I'll see you get a copy of the book. While most pay the Fates homage, too many lose their way and treat it as dogma."

"The Shade is a metaphor?"

He cocked his head. "Good question. I would say no, that it's literal."

"A place?"

"A destination." He scraped his hand across his chin, then took another sip of his wine. "The Journey to reach the Shade is arduous and dependent on the life you lived on Eleutia. A good life gives you many aids on the journey. A bad life, and you journey alone, without weapons or comrades."

"I'd like to read it. An audiobook would be better."

"A what?"

"A sound recording of a book?"

"Ah, a sonos. Your wish, my command."

"I like the sound of that."

He raised a brow, eyes laughing. "You do, eh?"

"Oh, yes, but we're sidetracked. What you said about your father, is it just a feeling of yours? Or has he said something?"

Rafe shook his head. "No, the old Wolf hasn't said a word. But for the past week he's stepped up my "Alpha lessons," which is what I call them. Preparing me. It feels wrong. I don't like what that implies. Giving up has never been his style."

"You'll become Alpha when he dies or relinquishes his Alpha-hood?"

"Not necessarily."

The night had grown chill, and Rafe strode to the fireplace, added some kindling, and set it ablaze. He remained crouched by the fire, though he turned to face her. "To become Alpha, you must meet challenges, both intellectual and physical. But all my life Ulfr has prepared me to assume a role I'm not sure I want. The protective stuff, the guidance, steering the Clan, I would gladly accept those burdens. The politics? I despise them."

"But it's a package. I understand. I saw that look you gave Max during the council meeting. Is that why?"

"No."

"Then what?"

A knock pounded the door. He gave her a brief kiss and went to answer it. Quiet voices came from the mudroom, while Paulo trotted into the living room and climbed onto the couch beside her.

"Rafe?" she hollered. "Is Paulo allowed on the couch?"

A bark of laughter from the other room. "No one *allows* Paulo to do anything. But he knows if he scratches my couch, he's one dead coywolf."

Paulo's jaws widened into what Kit was sure was a laugh, his tongue drooping out of his muzzle.

Moments later, Rafe returned, Max at his heels. "I've got to go. This won't take long. I should be back within the hour."

A pinch of disappointment, but she nodded and said, "Of course."

"Hey, beauty, don't look so serious." Rafe sauntered over, tipped her chin up, and favored her mouth with a succulent kiss that ended way too soon. "I'll always come back to you."

After he left, she snuggled next to Paulo and commanded the TV to turn on. She watched a nature show and waited…and worried.

Rafe and Max walked toward the barn, out of Kit's ear shot.

"You don't want Kit to know about this?" Max said.

"About the men I've assigned to guard her?" He swiped a hand across his jaw and couldn't stop his chagrinned smile. "Perhaps she knows. It's nothing we've talked about. The men haven't lessened their vigilance, have they?"

"Of course not, Commander."

"Good. I want you to step it up. Team them. Two at a time."

"You're seriously crazy."

"I have a feeling."

Max nodded. "I never like those, but they've proven dead on too often. I'll put your directive in place as soon as I leave you, but…" Max shook his head. "You should talk to her about it. Explain. Keeping things from your mate never ends well, Rafe."

"What do you know about mates? Just do as I say."

Max raised his hands. "Okay. Okay."

The deepened lines bracketing Max's mouth and the puffiness beneath his eyes disturbed Rafe. "You're not taking care of yourself, Ferret."

"Too much to do. Dusan is gone."

"Why? Dusan's a kid. Where would he go?"

"No clue. His room's cleared out. Even his armor and sword are missing from his locker."

"Perhaps to our Timberwolves?"

"I doubt it." Max tapped his lips, his discomfort obvious.

"Why?"

"I suspect he wielded the goddart's sting."

"Dusan?" Rafe said. "The one who's been after Kit? That makes no sense. He's loyal to the bone."

"I thought so, too," Max said. "But why would he leave, especially with war coming? What else could it mean other than that he shot her the first time, then used the sting?"

"First of all, Kit believes the archer who shot her was a woman. And where the Fates would Dusan get a goddart's sting?"

Inside the barn, the mistrals greeted them with nickers and whinnies. Moonrise allowed Rafe to pet her, which was a boon. Kit's influence, he supposed. Had her breeding taken? His father's stallion was potent, but breedings failed more than they succeeded where mistrals were concerned. Time to get the vet up to check on her.

Rafe leaned against Nightfall's stall door. "Damn... Dusan. There has to be another reason why he left."

"I don't see what else it could be." Max scratched Nightfall's forehead. "But my investigation's not done. I have a few more leads to track down. Any word from Calix?"

"We should be stepping up the pressure on the Alchemics. Instead, we're warring with those farking Cats."

"Are you prepared to fight Gato?"

A childhood friend turned enemy. "Absolutely." Daybreak snorted, bringing back memories of how he and the Cat had fought together against the dakos. How Gato had saved his life during the battle of Blazing Sky, and how he'd returned the favor in the next battle.

Max rested a hand on his shoulder. "I remember, Rafe. During the battle, I can take care of him."

"Can you? You look wrung out."

"I'm fine."

"Gato is mine." And he was. He'd been avoiding thoughts of his once-friend. Now he must plan how to end him and defeat the Cats. Though Kit was wrong about the war, he understood. The deaths, the loss, the injuries—both sides always suffered.

He saw no path to a non-violent conclusion. Yet who would win in this war? He suspected it would be the worst of all outcomes— boosting the Alchemics another notch higher.

"Gato is mine," he repeated. "Remember that, all right? And don't get so worn down that you stumble."

His chest puffed. "Me? Stumble?"

Max's bravado hid a gentle soul. He might be the best spy in WolfHome, but he'd been distracted lately.

"That's an order," Rafe said.

Max saluted, except his grin destroyed the gesture. "Yes, sir! Seriously, I'm being careful. They don't call me Ferret for nothing."

Rafe slapped Max on the back. "Truth. Have you finally started courting Tilde?"

Max's eyes danced. "I have. From the gifts I've left, she's convinced herself that it's Ted the Tank, a Wolf who holds no interest for her. I'm enjoying this."

"I can see that. But you've got to leave meaningful gifts, or she'll never send a reply of her interest."

"I know. But I'm having too much fun. There's time."

The Fates, they were out of time. Look how he'd farked up so bad with Kit that he'd almost lost her. "Watch yourself. You like games too much. You could lose her."

"Nope!" Big grin. "She's too hung up on me."

"You're an arrogant asshole."

"True. But Tilde's not. She's so damn smart and witty. Deep, like our caverns by the sea, with unplumbed depths that I can't wait to explore."

"Don't overplay your game is all I'm saying."

"I won't." His smile was self-deprecating. "I'm well and truly smitten. As are you, brother."

"That I am. But keeping up with Kit is like trying to grab smoke. She's more unpredictable than a moregul."

"But twice as sexy."

He laughed. That she was. And an image formed of Kit naked beneath his hands and lips. His heart went into overdrive and his hard-on was instantaneous and painful. "I'd better get back. Ma'am Curious will have about a million questions as to why you were here."

"Kit's a damned independent creature. I still think you should talk to her about her guards."

"And I think you should focus on your task and on that pretty redheaded Wolf."

Max strolled out of the barn whistling.

CHAPTER NINETEEN

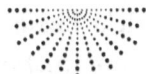

The following day, Rafe's concern for Max grew as he left the war room to check on an arms shipment from the Bear Clan. When they'd talked yesterday, Max had been too confident. Not that he didn't have the right to be so. He was their best. But overconfidence could lead to sloppiness that would get Max killed. Rafe knew his protective inclinations could steer him wrong. He might have corrected his course with Kit and his inexcusable reaction to his mam's death, yet worry for Max still nagged.

To assuage his concern, he found one of his Timberwolves and sent her in search of Max, as well as sending a Peacekeeper to check on the arms shipment.

Rafe changed direction to make his way toward the den of Dusan's brother, Georg. Max had checked, but he wanted to hear and taste the temper of the situation for himself.

Buying Dusan as the archer simply didn't fly. The kid was green as a newborn foal. Knowing the boy since he was a pup, he couldn't believe the Wolf would initiate such a vicious act.

Rafe was about to knock on Georg's door, when Inga appeared, limping down the hall.

"What happened?" he said.

Inga swatted the air. "Nothing big, I just twisted my ankle dismounting. A clumsy thing to do."

"Did you have the healers look at it?"

She smiled up at him. "I'd rather you look at it."

There she went again. Inga wearied him. "Go see Kicks, Inga."

When he moved to step away, her hand gripped his forearm. "Wait."

She had that look on her face, the hungry one that said she wanted to mate with him. He'd made it abundantly clear that the romantic attraction was not a mutual one. She'd also seen him kiss Kit in the council room, a clear declaration of his intent.

"This is beneath you, Inga."

"The only thing I want beneath me is you."

Fates, give him patience. "That's not going to happen."

She twined herself around him like a clamper vine. "It could. Your kitty cat need never know."

He stiffened and began to push her away. "And what kind of man or Wolf would I be if I deceived my mate?"

Inga smiled as she clung to him. "A happy one?"

Impossible to hide his disgust. "Do you know me so little that you would think I would consider such? We're friends, we grew up together, yet you still don't get my dislike of your games."

Inga's eyes widened, then her wrapped firmly around his neck. She pressed herself to him and brought her lips to his.

He turned his head. "What the fark, Inga!"

"You were destined for me, Rafe," she said. "Why fight it?"

A sad byproduct of the decrease in females was a few of those remaining grew entitled, so convinced of their desirability as mates, they lost sight of any wants or desires but their own. He'd thought Inga too smart for that pitfall. It appeared he'd been wrong.

Footsteps behind him. That floral fragrance he'd recognize anywhere.

Rafe shoved Inga away. She bounced off the wall and giggled.

Shote. Kit would rip him a new one. Should he punch Inga. Or flee.

Then warm hands slid up his back, rose to his shoulders, and slipped around his neck.

"Hungry, baby?" Kit said.

His laugh started as a chuckle, but rose from his belly through his chest until his laughter boomed around the hall. He turned to face Kit. "Always for you, beauty."

Her grin was blinding, and it included Inga, who'd begun to slink away from them, face blank, no limp in sight.

"I thought so," Kit said. "She touches you again, she'll be toast."

He nuzzled her neck. "Toast?"

"I'll explain. Later." She tasted his lips and destroyed him yet again.

Two days to war. Kit let Moonrise out into the pasture, then returned to the patched, rebuilt corral. She sighed. The idea that in forty-eight hours people would start killing each other circled her brain like a tracking missile about to detonate.

Kit had prepared as much as she could—provisions, clothes, transportation, and such.

Once she was able to read, she'd enhanced her lessons with Yuan by studying the history books of Eleutia in the library, as well as downloading several onto her tablet. She skimmed the oldest, uncertain if they'd help her with the modern Eleutia. Only the lack of mentions of magic surprised her. Had the books been edited by the Alchemics? Women had been plentiful. In fact, they'd fought as warriors. She'd delved into the more recent history, learning facts that interested her, particularly those about the Battle of the Dakos that Rafe had fought in. But it was Yuma, the librarian, who handed her a book that earned her greatest attention. He'd taken the slim, leather-bound volume from a locked case behind his librarian's counter and thrust it into her hands with the words, "Perhaps you will find this of interest, Ma'am Kit. I'd suggest you not share it."

When she'd gone to leave, he'd rested a hand on her shoulder, his bushy brows scrunched with concern. "I'm afraid you must remain if you wish to read that last book I gave you. It's an in-library book."

She nodded, took a seat, and opened the book.

The history it related concerned what the author—Anonymous—called The Transition—the time more than two-hundred years earlier when female births had begun to decline. Prior to that, according to the author, the Clans had only occasional conflicts. In fact, inter-Clan marriages were common. Yet during this transition period, intermarriages trickled off, then ceased. As the warrior women died out, their positions—from Commanders to Peace-keepers—were replaced by men. Within fifty years from the onset of falling female birthrates, all the Clans had barred women from fighting in any type of war, relegating them to support staff and healing. Simultaneously, inter-Clan wars increased exponentially until they were commonplace.

Eleutia had been a far different world before its women became rarities.

When she returned the slim volume, she said, "I'm curious why I couldn't take this out of the library."

He pursed his lips. "Because it's one-of-a-kind."

"And why Anonymous?"

His smile wasn't pleasant, and he leaned close enough that his warm breath tickled her ear. "Because the words in that book are banned."

"I see." She handed him the leather-bound book. "Thank you for sharing it with me. I found it quite illuminating."

The logistics of her escape were troublesome. Ever since she'd been shot in the barn, she'd had a Peacekeeper dogging her steps. An exaggeration. They'd kept eyes on her is all, when she was out and about alone. Paulo was the one Scotch-taped to her side.

She needed to cement her getaway plan.

Kit found Tilde in a large patch of outdoor space tending her herbs. Her friend was digging in the dirt, a scruffy straw hat on her head, spattered jeans on her legs, and wearing a bilious green t-shirt with the sleeves ripped off.

Sage, basil, and rosemary perfumed the air, recalling the time she, Bree, and Sybi had insisted on growing a pumpkin patch for Halloween. Their mother had been all for it, and so she'd unleashed her girls on a chunk of land behind the horse barn. The patch had proved a massive success, all because of Sybi. It turned out that Kit and Bree had brown thumbs, while Sybi's was greener than green. They'd been so jealous of their sister, but they'd admired her, too. And typical Sybi—the least outgoing of their trio—had insisted all three take the credit. Credit. Right. Kit and Bree somehow managed to clear out a quarter of the pumpkins by mistaking the seedlings for weeds. Sybi's "pumpkin hills" worked beautifully, while Kit's and Bree's collapsed. Kit over-pruned her vines, whereas Bree forgot to pinch off the fuzzy ends of hers and overpopulated her section. Bree complained about touching the manure, though she had no trouble lobbing it when Kit started a manure fight with the other two. She and Bree had been reduced to making signs for the sale.

That funny fight. That memory.

Kit kneeled beside Tilde, who was examining her rosemary.

Her friend tipped back her hat. "How come you look both sad and happy?"

"Because the memory is both," she said, smiling, and told Tilde about the pumpkin patch, including a painting Bree had done about their misadventures that had won a prize. They were both laughing by the time she finished.

Tilde angled her head. "You're not here to reminisce or talk about pumpkins, are you?"

"No."

Her friend pulled off her gloves and set them down. Her silence was speech enough.

"You know my feelings about the war," Kit said.

Tilde poked her glasses back up her nose. "I do."

"Swear you'll tell no one of our conversation?"

Tilde nodded.

"Say it aloud."

"Kit, what's wrong? What are you planning?"

"Please, Tilde, say it."

"I swear by the Fates I will divulge nothing to anyone about what we discuss."

Kit's long sigh relieved a bucket of tension. She brushed her hand across the rosemary, releasing its fragrance. "What would you say if a monster squashed your herbs?"

"I'd kill it!"

"What if the monster was just hungry, and you could prevent him from ever hurting your plants without killing him? What would you do?"

Tilde snorted. "That's not very subtle, Kit."

"I know. I'm not good at analogies. I'm going to turn myself over to the Cats."

"You can't!"

"I must."

"But Rafe."

"I'm doing it for Rafe. And for you and Max and little Vantha and everyone else. It makes sense."

"No, it doesn't. Not at all."

"Geesh, Tilde, think outside the box. There doesn't have to be a war! The Cats won't hurt me. They'll hold their stupid contest and—"

"And you'll go to the winner!"

"I have a plan for that, too. War doesn't have to be a given."

Tilde shrugged. "The Wolves and the Cats have been aching for a fight for years. You're just the excuse."

That pissed her off. "I won't be anyone's excuse."

"I can't betray the Clan, Kit. I'm sorry."

She gripped Tilde's shoulders. "It won't be a betrayal. All you have to do is distract my guard while I ride out."

"Will you fly?"

"Rafe can best me in any flight I take, but on Moonrise, I can outride most."

"You'll still be caught. Between The Keep and our wall, dozens and dozens of Peacekeepers are running patrols. There's no way you'll slip through."

"I will if you provide a distraction."

Tilde shook her head.

"Tilde. Picture this. Picture a world where Clans—humans and animals—don't fight with each other all the time. Where they work together to change the way things are run around here."

"Run around here?"

"The Alchemics pull all the strings. They are untrustworthy, autocratic, and devious. And they get away with it because the Clans constantly squabble among themselves. The Alchemics love when Clans fight. It keeps the focus off them. If the Clans unite under one banner and demand the Alchemics see reason and share their knowledge, your world could be infinitely better."

"The Clans are too different, Kit. Our symbiont creatures have different natures, too."

How to make Tilde see? "I know I'm new here. But I love the Clan, the Wolves. *My* Clan. I've seen and heard enough to know that the Alchemics are strangling your world. They keep tech from you, only doling out what they deem appropriate. They conscript any Clan child with a scientific bent and mold him into one of them. They make Made Ones without—"

"But we need you, we need Made Ones."

"You wouldn't if someone figured out why female birthrates are declining." *Gaak!* She was so frustrated she ripped out a clump of weeds beside the rosemary.

Tilde snorted.

"What?"

"Um, those were my chives."

Kit sniffed her hand. "Sorry."

Tilde clamped her in a huge hug. "I can't help you, Kit. But I love you, too. I will miss you."

She clung to Tilde, loving this exuberant, marvelous woman who was so generous with affection. "I'll return. Count on it."

When they separated, Tilde said, "I won't tell. I gave my word." She ducked her head. "Um… Well…"

"What is it?"

Tilde fisted the torn clump of chives. "I don't think the decrease in female births is genetic. I think it's deliberate."

"Deliberate?"

"I know it's a radical idea." Tilde's eyes were fierce. "I haven't spoken up yet. I don't have enough evidence. But I am beginning to think the female birthrate is being purposefully manipulated."

"How could that be?"

"I'll show you." Tilde rose, and they trotted back to her suite in The Keep. Done up in blues and greens, it reminded Kit of an underwater habitat. Tilde disappeared into her bathroom while Kit waited on a sofa covered in plush turquoise velvet. The water ran for a few minutes, and then Tilde emerged carrying a box and what looked like a set of VR glasses. She sat on the other end of the sofa, her hands trembling. She removed the glasses. "I've sworn to keep your secret, now you keep mine."

"I swear to the Fates I will."

"I have a strong scientific bent. My mam didn't want to lose me to the Alchemics." She grinned. "Mam and I practiced and practiced, so that the day they came for potential Aspirants, when the Alchemics walked into our home, my mam signaled the word, and… and I began acting the cripple who had seizures. I even drooled. They despise physical imperfections, and they were revolted by me. One even offered to fix me! But my mam, she said, 'Why? She's perfect.'" Tilde laughed. "When they left, I remember the one shaking his head and saying, 'You Wolves are crazy!' Ha! My mam, she was smart, so smart. She didn't give me the signal to stop my seizure, so I kept on with the act. One Alchemic returned, pretending he'd forgotten his tablet, which I'm sure he'd deliberately left. Since I was still in seizure mode, while my mam kneeled beside me, he fled." She inhaled, her eyes squeezed tight. "Back then, I didn't truly appreciate what my mam had risked and accomplished. She saved me from them."

"How old were you?"

"Seven. Years later, when I asked Ulfr to study mistral biology, I was shocked when the Alchemics gave permission. They have great interest in mistrals, but none in me! Though it's illegal, the Alchemics kill mistrals in secret for their bones and attempt to replicate their strength and pliability in their labs."

"That's horrible. Evil," Kit said.

"They are that. We've tried to catch them at it, though so far they've eluded us. But they've yet to recreate the bones. It's one of their greatest failures." Tilde thinned her lips, a flush racing across her face. "We Eleutians want to *study* the Magics, so we can understand them better, find their source, how and why the magics happen. Fukkes won't permit it."

"When Rafe was injured and you met Fukkes, weren't you afraid he'd recognize you?"

She giggled. "Not at all. They saw me—the child—as a twisted thing, not a person. They take no notice of that which they disdain. That which is imperfect." She lifted the lid off the box. "Come closer."

Kit scooched near Tilde and peered in. A tiny creature rested on a bed of cotton. "Here." She handed Kit the odd glasses, and Kit slipped them over her head. Everything was huge. Not VR, then, but more like a jewelers loupe.

"Now, look."

When Kit peered into the box, she wasn't quite sure what she was looking at. A bug? It resembled a dragonfly but made of metal, with delicate wings, a straight body, and legs like pincers.

"What's its purpose?"

"I don't know specifically. It's a carrier of some sort. See those grippers, like tongs? I found it caught in a spider's web spun across the hose nozzle I use for watering delicate plants. Do you see the pill?"

Kit looked again. Clamped in its tiny pincers was a clear, liquid-filled capsule. "Yes. Have you analyzed what's in the capsule?"

Her laugh was bitter. "Of course not. We have no instruments, no chemicals, nothing with which to perform any kind of analysis. It's not allowed. Though we have underground cells that keep the broken tech to study it, they're few and far between. No, all I could do were a few tests. I've activated the bug's minuscule switch. If it's turned on, it seeks water. Without water, it flies in circles going nowhere."

The capsule looked innocuous, a round globular thing near transparent. "The capsule. Is what you're saying possible?"

"I believe it is. Sure, it's a leap to think it has anything to do with our fertility issues. But what else could it be?"

In Kit's mind, many things.

"We Wolves have remnants of pack magic, you know."

"What's that got to do with anything?"

"Some people have more than others. I do. Healers must. Rafe certainly does. Ulfr, of course. And when my instincts spark an idea, I tend to listen. I've been wrong." She giggled. "Sometimes Max teases me about it. He's got a lot, too. My gut says this bug and that pill are connected to our lack of female births."

Was it possible? If true, it would be diabolical. "Let's say you're correct. Why would the Alchemics do such a thing?"

Tilde shrugged. "I don't know why. The idea of crawling into their minds makes me want to bathe."

"What are you going to do? Who can you tell?"

"Rafe. Thorn."

"The Viking? The huge fighter."

"Yes, him. A few others. I'll bring it to Rafe. But not now. Not until after the war."

She took Tilde's hand. It was smaller than hers, freckled and white. "Won't you reconsider my request?"

"I can't, Kit."

"I've got to go."

"You're so sure we Wolves will lose?"

"Of course not! My leaving isn't about winning or losing the war, Tilde, but about the loss of life and limb."

"You'll never make it to the border of WolfHome."

"Moonrise is faster than any horse and most mistrals."

"*Most* mistrals."

"Leave it to me."

Tilde wrinkled her nose. "What you're saying is after the contest, you'll willingly go with some 'dude,' as you call them, who wins you because of his brawn?"

She grinned. "Maybe a woman will win."

Tilde threw up her hands. "Don't be ridiculous. Rafe will be so mad."

"He will." A chill of fear rippled through her. He'd be furious, but would he forgive her? Perhaps. Maybe. She hoped. "I can't help how he reacts. I only know it's the right thing to do. I *will* see you again."

Tilde hugged her. "Don't die on me, okay?"

So many goodbyes. Again. She squeezed Tilde back. "Not a chance."

Kit headed up the hill aimed for the other side of the Keep. She'd planned on Tilde's rejection, but it still hurt. She also had to get it out there, so at least one friend knew she wasn't betraying the Wolves. That shouldn't matter to her, but it did. If everything went south, Tilde would talk to Rafe and explain why she'd done it. She hoped.

Now came the tricky part. She had to play this just right. Just like Tilde in her "palsy" story, she'd practiced. Given the bait, she anticipated a resounding yes.

Kit found Inga in her rooms fletching arrows. On the sofa table along with some two dozen newly made arrows sat bodkin tips, feathers, glue, and twine.

The blonde's eyes narrowed when Kit entered the suite. "Get out." Inga returned to her work.

"I've come to make your day." Kit smiled.

Inga's eyes brightened. "You're dying?"

Crossing the room, Kit brushed the arrows aside with care, and took a seat on the table to face Inga. "I need help in escaping Wolf-Home. You're it."

Inga's hands froze, and she stared at Kit. "You're crazy."

"No, I'm dead serious." *Oh, Inga, this is just what you want—to get rid of me.*

"I very much hope so, about the dead part, I mean."

Kit didn't understand this woman. Gifted with beauty, a quick mind, and many friends, she was nonetheless filled with vitriol, as if something unseen were driving her. Not just her desire for Rafe, but more. "You have hundreds of men begging for your attention, yet you insist on Rafe, who wants only friendship. Thus, you hate me. That's pretty sad, Inga."

The blonde shrugged. "It doesn't matter what you think. You're really leaving WolfHome?"

"I am, with or without your help."

Inga leaned back in her chair and crossed her leg. "This help. Can I do it without anyone knowing I aided you?"

"You can. You'll be a distraction, that's all."

A huge smile blossomed on Inga's face. "Count me in."

CHAPTER TWENTY

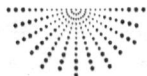

The countdown had begun, *her* countdown. Everything was in place, including Inga's aid. She simply had to get through these two days without giving herself away.

Kit left for the stables an hour before her shift began, needing to physically expend some of the energy pinballing around her body, like dozens of molecules desperate to escape.

With Inga's help, her scheme could work. *Would* work. Deep in thought, she hiked up the hill toward the barns, though the day's perfect weather and the scents of the sea for once failed to enchant her.

An odd sound whispered up ahead, to her left. She stilled. It came again, almost like an animal's sigh of pain. Or a human groan. She slinked off the path into the high grass, pulling her knife from its sheath. Fifty feet ahead Kit spotted an indentation in the grass, a large one. An anomaly that felt wrong.

She stalked closer, wary. Nearing the dip in the field, she crouched, parting the tall grass as she crept further.

Closer, closer still. The sounds of labored breathing. She parted the grass to reveal two men, one sprawled supine on the ground and red with blood. A second man lay on his belly nearby, bloodied as well, hand clutching a knife.

Kit swallowed hard, then scooted forward at a crouch.

Max! Bruises and blood covered his face, and a red stain spread from his right side. Her head spun. Max was clearly breathing, but the other man…

She scrambled over to where he lay in the grass and pressed her fingers to his throat. Cool flesh. No pulse. Dead.

Moving back to crouch by her friend, she said his name. His response was a moan. *Lucky stars.* She whipped out her phone, so shaky she almost dropped it, and called Rafe.

"Kit?" Rafe said.

"I'm in the field on the way to the big horse barn. Max. He's badly hurt. There's a dead man here, too. Send healers. Hurry!"

Her hand hovered over Max's shoulder, but she didn't touch him, so afraid she'd hurt him further.

"Max, it's Kit. If you can hear me, know it will be okay. Healers are coming. So is Rafe. Please, Max, stay with me."

She so badly wanted to *do* something.

A horn blew, and a dot appeared in the sky. Her fingers groped in the grass for the knife she must have dropped.

The dot arrowed toward her, growing larger. *Rafe.* Relief made her dizzy.

In the distance, half a dozen men ran toward them, flanked by two Timberwolves.

Rafe landed long before the healers crested the hill. He leapt off the mistral, stiffening when he took in Max's condition. Kneeling beside his friend, his eyes roved Max from head to toe. "Your knife, Kit?"

Her knife was raised, its tip pointed at Rafe's throat. *Oh.* She slipped it into its sheath.

"The dead man?" He wore his blank battle-mask.

"I have no idea who he is."

He strode to the body and turned him face up. "Georg." If possible, his face hardened further as he returned to Max's side.

"I know so little about these kinds of wounds," she said. "I... I saw Max didn't have arterial bleeding, so I called you. I was afraid to do more."

"You did fine. Another hour, he'd have been gone."

His steely presence anchored her, allowed the chaos of her mind to clear. If she hadn't left for work an hour early... The thought chilled her.

"Why would they fight like this?"

Rafe took his friend's hand in his. "Georg is Dusan's brother. Max believe Dusan shot the goddart's sting."

"Has Max been stung with the poison?"

"Perhaps. Hopefully cut, not pierced as I was."

"Can you call Fukkes?"

"I intend to."

Both of them knew the Alchemic might not answer.

The healers crested the hill.

"Oh, no," she said.

Rafe looked over his shoulder "Tilde."

Her friend was in the forefront of the healers, two of whom were carrying a stretcher. Tilde pumped her legs, racing toward Max, her face fierce.

"He's got to live Rafe."

His lips thinned. "Non-negotiable. Max *will* live."

Kit swallowed hard.

Tilde collapsed next to Max and raised her hands, hovering them over his chest. As she began to hum, tears coursed down her cheeks, splattering onto the bloodied flesh of her love.

Kit sat off to the side of the infirmary room, hoping for invisibility among the thick shadows shrouding her chair. Outside, night had fallen.

The small room was close and cloying with the heated breaths of Kicks and the three healers working over the injured man. The dim lighting suited the unnatural quiet—only occasional words and Max's labored breathing broke the silence.

Max was dying, just as Rafe was when he'd been stung.

This world of violence and passion, of flying horses and poison arrows. Life could be snuffed out far more swiftly here. At least it seemed that way.

Yet she felt more alive on Eleutia than she'd ever been on Earth, each moment fraught with danger, intense and real.

Which made Max's dying from the goddart's poison all too vivid. Tilde was in agony. She'd stopped crying, her grief replaced by grim determination. She would not fail, or so she believed.

Rafe stood sentinel beside the bed, one hand resting on Max's shoulder, as if he could imbue his friend with his bulwark of strength. He caught her eye, and his were filled with a feral pain and fury. That look would send most running. It made her want to hold him close.

Funny how the small things between them touched her most. How her toothbrush sat beside his that morning. How he'd insisted on bringing her a cup of precious coffee in bed. How he'd laughed at a joke from her old Earth life. Watching the evolution of his latest sculpture, a blessing he gave to no other.

His closest friend was dying. How could she leave Rafe? She *must*, the feeling like ice coating her soul.

Once, she'd faced a life with no choices before her. Here, with the impending war, she'd created her own choice. The right one. She had to believe that. All she needed was the courage to see it through.

Though she'd hoped Fukkes would bustle through the door, he hadn't. Without Fukkes help, Max would die. She cleared her throat. "Fukkes?"

"I left messages," Rafe said, his words bitter. "According to his staff, he's 'incommunicado.'"

Tilde began to crumple. Rafe caught her before she hit the floor, carried her to the healers' waiting-room sofa, and laid her down with care. When he returned, he began to pace, hands clasped behind his back.

"That child almost spent herself," said the Master Healer. "Bah. Look at her, passed out like some amateur. For what? He's destined to die."

Kit threaded her fingers together so they wouldn't throttle the man. Tilde would always give a hundred and ten percent. "Shame on you. Tilde should be applauded for her efforts, not denigrated."

The healer cast her an acidic look.

Rafe dropped to his knees beside the bed and pressed his hand to Max's forehead. He began to whisper.

The Master Healer drew himself up. "What are you doing?"

Was that panic in the healer's voice? Kit strained to hear Rafe's words, which were more like chanting.

He raised his voice, repeating the words over and over. "*Adrishta Dishtam aabhari aarogya gantavya addhaa alaukika kshiina pumaana.*"

"Stop!" The healer moved to place his hand over Rafe's mouth.

Rafe grabbed his wrist. "Do not dare."

The healer hissed. "It is forbidden."

Rafe ignored him, resuming his chant. Perhaps it was a trick of the room's dim light, but Rafe's body began to glow.

Tilde rose from the sofa and walked to the bed. Her hand slipped into Max's, her eyes saucer wide. Tilde took up the chant. "*Adrishta Dishtam aabhari aarogya gantavya addhaa alaukika kshiina pumaana.*"

Though Kit had no idea what they were doing, she crossed the room and pressed her hand to Max's other shoulder, joining in as best she could, repeating words that stumbled from her mouth.

Kicks removed Max's boot and sock, wrapped her hand around his foot, and took up the chant.

A tide rose, invisible, powerful, like an immense translucent wave reaching for the sky. The curved wall seemed to expand, arcing outward. Pressure filled her, her body too small for what grew within.

Fear rippled across the three healers' faces, and they scrambled from the room.

Rafe's eyes rose to Kit's as he mouthed the words again and again, and his approval shined like a beacon.

Blood dripped from his eyes, and Kit wanted to yell, "Stop!" just as the healer had. Instead, she tightened her hold on Max's shoulder. "*Adrishta Dishtam aabhari aarogya gantavya addhaa alaukika kshiina pumaana.*"

Mimi raced through the door. "I heard the call..." Her voice trailed off as she took in the room. "Oh!" She walked to the bed and pressed her small hands to Max's ankle. "*Adrishta Dishtam aabhari aarogya gantavya addhaa alaukika kshiina pumaana.*"

Rafe shook his head at Mimi.

"I must," the child said.

Five minutes. Ten.

Blood ran from Mimi's ears and in runnels from Rafe's eyes and nose.

Kit's chest compressed, as if she wore a corset, her breath coming in pants, her free hand clinging to the bedstead.

"*Adrishta Dishtam aabhari aarogya gantavya addhaa alaukika kshiina pumaana.*"

Glittering lights rose from each chanter, blending together to spiral above their heads. The translucent wave crested, and spiral shot into Max's chest.

Max jackknifed up. "Shote!"

The pressure vanished, and she thumped down onto the bed, while Kicks slid to the floor.

A door slammed. Rafe's father and stepmother blazed into the room, the Alpha leaping for Rafe, who wobbled as he pushed himself to stand.

Mimi's mother screamed.

The Alpha's fist slammed into his son's face. "You fool!"

Rafe staggered, his bloody grin stretched wide. "Fark you, Ulfr. I did for Max what you could not to do for me."

"Did what?" Max said in a hoarse voice.

Claws flashed toward Rafe.

Kicks tripped Mimi's mother, while Kit tackled her to the floor, landing with an *oomph*.

She was forcibly pulled off the feral woman. "She'll claw him!"

Rafe's arm banded around Kit's waist. "Not with my father here, she won't."

Ulfr gripped his mate tight, lifting her off the floor, and holding her still, his face the same blank one as Rafe's when he fought.

Somehow Tilde was beside Max, Mimi hugging his other side, all three grinning as if they'd just drunk a case of wine.

"Max?" she said.

He gave her a tipsy smile. "I feel great."

Yuan entered the suite in her hoverchair, a tray holding a pitcher and glasses balanced on the hover's arms. *"Finally."*

"Excuse us." Rafe kissed her temple and released her. "Mimi and I need to wash up." Rafe wobbled toward his sister, lifted the child into his arms, and vanished into the outer corridor.

With a calm that belied the emotions in the room, Yuan pushed aside the medical instruments and set her burdens on the metal table. She began to pour.

"Was Max just healed by our chanting?" Kit asked Ulfr.

The Alpha snarled, striving to hold his squirming mate's shoulders.

"It's good to see the taboo finally broken," Yuan said.

Rafe and Mimi reappeared, faces clean, Mimi cradled by her brother and sleeping peacefully.

Yuan turned her chair toward Rafe. "I see you followed my advice and studied our High Magics. You must have practiced, too."

Rafe winked.

"Take our child and go, Seelar." The Alpha notched his chin toward the door.

His mate shot Rafe a poisonous look, but she lifted Mimi and carried her out the door to the sleepy cry of "Want Rafee, Mama."

The Alpha whirled on Yuan. "You encouraged this?" He whirled on his son, jabbing his finger. "And you! It is forbidden. You broke our inviolate law."

"Not *our* law, those shoting Alchemics' law. I don't give a fark, either." Rafe hauled Kit close and pressed his lips to her ear. "Thank you for your help, beauty."

Kit slid her arms around his waist and rested her head on his shoulder. She breathed him in. When Rafe held her, nothing else mattered.

"What just happened?" Max said.

"Everything." Rafe's bloodshot eyes were smiling. He sank into a chair, lifting her with him and settling her on his lap.

"I agree with Rafe," Yuan said, her eyes narrowing on her Alpha. "Our ancestors' agreement with the Alchemics, bah! A fool's bargain."

The Alpha's head whipped around like a snake's. "The only fool here is you, old woman. What if the Alchemic Clan follows through on their threat? What if they will no longer create Made Ones?"

Yuan shrugged. "They've had us over this barrel for too many years, with their rules and regulations. I, for one, will be happy to again use our Clan magic, *all* our Clan magic."

The Alpha slumped onto the edge of the bed. He looked older, vertical lines carving his cheeks, his jaw slack.

"Alpha?" Kit said.

He flapped a hand at her. "Don't look so worried. My strength will return."

"Hey, guys, what's going on?" Max said. "Did you catch Georg? He's the one who shot Kitlyn."

Rafe laughed. "It seems you took care of Georg." Rafe nuzzled her neck as if he couldn't get close enough, his joy spreading through her like wildfire.

"Go, me!" Max beamed.

Yuan explained to Max all that had gone on, beating the Alpha to the punch.

"We're doomed," the Alpha said.

Rafe shot his father a dark look. "We are *not*." He turned to Kit. "The Alchemic Clan hates any magical powers, which were once the Clans' greatest strength. They have no magic. So they forbid us the use of our High Magics."

"How will they know we broke their law?" Kit asked.

The Alpha gave a bitter laugh "They'll know. All I've built, shattered in an instant. For what?"

"For Clan, Da," Rafe said. "Why else?"

So worth it. Kit's fingers skimmed Rafe's swollen jaw where the Alpha had punched him.

Ulfr swiped up one of the glasses Yuan had poured. "I need this."

But Yuan halted Ulfr's drink mid lift. "Wait." She handed the rest of the drinks around. "A toast—Ma'am Kit's tradition—to remembered strength and renewed bonds."

The Alpha paused, then he took in each member of the room. His eyes turned fierce, and he nodded. They all clinked glasses.

Max sucked in a breath, and though he looked drunk, his face was aglow with health and strength. "May they forever remain unbroken."

Every few days or so, Alchemic City moved to another location on Eleutia. Calix's stomach flip-flopped each time, and this one would be no different. He didn't understand their need to move, their disconnection from the land, to not have an aerie they called home.

He'd managed to plant a listener on Gabin, loving the irony. They'd developed the tech. The listener was quite brilliant—once activated, it would dissolve in sixty minutes, no one the wiser. How he enjoyed using their own genius against them.

A small dining table by the window was free, and Calix chose it to signal that he wanted to be alone, a common occurrence amongst the Alchemics. Gabin and Fukkes sat a few tables over. Once the server had taken his order, he drew out his tablet, prepared to take notes. He activated the listener.

Fukkes was laughing. It hurt Calix's ears. "Did you hear, Gabin? That fool Wolf broke the law."

"The one you cured?"

"Yes. It's delicious! He used that ridiculous Clan woo-woo to save his friend. They'll pay."

He was shocked when he'd finally learned it had been Radulfr saved by the Made One's blood. That the resistance leader had almost died shook him to his core. Thank the Fates the Alchemics didn't know they'd healed their greatest enemy.

His fingers sped across his tablet, making notes for the encrypted message he would send to Compass True. While the Alchemics were clever, they had yet to break the encryption or the cloaked device he used to send messages. Break it? Bah. Those arrogant farkers paid little attention to potential spies amongst them.

"I'm not so sure they'll pay," Gabin said. "What with war coming, Eleutians may not even learn of the breach. Who's to know?"

"Gabin, where is your imagination? I'll leak it, of course. Then after the war, we'll come down hard on them. We have every right."

"I still say they may not care." Gabin snorted.

"No respect," Fukkes said. "This world that's been ours for centuries is unworthy of us. On our new world, the people will treat us as kings."

"Like those Earthly rulers," Gabin said.

"Yes. As it should be."

"After we leave to inhabit our new flesh," Gabin said, "the Clans will die out. Is that what you want?"

Fukkes shrugged.

Die out? Fates, they were monsters. Calix had yet another reason to despise them. Fukkes' crystal smile appeared. It gave Calix the willies. Fukkes leaned close to Gabin and whispered, which the listener easily caught.

"I have a plan."

"Do you?" Gabin said.

Fukkes laughed. "Early days yet, and not to be enacted until the symbionts kill all the Alchemics excluded from the Eleven. The symmetry of it excites me."

Talk about farked up. Not only were they planning to steal the lives of Other Worlders, but they expected the Clans to kill the remaining Alchemics.

"I wish Nemrah…"

"You will have myriad choices on Earth."

"I suppose you're right, but she—"

"Stop your whining," Fukkes hissed. "She wasn't worthy to join us, and you are well aware of that fact."

Calix cursed but paused the transmission as his server approached with his food.

She set the dishes on the table. "Thank you," he said.

The woman's eyes widened.

Shote, he'd forgotten his manners, at least those for the Alchemics. Non-Clan servers were never thanked. As Alchemic Aspirants, along with their training, they were put through the meat grinder of onerous and endless chores to see if they had the rigor to become one of the elites.

"Go away," he barked, far more in character.

She backed away, but not before he garnered another concerned look from her. If she talked about his misstep… Good thing his time here was waning. He was slipping up, making mistakes. He'd been embedded for too long. He knew it, and his handlers had told him to get out. Which he would do, once he secured the Made One.

"Is there a problem, Calix?"

Fukkes stared down at him.

Calix rose. He towered over the peacock of a man. "No. Should there be?"

"Did I see you compliment the Aspirant?"

"You did."

Fukkes plucked his chin. "Because…?"

Holding out his hands in faux submission, he said, "I desire her in my bed."

"Really!" Fukkes gave the server, who was now waiting on another table, a long penetrating look. "Really?"

"I can't defend my actions." Calix shrugged.

Fukkes snorted. "You and Gabin, ruled by your gonads."

"It won't happen again, sir."

"Let's see that it doesn't."

One more day until war. It reminded Kit of the song from *Les Miz*. Not a happy thought.

She stood in The Keep's high tower, the scope fixed to one eye. She saw beyond the town, beyond the outer wall, beyond the first rise to where the Cat forces crawled like ants across the hills. The sea of vast numbers undulated, making the ridges and valleys look as if they themselves were moving.

Within the outer wall, the Wolves bustled, preparing for the coming siege. Their oil pots, stones, fire arrows, and bombs appeared and disappeared as they were strategically placed along walls and in towers. Horses galloped this way and that, while hundreds of men practiced sword play, the claws, and grappling one another.

Her hand slipped into her pocket, and she rubbed the lucky stone Rafe had left as a courting gift.

Rafe had explained how he'd known the chant and had the ability to wield a few of the High Magics, mostly the healing ones. He'd studied the magics in secret for many years, his interest having blossomed at college. Yuma the librarian had further helped his study, as Rafe was determined to flout the Alchemics' law. Without a teacher, his abilities were slow to grow. Healing Max was the first time he'd used them, daring to touch the other man's soul and spirit.

Today, though Rafe was in full Commander mode, he'd sprinkled the passing hours with small kindnesses, thoughtful moments that told her she mattered, not as a Made One, but as his love. She'd tried to do the same and wished the day might stretch to weeks and months and years.

Kit's actions would be seen as a betrayal of Clan. Her fingers squeezed the parapet. But perhaps something forgivable.

Sounds on the stone steps made her turn. Rafe held out a hand and she went to him, hugging him close.

"We're well prepared," he said, threading a hand through her hair.

"I know. I just wanted to see for myself."

"Up for a surprise?" He kissed the top of her head, released her, and took her hand.

"A good one?"

"Very."

CHAPTER TWENTY-ONE

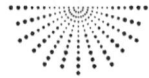

A door clanged down below. "You there, Rafe?" Talos called.
Rafe swore. Talos was a worrywart. "I am."

"You need to review the arms a final time," Talos said.

He shook his head, unwilling to release his Kit. "Coming, Talos! One hour, beauty. Meet me at the barn out back of the house."

"Yes, sir!" She saluted, thumping the side of her hand against her forehead.

"That's not a salute!" He grinned.

"It is in America."

He pressed her delicious body against his, and his lips found hers and closed on them, his tongue exploring her anew. She tasted of honey and love, and she was his.

"Rafe?" Talos hollered.

"One hour." He stepped away. "Sooner, if I kill Talos before then."

Her laughter followed him down the stairs.

Amidst supervising war preparations, stealing a few moments with Kit, and keeping his father in check, worry consumed him.

Kit was up to something. A sadness. Since she couldn't stop the war, perhaps she planned to fight in it. She might be courageous and fierce in more ways than he could count, but his Kit possessed a tender soul. She was no warrior. The Fates, what was she up to?

"Speed it up, Commander," Talos said.

"The armory isn't going anywhere."

"Neither are you if you don't move your feet."

Talos still treated him as a youth in need of training. To please the man, he picked up his pace.

The timing of the war was abysmal. His and Kit's relationship needed to heal from his stupidity at turning away from her. He'd been a coward.

Give him a sword to wield or a mistral to ride, and he possessed no fear. Give him a hint that Kit might be injured or die... Even the thought froze the marrow in his bones.

"Rafe!"

"Coming!"

She hated discussing the war with him, her unwillingness to make plans for her safety frustrating. When he'd asked her to relocate to his cabin in the mountains, she'd refused, which he'd half expected. He'd seriously considered kidnapping her. She'd probably stab him. She'd certainly never forgive him, so he'd tabled the idea. For now.

What was his old friend Gato thinking? Gato had changed, his sense of ethics and justice seemingly vanished. He'd always been confident, but when he'd come to the Wolves asking for Kit, he'd turned arrogant, essentially making a declaration of war—as if the Cats' triumph was predestined. Gato well knew the Wolves would never give her up.

The Cat was using Kit as a pawn to precipitate this conflict. Why? Where had this desperation come from? What had changed?

Imagining Kit in their clutches... Fark. No one since he'd reached adulthood had touched his soul as she did. *My darling Kit, you are my great weakness.* But she was his greatest strength, too, as well as his heart. She always would be, for she had unlocked a part of him dormant since the day his mother died.

He wondered if Kit knew wolves mated for life.

Rafe detoured on his way to the armory, much to Talos' annoyance, and put a third guard on Kit, this one an expert at ghosting. She must be safe. He would tolerate nothing less.

Ninety minutes later, Kit flew high in the sky atop Moonrise as she and Rafe on Nightfall soared above the hills to reveal the magnificent expanse of turquoise sea. Each flap of the mistral's wings pumped the air in a thrilling rhythm, and when they dove, she screamed her joy as wind plastered her face, Rafe's laughter ringing in her ears sweeter than a choir.

They circled high above the sea, spiraling downward to land on a flat promontory above a rocky beach made up of interleaved stone slabs. Ten feet below, tidal pools of turquoise puddled across the smooth rocks like a string of jewels. A few of the pools effervesced with mini geysers, though most were calm as a still lake. Beyond the sea wall, waves pounced on the jagged rocks, spray shooting high into the air.

She'd found a new favorite place in WolfHome. Well, not counting Rafe's arms.

They walked the mistrals beneath a shaded overhang, and Rafe removed the saddle packs. The mistrals would remain nearby while they went on their adventure.

She'd asked Rafe how he could take time off from his war preparations. He'd laughed. The Wolves were old hands at war. They were prepared. It would be the Cats who'd make the first strike.

"We are ready," he said. "I wanted this time, for us. Come on." His hand firm in hers, he led her to the middle of a rocky bridge carved over time by the ocean tides. Beneath them, a deep pool lapped the shore with water so clear she spied the sandy bottom, the fish darting this way and that.

Rafe had braided his hair, and she resisted the urge to undo it. She had trouble swallowing as he stripped, his golden flesh glorious in the hot morning sun.

"How do we get down to the pool?" Her voice was husky, and he smiled. Terrible man, he knew just what his striptease had done to her.

"Follow me." He dived into the pool far below. She peered around, not a soul in sight, and finally doffed her clothes, walked to the bridge's edge, and hovered.

Rafe broke the surface, and he waved. "Come on in! I'll catch you, beauty. I always will."

She let a smile meander across her lips. She'd show him a dive, all right. She pressed her hands together, lifted her arms, and arced her body, then she tucked and somersaulted, and for a moment she was flying around the circus ring, flinging herself far beyond reality's realm.

The warm water embraced her, and she plunged deep. Then hands pulled her to the surface and twirled her around, Rafe's salty kiss perfect.

"Your dive was grand," he said when they separated.

"It felt good."

"One of the perks of being a Wolf. The pools are all ours."

"Arrogant man."

He quirked an eyebrow. "Just speaking fact, Ma'am Kitlyn."

She laughed, and he pushed her away from him, face serious, eyes hot. The heel of his hand shot a cascade of water that drenched her. His eyes grew feral, and he growled. She knew just what that meant. She turned and swam like a monster was after her. Her monster.

Rafe broke the surface in front of her. Damn, how did he do that? She slapped her hand through the water, a huge splash covering him.

He was laughing again. "You dare?"

She went "Grrrr!," which sounded nothing like his growl, and he laughed harder.

They made love on a warm rock shaped like a giant platter, and afterward all she wanted to do was drowse in the sun.

"Come, you must see the caves," he said.

She squinched open an eye. "Now?"

"Let's go, sleepyhead." He slipped into the water, the pack he'd placed by the bank slung over his back, and held out his hand.

The chain of pools shone like an azurite necklace, one end fading into darkness. Rafe had told her about the caves—strange dark spaces leading to treasure, according to him.

Apprehension battled excitement. They could get trapped. Which was absurd. Rafe would never let that happen. The caves looked mysterious and alluring. She clasped his hand. "Lead on."

They swam beneath the high stone arch and away from the sun. The air became chilly, though the water remained warm, a refreshing change from the blistering heat.

"The Lucents are a series of caves, one leading to the other."

As they swam further, though the roof sloped downward, Rafe and she were able to walk in shallower water.

"Is your backpack okay?"

"It's waterproof, beauty."

He took her lips in a long, salty kiss, then they scrambled over a ledge and slipped into another deeper cave pool, and another and another, finally pausing to catch their breath. The interwoven system of pools grew darker, the air denser, until the cave entrance was but a pinhole.

"Just a little further," he said.

She wasn't eager to lose that pinhole of light.

They dove into the next pool, then swam around a bend, the pinhole winking out. Yet light filled the space, revealing a crystal cave-like grotto much like she'd seen on Capri—a giant geode.

"How?"

"Natural luminescence from the properties in the crystals."

She stood on the sandy bottom, the water to her neck, while lights from the myriad crystals around her sparkled with blue, purple, and yellow iridescence. Magical.

The water didn't wish to release her as she climbed the five steps to a large rock platform, perhaps eight by eight—a mini cave—and touched the crystals. "Oh, Rafe."

"I knew you'd love it." He spoke from behind.

She'd been so entranced, she hadn't heard him climb up behind her. He wrapped her in his arms, and she leaned back against his chest. "Magnificent."

"Yes, you are."

She laughed. "Silly man." But it was no small thing to be the focus of Rafe Wolven's attentions.

"This branch of the caves ends here. Worth the journey?"

"Every journey I take with you is worth it."

He loosed the waterproof pack on his back, unstrapped it, and pulled out thick beach towels that he laid on the floor and two water bottles. When he handed her a square of chocolate, he grinned, slow and warm. "For you, Ma'am Kitlyn."

"Share it with me?" She bit half, but not all the way through, and leaned forward. He leaned forward, too, and slid half the chocolate into his mouth. When they bit down, their lips met in a chocolaty kiss.

They lay on the towels, and Kit touched his chest with reverence. She had so much to say, but her words would seem false after she left tomorrow. So she spoke with her eyes, her lips, her body.

Rafe stared at her with wonder, his hands caressing her face, her arms, her waist, her legs. He paused and began again, the pads of his fingers grazing across skin that ignited at his touch. He paused, placing a light kiss on her neck, then licked her chin, behind her ear, the divot at her neck.

"I dream of this, you know," she said to him, her voice husky. "The way you touch me, look at me." Kit never imagined anyone taking that kind of care with her.

She reached out to him, but he shook his head. "Wait. Let me explore."

Her fingers ached, but she dropped her arms beside her. His lovemaking was so Rafe. Incredibly giving, never taking. He committed time to the things he loved. His people. His mistrals. Her.

Kit's blood was already warm in her veins, her anticipation growing when he spread his hands over her belly, his thumbs brushing where she wanted him to touch most. His strokes delicate, setting her on fire, making her ache for more. She wanted him inside her. No, not wanted, *needed* him there, needed him to fill her.

It all felt so strange, so delicious, both decadent and loving.

She needed so badly, and he'd explored enough, so she pressed her body to his, wrapped her arms around him, her hips grinding when her sex touched his cock. Rafe eased her back onto the towels and began to prowl down her flesh, dropping lingering kisses to her breasts, her belly, lower.

She tried to pull him upward, her need overwhelming. But he shook his head, took her wrists.

"I need some honey, love." He dipped his head and ran his tongue up her slit.

Oh, my lucky stars. Heaven. Rafe licking her clit was the most exquisite sensation. Feeling rushed from her sex to her head, and she couldn't stifle the moan amplified inside the cave.

"That's it, beauty."

Over and over his exploring mouth and tongue lapped and licked, sucking, flicking, grazing her clit.

She was going to die. It was simple. She pushed up on her elbows to watch the play of muscles across his back, a symphony she could study for endless hours.

Her moans echoed through the cave, and he groaned, his exhaled breath hot on her clit. She was climbing toward that peak, watching him, compelled by him, ensorcelled by everything Rafe.

"You are beautiful, my love," she said.

He raised his head, his lips slick with her juices. "Now you're just trying to get me to move faster."

Her smile was slow and wicked. "Perhaps."

He shook his head. "Won't work."

"No?"

His head dipped low, his tongue spearing into her, then twirling around and around the spot she wanted him to touch the most.

And there, she was *there*.

Pleasure jolted through her. "Rafe!"

He rose and crawled up her body, his color high, eyes bright and burning, and in one swift thrust he entered her. She gripped him tight, legs squeezing his hips, arms clutching his back, her inner walls clamping him tight.

He groaned, and then he moved in a sinuous dance, pumping in and out, rolling his hips, moving fast, then slow, then fast again. Kit answered his dance move for move, their rhythm perfection, bodies slick with sweat, breaths panting, voices a duet of groans and moans.

"I want you so farking much," he said. "Always. Forever."

Tears burned her eyes even as their pleasure spiraled higher. But she couldn't say the word, couldn't mouth "forever," so instead, "I love you, Rafe, Wolf of my heart."

He thrust harder, faster, and she broke apart again, her joy of completion accompanied by his hips moving faster, pounding into her, then his bark of pleasure that was her own personal music.

They clung to each other, offering butterfly kisses and love words, and Kit wished they could join for always.

But that wasn't to be.

That night before bed, Rafe took a pair of huge kitchen scissors from a drawer.

"What are you doing?" she said.

"Want to watch?"

"Um, sure."

"Come then." He gave her a quick kiss, then stepped around the corner and walked into the bathroom. He stood before the mirror, his face serious.

In a swift move, he snipped off his long braid.

She yipped. "Why did you do that?"

He faced her, one hand holding his braid, the other the scissors. He leaned toward her and gave her a long, slow kiss. "No worries, beauty, it will grow back."

"Why, Rafe?"

"We go to war in the morning. It's what we Wolves do before battle."

"I see." She scraped her fingers through his shorn locks. Soft and silky. Still Rafe.

He went to toss his shorn hair in the bin.

"Don't!" she said. "Can I have it?"

"Why?" He tilted his head, a smile teasing his lips.

"Because it's part of you."

"Good reason. Here." The long braid dangled from his outthrust hand.

She turned away, lest he see her tears, and went in search of a rawhide tie for the cut end. Once she crawled into bed, she laid the braid on her nightstand, then strapped on her wrist alarm and set it to vibrate. Unless Rafe was on call, he slept like the dead.

They cuddled, finding warmth and comfort after the day's pleasures. They didn't made love again but held each other tight, stroking and petting until Rafe's eyes drifted closed.

Neither she nor Rafe had mentioned tomorrow again or how their world could be ripped apart.

Paulo slept on his own bed at the foot of theirs. In her preparations, she'd forgotten he did that some nights. An unexpected complication. But she'd deal. Thank heavens she'd hidden a bag of clothes in the linen closet.

Tugging Rafe's braid from the table, she clutched it tight. Her eyes drifted closed. She needed sleep, to be fresh when she left before dawn. Her lids grew heavy.

Riding the ring atop Nessie. Falling, falling. Days blurring—can't walk, barely talk, can't smile, breath so hard. Bree, rocking her. Teaching—yes, that's it! Fingers shaking. Arthur's "You never loved me." Sybi's tears, trying to wipe them away. Boom! "Come on, lazybones!" Falling, falling. Cold. Icy. Frozen. Caramel eyes. The cliff Cat fight. Snarling teeth. I'm new. Am I? Lips lifted in a smile, eyes crinkling. Paulo's head on her lap. Rafe surrounding her, inside her. Sweet bliss atop Moonrise, autumn leaves fluttering far below. A sister hug with Sybi and Bree. Where are you? Hungry eyes, loving eyes, caring eyes. Rafe's eyes. Trusting eyes.

I will not betray you!

Tears leaked down her temples, burrowing into her hair, her

thoughts chaotic. Stroking the soft strands of Rafe's braid, she forced everything from her mind but her escape. Her focus grew heavy reviewing all the possible scenarios tomorrow might bring. Somehow, amidst Paulo's snores, she slept.

The vibration on her wrist awakened her. Her heart seized. No more tomorrows.

Dawn had yet to crack the night sky. She couldn't see Paulo, and Rafe lay on his belly, one arm wrapped around her waist.

Kit moved to slide from the bed. Rafe's arm tightened.

"Bathroom," she whispered in Rafe's ear, then kissed his cheek.

His arm relaxed, and she slid from beneath it, instantly missing the closeness. When her feet hit the floor, she clutched the braid and scooped up her phone.

Paulo's head popped up.

She pressed a finger to her lips and pointed to the bath attached to Rafe's bedroom. The coywolf's head drooped to rest on his paws, but his eyes didn't close.

Out the bathroom window it was.

Inside the bath, Kit texted Inga, then pulled on jeans and a long-sleeved t-shirt, then socks and boots, the older pair she'd gotten when she arrived on Eleutia. She waited, chewing a nail, forcing herself to stop, until her phone vibrated. Inga was in place. Kit's stomach clenched. The moment had arrived when everything changed. Again. She pressed a fist to her mouth, caging the sob.

All we have to decide is what to do with the time that is given us. Gandalf's wise words to Frodo, just before he fell with the Balrog. It was true, what he'd said. She could stay, be with Rafe, see how it all played out.

That way, all she saw was death. She signaled to Inga and cranked the recently oiled window open. Five minutes, four, three. She stood on the toilet seat, lifted, and leapt outside, somersaulting and rolling to a stand.

Forgive me, beloved.

Stop. She had to stop thinking about Rafe, worrying over Rafe, imagining what could have been. Focusing on the task ahead was all that mattered.

The two guards' backs were to her, tending to an "injured" Inga, who'd made her blood and scrapes look real. Bent low, Kit raced for the barn and slipped into Moonrise's stall. She saddled and bridled the mistral, then tied on her cloak and saddle bags.

Her armor and sword were in one bag, her knives and claws in the other, along with the rainbow crystal and the second Paulo carving Rafe had gifted her. She'd left the mistral carving behind, standing beside her letter for Rafe, as well as a note she'd written to Ulfr.

Once mounted, she wound Rafe's braid around her throat and tied it with a leather thong.

"We go." She pressed her heels to Moonrise's flanks, who leapt into a swift canter.

In the dark, Kit rode low over Moonrise, cantering up hills and down valleys where she'd done many a dry run, headed for Wolf-Home's outer wall. Every few minutes she glanced back. Dawn had begun brushing its rays across the land, though shadows still darkened much of the landscape.

On the flat, the mistral galloped over the ground with her massive stride. The inner wall loomed, and they took to the air, flying low above the trees, the pre-dawn light cloaking her. Halfway to the outer wall, she landed. Once the sun had fully risen, flying left her too exposed. At her reined command, the mistral climbed a hill toward the wood. When they reached the cover of the trees, she stood in the stirrups and looked behind her.

A dark figure, a rider, crested the far hill, a finger of light splashing him. Max.

He'd never catch her, but she'd bet he'd alerted Rafe.

Inside the wood, enfolded by darkness, they picked their way among the trees, zigzagging around rocks. When the outer wall loomed a football field away, they rode back to the hill's crest, then downward.

Max continued to follow, but he wasn't closing the distance, rather keeping her in his sights as she galloped across the final valley. Far to her left, three riders raced toward her.

Shit shit shit.

She pressed Moonrise's flanks, leaned further forward, gave her more rein, anything to get to the outer wall before her pursuers. Three falcons circled above, and she wondered if they'd been tracking her this whole time.

Over lush wild-flowered grass, up another small hill, then downward again.

They were almost to the gate when... Movement on her right. Rafe raced toward her atop Daybreak, the massive stallion pounding the earth beneath his hooves. Her lover's face was carved intensity, his newly shorn hair wild. He would cut her off long before she reached the wall.

Forgive me.

They'd blocked the outer door. But she'd planned for that.

Daybreak ate up the ground between them. She reined in, and Moonrise squealed in protest, chest heaving.

Timing was everything. Rafe was almost in front of her now, cutting her off.

She kicked the mare's flank, and Moonrise leapt forward, straight for Rafe and the gate.

Rafe stood in the saddle, the mistral galloping beneath him. "No!"

He knew her too well.

On her left, her pursuers closed in. It would be tight. Wind tore her hair, and she patted Moonrise's neck. They'd practiced this maneuver, too. "Let's see how this goes, girl! Fly!"

She wrapped the reins once around the pommel, squeezed Moonrise's flanks, and gripped the knobs behind the mistral's ears. Going near vertical, Moonrise leapt into the sky, wings pumping with mighty strokes.

Rafe beneath them, Daybreak's wings spread to launch.

But he couldn't catch them, not before they crested the wall where the Cats lay in wait.

The wall blurred beneath them.

Down below, the Cats' army stood in wait. Troops upon troops, they watched her flight with rapt attention.

"Down!" she said to her mistral.

Moonrise banked, preparing to land.

"Kit, no!" Rafe shouted as he soared over the wall.

Moonrise thundered in for a landing amidst shouts and screams, the Cats rushing away to avoid being crushed.

Kit leaned on the saddle, gasping, shaking, Moonrise wheezing harsh in her ears, the mare's head hung low.

The Alpha Cat sauntered over. He raised his hand to pet Moonrise, and she snapped her teeth to bite him. Gato laughed. "Quite an entrance, Princess."

Overhead, Rafe spiraled downward, as if he were about to land.

The Cat archers raised their bows.

"No!" she screamed. "If you shoot him I swear to the Fates I will vanish from those damned games of yours."

Uncertain, the archers looked to their Alpha.

"As you command, Ma'am Kitlyn," he said to her in a low voice. "Hold your fire!"

The Alpha clamped his hands around her waist and held her aloft for his troops to see. "The Made One is ours."

"Not for long!" Rafe wheeled Daybreak back toward the wall.

CHAPTER TWENTY-TWO

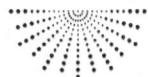

"Let go of me, idiot!" Kit elbowed the Cat's Adam's apple.

"Oof." The alpha dropped her.

She stuck the landing. Though her eyes ached for a glimpse of Rafe, he'd disappeared beyond the wall. She'd done it. Left Rafe and WolfHome behind.

Don't think, just do. She brushed herself off, turned to the Cat Alpha, and slapped her hands to her hips. "You wanted me, now you have me."

He smirked. "That we do."

"The deal—no war. We return to CatHome. And in four weeks, I'll submit to your contest."

He scratched his chin. Too bad he didn't have a mustache. He could twirl it, which would match his sly eyes and crooked smile.

The Alpha held his arms wide. "But we're here. And we Cats do love to wage war."

"Then you lose me, asshole."

"I think not."

"Think again. I'd sooner die."

He tilted his head. "You're not serious."

"Deadly."

The blonde who'd accompanied him to dinner approached. She punched the Alpha in the arm. "You gave your word."

"Everyone best stop punching me." He rubbed his bicep. "You didn't have to hit so hard, Arina. I was pulling her chain."

"What's that supposed to mean?" Arina said

"Teasing," Kit said. "It's an Earth expression. Heaven knows where he learned it."

"I know many things," the Alpha said.

"You sound like a B-grade movie actor."

He laughed, which wasn't what she'd intended at all.

The Alpha signaled a man holding a long horn. The soldier raised it to his lips and blew three blasts.

"We will parlay with the Wolves," the Cat Alpha said.

Quiet descended. The day had lightened, the sun streaming down on them, the cloudless sky bluer than blue. Sweat greased her every-where, and she was tired and sore and not up for any posturing.

The Alpha tugged a kerchief from his hip pocket and dangled it in front of her. "Keep it. CatHome is far warmer than the Wolves' environs. For so many reasons." His lascivious smile made her fingers itch to strangle him.

Waiting was horrible. Worse would be staring into the eyes of Rafe and Ulfr. No matter. She'd stuck to her course. The best course. The only course.

But facing them...

"Give me a guard," she said to the Cat Alpha. "I'll leave for CatHome now."

The Alpha straightened, assessing her with those calculating eyes. "No."

"You want them to suffer. You want me to suffer, too."

That sly smile of his. So easy to smack him in the jaw. She suspected that urge would arise often.

The immense gates to WolfHome groaned open.

Ulfr, Rafe, and Max stood shoulder to shoulder as they stepped through the gates of WolfHome. Paulo, too. And stars alive, there was Yuan in her floating chair, and Arne and Talos, and behind them scores upon scores of battle-ready warriors.

"Greetings, Wolven," the Cat Alpha said. "We have what we came for. We leave."

Rafe stepped forward, but his father's outthrust arm blocked him.

"Return her to us," Ulfr said. "The Made One belongs with us."

The Alpha Cat clasped his hands behind his back. "I think we will keep her. After all, she came to us of her own volition."

Rafe shoved his father's arm aside and moved toward their group. His black leathers gleamed in the light, a crested horsehair helmet atop his head, his hand white knuckled on his sword. "Kit, come home."

An order, Rafe's face wearing that emotionless battle mask. But his eyes blazed.

She took a step toward him, tethered to him in so many ways. It was just the two of them, surrounded by a cloak of intimacy. Rafe was hurting. How could she do this?

How could she not?

"I can't, Rafe."

She'd never wanted anything so much as she wanted to return to Rafe and the Wolves. But if she did... Now was the time for strength. She stood her ground.

Rafe's eyes fastened on the Cat Alpha. "Fight me for her, Gato. Just you and me. Here. Now."

"No!" Kit straightened her shoulders. "I choose to go with the Cats."

Rafe's eyes widened, and his quick flash of hurt near broke her. Her hand flew to the braid at her neck.

"As Ma'am Kitlyn wishes." Rafe bowed and stepped back.

"I'm leaving." Kit didn't bother to wait for any of the Cats but walked toward Moonrise, her back rigid. No one held the mistral's reins. She'd bet they'd tried, and Moonrise either bit or kicked them. What a good girl.

She mounted and turned Moonrise away from WolfHome, away from those she loved.

The Cat Alpha appeared beside her atop a sleek black mare. "No going back now," he said. "I suspect your reception would be less than hospitable. Shall we proceed?"

Kit nodded, and she kept her head high.

The Alpha turned in his saddle and raised his voice. "The Challenge is open to one and all. If you dare, Wolven." He laughed.

"Are you always such a jerk?" she said.

"A 'jerk?'"

"Never mind." *I've a surprise for you, big boy. Just you wait.*

She put her heels to Moonrise and galloped toward CatHome.

That evening in the big barn, Rafe was removing the new saddle he'd been testing on Nightfall. Across the arena, Inga and Neff were saddling a pair of warmbloods, talking softly, secretively. But the arena's acoustics amplified sound.

"After all we did for her," Neff said.

"She's an ingrate." Inga slipped the halter over her horse's head.

"An ingrate? Bah. The Made One is an arrogant bitch."

Rafe stalked across the arena floor, grabbed Neff's shoulder, and leveled him with a single punch.

The man landed on his ass with a thud.

"Rafe!" Inga said. "What is your problem?"

Neff sat up, massaging his chin. "Fark, Rafe!"

"You dare talk about my mate that way?" he said, his voice a growl.

"She's not your mate." Inga laid a hand on his chest. "She betrayed us. She has no loyalty."

Rafe slapped Inga's hand away. "Be glad I didn't punch you, too."

Neff spat blood. "Inga's right. She's disloyal. I heard the Alpha's going to expel her from the Clan."

"You heard wrong." His head began to cool. What did it matter what they said? No point in arguing with idiots.

"I'll report you," Neff said.

Rafe grinned. "Do that. I'd enjoy watching the Alpha rip your head from your shoulders." He walked off, giving both the middle-fingered salute Kit had taught him. Kit was right, it was satisfying.

The ride home cooled him further. Rather than be proactive back in the barn, he'd *reacted*, something that was unlike him. But any disparagement of Kit turned his vision blood red.

Those who'd gotten to know Kit understood her truth. His Clan-mates found war with other Clans normal. Kit did not. Hard to fathom.

Kit had not betrayed them. In her mind, she'd saved them.

He was sick over what she'd done, and he'd rectify it. Fark knew how he'd survive the weeks until The Challenge, but his training would take up much of the time. He flexed his bruised hand.

Once home, he strode to the bedroom. He hadn't changed the sheets, wouldn't do so until she returned. The cotton held her scent, filling the room with it. He lifted the carved mistral that rested beside her letter.

Paulo leaned against him and whined. The coywolf missed Kit, too. Her letter had said she'd wanted to take the carving but feared it would break. She should have done. If it broke, he'd carve her another and another and another.

He'd been blind not to see how determined she was to end the war. She'd accomplished her mission, just not in a way he could accept.

And she'd known—*fark*—known how much it would pain not just him, but her, too. When he'd faced her across that space, the Cat Alpha at her side, he'd felt her sorrow like a knife being dragged down his chest.

With shaking hands and great care, he set the carving beside her letter, because he really wanted to throw the mistral against the wall and watch it smash to pieces. He slumped on the bed.

Paulo crawled up beside him. *We must get her back.*

"We will, old friend."

He'd thought he'd been fine before Kit. Once he met her, it was as if she'd added bright colors to his black-and-white life. He hadn't understood. Now, he had trouble breathing without her.

Who would watch over her? Who would keep her safe?

He rested his hand on Paulo's head and smiled. Perhaps there was a way.

The Cats rode hard, the army camping for the night beneath trees reminiscent of Southern live oaks. When she'd laid out her bedroll, everything ached. No one bothered her, for which Kit was thankful, her heart a lump of desiccated flesh.

Arina brought her some of the necessities—a toothbrush, soap, washcloths—and sat beside her on the ground, folding her lithe body with ease. "You'll like Catamount. It's far more lavish than the Wolves' den."

"I've never been one for lavish. Thank you for the toiletries." Kit washed her face and hands, rinsing them in a bowl of tepid water.

Arina toyed with her knife hilt. "Everyone is one for lavish once they get used to it. We Cats like our amenities."

"Sorry about that, kitty-cat, but I've always been a canid person."

With a smirk much like her Alpha's, Arina said, "Odd for a woman named Kit."

"Only the truth."

"That perception will change."

Her mother had often quoted, "Be the oak, and bury your taproots deep in the soil. But also be the reed, that bends with the wind, and does not break."

She would.

As they rode toward CatHome, the elevation dropped, and the land turned increasingly arid, reminding Kit of the Mediterranean region. A breeze brought the tang of sea. Her spirits lifted a bit knowing it remained close.

She replayed her day with Rafe in the tidal pools again and again, which only made her longing worsen.

By the fourth day of riding, she was sore, tired, and badly in need of a bath. But the end was in sight, the gates of CatHome yawning before them. The coming weeks with the Cats would test her patience. Her mood only worsened when the Alpha pulled up beside her.

He raised a hand, the horn sounded, and they reined in to a walk as they passed through CatHome's gates amidst raucously cheering troops and Clansmen who dotted the ramparts.

When her eyes cut through the sea of greeters to the town itself, she was struck by its difference to WolfHome. Here, many of the houses were angular and modern, with much glass, while others reminded her of Southwestern adobe ones, sprouting curved chimneys and painted bright colors. The streets were angular, too, unlike the sinuous ones of WolfHome. Gato pointed with great pride to the keep, Catamount. It sprawled on a bluff above the town, its design reminiscent of Frank Lloyd Wright's Fallingwater, only five times larger. Acres of glass overlooked the town, and beneath the keep, waterfalls cascaded to a river below.

Catamount was spectacular, not that she'd tell the arrogant Alpha that.

"Well?" said the Alpha.

"Pretty."

"*Pretty?*" he said, disdain curling from his lips. "The splendor of Catamount transcends such banality."

She shrugged.

Groomsmen rushed toward them, one about to take Moonrise's bridle.

"Don't!" Kit said. "She'll bite you."

"I've handled worse." The groom's swagger matched his Alpha's.

Was arrogance injected in the Cats' DNA at birth? "Not like this one you haven't."

"Leave her be," the Alpha commanded. "Always heed Ma'am Kitlyn's words. Understood?"

The groom cut her an obsequious look and bowed to his alpha.

She suspected she'd made another enemy. "I'll follow you to the stables."

The Alpha dismounted and handed his reins to the second groom. She slipped from the saddle, forcing herself not to massage her sore bum. "Time to rest, girl." She scratched Moonrise's chin and followed the surly groom.

"Behave yourself, Kitlyn."

The Alpha's words didn't deserve a reply, but she stretched her arm out and flipped him the bird.

The Alpha's laughter was his only response.

Settling into her new quarters at Catamount took fewer than fifteen minutes. Once Kit removed her boots, she lay down on the luxurious bed and closed her eyes.

All she wanted was to make it to the competition in one piece. Four weeks of annoying Cats surrounding her would test her resolution, not to mention her patience.

Back home, she'd handled gaggles of overly enthusiastic teens. If she could deal with them, she could deal with the Cats.

She kept telling herself that.

As Arina had said, her rooms were lavish. Massive windows overlooked the town and valley below, the sounds of falling water soothing. The Alpha and his "pride"—his commanders, close advisors, and family—dined in a small hall within Catamount. If there was a central hall where his Clan ate, she hadn't seen it. Most days she chose to eat her meals in her room. In the halls, she'd often encounter numerous small cats, like on Earth, but she'd yet to see a large one.

Kit used her notebook to make a calendar, crossing off each day that passed, the competition dates circled in red. The games would occur over three days, with contestants and observers coming from all corners of Eleutia.

Week One was horrible. The days dripped by like Chinese water torture. Even when she'd first arrived at WolfHome, knowing only Rafe, she'd never felt so alone. The walls of her rooms had started to close in, though her suite was far more expansive than her rooms at WolfHome.

The jetted tub in her bathroom soon palled, as did the huge bed with the down coverlet, and the luxurious chairs, chaise, and sofa in her living area. She mostly ignored the full kitchen. Her isolation chafed, but it was better than spending time with the Cats.

She kept fit practicing her martial arts, mostly in her suite, though she performed her Tai Chi forms outdoors on occasion.

Unlike WolfHome's keep, with Clan members living in myriad rooms and suites, Catamount was mostly ceremonial, with few inhabitants. From what she gleaned, only the Alpha Gato, Arina, and Gato's Pride lived there, the other rooms given over to public functions and meeting rooms.

The Alpha, thankfully, left her alone for the most part. But a week after she arrived, he appeared at her door.

"Come, I would show you the competition grounds."

She nodded and followed.

The Alpha had left his midnight hair free of ties, and his black shirt and pants clung to every muscle. Standing in the elevator that took them to the valley floor, his sultry glances made her itch. He stood too close, loomed too often. His scent wasn't unpleasant, but it wasn't welcome, either.

"Do you always hover like this?" she asked as the elevator took its time.

"Most women enjoy my attention."

"See? You nailed it. I'm not most women. So, give me some space."

"As you wish, Ma'am Kitlyn." He stepped back to lounge against the elevator's glass walls.

Three more weeks of this banter would have her nerves scraped raw.

Heads turned as they crossed the square, headed for a distant structure at the town's edge. She'd expected the stares, but they still made her uncomfortable. The paths were prettily arrayed with desert flowers and cacti, but she longed for WolfHome's more lush plantings.

"Orderly," she said.

"We prefer it that way." He walked with his hands clasped behind him, occasionally nodding or speaking a few words to the Clanfolk who greeted them. All too often he'd press a hand to the small of her back, as if she belonged to him.

The more he spoke, the more her certainty solidified that he was the man who'd stalked her in the movie theater. "Why did you speak to me in the movies, then run away?"

He grinned, scraping a hand across his chin. "We Cats love to play. Hard to resist taunting you and getting away with it inside WolfHome. Harmless fun."

"You pricked me with your claws."

"That wasn't intended."

She nodded and walked on. Play, was it? Not to her.

It was Rafe who'd said some of the Cat-held competitions for Made Ones might be fixed. She'd keep a sharp eye.

There was no escape, of course. One didn't "escape" from something one had voluntarily chosen. In any event, where could she go? What would she do?

The Cats would come after her should she leave. And the only place she wanted to go was back to WolfHome, where she suspected her welcome would be less than warm. Gato would renew his threat of war in a heartbeat.

They arrived at a huge open-air stadium, where they walked an aisle beside the wooden bleachers overlooking the inner arena. Easy enough for someone to slip beneath the seats and escape.

She jerked to a halt. It was all too real. The competition was happening, really happening, The Challenge no longer an imagining in her head. Perhaps not as barbaric as the Roman games, but primitive enough with *her* as the prize.

The idea was so absurd, she almost laughed.

Six pillars crowned with a variety of big cats, apex predators all, hugged the walls surrounding the inner playing field of hard-packed earth. Across the field sat a lavish grandstand of padded benches for exclusive spectators. Like something out of *Game of Thrones*. Now if she only had a dragon.

"This seems permanent," she said.

"We often hold games amongst ourselves, as well as with the other Clans."

"When you're not waging war?" she said, her voice dust dry.

His smile was one of pride. "Exactly. We are the mightiest Clan on Eleutia. Never doubt it. I am the strongest alpha, as well."

"And humble, too."

He laughed. "Oh, I see my modesty precedes me."

Unable to help herself, she joined in his laughter. He was an outrageous man. The idea that this Cat could be likable flashed in her mind. Horrible thought.

"I'm working on a surprise for you," he said.

Oh goody. "And what might that be?"

He grinned, all teeth and self-satisfaction. "You know the cliché. It wouldn't be a surprise if I told you. But you will *love* it."

With a fat, red X, Kit marked off day eight of twenty remaining on her calendar, time moving with the speed of a slug. The only saving grace was Moonrise. Each day she'd escaped to the stables and groomed her, threading her fingers through the mistral's curls, feeding her, though Gato had "requested" she not go for any rides. So far, she'd obeyed. Simply being in the presence of the mistral offered comfort.

Afterwards, in the shade of a huge mesquite tree, she would run through a series of Tai Chi forms. Slow and passive-appearing, they didn't alert her guard, Taz, to her plan. Practicing her more aggressive katas out in the open was impossible. They'd reveal too much.

She did push-ups, sit-ups, and jumping jacks, while Taz made a valiant effort not to gawk. That day—nineteen to go—she broke through Taz's stoic demeanor amidst lifting weights with found rocks.

"Ma'am Kitlyn, what are you doing?" He waved his arm at the rocks.

"I…" She panted between words. "Need to stay fit."

His look of shock pleased her. "Why?"

"I'm surrounded by people I don't know in a place that speaks of danger and death. Why not?"

Of course, her words had precipitated the Alpha's appearance in her rooms. He stalked in, face furious, smoke coming from his ears. "You fear danger and death?"

Why had she said that to Taz?

She returned to her journal writing. "Yes. I'm in hostile territory."

He clasped his hands behind his back, frowning. "We only want the best for you."

With care, she laid down her pen. "Do you? If that were true, you'd have let me stay with the Wolves."

Gato snorted and began to pace. "No, I would not. They are not deserving of you."

"Aren't you the judge-y one." She leaned back in the chair, stretched out her legs, and crossed her ankles. "And might I ask, who are you to decide that?"

He halted his pacing and stared at her, eyes incredulous. "Alpha of Eleutia's mightiest Clan."

His posturing reminded her of Inigo Montoya. Any minute he'd say, "Prepare to die!" She began to laugh, which caused a mighty scowl to mar the Alpha's face.

"You are a ridiculous woman," he said.

She laughed harder.

Gato glided out of the door. If he'd been any other man, he would have stomped. But Cats didn't do that.

Her laughter died. Rafe didn't stomp, either. Well, she admitted, he did sometimes. What was he doing right then? How was he feeling? She saw him so clearly, different scenes from their time together flashing by like a stupid PowerPoint presentation. Her heart did that withering thing that sent her flying to the shower so the water might pound her senseless.

It never worked.

CHAPTER TWENTY-THREE

The days blended together, and she was fitted for gowns, when all she wanted to wear were jeans and a t-shirt. Shoes appeared, lavish ones with five-inch heels that she couldn't possibly walk in, and supple boots that fit like they were made for her. She supposed they were. Jewels arrived in her rooms, too. Yet she remained isolated until the day a boy approached her while she was reading in the library.

Now that she could read Eleutian words, she was thankful the written language of the Cats was the same as that of the Wolves. She read about the trees, the plants, and the animals of Eleutia and gobbled up information about the different Clans inhabiting the world. She even dove into a work of fiction on this strange and wonderful and terrible planet. Yuan would be proud.

Taz nodded to the hovering teen to approach.

"May I sit?" The boy had an open, eager face, with freckles and a shock of red hair that fell to his shoulders. He looked to be about fourteen.

"Please, do."

He took the chair beside hers. "I'm Mateo."

"I'm Kit."

His chest puffed out. "Oh, I know. Everyone knows, Ma'am Kitlyn."

She hoped her smile made him feel comfortable. "Just call me Kit."

"You like reading?" Mateo said.

"I do."

He beamed. "Me, too."

Where this was going? From Taz's nod, she assumed he was a Clanmate and one of the Alpha's Pride, though she hadn't seen him before.

"I saw you reading a book on our fauna," Mateo said. "Did you know we have the biggest trees on the planet?"

Ah, another humble Cat. "Do you?"

"Yes, in the high forest behind Catamount. They're huge, some more than four-hundred feet tall. And old, really old. Our giant reds are the best trees in the world."

"I'd love to see them." If they were anything like California's redwoods, they'd be spectacular. He was a likable kid, full of enthusiasm. Yet her innate wariness of the Cats wouldn't let her relax. He could have an agenda, one she couldn't imagine.

Mateo leaned close. "Some say, they were once Eleutians who reached too high for the Sky."

"What do you think?"

"I think they're just trees."

They chit-chatted for a few moments more, and she learned he hated math, loved girls, and practiced wrestling and swordplay to enter the competition—for her.

"How old are you?"

"Fifteen."

"Then why enter The Challenge against older and stronger men?"

His eyes grew sultry. "You need to ask that?"

Lucky stars, save her from teenaged boys and their hormones. "Your Alpha is entering, too, as are warriors from all of Eleutia. Do you think that wise?"

His lower lip thrust out. "I may not win. But I must try."

"I'm not disparaging your abilities." She took his chin in her hand. "Just don't die." His look of ecstasy made her snatch her hand away. "Hear me, Mateo?"

A big sigh, then the boy nodded, slipped out of the chair, and ran as if on Nike's wings.

After mid-day, Kit mentioned to Taz about Mateo entering The Challenge.

His shy smile flashed, then disappeared as fast. "Do not worry, Ma'am Kit. When boys enter, we make sure they're not seriously damaged, and he won't make it to the final three." He waved a hand. "It's a right of passage for our kind."

She blew out a breath that she hadn't known she was holding. "Good. Very good. I'd like to see the trees. Mateo called them 'reds.'"

"It's a tough hike, Ma'am Kit. Up to the high mesa above Cata-mount and beyond."

Taz was a big guy, a good soul, and a worrier. An adventurer he was not. "Let's go."

He sighed. "If you insist. Put on sturdy shoes, pants, and a rain jacket in case—"

"Taz, we're not exploring uncharted territory, but the mesa in CatHome. We'll have fun."

"Fun?"

Oh, dear.

To make him happy, Kit wore boots and pants, and she carried a light jacket and a bottle of water.

An hour later, they walked the narrow serpentine path above Catamount. The track that ran alongside one of CatHome's epic waterfalls led to an immense boulder that Taz told her lay at the end of the trail. The soaring "reds" shaded the ground, cooling the air and peppering the earth with ferns. It reminded her of Big Sur, one of her favorite places on Earth.

At first, Taz hovered like a mother hen guarding her chicks. He finally agreed to stay a good distance behind her but to always keep her in sight. Kit pretended she was on a hike with her sisters. While she'd seen the California redwoods, neither Sybi nor Bree had. They'd be enchanted, too. Bree would want to picnic on one of the fallen trees. Sybi would hug them.

Rounding a bend, she stumbled over a dead branch in the path, tumbling to her knees. "Damn!"

She looked up and froze. She was face-to-face with a mountain lion.

Huge. Grayish tan. Scarred muzzle. The cat's jaws widened, and it raised its lips in a low, throaty hiss.

Shote. The branch was too heavy to use as a weapon, and the Cats had taken all of hers. Taz was around the bend, unable to see her and too far away to help. She herself was a weapon, but beginning on her knees opposing a mountain lion would end in disaster. Hers.

The world dimmed. She bit her lip *hard.*

Don't flash back. Don't flash back. Don't flash back.

Clarity returned, and she sighed. "Hello, Mr. Mountain Lion." The wolves were friendly in WolfHome, maybe the cats were the same here.

Except the cat's muscles bunched, as if he were about to spring.

Time slowed.

She braced her hands, ready to engage. Not the ending she'd expected. She'd fight. An uppercut to the chin might work or a sweep of her leg. But fear was ascendant, never a good thing.

Why had she asked Taz to maintain his distance?

The cat's head snapped to the left, his mouth widened, and he screamed in fury.

Paulo ghosted from the trees, trailed by three huge wolves.

Her heart thundered. A mirage?

The fur on all four canids rose in aggression, and they moved forward, snarling at the mountain lion.

The cat took one long look at her, and she'd swear she saw regret. Then he flipped around and bounded off through the trees.

She sat hard on her ass.

Her near death and salvation had all happened in a matter of seconds.

The wolves and Paulo surrounded her, nuzzling her, Paulo licking her cheeks. She hugged them all.

"Thank you!"

Pounding footsteps.

We remain, Paulo said in her mind.

"I'm so glad. I missed you."

Just as Taz rounded the bend, they backed into the screen of trees.

When she arrived home, Gato was waiting for her, insisting she tell him all that had happened on her walk. He sprawled on one of her lounge chairs, wagging one finger back and forth. "You exaggerate."

"I do not. One of those huge mountain lions—"

"Puma."

"Gah! Fine! A puma, then, almost ate me."

His smile was obsequious. "That is impossible. Our cats know not to approach strangers."

"Approach? More like nose to nose."

"Where, might I ask, was Taz?"

"Around the bend. He couldn't see me."

"Tell me your tall tale again."

If she could throttle him, she would. "A huge branch was in the path, and I tripped and fell to my knees."

"Already exaggeration. No wood mars our walking paths. We keep them clean at all times."

She threw up her hands. "Why bother telling if you're going to negate everything I say?"

He nodded. "Apologies. Continue."

"Like I said, I fell to my knees and the cat was there. He looked pretty hungry to me."

"You appear unscathed. On your knees, you say. So how did you fend him off?"

She'd prepared. "I love rocks. I'd picked up a pretty one just off the trail and smashed it into his nose."

He pressed a finger to his chin. "Describe the cat."

"Big. Almost as big as a wolf."

"Our cats are bigger than wolves." His soft chuckle grated.

"Will you just shut up and let me speak."

"Continue."

"This one was grayish tan, with a badly scarred muzzle."

His languid pose vanished, and he sat up. "Scarred muzzle, you say?"

"Yes."

"Did he speak with you?"

"Mind to mind? No."

"Hum." He leapt out of the chair. "No more walks."

He stalked out the door, leaving her curious as to why the cat's scarred muzzle had lit his fire.

Sweat still coated Rafe's body, his hair made sticky by the heat and effort. He smelled. He was also filthy and bruised, and he didn't give a shote. He ate alone, no one daring to approach him, his mood foul as he shoveled meat and pasta into his mouth.

Thorn was next up as his sparring partner, a warrior who outweighed him by fifty pounds. Finally, a true test of the bulk and muscle he'd added over the past two weeks.

If he didn't win Kit, he'd... He growled low in his throat.

Worry consumed him. One of the wolves he'd sent with Paulo had returned yesterday. Which was when he'd learned a wild puma had almost attacked Kit. The Cat Clan was secretive, yet he knew the wild cats who roamed their territory were charged not to attack humans. Not unless bidden.

A Clan member had to have set that cat on her. He wondered if Kit knew that.

Max slid into the seat beside him.

"Leave," Rafe said, his tone harsh.

"You need to—"

"Go away, Ferret, unless you want a swipe of my claws." Rafe lifted his left hand with its clawed bracer.

Max reared back. "Fark, Rafe, why are you wearing claws to mid-day?"

"Because I feel like it."

"I need to show you something important."

Rafe looked him up and down. "I see nothing important. Leave."

"Fine!" Max smashed his fist onto the table, rattling the dishes. "I've had it with you. When you're ready to listen, look me up."

Rafe returned to eating, though the food—all food—tasted like dirt. He cleaned his plate and went for another round. He had two hours before Thorn, enough time for a shower and to do some squats, pull ups, and weights. As long as he didn't puke.

The line for food wasn't long, but it took all his will not to barge his way through.

A hand on his shoulder made him whip around, claws extended.

"You're a farking mess."

His eyes burned into those of his friend and favorite doctor, Kicks, her spiked pink hair and leather bandoliers reflecting her badass attitude. "Fark off."

She crossed her arms, her lean muscles standing out in harsh relief. "As if."

He growled, vision a blinding red.

A surprise blow to his solar plexus had him bent in half, pain coming in waves.

"You are out of control, Commander," Kicks said.

Rafe prepared to spring and rip out her shoting throat. But as he moved, hands banded his shoulders, waist, and thighs.

"Bring him to my office, boys," she said.

At first, he struggled, almost freed himself, and landed a fist to Talos' nose. But his temper gradually cooled as he was hauled like a sack of meat through The Keep's corridors. "Release me."

Kicks pivoted. "You'll behave?"

He nodded.

"Do it."

The men put him down, and he straightened his shirt while his captors beat a swift retreat. "Was that necessary?"

"You missed your physical. The Alpha sent me."

"The Alpha's a pain in my ass."

She slapped his back. "Isn't that the truth."

"I spar in two hours with Thorn. I won't miss it."

"Then c'mon, so we can get this over with."

Rafe checked his phone. Kicks was halfway through the exam, and an hour remained before his bout with Thorn. The receptor Kicks pressed to Rafe's chest made him jerk. "You could warm the thing up."

"Where would the fun be in that?" She ran a hand over the tips of her spiked hair. "I don't like this. The reading's high."

He grabbed her wrist. "Will it kill me?"

"Let. Go."

He stared at his hand wearing claws capable of ripping open Kicks' wrist. He'd really just done that. *Shote*. With care he released her. "Sorry. I'm not myself."

She removed the receptor, made some notes on her tablet, then wrapped the cuff around his upper arm. "To answer your questions, no, the readings on the receptor won't kill you. The Made One might."

"Kitlyn."

She spat into the sink. "For that one."

"Don't, Kicks." He couldn't promise not to throttle her if she continued. "I thought you liked her."

When she raised her eyes to his, they burned. "She broke faith with you. With all of us."

Yup, he'd throttle her, except then he'd have to do the same to half of the Clan. He was calm now, ice coating his heart and mind. "She did not."

"What do you call her going with the Cats?"

He called it sacrifice.

"I see that look on your face." Kicks slammed her fist into his bicep. "Wake up!"

He'd listened to this crap for the past two weeks. Kicks wasn't saying anything new. "We done here?" He slid from the exam table.

She ripped off the cuff, then stabbed the tablet hard enough to break it as she made notes. "Your quaylights are out of balance. More water, less sodium, more bananas."

"Bananas."

"Your potassium levels are also low. Spinach, dried apricots help, too. I'll send a list of foods to your tablet."

He tugged on his pants and balled his filthy shirt in his fist. "You're wrong."

Kicks raised a perfectly pink eyebrow. "You're questioning my medical expertise?"

"You know who I'm talking about."

She massaged his arm where she'd just struck him. "For your sake, Rafe, I hope I am."

Rafe leaned against the cage, sipping the quaylight drink he'd snagged before his bout with Thorn. If he were the kind who fist pumped, he would have. Then again, he wasn't sure he could raise his arm that high. They'd fought without weapons, hand-to-hand, and he was bruised and bloody in ten different places, his gut screaming at him. But he'd scored a clear victory. A first.

In two weeks, he'd face Gato, who was certain to make the finals. True, a falcon or bear might take Rafe out, but it was unlikely. No, Gato was his true opponent.

He leaned over and spat blood. Someone shoved a clear serus-bagged piece of paper in his face. He was about to slap it out of the way when the words came into focus.

Kill the Made One.

"Where did you get this, Max?" Rafe straightened, and spots

danced before his eyes. He pressed a hand to his throbbing abdomen.

Max bared his teeth as he tucked the paper back into his pocket. "Georg's room, the shote-head. I went over it again and found this jammed between the drawer and the side of his night table."

The throbbing in Rafe's head increased. "Forensics?"

"On my way there."

He grabbed Max's forearm. "Sorry about earlier. I'm an ass."

"Yeah." Max grinned. "But we always knew that."

He went to squeeze his friend's shoulder, but his world went black.

One week to go. Kit had plans. First, she'd return to her rooms sweaty and stained and take a shower. She'd think of Rafe, make herself come, and pretend that helped.

But when she breezed into her rooms, thrilled to be leaving Taz at the door, she found Gato draped across her sofa reading a magazine.

"Excuse me?" she said.

Gato held up at finger. "One sec. I want to finish this article."

That pompous dickwad. She threw her filthy towel at him and made her way to the bathroom, shutting and locking the door. Once she'd switched on the shower, she doffed her clothes and stepped inside the cavernous space. The pounding spray gave her a few moments of solitude before she went out to see what the jerk wanted.

Whenever Gato visited, he wanted *something*—information, usually, though he'd often use words of seduction to convince her that she was meant for him.

She soaped her hair with the urge to cut it all off. That would show him. Except Rafe loved winding her curls around his fingers.

Gato did nothing like that, not that she would let him, but he hadn't even tried. In fact, if she thought about it, he never showed any genuine interest in her. Oh, he spoke pretty words, said all the right things, yet there was no true heat, no authentic emotion other than that she mattered to the Clan. For all Gato's blustering and braggadocio, his devotion to Clan was evidenced in the man's every action.

But for Kit herself, as a person or mate? He didn't desire her, which was just fine.

When she walked back into the living room, Gato was staring into space. "You no longer smell."

"And that's a phrase that would win any girl's heart."

"Why don't you wear the gowns we've made for you?"

"Because I don't like them. Plus, they restrict my movements."

"Movements. Ah, yes. Taz tells me that you've stepped up your practice to 'keep in shape.'"

"So?"

Eyes half-lidded, he asked, "Why, princess, when you needn't lift a finger? I am somewhat skeptical of your motivation."

"Honestly?" Her huffy expression masked the fear that he'd discover her plans. "Because I haven't anything else to do here. Because that puma scared me. Because I like to exercise."

"Because your former illness still makes you feel death's hand at your throat."

A chill rippled up her spine, and she walked to the bank of windows that overlooked the village. She recalled the disease's hunger for her death only too well.

Yet on that hike, she'd staved off her flashback. More and more she'd been able to keep the past at bay, while becoming stronger, more present.

Her hand pressed the glass. Outside, the sun still blistered the dry earth. The heat made her workouts twice as hard, and yet inside Catamount, the air was cool and fresh and scented with growing things.

"Forgive my harsh words," Gato said. "And my unkind reminder. I've been distracted."

"Alphas often are. No worries." Kit glanced over her shoulder. "What's up?"

"Do you never glide gently into conversation?" He shook his head, lips twitching a smile.

"What's the point, since I know you're here on a mission."

"You've been tainted by those Wolves." He spat that last word.

She whirled on him. "What is wrong with you people? Why is it so hard for your two Clans to get along? Centuries ago you did. Why not now?"

He chuckled. "Get along? What an amusing idea. As the dominant Clan, why bother?"

Gah! "Do you never get tired of posturing? Why does it matter who's the dominant Clan? Getting along could enhance both Clans' lives. Instead, you act like testosterone-driven idiots."

"War is better." He wiggled his brows.

Everything was a joke, and he'd said that just to rile her. She calmed, her efforts at negating his button-pushing not entirely successful. "No, war isn't better. Death is not preferable to life."

He ran a hand over his face, and he abruptly looked tired, with fresh lines of strain about his mouth and eyes.

"As you pointed out, we were comrades, once. Or so the histories say. That was before our women began to decline in numbers." Gato grew still, utterly serious. "Before our world began to die."

CHAPTER TWENTY-FOUR

Kit took a seat across from Gato and leaned forward. "What I don't understand is if your scientists can perform such amazing feats as bringing me to this world, why can't they discover what is causing the female decline and correct it?"

Gato's too-familiar smirk reappeared. "Do you think we have not tried to convince them that is the path they should take? The Alchemic Clan... Cruel men and women who hold our balls in their fists. They squeeze them, frequently. We cannot direct them, nor will they listen to our pleas. They are fixed on 'more important matters.' Something as small and inconsequential as Eleutia dying gives them little pause. Or so our spy tells us."

"Spy. Within the Alchemic Clan?"

"Indeed. I assure you, the Wolves and other Clans have the same. She can't breech their inner circle, but she learns things. Would our world die, our spy conjectures that the Alchemics would leave."

"Leave Eleutia? How?"

"They would transfer their Essences to another parallel world, other flesh, and begin anew. As outlandish as it sounds, she may be correct, for they pursue knowledge and worship the intellect as if they were the food and drink of the Fates."

"There must be Alchemic outliers who would help Eleutia."

"Perhaps, but they would be frozen out, unable to access Alchemic machines and the knowledge needed for deep study and experiments."

"You seem to know an awful lot about them."

He grinned. "She's a good spy."

"They sound like inbred assholes."

His booming laugh transformed him from distant to approachable.

"Release me." Kit had spoken softly, her words measured. She laid a hand on his and captured his eyes. She hoped he'd see her terrible desire to leave. "Cancel The Competition and allow me to return to the Wolves. Please."

The compassion in his eyes hurt. "I am truly sorry. The wheels are in motion, the games announced. Nothing but a cataclysm would prevent it from going forward."

She leaned back, sliding her hand away. She'd guessed as much, yet it felt like the final door had locked on her hopes, her personal scheme for victory a frail thing. "The Wolves say you've had many Made Ones."

He took a long time to respond, as if he were searching his memory for something elusive.

"Perhaps that was true decades ago. Has it been three years? Five? It matters not. Two years have passed within our Clan with but ten girl children born."

Ten. In a Clan of thousands. Shocking, and sad, which would explain his precipitous move for war, his demands outsized. "Why not simply keep me for yourself?"

"I would, were it at all possible. If I did so, the other Clans would band together to attack us. We are strong, but no. Winning the games, and you are our best chance—"

"To breed girl children."

"Yes. And I will win. You will be mine."

Not if she could help it.

· · ·

319

During the few days remaining before the competition, Kit forced herself to eat, afraid she'd lose weight she couldn't afford. That would be disastrous. But she was tired, the tension wearing on her.

Over the past weeks, she'd tried to reconnect with the wolves and Paulo. She hadn't had the opportunity. That was, until today, when a friend had pulled Taz aside in the market, and she'd escaped her tether to climb the trail where she'd met the puma. She ached for any news of Rafe and WolfHome.

The day was cooler, harkening to the coming fall, or what the Cats might call fall in this dry, desert land. The minute she'd hit the path, she'd begun whispering Paulo's name. If he was around, he'd show himself.

A right turn took her into the trees, where the temperature dropped further, that morning's workout sweat chilling her flesh.

"Paulo," she repeated, stepping further into the forest.

The towering trees dampened sound, and she raised her voice, repeating his name. Normally she'd love this dark place filled with quiet and solitude. Today, all she wanted was to see Paulo's bright blue eyes.

Ferns brushed her legs, making a scratching sound against the rough weave of her leggings, the trees themselves mute.

Too mute. Too quiet. No bird caws or rustle of small creatures disturbed the forest.

Her throat dried. She touched the laseblaster she'd brought for reassurance, its handle smooth with wear. She'd been shocked when Gato had insisted she carry one since the puma attack. Would she hear an approach from behind?

She whirled, blaster out. Nothing.

When she turned back, Paulo and the three wolves stood before her. She hadn't heard a sound.

Kit dropped to her knees and hugged the coywolf. "Paulo, what news?"

If she could read his eyes, she'd say they were sad.

WolfHome is as always.

Vague wasn't what she needed.

"How is Rafe?"

Paulo's eyes dropped to her chin and he licked it.

"Tell me. Please!"

He is injured.

"What happened? Why?"

The coywolf tilted his head.

She'd asked too many questions too fast. "What happened?"

A fight.

"Will he recover?"

The wolves' hackles rose. Something was coming. Whatever it was, she had to know about Rafe. "Will he get well?"

Paulo nodded, but he was no longer looking at her. A snarl crawled from his lips.

"Rafe will be okay?"

Yes! His annoyance was drowned out by the increasing growls of the wolves.

Run, my Kit!

"No!" She spun.

Two pumas loped toward them, mouths agape, yet silent.

"She's here! We've got her!"

A boy and a man thundered out of the wood. The teen she'd met in the library. "Mateo?"

The man shouted, pointing at her, "Attack!"

The pumas leapt off their hind legs, the wolves and Paulo doing the same.

No, no, no!

She raised the laseblaster as the canids slammed into the cats midair.

Howls, screams, screeches.

They fell to the ground in a tangled heap of claws and teeth, the jumbled five moving too fast for her to get off a clear shot.

The large man raised his own blaster. At her.

Kit pulled the trigger.

Missed!

She pulled again, but nothing. Kit dove for the trees just as the man fired.

Her hair was on fire! She beat at her head and hair, while her shoulder and neck burned with agony.

Someone was howling in pain.

More voices. *Damn.* She fiddled with the laseblaster, couldn't get it to fire. She tossed it to the ground, found a sturdy branch, and dashed from the tree, weaving as she went, praying she wasn't shot. With a heave, she swung the stick into a puma's side.

Shouting from somewhere, her attacker raising his blaster. She dived, simultaneously flinging the branch at him.

Score! The branch had hit him in the head, knocking him to the ground.

She lifted a rock and ran toward the man. As he rose, lifting his laseblaster, she jerked to the right. Pain seared her arm, but she powered through it, running hard, raising the rock. The man raced toward the cats. Mateo leapt for her, and she kicked out and sent him flying. She whirled.

One puma was down, the other nearly so, the wolves and Paulo's attack frenzied.

"Halt!" Gato's voice.

The puma froze, as did the man and Mateo. The wolves did not.

"Paulo stop! Stop the wolves!" Her words to Paulo went unanswered as Gato, Taz and Arina blazed into the clearing.

Without thought, she leapt between the wolves and Gato, shouting, "No!"

Everyone froze.

All the adrenaline leached from her body at once, and she grew lightheaded from the pain in her neck and shoulder. As she was about to topple, Paulo leaned against her, steadying her. She braced her hand on his back and felt the stickiness of blood.

Gato, Arina, and Taz stood in front of her. "What is going on here, princess?" His voice was soft and deadly.

"I can explain."

Arina looked feral with fury, Taz little better.

"Can you?" Gato said. "You dare attack our people. Kill our cats."

Both pumas lay on the ground, throats ripped out, bellies open, entrails exposed. Arina knelt beside them, taking a silver device from her pack and running it across each cat. She nodded to Gato.

A groan from the man who'd set the cats on her. Taz hoisted him to his feet. Her aggressor pointed at Kit. "The Made One attacked my son and me with her wolves."

Her knee-jerk was to respond. She curled a fist and waited to see what tale he spun.

Mateo limped over to his father and slung an arm around his waist. He stroked his son's head.

"The pumas came to our rescue," Mateo said, face pale. "They were only trying to protect us."

Well, well, well. What a bunch of lies.

She glanced at the three wolves who'd saved her. Two appeared bloody but okay. *Oh, no.* She rushed to the panting wolf who lay on its side, and she knelt beside her. Beneath the wolf's bloody and matted fur, claw marks had opened a large flap of flesh, exposing her ribs, and her right hind leg was twisted at an odd angle. "Gato, please, we need to help this wolf. She's badly injured."

"I think not until we learn the truth of the matter." He crossed his arms.

The wolf could die. Kit sprang up and stalked toward the Alpha. "The truth of the matter is they attacked us." She pointed to Mateo, and his father. "That man and his son *commanded* the pumas to attack us."

Gato's arched brow said it all.

"Just to clarify our situation," Kit said. "You believe father and son were out for a stroll and we attacked them for no apparent reason."

"Because we saw you conniving with the wolves!" the father shouted.

"Ah." She smiled. "Of course. And that laseblast you shot at me?"

"We didn't," Mateo said.

Arina spat. "I see no injury."

She walked to Arina, brushed her singed hair aside, and showed the woman her blistered flesh.

Arina hissed and raised her face to Gato. "She was hit. Only a laseblast could do this."

Gato pivoted to focus on the man. "You brought a laseblaster for protection in our woods, Santiago? Correct?"

The boy looked to his father, who nodded. "We did."

Kit's heart sank. She might be too valuable to kill, but they'd end the wolves and Paulo in a blink. "I gave you the truth."

The Alpha walked to Santiago and swung an arm around his shoulder. "And where is this blaster now?"

Santiago shrugged.

"Taz, find it," Gato said.

The soldier began searching, and Kit kneeled again by the fallen wolf, whose breath had become labored. She ran a hand across the wolf's head. "Please, can't we get some help for her while we talk?"

Gato opened his phone and made a call, one too quiet for her to hear.

"Got it," shouted Taz, who returned to Gato and handed him the blaster.

Arina stepped beside her Alpha and held out her hand for the weapon. She turned it over in her hands, sighted it on a dead tree, and fired. The tree broke into flame, which Taz extinguished. She raised her eyes to Gato. "I see."

"Are we in agreement?" Gato said.

"We are," Arina said.

They would not kill the wolves or Paulo. They'd have to go through her to get to them, and the canids were fast. As she petted the dying wolf, she turned her head toward the other two and Paulo, and whispered. "Run."

No. We will not leave you.

She pressed her face to Paulo's muzzle. "Run, I said. Do as I command."

"If they run," Gato said. "We will kill them."

Arina raised the laseblaster and aimed it at the wolves.

Kit climbed to her feet. "Don't you dare. They have done nothing but protect me, your precious Made One."

Three men trotted into the clearing, two carrying a canvas stretcher, the third holding the handle of a large box.

Gato pointed to the now-unconscious wolf, and the man with the box knelt beside her. A healer.

The other two wolves growled, and the healer jerked back.

"Let him," Kit said to the wolves. "He's here to help her."

The man opened his box and began to see to the wolf's injuries.

"What the...?" Santiago said. "They tried to kill us! Why are you helping that wolf?"

Gato's smile was cruel. "Because you attacked them."

Relief whooshed through Kit. Though she didn't understand why, Gato believed her.

Both father and son protested.

"Quiet!" Arina commanded.

The healer signaled to the men holding the stretcher, and they lifted the unconscious wolf onto it and carried her off. The healer stood and walked toward Kit.

"May I touch you?" he said.

"Yes, of course."

He cut away her burnt hair and rubbed a cooling salve across her blistered skin.

"Thank you," she said, though her eyes locked on Gato's.

The healer kneeled by the two remaining wolves and Paulo, but when he reached for the largest male, the wolf curled his lips and growled.

Paulo yipped, and the wolf lay down, burying his nose between his paws. The healer went to work.

Kit walked to Gato, who took the laseblaster from Arina.

"This blaster," Gato said, holding it up. "It is military grade."

Santiago raised his palms. "I was—"

"Quiet," Gato said. "I know well you were in the military, Santiago. But no longer. Civilians are not allowed these."

Santiago dug his hands into his pockets. "I know, but—"

"Also, the serial number tells me this is of recent make. Not a weapon from your military days."

Mateo's eyes went back and forth between his father and Gato. "Alpha, please, my dad got it for protection."

"Ah." Gato nodded, eyes blazing. "Tell me, did you also chip those pumas...for protection?"

"Chip?" Santiago said, eyes widening.

Arina laughed. "Gato, end this game. You're enjoying it far too much."

He nodded. "Taz, Arina, take them."

Santiago raised his hands. "But—"

"Not a word," Gato spat. "Do you take your Alpha for a fool, Santiago? You chipped and trained those pumas. To do so is illegal for anyone other than myself or the CatGuard. The penalty for doing such is death."

Santiago paled. "I didn't."

"You most certainly did." Arina flashed Santiago a look filled with hate. "I scanned them. The chips are not in our possession but from a batch pirated last year. Now it's our turn to find out why."

Santiago clasped his son to him.

"Taz, Arina, take them and go," Gato said, his eyes on Santiago. "We will discuss this later."

The father and son didn't resist as Taz and Arina zip-tied the teen and his father and led them off.

They must have followed her for days, and at the first opportunity when she'd been alone, they'd taken their chance. She had no idea why they'd attacked her. But then she hadn't understood the attacks at WolfHome, either. Who were these people who wanted her dead? If it hadn't been for the wolves and Paulo, she would be.

Once the healer finished with Paulo, he stood, his smile one of exhaustion. "These three will be fine."

"Thank you." Kit put a hand on her heart and bowed. "And the one you took on the stretcher?"

The healer shrugged. "Up to the Fates. She'll be in our infirmary.

You're welcome to visit." He lifted his medical kit, nodded to Gato, and left.

Paulo licked her hand, and she stroked his muzzle. "Thank you, good friend."

We will continue to watch.

They bounded off, Paulo favoring his injured leg.

"Now," Gato said, turning to Kit. "We talk about why you were meeting wolves in our wood."

CHAPTER TWENTY-FIVE

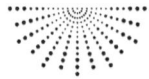

R afe walked with a slow, measured pace, a hand pressed to his side. Once he neared the council chamber, he dropped his hand and straightened. The stitches pulled, the ache in his side worsening. He was healing too slowly for his liking.

The council chamber was abuzz about The Challenge for the Made One. His Kit.

Behind him, the council doors closed. It took him long minutes to make it to his seat beside his father.

"What are you doing here?" Ulfr said.

"Isn't it obvious?"

"You can't compete." His father hissed his words, low and fervent.

"Of course I will." He almost smiled at his father's struggles to keep calm. Without a doubt, smiling would set him off. So tempting.

Meela chimed the bell, and silence descended.

The Alpha rose. "We are here to discuss who will be our candidates at the CatHome competition for the Made One. We are allowed three entrants."

Inga stood. "I've spoken to Thorn. He's our strongest. We send him."

"Giving Kit to him if he wins?" Rafe barked a laugh.

"Of course not," Max chimed in. "He would fight in your stead."

"I disagree," Inga said. "If Thorn wins, she's his."

"Not in this lifetime," Rafe said.

His father growled words meant only for his ears. "Which will be unnaturally short if you fight in The Challenge."

He spoke low. "Again, you underestimate me, Da."

Eevon stood. "I would like to compete in Rafe's name."

Rafe stood and bowed to Eevon. "Thank you, friend." He scanned the room, catching the eye of each council member. "Know that I will also compete."

Silence.

His father was silent, too, but fuming.

Inga stood. "Your operation was no easy thing, Radulfr."

"Agreed," he said. "But Kicks' spleen surgery has me back to near full strength."

Tilde nodded. She'd agreed to bind the area, which would help guard against further injury.

The Alpha rose. "I forbid it." The force of his power filled the room.

"I'll go in Rafe's stead," Max said. "When I win, the Made One will be his."

He and Max had discussed this. A ruse. He would take Max's place if the Alpha forbade his attendance. "I concede."

Ulfr's side-eye told Rafe his father wasn't convinced of his surrender. The Alpha nodded to Meela, who chimed her bell. "We vote. A show of hands."

All three—Thorn, Eevon, and Max—were unanimous choices to compete.

"The Wolves are my Clan." Kit said to Gato, raising her chin. "I miss them." She wanted to go home, to be with Rafe. He was injured, Paulo had said. She bit her lip.

He spat. "They are not your Clan."

A soothing breeze ruffled the trees. She couldn't run off to Wolf-

Home, no matter how badly she wished to. Somehow, she'd find out the details about Rafe.

She leaned against a trunk, needing the support. "The Wolves made me Clan when I arrived. Don't act like you don't know. You can smell it on me."

He gripped her upper arm and hauled her close. "Their scent will be erased by ours."

She pushed away from him, but he didn't release her. "In your dreams."

"No more walks. Hear?"

"Fine. Good thing the wolves were here, or I'd be dead."

His eyes bored into her. "I am aware, though if you hadn't escaped your guard, none of this would have happened."

"I'm not so sure." Gato was furious, but he was sincerely concerned, too. He'd also acted fairly, when it would have been expedient to blame her as the attacker. "Why? Why would your people try to kill me?"

"Bah, fanatics. A movement, and you know how they go. They find Made Ones anathema. 'Unnatural,' they call you. They wish to end you all."

"Given our purpose on Eleutia, that seems rather shortsighted. Can I have my arm back?"

He released her. "They are all fools. So, no more walks."

"I already agreed."

"You will stay within the walls of Catamount."

That wasn't good. "I need to feed and groom Moonrise and to work out, too."

"To care for your mistral, yes. But other than that, it's decided." He made a swiping motion with his hand. "Not under discussion."

From Gato's stiff posture and rigid muscles, she knew he wouldn't relent.

Rafe walked into his home, blistered with frustration. The day of the competition dawned bright and hot, a definite advantage for the

Cats, who were most acclimated to the searing heat of their land. The opening ceremony would be held at noon, with a feast after that for the competitors and dignitaries in attendance. Ulfr would be there, along with Seelar, who always attended high-profile events. By the time his father spotted him, it would be too late, not to mention too humiliating for Ulfr to force him to withdraw.

Ulfr, along with Max, Thorn, and Eevon, had ridden four of the mistrals to CatHome. When Rafe went to saddle Nightfall, he discovered Ulfr had set guards on his stable, much to Rafe's annoyance. A hovercraft, its speed far less than a mistral's in flight, wouldn't get him there in time. Ulfr knew his son.

He no more wanted to hurt the guards than he did his father, but he saw no other way. He splashed cool water on his face, and when he reached for a towel to dry off, his hand encountered an anomaly. A note sat propped on the towel rack leaning against the counter. The script with his name on the envelope was Ulfr's.

His fury boiled when he took the note in hand, wanting to rip it to shreds. Instead, he pressed his thumb to the seal, and the flap popped open.

Radulfr -

I know you, my son, and I know you plan to attend The Challenge, no matter the council's choices.

As your Alpha, I oppose this, your life too at risk. Were I to perish, you, as my First Commander, must take charge of the Clan until a new Alpha is chosen.

As your father, and after much thought and soul searching, I find I must support you, foolish though it may be. When you took her to the caves, those sacred caves special to your mother, I knew. You love Kit as I once and still love Juliette.

Go to the shore by the caves. I have tethered Mistralys in the shelter of the Battons cave. If you can ride him, which is questionable, you will make the games.

Your displeased father,

Ulfr

He stared at the letter, read it once again. Had his father really done as he said? Or was this merely a time-eater to prevent his attendance? Only three from each Clan could participate. If he didn't show, Max would stand for him. And lose. Once Gato signaled for the games to begin, they could not switch.

He'd prepared his gear, and Tilde had bound his injury. He was ready.

Rather than heading for the caves, he walked to the big barn, needing confirmation. One more day of healing, and he could run. Right now, he wasn't about to rip himself open.

Assuring the guards he had no intention of stealing a mistral, he headed for Mistralys' stall. The huge stallion was gone. So were three of his father's other mistrals. If his father's letter spoke truth, he would have ridden Nightfall to The Challenge. If it wasn't a ruse.

Yet hope tightened his chest. A nod to the guard on the way out, and he returned home, double checked his sword, knives, and leathers, then ambled up to the barn.

He barely knew the guard, Borne, which was smart of the council. They didn't want him twisting a friend's duty. Borne opened his mouth to speak.

Rafe held up a hand. "I'm only here to take Baloo out for a ride."

"Sorry." Born's chagrinned face smiled back at him.

"Not a problem."

When he entered, he noted Nightfall's empty stall. He saddled and bridled the black mare, then led her to a corner of the house hidden from the barn to retrieve his gear. He settled it onto Baloo, ignoring the uncomfortable tug in his belly, and phoned Tilde about collecting the mare from the cave. He also grabbed several apples from the house.

Forced to walk Baloo away from his destination, he was finally far enough to circle back around toward the sea.

They galloped for the caves and Mistralys. What his father had done—it was out of character for Ulfr. But what he'd written about his love for Rafe's mother, that had been real. Ulfr had changed greatly after her death. They both had.

Perhaps Rafe had been so self-absorbed since his mother's passing, he'd failed to see the deep pain his father still bore. For years he'd distanced himself from Ulfr. Years that gradually ate away at the love he bore his father.

If Ulfr wrote true in his note, Rafe resolved to take better care with his father and to probe further beneath Ulfr's crusty exterior.

Battons cave sat in the opposite direction from the pools where he'd taken Kit. Larger, and not as tidal, Battons sat on a small spit of land that curved toward the sea.

Arriving, he reined Baloo in. The cave's sandy floor beckoned, but he didn't see Mistralys. Nonetheless, he walked the mare toward the cave, and over the sound of the breaking waves, he heard several neighs from within. He laughed aloud.

After he secured the black, he approached the fiery stallion, who stood saddled and bridled. When he neared, Mistralys snaked his head around to bite Rafe.

"Do not."

The mistral snorted.

He wasted endless minutes as he cajoled and bribed Mistralys with the apples. Each time he tried to mount, the stallion danced away. Rafe could vault onto his back, but if Mistralys didn't want him there, he wouldn't remain in the saddle for long.

Mistralys was one of the few mistrals who failed to respond to him. The mistral's behavior was all a play to assert his superiority as the leader of the herd, but too much time was passing. He almost punched Mistralys in the snout. If he was late to the games, all was lost.

Finally, Rafe grew desperate. Every horse and mistral had a key. He must find the stallion's. The creature reminded him far too much of Ulfr. Perhaps…

He bowed before Mistralys. "Yes, you are mighty and powerful. I concede your superiority. And I would deeply appreciate your assistance." Mistralys tossed his proud head and pranced. Then he stilled. Rafe stepped close, crooning to the mistral, and put his foot in the stirrup. The mistral danced, but without anger. Rafe swung himself onto his back, and they trotted from the cave into the open air. Mistralys' incredible leap into the sky took him by surprise.

"Okay, boy, we're off."

They soared, Mistralys' massive wings devouring the miles. He would arrive in time. He must.

Arina accompanied Kit when they entered the arena, now full to bursting. Perhaps five thousand people filled the stands. Pennants flew and banners proclaimed, and Kit swore she saw men moving among the stands offering refreshments.

Just like a Red Sox game at Fenway, except with more blood and gore.

Canopied rectangular stations circled the floor of the arena, hugging the walls, each bearing pennants of different colors. Blue and gold for the Cats, green and yellow for the Wolves, and numerous other color combinations. In the stands behind each station sat Clan members, in their Clan colors, ready to root on their team. Yet she saw myriad Clan members mingling with other Clans, exchanging greetings, laughing.

It should be like this always, the interweaving of diverse Clans. Just not when she was the trophy.

Arina led her to the grandstand, their box center stage, where the Clan alphas and other dignitaries held court.

Fukkes! He sat off to the side with another Alchemic Clan member, both dressed in white. She needed to grill him for information. He knew where her sisters were, she'd bet on it. It would have to wait. Oh, the frustration. One plan at a time, she told herself.

She had donned one of the glittery dresses Gato insisted she wear, but also made sure to wear her voluminous cloak. The fabric was light, yet strong, and the red complemented the pale rose of the toga-like dress that fell to her ankles. She'd defied Gato by wearing, not the jewelry the Cats had given her, but Rafe's braid around her throat. He'd been furious, but he didn't dare rip it off her.

Now Gato stood beside one of the throne-like chairs, hands clasped behind his back, observing the crowd. Resplendent in formal black and silver leathers, he would change clothes to compete. The egotistic jerk expected to win.

Not on her watch.

Arina directed her to a seat at the very center in a "throne" made of wood painted with gilt. Absurd. The whole thing was absurd, like one of those old Roman gladiator arenas where the crowd pointed thumbs up or down.

Gato had assured her the bouts didn't go to the death. Mostly. Accidents happened, he said. And wasn't that swell.

A uniformed Cat Clan member passed binoculars to the observers in their box. Once she received hers, she peered through them, hunting for the Wolves.

In front of their canopied station, Eevon paced back-and-forth. Kit dared hope Rafe would be one, though she worried about the injury Paulo had mentioned. But she knew her Wolf, and she'd bet he would compete. She spotted Tilde in the bleachers behind the Wolves' station, sitting beside Kicks. Arne, Inga, and Yuan were there, too, along with Talos, several council members, and dozens more attendees. And wasn't that Yuma, the librarian?

"Kit, would you like refreshment?"

She bit her tongue so she didn't snipe at Arina. "Not right now, thank you."

Two rows below Kit's, Ulfr was ensconced beside Seelar, one arm slung over the back of his mate's chair. Given Seelar's contempt of Kit, she could only imagine what the female Alpha was thinking. Thankfully, they hadn't brought Mimi to watch the violence.

Gato turned and raised an arm, signaling to the row of drum-mers seated across the arena, their thighs cradling immense wooden drums.

Boom. Boom. Boom. The processional began, with men emerging from the stations in an array of fighting gear, lining up, each contestant wearing his Clan colors as a sash across his chest.

She perched at the edge of her seat to see who was competing for the Wolves. There was Eevon, who was dwarfed by Thorn the Viking. Her heart clenched, muscles tight with anticipation. Another man strode out behind the Viking. Tall, but lean. Too lean. Max.

Her body melted back into the seat, trying to leash her distress. Rafe must be hurt badly not to be here. Or maybe he didn't care anymore. Or he believed she'd betrayed him.

The team members marched single file, hugging the arena perimeter, until they met at the far end where they converged. Now, each team walked three abreast down the center of the field toward the grandstand.

The drums boom-boomed, the procession painfully slow. The Wolves were last, making Kit glad there wasn't a Zebra Clan.

Though it took forever, Eevon, Max, and Thorn finally reached the stands opposite hers. Shoulder to shoulder, they moved toward her. She raised the binoculars. Eevon's harsh face bore a rigid determination, while the Viking's gleeful grin spoke of confidence. Max's frown worried her, and he kept raising his eyes to the blue sky.

She followed his gaze, but the sky was clear.

As each Clan made it to the grandstand, the contestants paused, bowed, and Gato raised his microphone and announced the participants' Clan and their names. The Wolves came closer, then they were two back, then one, then...

Max, Eevon, and the Viking stood before her.

"The Wolf Clan's Thorn." Gato announced. As with the earlier contestants, Thorn bowed to Gato, and then to Kit.

A rumbling in the crowd, with people shading their eyes and peering skyward.

"Maximus," Gato boomed. Max bowed to the Alpha, and as he did to her, he winked.

"Eevon," Gato announced.

A blurring of time and space.

People screaming.

Eevon throwing two knives shouting "Kill the Made One!"

Arina knocking her sideways.

As she toppled, she caught a black mistral bulleting toward the grandstand, Rafe leaping off its back onto Eevon, bringing them both crashing to earth.

Kit pushed herself up, side aching where she'd hit the arm of the chair. Far below, she saw Rafe and Eevon grappling on the ground.

"Are you hurt, Made One?" someone shouted.

Blood speckled her right arm. But she was fine.

Arina!

A knife buried to the hilt protruded from Arina's shoulder. Gato was there, as was a healer. Kit moved close, thankful Arina's chest continued to rise and fall. A second knife lay on the floor, having missed its mark.

Men appeared with a stretcher.

"Take her to the infirmary," Gato said.

"Arina." Kit touched the woman's hand.

"I'll be fine," Arina said, her voice thready. "We Cats are tough."

Arina was carefully lifted onto the stretcher and borne away,

Kit had been saved by Arina. Just as Rafe had done, the wolves and Paulo, even Mimi, and now a Cat. How many times had her life hung by a thread on Eleutia? She rubbed a shaking hand across her forehead, knees wobbly, and sat back down. Well. Life was certainly different on Eleutia.

Eevon. Her claws instructor and tablemate had tried to kill her. She sucked in a deep breath.

Rafe!

The two men were surrounded by soldiers, Rafe gripping Eevon in a punishing hold. The stands were hushed, the crowd waiting, breathless.

"Take him to the cells," Gato said.

Rafe released Eevon to the guards.

"Kill the Made One." Eevon's voice might be hoarse, but his words rang with fervor. "All Made Ones will die. They are an abomination to our world, to our way of—"

A guard strapped his mouth with a cruel bit of leather and tightened it.

Her eyes cut to Rafe's. A flood of longing choked her, Rafe's face unreadable. He broke their eye contact to lock onto Gato. "I will be the third member of the Wolf team."

"I'm afraid not, Commander," the Alpha said. "The teams have all reached the grandstand. You're too late."

Rafe's grin could only be called wolfish. "Do check the rules, old friend. Not until you've called The Challenge's start does that one apply."

"Ah. Yes." A slow smile meandered across Gato's face. "Of course, you are correct, *old friend*. I must have forgotten."

"A pity how memory can fail like that," Rafe said.

"Isn't it?" Gato said.

She'd swear the two were enjoying their exchange.

The Cat Alpha took up his microphone and proceeded to announce Rafe's name as a contestant, replacing Eevon for the Wolves. When Rafe bowed to Gato, then to her, she wanted to smile, but her lips trembled too much.

The teams formed a semi-circle around the grandstand. Gato raised one arm and chopped downward, shouting, "Let The Challenge proceed!"

A roar filled the arena as the teams filed back to their stations. When Rafe passed in front of her row, he gave a brief nod to his father, who nodded back. No other contestant had nodded to their alpha, making Kit wonder what that was all about.

Rafe veered off the recessional toward the guards encircling a horse. No, Mistralys! Had he stolen him? Rafe clasped the mistral's reins, and the stallion snorted and pranced as Rafe led him toward the Wolves' canopied station, where he handed off the mistral to Arne.

It finally sank in. Rafe was here. He would compete for her.

She tried to imagine what he'd think of her plan. She failed.

CHAPTER TWENTY-SIX

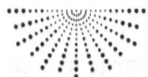

Two days watching blood and guts spill onto the hard-packed earth were two days too many for Kit. Some men wore full leathers. Others, including Rafe, fought in leather loincloths, chests bare, with metal shoulder guards, cloth and leather wraps for arms and wrists, wide leather belts, greaves with leg pads, and soft boots. Watching Rafe fight, she hurt with each prick of a knife and black-and-blue to his flesh.

Kit never would have made it in ancient Rome. The men's injuries and pain nauseated her and, sadly, two had died, the unintended consequence of their bouts. The only bright note was Arina returning to the games on day two, her arm in a sling.

Early that final morning, Kit wore a tank and panties as she stared out the suite's window to the town square below. Normally, it would be bustling at this hour, but because of the games, the place was near empty of life. Already, the broiling sun beat down at dawn of that last day.

A soft knock.

"Who is it?"

"Arina!" Then she breezed in, teeth bare. "Why are you not ready? You are the most frustrating woman!"

"My sisters thought so, too."

A shadow flashed across Arina's eyes. Perhaps she'd also lost a loved one. "Be that as it may, we have less than thirty minutes to make it to the grandstand, and you're still wearing…that."

Kit picked a piece of lint off her tank. "All right, except I'll change in the bathroom. I need privacy."

Arina's lips pinched, but she nodded her assent.

Kit hefted her bag from the closet and made for the bath. No fancy dress today. She brushed out her long hair, plaited it, and tied it off with a bow, a nice ironic touch. Then after she bound her breasts, she squirmed into her supple leathers. She'd worn them often in the privacy of her suite at WolfHome to be certain they'd bend to her will and not vice versa. One look in the mirror made her smile.

Her three knives slipped into their waist and boot sheaths with ease. Hot though it was, she'd deliberately chosen a green full-length cloak that day. She donned it with a swirl of anticipation. She'd sewn deep pockets and loops into the lining of her cloak, which was where she stowed her hood, the foldable stick Talos had cleverly made, and her pennant. The trickiest part was her short sword, but it slipped perfectly into the leather loops lining the cape. Finally, she wound and tied Rafe's braid around her neck.

Her leathers and weapons were merely a costume covering her true arsenal, which lay within.

She did up the cloak's buckles and checked herself in the mirror.

The cloak hid her leathers, but her first test would be Arina's inspection.

Arina's eyes bugged out when Kit entered the living area.

"All set," Kit said.

"You wear the color of the Wolves," Arina said

She'd pissed Arina off, but her color choice had been purposeful. "I do. They are my Clan, and Rafe is my mate. Why would I not wear green?"

"Perhaps so you didn't infuriate Gato?" Arina's hand snaked out.

Kit jumped back, but Arina was fast. The Cat gripped one side of the cloak and flung it over Kit's shoulder, revealing her leathers in all their white glory.

"What the…" Arina's nostrils flared, her chin lifting. "What are you playing at, girl?"

Kit's lips tightened, and she deliberately stepped into Arina's space. "This has nothing to do with play and everything to do with survival."

Arina's mouth fell open. "You plan to compete."

"I do."

Laughter rocked the room, the Cat's eyes streaming with tears. "There is a dumb, and then there is truly stupid. You have surpassed both."

"All I ask is that you not reveal what I'm wearing or that I plan to compete."

One silver eyebrow rose. "Why should I keep quiet? If Gato learns I knew—"

"He won't. Please."

Arina smirked. "And do you fight on the Wolf team?"

"You know I can't. The team is complete. No, I fight for myself, which is allowed for last-minute entrants according to the rules. I studied them thoroughly. I'm right, aren't I?"

Arina shook her head, muttering to herself. "Gato will kill me."

"If you're so sure I'll lose—"

"Oh, there is no doubt about that."

"Then what difference will it make to keep my secret?"

"Gato removing my head from my body?" Arina checked her phone, grabbed Kit by the arm, and hauled her down the hall.

"Well?" Kit said. "Will you?"

"We must make it to the grandstand before the herald's call."

Kit stopped dead. "Will you keep my secret?"

"I will give you this. I will consider it."

"Give me the chance, Arina," Kit said, "to make my own choice. To be my own person."

"Bah. What are you babbling about?"

Kit straightened. "On Eleutia, just about every choice has been made *for* me. This one, this choice, is mine."

"Come, or we will be late." Arina took off at a run, and Kit did the same.

Of the Wolf team, only Rafe remained as a contestant, even the mighty Thorn having fallen to a Falcon. A mere third of the teams remained in the games, and of those, only a single combatant prevailed from each. Unsurprisingly, Gato was the last Cat standing. While leaner than many of the fighters, his speed, cunning, and skills were unmatched.

The day's contests began, with wrestling, swordplay, running, javelin, and boxing taking place.

The contestants in the boxing match used no gloves, merely wrapped strips of leather around their hands. Copious blood flowed, and one of the Ferret Clan sustained a fatal injury during a bout.

As Arina had told her, when the field had been winnowed to eight contestants, all would engage in freestyle pankration, which combined wrestling and boxing. A no-holds-barred fight, with biting, gouging, and other unpleasantries permitted, most similar to an MMA bout. When only two were left standing, a final pankration between them would decide the matter.

She had to wait until only the two combatants remained, and it was killing her. If she joined The Challenge earlier, she feared they'd suss her out and disqualify her for being a woman.

The day inched along. Rafe took a mean blow to the kidney from one of the Eagle Clan. He was tired. All the contestants were, and more mistakes meant more injuries.

They broke for mid-day, and Gato joined them, appearing doctored, showered, and wearing fresh clothes. She prayed the same was offered to the other teams. Servers entered the grandstand bearing drinks, cold meats, and fruit. When Gato took his seat beside her, she was careful to keep her cloak closed. Her sword hilt poked her in the boob. She wasn't sure how to fix it without bringing attention to herself. She'd had enough of that, the crowd having had two-and-a-half days to gawk at her.

"Take off that awful cloak," Gato said between bites of food.

"Later." Her hand snaked out from a split in her cloak as a young Cat bearing a tray passed, and she popped a hunk of cheese into her mouth.

He chuffed his annoyance. "What are you wearing beneath?"

"It's a secret."

Gato leaned close and whispered in her ear. "Today is our day, Kitlyn."

She tried not to, but she couldn't keep her smile at bay. "I couldn't agree more."

Gato rubbed his chin. "You're in a strange mood."

"I am. How would I not be?"

His green eyes grew distant, then sharpened. "Indeed."

Eight. Then six. Then five. Three. Rafe, a Jackal, and Gato.

Rafe and the Jackal fought. She'd known Rafe was a warrior, but she hadn't realized how adept he was at defeating all comers. *Stars alive*, how he'd fought, with tooth and claw, brawn and strategy. He'd put on muscle in the month she'd been gone, and he was clever and incredibly strong. As was Gato, though he was a whip to Rafe's hammer.

The crowd went crazy when Rafe defeated the Jackal. He bowed to them, which was when she noticed Rafe favoring his side. Gato would have seen it, too.

A bell chimed for the brief rest period and some doctoring before the final bout. A group of fire dancers streamed into the arena to perform for the crowd during the break.

Kit's mouth dried. It was time.

Arina sat beside her, and Kit leaned close to the Cat. "Allow me to surprise you."

As if Arina hadn't heard her, she remained face forward watching the fire dancers.

Kit slid between the open space between the bleacher seats and dropped to the ground, landing softly on bent knees.

She pinned up her braid, then slipped her hood over her head, the eye, nose, and mouth holes in alignment. She slid the edge of the hood beneath her leathers, then zipped them to the throat. A perfect fit. Talos knew his business.

The last thing she did was attach the rainbow pennant to the long stick, though she waited to unfold it. She'd sewn it herself, her skills rather abysmal, but it worked. Symbolic in so many ways, it identified her as being of all Clans.

The five-minute warning bell chimed for the commencement of the competition.

This was such a gamble. She could be wrong. What if she was wrong?

She raced from beneath the bleachers.

On the ground, sight was different than up in the stands. She couldn't see much, and it was hard shoving her way through the crowd that clustered by the stadium entryway.

When she could finally see the arena, Gato was grappling with Rafe and pummeling him in the kidney, the area Rafe had been favoring.

She raced for the arena floor, but two guards with crossed spears stopped her, not even bothering to look at her.

"Let me through," she said, making sure to deepen her voice. "I plan to compete." She tossed off her cloak.

The guard who turned to her widened his eyes. "The Challenge is near ended. You are too late."

"No, I am not. Any unallied challenger can come forth at any time before the end of the games. I demand Final Challenge."

The pair exchanged glances, then the wide-eyed one ran up the steps to the judges' row.

She stood on tiptoe to see Rafe, who was standing again, thank the lucky stars. But the blood. He was covered in it, though Gato wasn't much better. He'd danced away from the Cat, which was when she saw a stream of blood down his side that hadn't been there earlier.

Stars alive, she had to get out there. She unfolded her banner stick and slid on her flag.

The wide-eyed guard pounded down the bleachers.

"Well?" she said when he stood before her.

He nodded. "You are correct."

Carrying her banner high, she raced into the arena.

Rafe had just landed atop Gato, who shouted a curse. Rafe's fist flashed, and he slammed it into Gato's face. Gato bit him. Rafe pressed his thumbs to Gato's eyes.

Gato screamed, released his hold on Rafe, and both men rolled away.

Kit ran to the front of the grandstand, planting her flag on the earth, pennant snapping.

Cries of "Rafe, rise. Rise!" stung her ears.

She pitched her voice low and shouted, "Judges! I challenge!"

The men gaped.

"Halt the competition!" shouted the red-sashed judge into his microphone.

She glanced over her shoulder. Gato froze, legs akimbo, fists balled as Rafe staggered to his feet. A chill rippled through her. She didn't dare look at Arina, and obviously Talos recognized her. If either gave her away...

She focused on the three judges and repeated, "I demand Final Challenge!"

A wave of silence rippled across the stadium.

Two of the judges muttered something to their red-sashed leader, who wore a faint smile.

"You cannot!" snapped the youngest judge, pointing a finger at her.

The leader leaned toward him. "He can."

"Remove your mask!" barked the young judge.

Terror froze her. Then she remembered. "No mention of masks is in the rules. I decline."

The younger judge forced a sour smile. "Out of courtesy, then."

"With respect, I will not."

Again, the red-sashed judge intervened. "Leave off, Milos. Your name, sir, and Clan so we may announce you?"

"Boadicea of no Clan."

The herald looked to the judge. "Proceed, just as he stated." The herald's horn silenced the crowd, and a cacophony of shouts and whistles erupted when he announced her.

Ignoring them, Kit bowed before the judges, pivoted, and walked toward Gato and Rafe across the blood-mottled sand.

Inwardly, she mantraed, *I will prevail*, over and over. It was a chant her sensei used often. It was all that mattered, all she needed, all her world. *I will prevail.*

Her steps brought her to the arena's center, and she halted and bowed to one side of the crowd, the grandstand, and then the other side. She resumed her progress.

I will prevail.

She was nearly to the two men when Rafe caught her eye, his stare blade-sharp, muscles tense as iron.

He knew.

She swallowed. Would he reveal her identity? He was a protector who would fear her coming to harm.

Revelation would ruin everything.

Certain she could do this and triumph, she squared her shoulders and held his gaze, aching for him not to interfere.

His hands curled into fists, his brow wrinkling. Then his muscles relaxed, and he blinked, nostrils flaring.

She reached the two men, and spun to face Gato. "Challenge."

"Accepted," he said with a smile and nod. "Prepare."

Rafe stepped back, giving them space.

She'd practiced her katas early that morning, and now she

performed her stretches, danced on the balls of her feet, shook out her arms, and rotated her hands, loosening her wrists. The crowd gawked, their eagerness for the fight rolling over her in a wave of expectation. When she and Gato were about four feet apart, she pressed her palms together and bowed.

"You must be kidding." Gato grinned, his scorn evident. "What team do you really represent?"

"My own team. And all teams." She straightened and waited.

He launched himself at her.

With a glide to the right, he missed her, landing in the dirt. She twirled, flew, snapped a kick predicting he'd have gained his feet. He had, and her kick landed. He staggered back, then leapt to pin her. He was so damned fast she barely escaped only to come at him from an unexpected angle. He wanted to grapple, which she definitely did not.

He was stronger and would last longer.

An unexpected punch to her jaw had her reeling, pain vibrating in waves, seeing stars. She spat blood as he followed up with a savage kick to her groin, which she deflected to her upper thigh. Still hurt like a bitch, and if she hadn't gone with the blow, she'd have been tasting dirt.

Time to end it.

She leapt, twirled, flashed out a kick, a chop to his neck. He flew sideways, then surged upward, bent to barrel into her. Using his own momentum, she flipped him over her head, came down on him with her knees just as he landed on his back.

Time, time. She could do this, she could.

In a move that momentarily shocked him, Kit pushed Gato's arm out of the way as she moved one knee to the side and onto the floor. She jammed her left arm across his neck, making it difficult for him to breathe. He began to twist in the opposite direction, screaming and swearing at her. She went up on one knee, brought her right arm around his, grabbed his tricep, jammed the heel of her foot in front of his face and stepped over the top of his head. He went for her with his left arm, so she punched her right foot onto his bicep right where the nerve was and flopped backward onto the ground, gripping his right arm, goose-necking it, his thumb pointing up to the sky. She had him in the arm bar, and she twisted.

"I'll break it," she said, "Admit defeat."

He spat at her, though the way his head was turned, it didn't come anywhere near her. He bucked. "Fark you."

She tightened her hold, twisted harder on the arm she held. *Shote*, she didn't want to break it.

His left hand scrabbled in the dirt, and she snapped her head away just as he threw sand at her face. Again, she twisted his right arm. A further twist, and it would break.

"Relent," she ground out, breathless with the effort.

His left palm slapped the dirt. But she didn't release him. Not yet. "Say the words!"

He spat several colorful swear words about her mother, her nonexistent children, and most especially her.

She pulled, just a little.

He howled, then, "I concede."

"Louder!"

More swearing. "I concede!"

His shouted words brought the roaring crowd to their feet.

"Don't move." She released him and backrolled to a stand. She landed all wobbly and bent, pressing her hands to her knees and panting, jaw killing her from that punch Gato had landed. Lucky he hadn't broken it.

She'd won. Done it. Moments later, she straightened her spine with effort. The fight had been fast, but she'd overextended herself. She felt disgusting, the inside of her hood and leathers greased with sweat. She wanted to rip the hood off, but not yet. Not yet.

Her eyes cut to Rafe. Though his face was impassive, his eyes—oh, those eyes—they smiled.

Gato pushed to his feet in one swift move. He studied her as if trying to figure out exactly what had just happened.

Ignoring Gato, the crowd, her aches and pains, the judges

arguing amongst themselves, the heat and the dust, Kit walked to Rafe.

The crowd hushed.

Rafe stepped forward, a mere foot away. Dried blood coated his face, bruises mottled his body, and one eye was swollen half-shut.

"I challenge," she said softly.

"I concede," he replied, his words as quiet as hers.

Neither of them smiled, but as she felt his joy, it infused her, too.

Then Rafe turned toward the judges and shouted, "I concede!" To Kit, he said, "Now, beauty, go show them."

She pivoted, walked to the center of the arena, and raised her arms in victory. The crowd whooped and screamed, threw flowers and confetti. A glance at the grandstand. It seemed no one noticed the Made One's absence, no one except Arina, who was grinning like a drunk fool.

The red-sashed judge stood, and the crowd quieted. "Boadicea wins the Made One!"

The crowd's cheers deafened. The judge looked toward her grandstand seat, but of course she wasn't there.

Kit unzipped the top of her leathers and worked her fingers beneath her hood. *Here goes.* She tugged the thing off her head, hair pins flying every which way, the day's cooling breeze washing over her.

A shocked hush blanketed the crowd. Gato swore. Rafe laughed.

People looked between her empty grandstand seat and where she stood dead center in the arena.

With deliberation she spun in a circle, speaking as she did so. "I am the victor of the Made One Challenge. I am Kitlyn, the Made One, and I get to choose. I choose me. I choose the freedom to have a choice. I deserve it, and I have won it. No Made One should be forced into commitment, rather than having a choice.

"You are a fair and just people. A good people. Heed my words. I choose me."

Pandemonium erupted. She ignored it and walked over to Rafe.

"Actually, I choose you." The next words came hard, and she swallowed. "Will you choose me?"

He might be bloody and bruised, but his swift grin was all that mattered. "Always." His left arm snaked around her waist as he lowered his lips to hers. "Always."

His kiss was like none other. She was home.

CHAPTER TWENTY-SEVEN

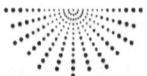

A tap on her shoulder had her whirling, ready to fight.

There stood Gato, wearing a poignant smile on his face.

"I'm sorry about your loss," she said. "But not really."

He laughed, his hands at his hips. "You are a menace."

Thank the lucky stars he'd taken her victory with good humor. "I've been called much worse."

Two men entered the arena carrying a huge bouquet of flowers.

Gato's eyes twinkled. "For you."

As the men moved toward them, Gato's eyes lit with more than humor. Cunning lurked beneath that warm expression.

His smile remained fixed, and he brushed a hand down her cheek. Rafe stiffened.

"You wanted a choice?" Gato said. "I will give you one. You may choose to go with your Wolf lover." He shot Rafe a disgusted look. "Or you may choose your sister."

"My...my *sister*?"

"Remember, princess, I had a surprise for you? Here she is." He swept his arm out. The guards blocking her view parted to reveal a woman seated in the grandstand, in the exact spot where Kit had viewed the games. The seating area had been cleared of everyone but the woman, Arina, and her Cat Clan guards.

Bree.

Kit began to run.

Bree's blue gown had been made for Kit, and she sat in a throne-like chair. She wasn't bound, wasn't silenced, yet she didn't move. Then Bree's leg struck out at a guard and got him in the shin. Good for her.

Of course Bree would kick her guards. Sybi would've remained composed while she thought up what revenge she could mete out.

A hand halted her dash toward her sister, and she swung around to deliver a kick to free herself. Except Rafe punched the Cat Alpha first.

"Don't touch her again," Rafe said, "or I will magic you out of existence."

"Bah," Gato said, swiping the back of his hand across his bloody mouth. "All Clan magic is but a shadow of what once was."

Rafe grinned. "Are you sure?"

Gato spat, then worked his jaw back and forth. "You talked about choice, Kitlyn. Then choose, Made One. Your sister is ours, and you will not see her, nor speak with her if you pick the Wolf."

"I didn't imagine even you were that cruel."

Gato shrugged. "Choose."

She shook with the desperate urge to touch her sister, to hug her, to hold her.

Kit *had* to be with her sister.

But Rafe. How could she leave him?

Solomon's Choice, except there was no baby to cut in half, only her heart.

"Go to her, Kit," Rafe whispered in her ear.

She didn't know how to make this terrible decision. She stared at Bree, drinking her in with her eyes.

"Go," Rafe repeated, and stepped back.

Which was when Bree landed a punch to a guard's balls.

Gato swore. "That insufferable woman!"

Bree winked, and her familiar smug smile squeezed Kit's heart. Her sister gave Kit a thumbs up, then her hands began to talk the language they'd learned to communicate with their long-dead sister, Marie.

Go, Bree signed. *I've got this.*

No, Kit replied in rapid ASL. *I must—*

Bree interrupted. *I want to stay. I'm intrigued, big sister. I'll be ruling CatHome before I'm done.* She grinned.

This isn't a joke, Kit signed.

Who said I was joking?

Her sister made a brushing motion, winked, and mouthed, *Go!*

Bree was such a badass, far more so than Kit, and crazy to boot. But she couldn't help worrying about her. Kit lifted a hand to her heart. "Love you, Bree!"

Her sister returned their time-honored sisterly gesture. Bree was alive, which gave hope that Sybi was, too. No matter what Gato said, she'd be with Bree soon.

And in the meantime, Bree would take Gato to his knees. She laughed. He had no idea who he'd unleashed.

She almost pitied him.

"You are being a bastard," she said to Gato. "And here I thought you weren't such a bad guy."

He spread his arms wide. "I'm a wonderful person."

She set her jaw, pushed back her shoulders, and locked her eyes on Gato's. "I choose Rafe."

Gato's face hardened with fury. "Be very sure, princess."

"I am. And if you hurt a hair on my sister's head, you will die."

Gato laughed, looked at Rafe, and deliberately kissed her on the mouth.

Instead of barreling into Gato, Rafe smiled. "You wish she were yours, *old friend*. Kitlyn is *mine*." He turned to Kit. "And I am hers."

When she looked back at the grandstand, Bree was gone.

She walked to Rafe and slid her shoulder beneath his left arm. "Shall we?"

"Here's hoping I don't pass out."

"I can't believe you fought injured. I could shoot you for doing tha—"

His piercing whistle effectively cut her off. A stagger, then he righted himself. "Watch."

The sounds of a mistral's fury, then Nightfall soared above the stands to land in front of them, tossing his head, eyes wild, gorgeous black wings glistening in the sun. They limped toward the mistral a few yards away.

The contrary judge ran toward them across the arena.

"Moonrise," she said to Rafe.

"Patience." Rafe's voice had grown faint. "Let's just get me on Nightfall."

More animal shrieks, men's screams and curses, then Moonrise appeared high in the sky.

The judge reached them, breath puffing. "What are you doing?"

"Isn't it obvious?" Rafe said.

"But you can't! We have ceremonies, the evening gala, your award, Ma'am Kitlyn."

"I hope everyone enjoys themselves," she said. "We're leaving."

"But... No!" the judge said.

Rafe arced his free arm downward, and Nightfall fell to his front knees as Moonrise landed. Kit helped him atop the mistral, and Nightfall stood. Then Kit vaulted up behind Rafe, worried he wouldn't be able to stay atop the stallion's back alone.

It seemed Nightfall wasn't entirely pleased with the arrangement, as he danced for a moment, terrifying the judge.

"Stop it, Nightfall!" she said.

Rafe laughed.

"This isn't funny. He's being a pain."

Rafe whispered to the mistral, and he settled.

The young judge reached for Nightfall's halter. "You can't leave. I forbid it!"

The mistral bit him.

Rafe laughed harder as he squeezed Nightfall's sides. They rose into the air, fortunately without the judge attached.

. . .

Rafe had to be operated on again, and it went smoothly. The four weeks of healing afterward did not. He was a horrible patient, restless and frustrated at the four-week wait for their Mating ceremony, his insistence on learning martial arts the carrot she used to keep him from overdoing things while he recovered.

Though an awful patient, those weeks gave them time to talk, to explore each other, to make love. They'd swum to the crystal cave again, had a picnic with Tilde and Max, and flown far and wide on the mistrals. They'd also worked, and together they discovered Eevon's deep involvement in the Anti-Made Ones' faction, as well as Inga's with the Alchemics, which shocked them both.

Inga had vanished, leaving only a note for Rafe saying that she'd left, but they would "be together again someday."

"No, we won't," Rafe said, tossing the note in the fire. "She's a traitor to the Clan."

Kit snatched the note just before it landed. "Ouch. We need this for the council."

Rafe slapped his hands on hips, fuming. "Fark her. Just fark her!"

"Rafe."

"We were friends. Always. Got each other out of scrapes as kids and... Fark it!"

He stormed out of the house, Kit traipsing after him. When he slowed on a high ridge overlooking their farm, close to where the tree had fallen and near crushed her, she trotted up to him.

"I'm sorry about Inga. I really am," she said.

He sat, pulling her down with him, their hands threaded together. "I need to explain Compass True and my role in it."

Which was when Rafe revealed he headed the revolutionary group formed to end the Alchemics' hold on Eleutia, shocking Kit further.

As the days moved closer to their Mating Ceremony, they talked about everything, especially Sybi and Bree, and Rafe assured her Ulfr was pressuring the Cats for a meeting. Thankfully, the Wolves had no plans for war over Bree, and Ulfr's Cat Clan spies had told him that her sister was well, had freedom of movement, and much to Kit's delight, was running circles around the Cat Alpha. No surprise there.

No more secrets, either, Rafe had said, his eyes filled with the memory of her escape to the Cats, a deep love, and a terrible fear.

No more secrets, she'd replied. *Promise.*

After the huge Clan victory celebration, they eased back into a normal rhythm, as normal as the preparations for their Mating ceremony could be.

"You can pull one more Made One before we go," Fukkes said.

Gabin cut the air with his hand. "I cannot. There is not time."

"We are set. All we need do is twiddle our thumbs until the alignment. We will be bored. She will entertain us."

When the fark was "the alignment?"

Weeks had passed since Calix had heard that conversation, and time was growing short for him to save the Made One, yet he'd been forced to wait. The Watcher they'd set on him was clever, but Calix was more so. He'd been tempted to take him out, but that would raise too many questions.

Yet if he hadn't had to wait, Calix would never have learned of the *unsanctioned* Essences the Cabal of Eleven Alchemics had stolen from their home world. They'd stored them in the secret vault known only to the Cabal and now to Calix.

He'd been deeply shaken. The Alchemics didn't plan to create Made Ones. No, they would acquire the Stolen Ones' memories, their skills and attributes and stations in life. One country's president, another's religious leader, yet another's corporate titan. On and on. Eleven souls stolen. Eleven luminaries from Earth.

He'd imagined they'd left them for dead, as they did with Made Ones. No, he'd learned they were merely comatose on their home world. Thus, when the Alchemics transferred *their* Essences into the Stolen Ones' bodies and arose, they would act and behave the same.

Once the transfers were complete, the Alchemics could interact—walk, talk, eat, make love—on that parallel world. And they would be world Alphas, prepared to rule. Diabolical.

The Alchemics had dared steal healthy lives. Not only was it unethical and cruel but forbidden by the Alchemical Code. They would commit murder, and he'd heard Gabin and Fukkes laughing about it.

"We are explorers," Fukkes had said. "You can't constrain us with rules and regulations."

That louse Fukkes still hadn't awakened the Made One in the capsule. Even with the sustaining gas, her body had grown painfully thin, her blonde hair beginning to fall out. He'd been all set to liberate her, and damn his handlers, until he'd learned of the Stolen Ones. Now. He must do it *now*.

Right beneath the Watcher's nose, he'd gathered the necessary elements to awaken her. A datafene here, a cornishe there, plasos and formulon and balastree—he needed one more ingredient for her Making before he stole her away. Which was why he slipped into the room where she slept, cocooned in her glass pod.

Calix spared her a glance. More than a glance. He drank her in, picturing her healthy and animated with life. At Gabin's insistence, he and Fukkes had transferred her Essence into her flesh. Yet she slept on. Fukkes hadn't budged in Awakening her, much to Gabin's displeasure, not to mention Calix's.

With effort, Calix tore his eyes from the painfully thin Made One to the safe at the opposite end of the room. Were it simply a matter of deceiving the lock, as he'd done acquiring the other elements, he'd already be in possession of the final ingredient. But palladious was so rare and precious, only three Alchemics had access to the safe. Fukkes and Gabin were incorruptible, and too clever by half, but in his friend Darva he'd found his unwitting prey.

He took the case from his lab coat pocket and opened it. Inside lay a tissue-thin sheet of fauxflesh with Darva's palm print. Unfolding the sheet, he smoothed it across his right palm, then tapped in the numbers to open the hidden panel. That accomplished, he raised his palm to the inner lock.

A click of the lab's outer door handle.

He snapped his hand back, closed the hidden panel, and stepped toward the glass cabinet full of heat syringes.

"Calix!" Harper's busy eyes darted around the room. "I'm surprised to see you here. No mid-day meal?"

Calix thrust his hands into his lab coat and wrapped his fingers around his knife. He donned a bemused mask for his Watcher. "I promised Neela I'd retrieve her cursed notebook. She said she left it near the heat syringe cabinet, but I don't see it anywhere. Maybe you can find it."

Harper's laugh grated. "Neela loses things hourly."

"That she does. I've looked, but it's not here. I'm off to mid-day. Care to join me?" Calix stepped closer to Harper.

"Can't," Harper said. "I've a formula to work up."

Calix nodded. "I'll leave you to it, then." He thrust his knife through his lab coat and into Harper's chest, shoving it upward to pierce his heart.

The shock on Harper's face transformed to blankness as his spirit left his flesh. Calix eased the body to the floor with the whispered words, "May the Sky welcome you."

He leapt to the door and locked it. Blood covered him, and taking care with the fauxflesh palm print, he swiftly cleaned his knife and threw his ruined lab coat over Harper, donned a clean one from the supply shelf, and opened the safe.

Once he secured the palladious, he added it to his case of essentials that held the ingredients for Awakening. Swinging his case onto his shoulder, he then pressed two buttons beneath the Made One's pod to activate its hover mode. He opened the door to the dusty corridor that led to the extermination chamber, glad he'd oiled the door to the chamber's outer disposal area. Without a backward look, he pushed the hoverpod into the corridor filled with cobwebs and detritus and silently closed the lab door behind him.

CHAPTER TWENTY-EIGHT

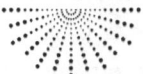

K it had embraced the whirl of preparations for her and Rafe's Mating Ceremony and Gala, taking time to create a special surprise of her own for Rafe.

The Made One dissenters remained a threat, albeit they'd been quiet these past weeks, and she still hadn't seen Bree, but in one hour, she would officially become Rafe's mate. She was a bit terrified and a lot thrilled to be united with the man she adored. According to Tilde, theirs was a big "do" because Rafe was the Alpha's son and she was a Made One. Alphas from around the territory had been invited, as had Alchemic Clan members, heads of the trade guilds, and a bunch of overseas friends from other Wolf Clans. Of course, the WolfHome residents would be the celebrants who mattered most—her family and friends.

There was no aisle, there were no pews, and she wouldn't throw a bouquet, but nonetheless the vibe felt much like a wedding. Talos' metalsmiths had crafted golden rings at Kit's request, though mated pairs didn't usually exchange rings. Rafe understood her desire for a symbol that echoed her Earth traditions. She hadn't seen the rings yet, as Talos intended them as a surprise.

Kit sat on the toilet lid while Tilde arranged her auburn hair, then she donned her diaphanous leaf-green gown reminiscent of 19th Century Earth's Empire style. The Eleutian dress was very Jane Austen, with embroidered flowers rising up the sides and trailing beneath her breasts. Kit loved it. What she loved almost as much was that the women of WolfHome didn't wear high heels.

She looked in the mirror as she fastened Rafe's braid around her throat. Not that she wore it all the time. But tonight? Her fingers stroked the soft plait. While she missed his long hair, it would grow back, and she prayed he'd never have to cut it and go to war again.

"All set?" Tilde said as Kit left the bathroom.

"Yes. Are *you* ready with our surprise?"

Tilde straightened her glasses. "Everything's in place and arranged. You are sure about this?"

"I am."

Her friend hugged her. "Good."

Kit twirled. "What do you think?"

"Perfect. Here." Tilde wrapped a band of emeralds around her wrist and snapped the clasp.

The bracelet was gorgeous and must have cost a fortune.

Tilde handed her a set of matching earrings. "From the Alpha."

She slipped the wires through her ears. "I… I… Wow."

When Rafe walked into their bedroom, he looked handsomer than sin and twice as dangerous, his tunic an earthy forest green, his pants black, his honey-gold hair bound by the First Commander's thin gold circlet of office. Except he was scowling.

"You don't look like a man about to celebrate our mating."

He shrugged, his shoulders and arms bulging with tension. He notched his head for Tilde to leave, and Kit grabbed her for a hug before she scurried from the room.

Kit held out her wrist. "Look what your father gave me."

All he did was nod, as if too distracted to pay attention.

She put her arms around his waist and tilted her head so she could look into his eyes. "Rafe? What's wrong?"

"Ulfr invited the farking Cat Alpha, and the shoting Cat accepted." He sighed and kissed the top of her head. "I have no idea who will accompany him. He's allowed three guests." He took her chin in his hand and kissed her hard and deep. "I'm sorry to put this on you today."

"Maybe he'll bring Bree."

"With Gato, one never knows what schemes he's hatching."

Right after the games, she'd called Gato in hopes of having him unbend about her sister. He'd changed his number, as had Arina. So Kit had written him, and written Bree, too, along with Arina. Her letters to Gato and Bree went unanswered, while Arina wrote back chatty ones, never mentioning her sister.

All that time, though the Alpha and Rafe continued to put out feelers, they'd gotten not a hint of Sybi.

At least they knew Bree was alive. "I hope…"

Rafe's arms tightened around her. "I know."

"Is Fukkes coming? If so, I plan to ask him where the hell Sybi is."

"No word from the Alchemics whether they plan to attend or not."

She tucked her head beneath his chin. "Forget about the Cats, the Alchemics, the dissenters. Today is about us. Let's make it a true celebration."

He barked a laugh. "This gala is a state event. Afterwards, beauty, that will be our true celebration."

She was distracted. She shouldn't have been, given the import of the event, but she kept watching the doors of The Hall now decorated for the festivities. Flowers festooned the space, fine tablecloths draped the dining tables, and a dais had been set up with four chairs, the middle two for Rafe and herself, the outer two for Ulfr and Seelar.

Mimi had pleaded to sit with them and had been told it wasn't appropriate. To soften Mimi's hurt, Kit had promised her a dance, as well as a ride on Moonrise. Much to Kit's joy, Mimi had forgotten all about the dais in her excitement.

The evening proved full of surprises. Yuan, as the Fates' curate among the Wolves, opened the event with a call to the Sky. During the Wolves' Salutation of the Fates Ceremony, Rafe and Kit faced each other. They clasped hands and raised them to their chests, threading their fingers together, palm to palm, as the Alpha wound a forest green ribbon around them that signified their mating. Blessings and praise flowed, first from the Alpha, then from others who stepped forward and spoke of Rafe's accomplishments and hers. She was so proud of Rafe, so in awe of the man who was now her mate. Her heart filled to the brim, her eyes burning with the impossibility of it—the wonder, the terror, the love—of all that had happened to her in her months on Eleutia.

When Ulfr told Paulo he was "on," the coywolf faced those gathered and sent out a Call, *the* Call, a command to WolfHome's every wolf and human to unite the couple in the Power of the Clan. Kit was relaxed, thinking the "Call" metaphorical. How wrong she was. She felt it. She felt *them*, thousands of souls, each a tiny spark igniting within her, filling her, saturating her entire being. The Call ended with her gasp, and she staggered. If not for Rafe, she would have fallen.

Her mate whispered, "High Magics, that. Not used at a Mating for hundreds of years. It seems my father has seen the light."

Once Ulfr removed the ribbon, Rafe and Kit added the ring ceremony, surprising many. Her gold ring bore a platinum mistral in the center, with wolves gamboling about the band. Rafe's was the opposite of hers. Murmurs filtered through the hall, and applause and cheers when they finally kissed.

The love in Rafe's eyes exploded inside her—this joy was new and fresh and incandescent. He was *hers*.

They ate and drank and watched their Clanmates perform. Max did Simple Magic tricks, delighting the entire crowd. To her surprise, Yuan juggled six knives in an awesome display. Tilde's haunting love song stunned her.

Once the applause for Tilde died down, Paulo pranced forward, flanked by the three wolves who'd guarded her while she'd been at CatHome.

Joy to you and Rafe.

"Oh, Paulo, thank you and the wolves for everything!" she said.

The canid quartet sat, raised their heads, and howled a song filled with wild beauty. It was almost too much, and Kit squeezed Rafe's hand tight so she wouldn't come apart. When they fell silent, the hall broke into thunderous applause.

Kit left the dais to kneel in front of the canids. She embraced each wolf, leaving Paulo for last. He didn't wait for her hug but lifted his paws to her shoulders and licked her face in that full-on coywolf way of his that left her giggling. Apparently pleased with himself, he yipped once, and the quartet dashed away.

Rafe handed her a handkerchief, and she wiped her face, laughing along with the crowd.

"I have a surprise," she whispered to Rafe. "Would you get everyone out to the lawn? I'll meet you there."

He gave her that look—*you and your surprises*—but announced to the crowd that a treat awaited them outside.

Kit ran to the bathroom and changed into a tight-fitting gold top and green leggings she'd sewn with the help of a Clan seamstress. Once outside, she instructed their guests to make a large circle, leaving a good-sized chunk open inside the circle.

She whistled. Moonrise cantered from the trees, and Kit readied herself. She'd practiced when Rafe was gone, Tilde helping, and she was as prepared as she'd ever be. Nerves be damned. She smiled and caught Rafe's eye—*For you, beloved, just for you*—and focused.

Moonrise's hooves thudded a slow canter, and as she neared, Kit began to run, then she vaulted onto the mare. She slipped her feet into the special stirrups she'd made for the custom saddle and stood. They cantered around the circle, Kit standing tall, arms wide, and it felt so right.

Next, she did the spritz, shoulder, and hippodrome stands, then spun the horn, moving from trick to trick as if the circus were yesterday and not a lifetime ago. Last, she flowed into the Cossack drag, the trick where it had all changed.

Moonrise cantered as Kit hung off the mistral's side, right ankle secured by one stirrup, left leg stretched outward, the sounds of Moonrise's hoofs on the grass, the crowd's awed silence, music.

As she rose back into the saddle, her heart clenched.

She'd done it! And her face split into a grin as she took one more circuit around to the crowd's roaring shouts and whoops and applause. Her eyes searched for Rafe. Where was he? When she slowed Moonrise to a trot, she finally spotted him standing alone beneath a tree, squeezing the bridge of his nose.

She vaulted off the mistral's back and ran to him. "Rafe?"

"Don't," his voice low and growly. He dipped his head. "Don't, or I'll weep in front of all our Clansmen and guests."

"I performed for you, Rafe. *You.*"

"The Fates, Kitlyn." He buried his face in her shoulder, his arms banded around her, and she felt his tears dampen her skin.

"My love," she said. "All is well. It was wonderful, exhilarating… and different. *I'm* different. I'm not that girl who rode under the big top. I am more, because of Eleutia and you."

A shudder went through him, and he raised his face, his hand cradling her cheek. "The gift was incomparable, though you will be the death of me. It will be the sweetest of ways to go. Forever, love of mine."

"Forever." She stood on tiptoe and kissed him, shutting out everything but Rafe.

He finally stepped back, his face that of the strong, wonderful man she held so dear. "I'll see to Moonrise."

"No need. Tilde's tending to her. Just for tonight." She bit her lip and smiled. "I owe her a vaulting lesson."

His laughter rang, and someone handed them each a Fafner ale.

Raucous celebration ensued. The Eleutians could party hard, and after hours of dancing—and to her joy, Tilde dancing with Max— eating, and drinking, the evening finally wound down.

Ulfr stood atop the dais, his hands waving to silence the crowd. "A memorable evening for WolfHome!"

Wild cheers, whistles, and shouts.

Next, she thought, the receiving line and home. Huzzah.

When the room hushed, Ulfr continued. "I have been your Alpha for many a year.

Some in the crowd wore surprised faces, others questioning ones.

Ulfr had gone off script.

The Alpha's steely eyes took in the room's many hundreds of Wolves. "Being Alpha has been both a burden and a joy, yet I've realized these last few months that something was missing."

"Come, child." He waved to Mimi, seated at the first table.

She dashed to her father, and he clasped her in a furious hug. "I knew when I took on this honor and task, that sacrifices must be made. And I willingly made them. But I have also missed out on much."

He gestured to Seelar, and when she stepped by his side, he grasped her hand in his.

"Tonight, I announce my retirement as Alpha."

Gasps from the Clan, with Paulo and the wolves adding yips.

Kit turned to Rafe and whispered. "Did you know?"

Jaw tight, he shook his head.

Ulfr looked to Rafe. "I nominate Radulfr, son of Juliette and Ulfr, for the Alpha trials."

Booming cheers filled the hall.

"Rafe!" she said.

"I know. Farking Ulfr." He laughed and took her hand. "Here we go."

"I will remain as Alpha," Ulfr continued, "until the challengers for Alpha have been winnowed to one and your new Alpha chosen. So be it!"

"So be it!" echoed the crowd.

As somewhat of an anticlimax, Kit, Rafe, and Ulfr's family formed a farewell receiving line. Kit was wrung out, but so very happy. Until Gato stepped in front of her wearing his typical smirk. She hadn't seen him arrive.

"Congratulations are in order." He bowed. "I suppose."

"You suppose correctly. I'm glad you came."

Rafe was giving them the side-eye while he spoke with Arne. The last thing anyone needed was Rafe going all Wolf on Gato.

Kit had to see her sister. "Will you—"

Gato cut her off with a raised hand. "I have a gift for you."

At that, Rafe broke away from Arne to give Gato a lethal stare. "Don't toy with my mate."

"Would I do such a thing?" Gato said.

The crowd parted, and Arina appeared with her hand on Bree's shoulder.

Gato was saying something to Rafe, but all Kit could do was take in her sister, her gown of shimmering silver swirling around her, her red hair crowning her head, her smile megawatt. Youth and health bloomed in her cheeks.

Tears burned Kit's eyes. The closer Bree came, the more Kit's throat dried with hope and anticipation. Breena was here, real, and almost within touching distance. Kit could stand it no longer. She rushed forward, arms wide, and Bree did the same.

Gato stepped between them. "Five minutes. That's all." He stepped away.

And then they were in each other's arms.

"Are you okay?" Kit asked.

"Hell, yeah. Is this a trip or what?"

She stuttered a laugh. "That's an understatement." Kit pressed her lips to Bree's ear. "Is he forcing you to stay? Being cruel? Demanding things?"

Bree's head reared back, her heart-shaped face wearing a huge grin. "Not to worry, big sis. All is well in hand."

"Bree, I'm—"

"I'm fine. It's fine. I haven't had this much fun in years."

"We will find Sybi. She's here. I know it."

"Hell, yes, we will."

They babbled to each other until Gato separated them. He pressed his hand to the small of Bree's back and went to move her away. Kit leapt forward, enfolding Bree in her arms once more.

She clung tight to her sister. Gato couldn't take her away. "Love you."

"Love you, too, Sis."

"We can offer you sanctuary. You can stay here, with me, with the Wolves. Don't go."

"It's all good, Kit." Bree pulled away, her face full of humor and a touch of irony. "I've got lots going in Catland. No worries, huh?"

"No worries." But Kit's voice was faint.

They stepped apart, and Gato steered her sister from the hall. When Bree glanced back, she flashed Kit *Love you! See you soon!* in ASL.

Hours later, she lay limp in Rafe's arms, spent from the fierce love they'd shared.

They talked far into the night about his plans to overthrow the Alchemics and what it would mean if Rafe became Alpha.

"We'll find Sybi, Kit," Rafe said. "Get Bree back, too."

"We will. I know my sister. She's a force of nature. If she wanted to leave, she would find a way. Whatever's going on, Bree is up to something." Her sister was healthy, and she'd seen satisfaction in Bree's eyes, and laughter. She grinned. "Like I said before, I almost feel sorry for Gato. He might be a Cat, but he's got a tiger by the tail."

"If she's anything like you..." Rafe nuzzled her neck, sending sparks through her.

"Oh, she's much, much worse."

His hot breath of laughter made her squirm. He knew exactly what he was doing. Her turn. She bit his nipple.

"Evil woman."

"Have to be, if you're to become Alpha."

"Worried?"

"Only a little."

"You'll have to take on more in the training of our mistrals."

"I'm looking forward to it."

He laved her breast, and she moaned. "I can only imagine."

She carded his hair with her hands. "Mimi will help."

"May the Fates protect us."

"You'll defeat the challengers."

"I intend to do just that."

She shivered at the certainty in his voice. Or maybe the shiver was from his hand roving downward across her belly. She bit his shoulder.

Rafe's laugh was deep and long. He grew serious, his hands mapping her body while he focused on her lips, lowering his to where their breaths mingled.

"To all our tomorrows, my sweet Kit."

"To all our tomorrows."

And then those warm, beautiful lips brushed hers, and her world dissolved to Rafe, only Rafe, and the wonder of it all.

THANK YOU! AND NEWSLETTER

Thank you for reading *Altered*!

Reviews mean everything—they're an author's lifeblood. If you enjoyed the book, leaving an honest review would be a kindness.

Would you like a free book? I'd love for you to sign up for my newsletter and receive my bonus novel, *Body Parts*. My monthly newsletter contains info on The Made Ones Saga, the Afterworld Chronicles, life in L.A., and lots more yummy stuff.

Come visit with me... VickiStiefel.com
Facebook • Instagram • Twitter • BookBub

CHANGED

EXCERPT—BOOK 2, THE MADE ONES SAGA

Breena Boadicea Balážová pushed herself up from her prone position on a scratchy bed of leaves and spat. Somehow, a clump of what tasted like dirt had ended up in her mouth.

Well, this sucked. Where the hell was she?

A tendril of long hair slithered from her shoulder to dangle in her face. She went to swipe it away and… "What. The. Fuck?"

She pushed to a sitting position. Everything ached. And she was hot. Then cold. Then dizzy.

Screw that. Bree grabbed a plait of hair and held it in front of her, revulsion making her frown. Orange. Others might call it strawberry blond, but it was a loathsome color, a clown color, her *natural* color. Which was ridiculous. Her hair hadn't been natural since she'd dyed it black at fifteen.

Her nails, too? She curled her fingers. No polish, nails cut short and squared. She'd chosen blood red for last week's manicure.

"Kit! Sybi!" Where had they gone off to?

Bree was having some out-of-body experience.

They'd been hiking in Maine's Acadia. Right. They'd fallen, the ledge where they'd stood giving way. No, not exactly. The ledge had *vanished*. She could still hear Sybi's screams.

371

With precision and deliberation, she took the monster Fear and tucked him into the box she'd crafted eons ago. Good.

That done, she pushed to her feet and stumbled, her legs tangled in some weird fabric. She plucked at the hideous thing, an unbecoming sack of blue. The damned dress covered her from ankle to neck, shoulder to wrist.

She lifted her hand to her forehead to shade the sun that blazed above rows and rows of dead corn stalks. Aware of a burning thirst, she strode across the field toward a distant pond, wincing at the small cuts and pains her bare feet endured. She *could* still be in Maine. But she wasn't, that much was obvious.

If she'd been abducted, then where were her abductors?

Why weren't Sybi and Kit with her?

What was happening?

Bree kneeled beside the pond, its crystal waters making her salivate, and leaned forward to scoop up the much-needed liquid.

She screamed, and a murder of crows startled into flight.

She dug her fingers into the muddy earth at the pond's edge and cautiously leaned above the still water.

The Bree who stared back at her wasn't her at all. At least not 56-year-old her. She turned her face left, then right, the reflection echoing her movements. She sat back on her haunches, and her trembling hands traced the contours of her face and throat. Not possible. Leaping to her feet, she flung the dress over her head, tossing it away. Her body. She couldn't stop staring.

The lines and curves of her twenties flowed across her flesh. She touched her arms, her belly, her hips. All taut with the firmness of youth. Gone was the middle-aged pooch, saggy neck, and drooping ass. Now, the muscular thighs from her aerialist days flowed to strong calves and high-arched feet. Except they were hairy! She needed to shave her legs. Her hands cupped her breasts. Oh, no. They were pre-implant, small and pert.

Her nails, her hair, her breasts… Her armor was gone. Whatever had happened. Whatever had dragged her back to her pre-makeover body. Whatever was going on. It was horrible. She *needed* her armor.

Except she didn't see any handy chain mail lying around. A welcome breeze played along her skin, the scrim of trees edging the field swaying. Nothing to do but scope out the terrain. The large field where she stood was rimmed by a forest of huge conifers, and in the distance at the forest's edge, smoke curled into the blazing blue sky. A cabin, perhaps.

Though the ugly thing made her swelter, she fussed with the dress until it was right-side out again, pulled it on, and strode across the field toward the curl of smoke. People must live here, given the cornfield, and they'd tell her where she was. Once she figured that out, she go find her sisters.

She smiled. In the same predicament, Kit would give orders, Sybi would ponder. If they were around, she could finally bitch at someone who would understand how messed up this all was.

Nearing the smoke's source, her eyes snagged on some wooden posts just inside the forest. A house, maybe. She paused, allowing the dead stalks to screen her from view. Taking care not to step on a rock or in a hole, she moved forward. A bright yellow building much like Southwestern adobe houses came into view, surrounded by cactus and other succulents.

Shit, Dorothy, I'm not in Kansas anymore.

A flagstone path led her to the front door, and she pressed the buzzer.

After long minutes, seemingly hours in the dry heat with no one answering, she swore. She circled the home, and when she came to the rear, with its glass door, she cupped her hands to see inside.

A *huge* tan cougar slapped its dinner-plate paws onto the glass, startling her so much she fell on her bum. Good thing it was on the *inside* and she was on the *outside*. The cat pressed its nose to the window and snarled, its breath fogging the glass. Who keeps a mountain lion as a pet?

On her feet again, she backed away from the door. No swift movements. The cat looked big enough to break the glass. Her head bumped into something, and she turned.

The owner's clothesline was strung from the house to a tree and held half-a-dozen pants, shirts, underwear, and skirts that snapped in the breeze.

Goody.

She bit her lip. She shouldn't steal. But the damned dress made her feel like she wore a boa constrictor. A pair of jeans, several t-shirts, and underwear proved too tempting to ignore.

The jeans were too big, the shirt too small, but both were better than the dress, which she hung on the line as sort of an apology for taking the owner's clothes.

With one eye on the cat, whose growls had escalated, she continued her survey of the cabin's perimeter. That capricious lady luck, who'd once blessed her with great bounty but in recent years had abandoned her, shined once more. She found a toolshed, and inside a pair of gardening boots sat amidst the hardware and potting soil. She pulled them on, wishing they were a size larger, but thankful for favors. As she left, Bree plucked a pair of pointy hand shears from the wall. Every girl needed a weapon, especially with that giant cat pressed against the door, drool dripping from its open mouth.

So, you'd like to eat me, would you, buster? Not today.

Cool shade enveloped Bree as she crept deeper into the forest. Ferns grew beneath massive trees so tall she could barely see their tops. Kit had visited the redwoods of Big Sur and Marin, and these giants resembled her descriptions. Her rational mind told her she couldn't be in California. They'd been in Maine when they'd fallen.

Her rational mind... She touched her abdomen. Still taut and firm, with a hint of abs. *Oh, boy.* Though her fear was demanding release, she made sure it stayed put inside that internal box. Not yet. She couldn't freak out. Yet.

She had to find a hidey-hole.

After hiking over moss and ferns and rocks, Bree found a hollowed out tree with burnt edges most likely from a lightning strike. Perfect.

She plucked half-a-dozen huge ferns from the base of a living giant, then slipped inside the hollowed-out tree. Sitting on the dry earth, she uncoiled her legs so they sprawled inside the tree's base, her back against its trunk, then lay the ferns atop her for camouflage. Safe. Sort of.

The shaking began at her toes, creeping up her legs and torso until her entire body trembled. Fear had broken out of its prison, and its grip felt lethal.

"Unproductive," Sybi would say.

"Control it," Kit would encourage.

And so she did, refusing to think about the next hour, the next minute, the next second. She needed to sleep.

And so she did.

Fark! Gato was disgusted. Kitlyn had almost gotten herself killed by two traitors who illegally control-chipped a pair of their cats. Now the shoting Alchemics said *another* Made One was in his territory, and he, Gato, was to retrieve her.

Where? he'd asked.

In your territory, they'd replied.

CatHome is near 10-million acres!

Find her, was all they'd said.

Kitlyn couldn't know that most likely what he called those "Mad Scientists" had inadvertently pulled one of her sisters to CatHome. Somewhere. As if he needed this, with The Challenge to win the MadeOne, Kitlyn, to begin in a few days. A Challenge he *had* to win.

He paced his lair like one of his beloved cats, those symbionts who shared their lives and their spirits with the men and women of CatHome, Bartholomew keeping pace. Catamount's immense keep suddenly felt too small, too confining. He strode out of the building, Barth at his heels, up the hundreds of stairs, until he reached the reds' mesa in a matter of minutes. The giant trees cooled him, let him think. Manageable. It was all manageable.

He'd find her, then hand her off to her makers, the Alchemics. Two Made Ones were one too many.

Voices startled Bree awake. They spoke English, which was good, though their accents were none she'd heard before, almost Spanish, but not quite.

She stayed very still as the two men walked right past her hidey hole. When their voices trailed off, she relaxed. Maybe she should have said something, but they might have hurt her, kidnapped her, raped her. She clutched the garden shears tighter.

They were gone. It was all right. She'd find a town, which would be a safer alternative.

A giant black puma shoved its head into her space, its frosty blue eyes gleaming like shining stars, the sounds of it sniffing loud, its teeth glistening. The tip of its nose was pink. How very odd.

She stretched her arms out, the points of the shears aimed at the cat's face. "Go away. Leave me alone. I don't want to hurt you, but I will."

The panther tilted its head as if it were actually listening to her words.

Its huge tongue snaked out and it licked her arm.

"Ow!" Sandpaper was softer.

She made herself small, tucking her legs beneath her. "Leave."

The panther shook its head.

Oh, goody, she was talking to a cat who seemed to understand her.

Mens' voices again.

"Bartholomew, don't scare her!"

"Bartholomew?" she said.

The cat nodded.

She bit her lip, the fear pounding for release.

Tears spilled down her cheeks. Not what she needed, dammit.

"Back up, Barth," said a deep voice from outside the tree. "Let us talk with her."

The cat was half in, half out the trunk. It didn't move.

"C'mon, Barth."

The cat didn't move.

"Am I supposed to say something?" Bree said.

The nodding cat raised its muzzle, as if to eat her or smile. Hard to tell.

"Okay, um, I'll talk to them."

The cat didn't wink, but it sure looked like he wanted to. He backed out of the tree.

A man wearing leather, lots of leather, poked head and shoulders inside the tree. He had a hook nose, warm eyes, and blond hair. "Hello."

"Hello."

"That was Bartholomew, one of Catamount's CatGuard."

"Oh, really?" She hadn't a clue.

"Clever, hiding out here. Without Barth, we'd never have found you."

Goody. "Why are you looking for me?"

He scraped a hand across his stubbled chin. "We, ah…"

The jingling of horses equipage and, "Move, Eldoro!"

Relief surged across Eldoro's face, then he backed out the opening. With all these people arriving, not to mention the huge panther, she was starting to feel foolish hunkered at the back of the hollowed-out tree.

Her hands had grown sweaty from gripping the shears, which she suspected were pretty useless at this point. Not going to give them up yet, though.

Another man crouched low and entered her hidey hole, uncurling his hand to reveal a round ball of light in his palm. Dressed all in black leather, he scooched down on his haunches, his piercing emerald stare slicing through her. "I am Náshdóítsoh, Alpha of the Cat Clan. My name's a mouthful, so call me Gato. How are you feeling?"

The strange light gave his stark features a malevolent cast, and she pressed her back against the rough wood. "Feeling?"

"Yes."

"Hungry. Thirsty." Terrified.

"You arrived precipitously."

"Did I, now?"

He scraped a hand across his chiseled face, with its prominent chin and lush mouth, similar enough to Malachi's the memory shivered down her spine. "Your arrival was unexpected. I would like to help you, to take you to Catamount, and to explain. Will you come with me?" He held out a hand.

She raised the shears. "Why should I trust you?"

His face tightened with anger, then he shook his head. "Because you have no other option."

The shears glinted in the soft light. "I have these." She held them up. "They're an option." Much as she'd love to go to someplace safe where she learned what was going on, where she was, and how the hell to find her sisters, she couldn't. They might sell her or rape her or something else equally horrible. Though why they'd want some broken-down fifty-something eluded her. Except... She'd looked different. Her body was different. And though the pond hadn't been much of a mirror, she'd seen enough to know something very strange had happened to her.

His hand shot out and her shears were gone. She stared at her empty hands. "They're mine!"

"True. But I wished to show you they are *not* an option."

A low-pitched hiss came from outside.

"Bartholomew is getting anxious. We must go before the cat loses patience. As I said, my name is Gato. What is yours?"

"Breena. Bree."

He again held out his hand.

Bree shook her head. "You go first."

"All right. For trust." He handed her back the shears and scooted outside.

Shears clutched in one hand, she crawled out of the tree. Oh, my.

The pony-sized puma stood beside Eldoro, while two men on horses, also wearing lots of leather, stared down at her, with two riderless horses standing beside them.

Bree pushed to her feet. "Now what?"

"We ride to Catamount," Gato said. "Can you ride or shall you come with me?"

"I'll ride." She might be half asleep, but she didn't want to ride with this imperious man. She walked to the pale dun nibbling a fern. The other riderless horse, a huge black, had to be Gato's.

"Hello, boy," she said to the dun. A friendly sort, he began to lip her hair. She laughed.

The four men tall, rangy men surrounding her froze.

"What?" she said.

Seeing Gato in the daylight shocked her. He was by far the tallest of the group, his muscled frame long and lean. He stared at her, his eyes narrowed. "Ready?"

She nodded.

"Let's go. We wish to be back at the keep before dark. Do you need assistance to mount?"

"I've got this." The dun wasn't a big horse, and she mounted easily. Once in the saddle, she took her place in the middle of their group, and they rode forward.

The saddle was strange, similar, yet different to those she'd always used, and a combination of English and Western. No one spoke as they rode, while the huge panther Bartholomew trotted beside her horse.

Gato dropped back to ride beside her. "You have a good seat."

"Thank you." Kit had perfected Bree's seat over the years, with all three of them loving the circus "ponies" kept first by her parents and then by Kit.

An awkward silence descended, as if the men wanted to speak, but refrained. Once she got to this Catamount, she'd get answers to her questions, get a good look at herself, and get food. This was all so weird.

The problem Gato held in his arms wasn't going away. The woman had fallen asleep in the saddle. Sure she'd topple, he'd pulled her off her horse to ride in front of him, her sleep so deep she hadn't awakened.

She'd hit him like a thunderbolt striking an enemy. Beautiful, ferocious, perhaps deadly, she fired his blood. That sunset hair of hers, those glorious eyes, and generous curves had given him pause. Dangerous ground, given he was about to battle for and *win* the Made One, Kitlyn. When she'd laughed, the rich, full sound had sparked an answering joy inside him, a strange and unfamiliar feeling.

The vague family resemblance said this Made One must be a sister to Kitlyn. He could use that to the Cats advantage, and so he set his mind to discovering the best way to do that. He must keep them separated until after The Challenge, that much was clear.

TO BE CONTINUED...

ACKNOWLEDGMENTS

Thank you, my readers, for your inspiration each and every day! You're the best.

I offer thanks to so many for helping me see *Altered* through to the finish line. My incomparable editor, Aria Jones, worked her magic in the best possible way. Thank you! To the extraordinary Camille Cotton—this book wouldn't exist without you. To the amazing Rosemary Hill, whose aid and insights are both invaluable and inspirational. To my much-loved and highly accomplished Betas —Wayne Page, Genevieve St. Yves, Pilar Seacord, and Debi McCarthy—for their invaluable Beta critiques and friendship. To Lorelai—who keeps me smiling.

To my exceptional cover artist, Mirela Barbu—you turned my dreams into reality. Thank you!

To Award-winning Master Karen Darabedyan of KD Mixed Martial Arts Academy. Karen (pronounced *Car*-en)—You are not only one of the kindest gentlemen I've ever met, but without you, *Altered*'s fight scenes would have been a hot mess.

To the Illuterati group and my Facebook pals. All of you inspire me with your warmth, your humor, and your truth-telling. To Wayne Page, whose friendship means so very much. To Monica,

Kiona, Mike, and Mikel, who always have my back. To Norah, Ro, and Karen, for their friendship, support, and knitting expertise. To Sheila Ryan, for her lasting and beautiful friendship, and Marc Ryan, who continues to inspire me. To Andrea Urban, Suzanne Hendrich, Pat Murphy, Donna Cautilli, CJ Williams, Linda Windels—love you. To Cindy's Knitters for the many stitches we wove together. To Betsy Bair, Georgi Mueller, and Karen Waxman for your love and friendship. To Cynthia Michaels, for her friendship and who continues to cherish my dear Cranberry.

To Peter, Kathleen, and Summer—your enduring love and profound support mean the world. Love you! Finally, and always, to my beloved boys, Blake and Ben—for all that you are, for all that you have gifted to me, and for all your abiding love. I'm the luckiest mom in the world.

I don't write alone in some crystal tower, but with the support and help of everyone mentioned above and so many more. Thank you!

Please know that any errors or screw-ups are mine alone.

ABOUT THE AUTHOR

Award-winning author Vicki Stiefel's science-fantasy romance series, The Made Ones Saga, launches with *Altered*. Vicki continues work on her Afterworld Chronicles, a five-book series which began with *Chest of Bone*. Her mystery/thrillers feature homicide counselor Tally Whyte, and Vicki's knitting love produced *Chest of Bone The Knit Collection* and *10 Secrets of the LaidBack Knitters*.

Having grown up in professional theater, Vicki planned to become an actress. Instead, she slung hamburgers, managed a scuba shop, and taught at Clark U. She's also a mom to two wonderful humans. Currently, she's playing with her pup, Penny, going wild in L.A., and pounding the keys on Book 2 in the Made Ones Saga, *Changed*.

Come visit with me...
www.vickistiefel.com • vicki@vickistiefel.com

www.ingramcontent.com/pod-product-compliance
Lightning Source LLC
Chambersburg PA
CBHW050903250626
47155CB00001B/90